GRAVIGNA,
A SMALL TOWN IN THE
CHIANTI HILLS

MURDER IN CHIANTI

CAMILLA TRINCHIERI

Allison & Busby Limited
11 Wardour Mews
London W1F 8AN
allisonandbusby.com

First published in Great Britain by Allison & Busby in 2020.
This paperback edition published by Allison & Busby in 2021.

Published by arrangement with Soho Press, New York,
with the assistance of Rights People, London

A CIP catalogue record for this book is available from
the British Library.

10 9 8 7 6 5 4 3 2 1

ISBN 978-0-7490-2656-1

Typeset in 10.75/15.75 pt Adobe Garamond Pro by
Allison & Busby Ltd

FSC
www.fsc.org
MIX
Paper from
responsible sources
FSC® C020471

The paper used for this Allison & Busby publication
has been produced from trees that have been legally sourced
from well-managed and credibly certified forests.

Printed and bound by
CPI Group (UK) Ltd, Croydon, CR0 4YY

CHAPTER ONE

Monday, 5.13 a.m. The sun wouldn't show up for at least another hour, but Nico got out of bed, shrugged on a T-shirt, pulled on a pair of shorts and socks, and laced up his trainers. Bed had stopped being a welcome place, both back in the Bronx brownstone he and Rita had lived in for twenty-five years and here in this century-old, two-room farmhouse he'd rented since May.

He set up the moka and, waiting for the gurgling to start, made the bed. Since he'd begun making his own bed at the age of three or four, he never walked away with it unmade. A neat bed started off the day with order, gave him the sense during childhood that all was well despite his father's drunken temper, his mother's fear. He knew it was all an illusion, but somehow it had helped then. And now, when he was trying to find order again.

A quick gulp of espresso shook him fully awake, followed by a forbidden cigarette that he smoked at the open window. Back in the Bronx flat, he had happily lived by Rita's house rules. Now he had the unwanted freedoms that came with being a widower. Bad language when he felt like it, dressing like a street bum, a cigarette after morning coffee. An extra glass of wine or two with dinner. A good night-time cigarette. Small stuff that would never be worth it.

The air was still chilly in the early morning, which Nico welcomed as he set off for his three-mile run along the winding road up to Gravigna. It was steep going and dangerous in the predawn light. And even at this hour, cars whizzed past in both directions, their drivers on their way to work. But Nico's morning run was like making the bed, a ritual that made him feel in control of his life, all the more necessary after the loss of his job, followed by Rita's death.

When the town appeared, perched on its own small hill, Nico stopped to catch his breath and take in the view of Gravigna, with its medieval castle walls, its two towers, the proud steeple of the Sant'Agnese Church. In the meagre predawn light Nico could, with the help of memory, make out the hundreds of neat rows of vines that covered the Conca d'Oro, the golden bowl below the town that had once only grown grain. He had marvelled at the sight the first time he'd seen it with Rita on their honeymoon. 'Our fairyland,' Rita had said then, and he had laughed, both of them dizzy with love.

Every three or four years, whenever they could afford the trip, they'd come back. It had been her childhood home town. Rita's parents, who had immigrated to New Jersey when she was six, had come back to die and be buried here. Rita asked to be buried next to them. He had obeyed, bringing her to her birthplace and immediately heading back. But he no longer had anyone in New York. An only child with parents long gone, ex-work colleagues who shunned him. And he missed Rita and her fairyland. He came back to be close to her and what family she'd had left – her cousin Tilde and Tilde's daughter, Stella.

A pink-grey light had begun to scale the surrounding hills. It was time to go back and prepare the tomatoes. No going off in his old Fiat 500 to the town's only cafe, Bar All'Angolo. The friendly bar owners; the schoolchildren, mothers and workmen crowding the counter; and the tourists sprawling over the tables made him feel less lonely, and the delicious whole wheat cornetti that came fresh from the oven made the place all the more tempting.

This morning, however, Nico was happy to break his routine. He had a job to do. Instead of his usual slow walk back, he started to jog home. Twin motorcycles rent the silence of the morning with their broken mufflers. A few cars passed, one honking loudly to announce its presence behind him. Another, a Panda, whizzed past, only a few inches away. Just another crazy Italian driver. Nico reached the stairs of his new home with a wildly beating heart and no breath left in his lungs. Maybe he was too old now for round-trip jogs. As he stretched his calves, he looked up at the sky. A cloudless blue vault, the start of another glorious Tuscan September day.

The dog relieved himself against a tree and meandered into the woods, sniffing for food that hunters or lovers might have dropped. The snap of twigs was followed by a chain of snaps. The dog froze, its ears at attention.

'Where are we going?' a voice asked.

The dog silently crouched down under a bush.

'I know these woods,' another voice answered. 'I'm taking you to the meeting place.'

'Why here, and why at this ridiculous hour?'

'You wanted privacy, didn't you? You'll only get that in the woods, when everyone is asleep. If it were hunting season, we couldn't even come here.'

'We've already been walking for half an hour.'

'Consider it a step towards repentance.'

'It hasn't been easy to live with what I did.'

'You've certainly waited long enough to make amends, but don't worry. The money will be enough to wipe away even your sins.'

'Are you sure this will happen? I have to fly back tonight.'

'Shh. Relax. You'll get what you came for.'

A ten-minute shower restored Nico. Cargo pants, a clean shirt, bare feet and he was ready. The previous night's pickings from the vegetable garden he'd started as soon as he'd signed the lease for this place awaited him in the room that served as both a kitchen and living area. Two baskets of ripe, luscious plum tomatoes sat on the thick pinewood table. He picked one up, felt its weight in his hands. A lot of work and love had grown these beauties. Nico turned on the oven and started slicing the tomatoes in half. After salting them, he drizzled extra virgin olive oil gifted from his landlord's grove, added a spattering of minced garlic, and spread them, cut-side down, over four trays.

A gunshot rang out just as Nico was sliding the first tray into the oven. The sharp crack made his arm jerk. Tomatoes spilt to the floor.

'Shit!' Hunting season wasn't opening for another week, but some hotheads were too eager for boar meat to follow the law. Aldo Ferri, his landlord, had warned him about the boars showing up en masse now that the vineyards were loaded with ripe grapes. The farmhouse Nico was renting was close to a dense growth of trees, the beasts' favourite habitat. They were mean, ugly animals who could grow to weigh over two hundred pounds. Aldo had suggested Nico pick up a hunting rifle to be on the safe side. No, thanks – he was through with guns of any kind. Last night was the first time he'd heard gunshots. They'd come in short, distant bursts. This one had been much closer.

Only one shot. If this guy was after boar, he must be a damned good marksman. A wounded boar would spare no one.

Nico stared down at the tomatoes on the floor. Some had landed on his shoes. Hell, what was the rule? Thirty seconds? A minute? Well, Rita would have to forgive him. He'd swept the kitchen two days ago, and he needed every single tomato for the dish Tilde was letting him cook at the restaurant tonight.

With the tomatoes back in the oven to roast, it was time to enjoy the rest of this new morning. Nico ground some more coffee beans, put the moka over a low flame, cut two slices of bread, and filled them with thin slices of mortadella and a sheep's milk caciotta. Probably a lot more calories than two whole wheat cornetti, but not caring about that was one of his new freedoms. He put his coffee and the sandwich on a tray, shrugged on a Mets sweatshirt, and stepped out to the best part of the house: an east-facing balcony overlooking part of the Ferriello vineyards and the low hills beyond.

There was just a slim ribbon of light floating over the horizon, enough light to see that the wooden beams holding up the roof were empty. No sleeping swallows. They didn't usually fly off so early. That gunshot must have scared them away. Or maybe early September was simply time to move on. He would miss them, if that was the case. The evenings that Nico wasn't helping Tilde at the restaurant, he'd got used to sitting out on the balcony with a glass of wine to wait for the three swallows to swoop in and tuck themselves in between the beam and roof for the night. He didn't mind cleaning up their mess in the morning. They'd become fond of each other.

Nico was halfway through his breakfast sandwich when he heard a dog yelping. A high-pitched, ear-busting sound that could only come from a small breed. Maybe it was the mutt that seemed to have made a home next to the gate to his vegetable garden. A small, scruffy dog that always greeted him with one wag of his bushy tail and then lay down and went to sleep. Nico had checked the garden the first time to see if the dog had done any damage. Finding none, he let it be.

Nico leant over the balcony and whistled. The yelps stopped for half a minute, then started off again, louder this time. Nico whistled again. No pause this time. As the yelps continued, Nico wondered if the dog was hurt. More than possible. The vineyard fences were electric. Or it could've got caught in some trap. The yelps seemed to be coming from the left, past the olive grove. What if a boar had attacked the dog?

With hiking boots on and the biggest knife from his new kitchen in hand, Nico traced the sound of the yelps. They led him past the olive grove, up a small slope of burnt-out grass and into a wood thick with scrubby trees and bushes. The yelps got louder and faster. He was getting close. Then silence. Even the birds were mute. Nico broke into a run.

The dog almost tripped him. There it was, between his boots, with a single wag of its tail. 'What the—' The dog looked up at him with a perky expression that clearly signalled, *I'm cute, so pay attention to me.* Toto, the cocker spaniel he'd had as a kid, used to give him that exact same look whenever he wanted a treat.

'I got nothing on me.'

The dog raised a paw. It was red.

Nico bent down to get a better look. Blood. On all four paws. The thick undergrowth had masked the prints. He checked the animal for cuts. Nothing. It was filthy, but fine. The mutt must have found the spot where the boar or other wild animal had been hit with that one shot.

'Come on, you need a clean-up.' Nico tucked the dog under his arm and turned to walk back. The creature squirmed and fought his grip, letting out a growl. 'Fine, suit yourself, kid.' Nico put it down and kept walking. The dog stood in place and barked. Nico didn't stop. The dog kept on barking. Nico finally turned around. Toto would do this when he was trying to tell him something. Once, it had been a nasty rat underneath the porch. No rats here, but maybe he should go along with it.

He turned around. 'Okay. What?'

The dog shot off deeper into the woods. Nico trudged behind him. 'This better be good, mutt.'

At the edge of a small clearing, the dog sniffed the air a few times, then lay down, his job complete. When Nico reached the spot, he let out a long breath. What the mutt had been trying to tell him was a blinder.

About twelve feet in front of them, at the far edge of the clearing, a man lay on his back, arms and legs spread out at an unnatural angle. What had been his face was now a pulpy mess of flesh, brain and bits of bone steeped in blood.

Nico's stomach clenched. It wasn't the sight that got to him – during his nineteen years as a homicide detective, he'd seen worse and quickly numbed to it. No, it was the surprise of finding a body here. He'd walked away from that job, his old life, and come to Italy to find peace. He wanted to be near Rita, near her family, and far from violent death. Murder seemed to have no place in the beautiful Chianti hills.

'Come on, let's get out of here.' His phone was back at the house. Nico bent down and swooped the mutt back up. No protests this time. He took another long look at the dead man without getting any closer. This was a crime scene, and old habits persisted. To blow off a man's face, you needed a shotgun, not a rifle. Close range, maybe four feet. So it was probable the victim knew his killer. Blood would have splattered all over him. Find the bloody clothes, and you had the perpetrator. Nico's eyes scanned the ground around the body. No shell that he could see. Either the murderer had picked up his brass, or it was somewhere in the underbrush. Not his job to go looking. His eyes shifted back to the body. A six footer at least, judging by the length of his torso and legs. Big belly poking out of his jeans and a grey T-shirt mostly covered in blood. Some dark-red letters on it, or was that more blood? Nico leant as far forward as he could without taking a step. Not blood. Two letters. *AP*. Blood covered the rest of the word or logo. At the man's feet were gold running shoes spotted with blood. Michael Johnson sprinters. If this man had ever been a runner, it was a very long time ago. White socks peeked up from the Nikes. On his wrist, more gold – a very expensive-looking watch. Maybe a knock-off. Hard to tell, even up close. Chances were the killer hadn't been interested in that. Unless something or someone had scared him away.

Nico looked down at the mutt huddled in the curve of his elbow. 'You?' He surprised himself by smiling. 'Sure thing.' He turned his back to the dead man and, with the dog tucked under his arm, started walking back to the house. About twenty feet back into the woods, Nico felt the ground soften. He looked down. He'd stumbled on a patch of wet ground. Elsewhere the ground looked perfectly dry. It hadn't rained in days. Nico took another step and spotted an upturned leaf. It held water. Pink water. The killer must have washed himself. There was no water source that he could see. Nico continued his walk home. Solving homicides wasn't his job any more.

Nico gave the dog what was left of his mortadella and caciotta sandwich and put it out on the balcony. He'd stick it in a bath later. He had a call to make: 112, the Italian emergency number, was the logical choice, but he'd prefer to talk to someone he knew first. Tilde was busy preparing lunch at the restaurant. She was a rock, but the news might upset her.

Maybe Aldo, his landlord, a cheery, likeable man who seemed to have a lot of good sense. It hadn't taken much effort to convince him the run-down farmhouse that hadn't been lived in for thirty years would make Nico a cheap new home.

'Gesú Maria! On my land?'

'I don't know. I found him about two kilometres into the woods past the olive grove.'

'Not mine, thank the heavens. The German who owned

it died a few years back, and the heirs put it up for sale. I wanted to expand and had the ground tested two years ago. You can't grow grapes on that land. Too loamy. Loamy soil makes for inferior wine. There's a rumour that some—'

'Who's in charge around here?' Nico interrupted. Aldo was a talker. 'Polizia or carabinieri?' He had no idea who was called when. All he knew was that the carabinieri were part of the Italian army, and that there was no love lost between the two police forces.

'Carabinieri. I'll call Salvatore, the maresciallo. The station is in Greve. If he's there, it'll take about twenty minutes for him to make the trip.'

'Thanks. I'll wait here.'

'I'll bring him over. Thanks for letting me know. Wait till I tell Cinzia. She's going to flip out! We're booked solid today. Seventeen Germans—'

'Someone has to get over there fast. Every second counts in a homicide investigation.'

'You sound like a TV detective.'

'I just want my part in this to be done.'

'I'll call Salvatore right away.'

'Thanks.' Nico put down the phone. He had to keep in mind that Tilde was the only one who knew he'd ever been a cop. And only a patrol officer, which was what he'd been when she had first met him. Rita had sworn her cousin to secrecy, afraid the townspeople would shun him. The Rodney King beating had happened only a few months earlier.

* * *

Sitting on a stone trough by the front door, Nico smoked the one of the two-a-day cigarettes he hadn't been able to enjoy earlier. The mutt lay at his feet, snout between his still-bloody paws. Clean-up could wait. The dog was a part of the crime scene. So were Nico's hiking boots. He'd changed into trainers, his boots next to the mutt. It was just past eight. The sun was warming things up, not a trace of cloud in the sky, and the tomatoes were nicely charred and out of the oven. He took another drag and felt the tension release. The morning's discovery would soon be over. A walk and a talk with this maresciallo, and he would return to his new Tuscan life.

A dark blue sedan with distinctive red stripes on its hood appeared at the top of the dirt road that led to Nico's rustic house. Nico quickly stubbed out his cigarette, forgetting that no Italian was about to tell him he was killing himself. The dog sat up and started a series of high-pitched barks.

'Shut up.'

The dog looked at Nico with what he would swear was a puzzled expression.

'You heard me.'

One last bark in protest, and the dog lay back down.

'Good boy.'

Christ! A man's face had been blown off not more than a few hours ago, and here he was, acting like his eight-year-old self when his mother had brought home Toto. Nico raised his hand to acknowledge Aldo in the back seat. In front were two men, the driver's blonde head tall above the steering wheel and the front passenger's head lying low.

Aldo came out first. He was a big man in his late forties with a round, jovial face and a wine-barrel paunch. He was wearing tan slacks and a bright leaf-green T-shirt with the purple logo for his wine on it. He waved back at the car. 'Who would have thought we'd have a murder on our hands today, eh, Salvatore?'

A dark-haired man in a tan shirt and jeans stepped out of the passenger seat. A black nylon jacket was tied around his waist. 'The murder is in my hands, Aldo. Yours have to make good wine.'

The maresciallo walked towards the house, recognising the man out front from his last visit to Bar All'Angolo. He had assumed then that he was just another American tourist, a man who'd held no interest for him. Now he saw the man as loose-limbed, big-shouldered, at least two heads taller than himself, on the short end of sixty with retreating grey-brown hair. He did not have the open, optimistic face he observed on so many Americans. Kind, naive faces bad at spotting danger. People who kept their wallets or cameras within easy reach of a thief and then came to the carabinieri with hope in their eyes. Hope the maresciallo was rarely able to reward. This man's face was closed off, though there was intelligence in his eyes, which were the colour of steeped tea leaves. Had he only discovered a body this morning, or did he have something more to do with it?

* * *

19

The officer was somewhere in his forties, at the most five foot six, with a full head of hair black enough to seem dyed. A stocky, muscled frame and a chiselled face, handsome, with large liquid eyes, thick lips, an aquiline nose. A face Nico had seen before but couldn't place. The man was smiling.

'Salvatore Perillo, Maresciallo dei Carabinieri. I should wear uniform, but no time.' Up close, Nico saw that Perillo's hair had too much shine to be dyed. Perillo offered a hand. 'Piacere.'

Pleasure it's not was on the tip of Nico's tongue, but he stopped himself. He conformed to Italian politeness and shook the hand. 'Nico Doyle.' Perillo's grip was strong enough to crunch bone. Nico squeezed back.

Perillo nodded as if to acknowledge a tie, then took back his hand. 'I have questions, but forgive, my English not so good.'

Before Nico could explain, Aldo stepped between the men and said in Italian, 'Nico's Italian is good. Italian grandmother, Italian American mother and Tuscan wife. Accent American.' He grinned, seemingly happy to impart information the maresciallo didn't have. Nico recognised the same proud tone Aldo used to explain the mysteries of wine-making to the busloads of tourists who came to his vineyards.

The fact that Nico was pretty fluent in Perillo's language didn't seem to affect the man one way or another. 'And the father?' Perillo asked in Italian.

'Irish,' Nico answered in Italian.

'An explosive combination, I've been told.' The maresciallo's Southern accent was strong.

'You've been told right.'

'I usually hear the truth when I'm in civilian clothes. With the uniform, not so much.' Perillo looked down at the dog sniffing at his heels. 'Is that blood on his paws?'

'Yes, the dead man's. The dog led me to the body.'

'Yours?'

Nico found himself answering yes.

Perillo bent down and scratched the dog's head. He got the one wag for his trouble. 'What's his name?'

Toto was the first idea that popped into Nico's head. No good. And they were wasting time. 'I call him OneWag.' He used English words for the name. To say the same thing in Italian would have required too many letters. 'I'll show you the way now.'

Perillo eyed him for a moment. Nothing showed on his face, but Nico suspected the maresciallo was surprised he'd taken the initiative. 'Yes, please lead the way. My brigadiere will stay here with the car. Is it far?'

'About three kilometres into the woods.'

'Ah, the woods!' Perillo's glance went down to his own feet. He was wearing brown suede boots that looked brand new. 'At least it hasn't rained.' He gestured towards the woods. 'Please. I will ask questions as we walk.'

'Maybe it's faster,' Nico said, not used to being on the receiving end of an interrogation, 'if I explain and then you ask questions.'

Perillo seemed amused by this. 'The Americans are

prisoners of speed. Tuscany, the whole Italian north, is closer to the American way of thinking, but I come from Campania.'

They started walking, Aldo trailing behind them, OneWag running ahead. Nico was surprised Perillo was letting Aldo tag along. The fewer people on a crime scene, the better, but again, he reminded himself, it wasn't his investigation.

'We have a different approach,' Perillo was saying, 'although in this case, you are correct. Time brings heat, flies, maggots. I'm sure it was a very unpleasant sight in the first place, one perhaps you are not eager to repeat and therefore wish to be over with. Best to deal with it quickly. As for understanding the story behind this death, I fear speed will not be possible. Our investigations are not like on *Law & Order* or *CSI*. And so tell me, Signor Doyle,' Perillo said, addressing Nico using the formal lei, 'what facts are you so anxious to remove from your thoughts?'

'A few minutes after seven this morning, I heard a single gunshot. It sounded fairly close by. I assumed it was some hunter who couldn't wait for the season to start. But it could be the shot that killed this man.'

'We will see. No need for you to speculate.'

'Of course.'

'Please continue, Signor Doyle.'

'Please, call me Nico.'

'For now, let us keep up the formalities.'

They stepped into the woods. There was no path. Nico was grateful that OneWag led the way. Under different circumstances, the walk would have been a pleasant one. The morning silence was now broken by bird chatter, the dark underbrush splotched with the sun breaking through trees. A light breeze ruffled the leaves. While Perillo kept his eyes on the ground, careful of where he placed his new suede boots, Nico explained that he'd been led to the body by the dog's desperate-sounding yelps. 'I thought he was hurt.'

'Where were you when you heard the dog?'

'On the balcony, having breakfast.'

'If the body is three kilometres into the woods, you have very sharp ears.'

'OneWag has a very sharp voice. It was early and quiet. It's possible I was on alert because of that gunshot. Just one – that surprised me. When I heard the yelps, I followed them and saw the mess. On my way back, I found a patch of wet ground and some pinkish water. My guess would be that the killer washed some blood off there. I don't remember where it was, exactly.'

'We'll find it. Did you step in it?'

'Yes. You'll want my boots.'

'Indeed,' Perillo said, looking at Nico with renewed interest. OneWag's barking stopped Perillo from going any further.

'It's just there,' Nico said. 'In the clearing behind those laurel bushes. The dead man's at the far edge.'

'Stay here, both of you, and hold the dog,' Perillo ordered. He squared his shoulders and walked ahead with a determined step.

The maresciallo was first overtaken by the thick metallic smell of blood and the frenzied buzz of the flies. And then he saw the body at the edge of the clearing. He shrank back a step, closed his eyes and crossed himself. It was indeed an ugly sight. What had he said earlier? *Time brings heat, flies, maggots. I'm sure it was a very unpleasant sight in the first place.* He regretted his pompous tone. It was an unpleasant trait that always surfaced with strangers. What Signor Doyle had discovered was a gruesome act of hate. The dead man's face and half his brain blown away, spread across the grass like pig fodder.

Who was this poor soul? What had he done to deserve such violence? Certainly not a local, not with those shoes. Perillo took off his new boots, his socks. He had forgotten shoe covers. Bare feet were easily washed. He took out rubber gloves from his back pocket and slipped them on.

Slowly, he walked in a wide arc below the man's legs, trying to remain on clean grass. He circled the legs and stopped near the man's hips. Perillo reached into the pocket. It was empty. He leant over the body and tried the other one. It had nothing that would tell him the identity of this poor man, but deep inside he found a hard object. He pulled it out, careful not to move the body, and studied it in the palm of his hand. With some luck, it would lead him to some answers. Luck and hard work.

Perillo slid the object into an evidence bag and took out his mobile phone. He punched in the number of headquarters in Florence.

Nico bent down and tucked OneWag under his arm, receiving a lick on the chin for his effort. Aldo waited a few minutes before tiptoeing forward.

'Oh my God.' Aldo's knees buckled as he peered beyond the bushes.

'I did warn you,' Nico said.

Aldo backtracked slowly, wiping his face with a handkerchief. 'You think he got shot in the face so he wouldn't be recognised?'

Nico had wondered about that himself. 'He may have had ID in his pockets.'

'You didn't look?' Aldo's hands kept kneading his handkerchief.

'I know not to mess up a crime scene.'

Aldo looked at his watch. 'I've got to get back. Seventeen Germans coming for a wine tasting and lunch, and forty Americans busing in from Florence for dinner. It's going to be a hard day.'

'The hard day's mine, Aldo.' Perillo walked through the laurel bushes with his suede boots and socks tucked under his arm. 'This murder makes it a good day for you. You have a much better story to tell your guests than how wine is made.' His tone was jovial, his face anything but. 'Regale them with a few details, they'll be thirsty for more, and you'll sell some extra bottles. Go home and enjoy a few glasses of your Riserva. It will erase the ugly sight you insisted on coming here to see.' He turned to Nico, who was staring at his bare feet. 'Blood and suede is a disastrous combination, Signor Doyle.'

Aldo asked, 'Did you find ID on him?'

'No. He was wearing white athletic socks and gold running shoes, which makes me think he's an American, although I might avoid telling that to your guests. He was also wearing a gold Breitling watch, worth around five thousand euro.'

'That eliminates robbery as a motive,' Aldo said.

'Possibly, if he was the kind of man who went around without a mobile phone, wallet, credit card or driver's licence,' Perillo said, 'although one can be robbed of many things besides expensive accessories. Their life, for one.' He turned to Nico. 'Thank you, Signor Doyle, for being my Cicero on this terrible occasion. I am sure your expectations of Tuscany did not include a gruesome death. I do request that you give your boots to my brigadiere, who is by the car. I also need you to come to the station in Greve this afternoon for a deposition. At that time, I will take your fingerprints and a DNA sample.'

'My fingerprints are on my residence permit, and I didn't go anywhere near the body.'

'I don't doubt your word, but nevertheless. The DNA requirement is fairly new and meant to eliminate confusion. A good idea, for once. We Italians often make more confusion than is strictly necessary. As for your fingerprints, it will save time. It takes a while for the carabinieri to gain access to residence permits. Leave the dog with me, please. He may have picked up something of interest in his paws and fur. The technical team and medical examiner are on their way. Don't forget, Signor Doyle. At four o'clock. The signage in town is clear. You won't have a problem finding the office.'

Nico glanced at the dog, who looked back with a sharp tilt to his head as if he knew something was up. 'I don't have a lead for him.' He was having a hard time letting him go. 'I could stay here until they come.'

'We cannot have you stay here while we do our work. Lay aside your fears. We will treat him with hands of velvet.' Perillo undid the nylon jacket tied to his waist and lay it flat on the ground. 'Put him here.'

Nico did as he was asked. Perillo quickly zipped up the jacket around the dog, tied the sleeves and lifted the bundle up. OneWag peeked out of the opening and barked at Nico.

'Go home, Aldo. You too, Signor Doyle.'

Nico gave OneWag a quick scratch behind his ear and turned to go. The dog barked louder.

'Try to forget what you have seen here. It is not representative of our beautiful country.'

Nico could not help thinking of all the Camorra killings he had read about in Perillo's neck of the woods, but the maresciallo was right about his expectations of Tuscany. They did not include murder or a stray dog.

CHAPTER TWO

It was eleven-thirty when Nico arrived at the restaurant with his pan of roasted tomatoes. At noon, Sotto Il Fico – Under the Fig Tree – would open for lunch.

'Buongiorno,' Nico said.

'Not for everyone, I hear.' Elvira, Tilde's mother-in-law, was in her usual armchair at the back of the narrow front room, which held the bar and a few tables. The draw of the restaurant was its large hilltop terrace, which held a huge sheltering fig tree and a serene view of a patchwork of perfectly aligned grapevines below. Elvira was wearing one of her seven housedresses – she had one for each day of the week. Today's was white with red and pink checks. She was a widow with crow-black dyed hair, a corrugated face that made her look older than her sixty-two years, a small, sharp nose and piercing water-blue eyes that didn't miss a single trick. Rita had nicknamed her 'the seagull' for the way she seemed to hover around people, looking for titbits to snatch up.

'Salve.' Behind the short bar by the door, her son, Enzo, Tilde's husband, reached for a grappa bottle. He had his mother's angular face and black hair streaked with grey, and always wore jeans and a Florentine football team's T-shirt. He poured grappa into a small glass and held it out. 'Poor Nico. This will restart your motor.'

So the news had already got out. 'No, thanks, I'm fine,' Nico said.

'I wouldn't be fine.' Enzo drank the grappa in one swig. 'No one's ever been murdered in Gravigna.' He gave the grappa bottle a longing look but put it back on the shelf. 'All over the world, people are killing each other for no good reason. This country is drowning in shit, and now there's a murdered man in our woods.'

'I'm sure it wasn't anyone you knew.' From what Nico had learnt of the town, only Sergio Macchi, the butcher with two restaurants, was rich enough to afford that watch, and Sergio didn't have the dead man's belly.

'Of course not.' Elvira turned her gaze on Nico. 'I hear the dead American had no ID.'

Nico walked up to her. 'Who says he's American?'

'I do,' Elvira declared. 'He was wearing gold trainers and thick white socks. You can always tell someone's nationality by his socks and shoes. Germans and Scandinavians wear brown or grey socks with sandals, of all things. Asian women wear little socks with drawings on them and feminine heels. The English, argyles and sensible leather shoes.'

Nico lifted up his pan. 'I'd better get this into the kitchen.'

'I was hoping you'd changed your mind about that dish of yours. The tourists want Tuscan food, not something invented in the Bronx.'

'Rita invented it, and she was Tuscan.'

Elvira waved him away. 'Go on, get yourself in the kitchen. Tilde thought you'd chickened out.'

'I did not!' called a voice from the kitchen.

'Ever since she heard about the murder, she's been acting like she's walked into a wasps' nest.'

'Mamma, she's upset. We all are.' Enzo reached back to the shelf and poured himself another grappa.

Elvira shook her head and went back to folding napkins. Nico sometimes marvelled at the relationship between the two women. It wasn't exactly a positive one, surprising considering how closely they worked together. Elvira owned the restaurant, and her contribution to the place was folding napkins from a rickety gilded armchair rescued from the dump – one that she would forever claim a Roman contessa had bequeathed her. When she wasn't folding, she solved the crossword puzzles in the weekly *Settimana Enigmistica*, eyes ready to snap up at every arrival. Enzo, her forty-year-old son, manned the bar and cash register. When he was feeling energetic, which from what Nico had seen wasn't often, he'd slice the bread as well. Tilde and Stella ended up doing the hard work, cooking and serving with part-time help from Alba, a young Albanian woman. Nico was only too happy to lend a hand.

Tilde was in the kitchen, a long, narrow room with scarred wooden counters and walls covered from hip level to ceiling with worn copper and steel pots and pans. She was rapidly slicing mushrooms for her apple, mushroom and walnut salad, a lunchtime bestseller. She pecked Nico's cheek while spritzing the just-cut slices with lemon juice. 'I heard. Sorry you had to go through that.'

'You mean Elvira or the dead man?'

That got a half smile out of her. 'Both. Are you okay?'

'Yes.' Nico put the pan of tomatoes in a far corner. He didn't need them until this afternoon. 'Are you?'

'The wasp bit me, but then it died.'

Nico grinned. 'I believe it. We all know you're armoured in granite, but it's still only armour. Having a murderer nearby is scary. There's nothing wrong in admitting that.'

Hearing about the murder was horrible, but it was mention of the dead man's shoes that had stuck a knife in her chest. It had been twenty-two years. Tilde had managed to almost entirely erase the thought of Robi, but now his drunken boast haunted her. *I'll return covered in gold.*

'Was the dead man really wearing gold trainers?' she asked.

'Yes, and a big fat gold watch.' Nico walked past the small window overlooking the dining terrace and saw Stella under the fig tree, setting tables. He waved at Rita's goddaughter. 'Ciao, cara.' He was hoping for her usual heart-warming smile but only got a nod. Understandably, the murder had got to her too.

'Let me do this.' Nico slid the pan of courgette lasagne ready for the oven to one side and stood next to Tilde.

She handed him the knife. 'Very thin. And don't forget the lemon.'

'Yes, I know, I know.' It wasn't the first time he'd done the slicing. 'I'm aware that news travels fast in a small town, but how did Elvira know about the socks and shoes?'

Tilde waved a dismissive hand in the air. 'She found out from Gianni. He works for Aldo. I thought you knew that.'

Gianni was Stella's boyfriend, a handsome young man with the arrogance of youth. Stella liked him as much as Tilde disliked him. Tilde stirred a pot of cooling navy beans that she would serve with tuna and the sweet red onions from Certaldo, Boccaccio's home town. Beans of any kind were a staple of Tuscan cooking.

Tilde offered him a spoonful of the beans. 'You need reinforcement after what you've been through. Help yourself to anything.'

He was being offered food as tranquilliser. Looking would have to be enough for now.

Next to the pot was another Tuscan staple, also a Sotto Il Fico bestseller – pappa al pomodoro, a thick soup of stale bread, tomatoes, garlic, basil and vegetable broth, topped by a generous squiggle of extra virgin olive oil. Tilde's pappa surpassed all the others he and Rita had tasted over the years. If Tilde had a secret ingredient, she didn't share. Every time he walked into the kitchen, no matter the time, the pappa was already made.

Tilde saw him eyeing the pot. 'Maybe someday I'll tell you,' she said.

'I won't hold my breath.'

'That's wise. Does Salvatore know you were a police officer?'

'No, and you're not going to tell him. You're on a first-name basis with him too?'

'Everyone knows him. He goes to Bar All'Angolo whenever he gets a chance. That's where the cyclists hang out. He's an avid cyclist. He and his pals sometimes drop by for a late lunch after a Sunday race.'

Cycling was an Italian passion, Nico had quickly discovered on his first visit. On the weekends, there wasn't a road in Tuscany that wasn't overrun by racing bikes either whizzing downhill or straining uphill.

Tilde said, 'You must have seen him before.'

'He did look familiar.'

'Salvatore Perillo is a good man. Solid.' She turned to look at Nico. She had a small face with wide, caramel-coloured eyes that softened her severe expression. The red cotton scarf wound around her head covered the same beautiful long, chestnut-brown hair that had been Rita's pride before it turned grey. Tilde was forty-one, and her hair had not lost its rich colour. She had been a stunning, smiling beauty in the photos Nico had seen of her as a teenager. With the passing years, her soft beauty had changed into something harsher, unsmiling. And yet she claimed to be happy. Rita had blamed the change on too much work.

Tilde wiped her hands on the long white apron that sheathed her perfectly ironed beige cotton dress. Nico had never seen her in slacks or in a wrinkled item of clothing.

'You could help him solve the crime,' she said.

'Why?' The last of the mushrooms were done. He picked up a green apple.

He wanted to add *I have no experience in solving crimes*, but Tilde didn't deserve a lie. The omission was bad enough. Tilde had never been told he'd moved from being a uniform to homicide detective.

When he'd protested years ago, Rita said, 'You don't know Italians. All they'll want to talk about are your cases. It would ruin our holiday. You deal with such gruesome, ugly stuff, and I'll never understand how you stomach it.'

He'd been angry at the time, unaware until then how much she disliked his new job. He didn't have much stomach either for the gruesome part of homicide, he explained, but he wanted to right what was wrong, give the victims' families justice.

Rita accused him of wanting to play God. He reminded her a detective's salary was better than a patrolman's. They'd hoped to start a family. Twenty years had passed since then.

Tilde opened a big jar of Sicilian yellowfin tuna. 'We need this murder solved quickly. The whole town is scared, excited, curious. Enzo's phone hasn't stopped ringing. I had to turn mine off. Just what we need right now, for the tourists to get scared and leave. Besides, I'm worried you'll get bored and go back to America.'

'It's hard to be bored in such a beautiful place,' Nico said. He was sad at times, which was to be expected. His footing here wasn't solid yet, but he was working on it. When he wasn't helping out at the restaurant one of his three shifts a week, he walked the streets, listening, striking up conversations at the bar, at the newsstand, at the trattoria in the piazza. He had nothing to take him back to New York. His police career was over. 'You're the only family I've got, and I'm staying right here. I like helping you with the restaurant.'

'But I feel bad I can't pay you.'

'What I need is friendship, not money. Besides, you feed me when I'm here.'

'We close in October and won't reopen until April. What will you do then? Of course, you're welcome to eat with us anytime you want, but still, the winter months here can feel very long.'

'I'll perfect my cooking skills and hire myself out to the competition.'

'Such a man. Your dish tonight better be good.'

'It will be. I wish I could reassure Stella she has nothing to be scared of.' He'd been watching her weave through the tables with sagging shoulders, head down.

'It's not the murder. She had a fight with Gianni.'

'Serious?'

'Very, and I hope she has enough sense to break it off.'

'That's harsh. She loves him.'

'She'll get over it.'

Tilde's angry tone made Nico pause and study her. He

knew she loved her daughter very much, and he wondered what could make her dismiss Stella's feelings so quickly. He watched her put the courgette lasagne in the oven and waited.

She slammed the door shut. 'Stop staring at me. I'm not a witch. Stella has a university degree in art history, but Gianni wants her to stay here and be a waitress. Yesterday she disobeyed him and went to Florence to apply for the competition exam to be a museum guard.'

'I would think her degree was enough.' From what he'd seen of Italian museum guards, all they did was sit in a chair and make sure visitors didn't get too close to the art. At least they had the advantage of sitting, a privilege American guards didn't seem to have.

'All state jobs can only be won by passing a competition with flying colours,' Tilde said. 'Even if Stella gets top marks, there's no guarantee she'll get it. Here, people get ahead because of nepotism or bribes. Stella wanted to teach art at the university level, but her professor wasn't esteemed enough to mentor her, so now we have to pin our hopes on the guard job. A state job is good. I think they have about twenty openings and more than three thousand people are applying. I don't hold much hope, but at least she should be encouraged to try. Gianni told her he'd leave her if she got the job.'

'He's just scared of losing her.'

She pointed a serving fork at Nico, eyes narrowed. 'Don't you side with him.'

It was the first time he had seen her this upset. 'I'm just saying. Want me to talk to him?'

'No. I want her to get to her senses and leave him.'
Laughter and German words drifted in from the front room.

'Enough talk,' Tilde said. 'Our first lunch guests are here.'

'I'll help Stella serve.'

'You're a gift from God,' Tilde said with a peck on his
cheek and a push out the door.

There had been quite a crowd at lunch today, thankfully
unaware of the murder in the area. Nico and Stella
were too busy rushing about to talk to each other until
it was time for him to go to the carabinieri station. The
maresciallo was waiting for him by now, but Stella was
more important. They had just finished clearing all the
tables. He took her hand and led her to a seat under the
shade of the fig tree. Before sitting down, he kissed her
cheek. 'How are you?'

Stella was almost a young replica of Tilde. The same
oval shape of the face, full mouth, straight nose, a fair, clear
complexion, thick chestnut-brown hair she had just had
cut to intentionally uneven lengths, one side covering her
ear and the other barely touching the top of her ear. Nico
had watched Tilde blanch when Stella came back from the
hairdresser. 'Good cut' had been her only comment. What
was different was the colour of her eyes, a transparent jade
green that no one else in the family claimed.

Stella furrowed her brow. 'Did Mamma ask you to
talk to me?'

'No. My feet hurt, and I want to see that beautiful
smile of yours.'

She responded with a quick, throaty laugh. 'Sorry, I've dropped it somewhere and now I can't find it.' She leant over the chair and clasped her arms around his neck. 'Poor Nico, it must have been terrible for you. Weren't you scared?'

'No reason to be. He was dead. I would say repulsed is more accurate. What's truly horrible is the cruelty we are capable of.'

She dropped her arms. Fingers started twisting at the hem of her top. 'It's scary. You found him in the woods behind Aldo's place, right? Mamma has always forbidden me from going there by myself. I don't know why. Nothing bad's happened there before today. Gianni thinks it's just a power play on her part. Says it's a great place to pick mushrooms.'

'And I suspect a good place for lovers too.'

Stella shook her head. No smile, no blush. 'There are other places. I do wish Mamma and Gianni got along. I feel pulled in two.'

'She's thinking of your future.'

'I know. So am I, and Gianni's being a perfect pill about it. Zio Nico, are you sure you're okay?'

'I am, and please don't be scared. The carabinieri will find the killer quickly.' Nico stood up. 'Ciao, my bella. Thanks for worrying about me.' He kissed her cheeks. 'See you tonight. You'll have to tell me if you like my dish.'

She stood up too, pulled the now wrinkled hem of her top down over her jeans. 'I'm sure it will be delicious, and there will be none left for us.' The shadow of her beautiful smile appeared on her face.

'Ah, the light is coming back.'

'Your doing. I love you.'

'Me too.'

A quick hug and he walked away. He was going to be very late for his appointment.

Nico got on the panoramic 222 road that snaked from Siena through the Chianti hills, ending just south of Florence. The 500 started belching as soon as he floored it, and what should have taken only fifteen minutes took twice that. He knew from the start that the price Enzo had asked for the car was over the top, but they both understood that Enzo was asking for help in buying a new espresso machine for the restaurant, and Nico had gladly paid. Now he felt like cursing.

Once on the main road in Greve, the car stopped belching, but traffic slowed to bumper-to-bumper pace. He read the banner flying over the street. The reason for the traffic jam became clear. The Chianti Classico Expo, the biggest wine-tasting event in the region, was starting in three days. As he neared the intersection that led to the big medieval piazza that was the heart of the town, he heard shouting punctuated by hammer blows. He had read about the event in the local paper, but this morning's discovery had wiped it from his mind. Even if he'd remembered, he hadn't been about to leave Stella with more than thirty diners to take care of all by herself. For once, even Enzo had been busy pouring glasses of wine and making espresso drinks at the bar. There was nothing Nico could do about it now. The maresciallo would understand. Or not. He didn't care. This was a courtesy. Anyway, Italians were always late.

The red light was taking forever to change, and he couldn't see any signs telling him where to go. Nico leant out the window and asked a woman overloaded with shopping bags where he could find the carabinieri station.

The middle-aged woman, dressed in a rumpled yellow linen suit, beamed at him. 'Ah, thank the heavens. I will show you.' She quickly walked in front of his car, opened the passenger door, pushed the bags to the floor, and dropped herself onto the seat. There was barely enough room for her.

Nico stared. She smiled. 'Trust me.'

He hated those two words because they rarely delivered, but her face was kind, which reassured him. Not that he thought he was being carjacked. Manipulated, maybe.

The light changed to green.

'Turn right here,' the woman said, pointing a red-nailed finger. 'Cross the bridge. Turn left at the next street. See the sign?' She said it slowly, in a soft, low voice, as if addressing a foreign child. His accent had given him away.

Nico did as she said. Halfway up the hill, she asked him to stop. 'I live in that villino.' She extended a hand to him. 'Maria Dorsetti.' Nico shook it and mumbled his name. Something about this woman flustered him.

She did not ask him to repeat it. 'Thank you for saving me the climb. At the top of the hill, turn right, then left. You'll see a cafe to your left, a park to your right. The carabinieri station is just across the street from the park.

I hope your business with them is not unpleasant.' She tilted her head, waiting for him to respond.

He said, 'Thank you.'

Clearly disappointed by his terseness, she gathered her shopping bags and struggled to get out of the small car. She waved at Nico as he took off.

As he climbed the hill, he noticed in his rear-view mirror that she stayed on the pavement and watched him drive off. Nico remembered the time he and Rita had got lost trying to find Dal Papavero, a famous restaurant in a village above Gaiole in Chianti. Rita had asked for directions from the only person they could find on the road – a teenager kicking around a football. The boy offered to take them there. Rita accepted before Nico could stop her. 'He's going to take us where he wants to go,' he had muttered in English. Rita had laughed, her way of shutting him up. The boy got in the back seat, gave Rita directions, and seven winding uphill kilometres later, Dal Papavero came into view. The boy didn't live in the tiny town, wouldn't accept a meal or money. He said he did it because they were lost and he was bored. Rita watched him kick his ball back down the hill.

With dessert, a delicious torta della nonna, 'grandmother's cake,' Nico had got a lecture on trust.

'Buona sera, Signor Doyle.' Perillo stood behind a large desk placed at the end of a deep room. The distance from door to desk gave him the time to study the people who came to complain, snitch, lie, or tell the truth. It gave him a head start.

41

Perillo watched the tall man stride confidently into the room. Not smiling, but at ease with his surroundings. Most people, even honest ones, were nervous walking into the carabinieri station for the first time. Not this man. Perillo had discovered several interesting facts about Signor Doyle, thanks to the Internet.

'I'm sorry I'm late. I wasn't expecting so much traffic.'

'An apology is not necessary. Your dog is waiting for you under the desk. He behaved very well.'

'Hi, pal.' Nico bent down.

The dog ignored him. His coat had turned into sparkling white fluff. His paws were clean too. Some fur had been trimmed off.

'Somebody gave you a bath.' He reached down and stroked the dog's long ears. 'You look good.'

Still no response. Was he hurt? 'What did you do to him?'

'The technicians examined him with great regard. His fur was carefully combed out to catch whatever might have been trapped there. His paws meticulously scrubbed. I do not believe he will solve our murder, but it is best to be thorough. We also took an imprint of your boots. As you seemed anxious about the dog, I brought him back to your house when they were through. You weren't present, so he came here. I was afraid he might run away. I left your boots by your doorstep.'

'I was at Sotto Il Fico.'

'Good restaurant, but I find their courgette lasagne too thin. Only three layers of pasta, no tomatoes, no ricotta, just courgette, herbs and béchamel. A poor man's meal, which is what Tuscan food is all about, after all. In the South, where we are far poorer than the Tuscans, our lasagne is small mountains of pasta filled with a richness for which we can only thank Apollo, the sun god.'

'You washed him.'

It sounded like an accusation, something Perillo was used to from indignant tourists and, too often, his wife. 'My wife took it upon herself. We live upstairs. I didn't think you would mind. He needed it badly.' He said it with a slight reproach in his voice. Tit for tat. 'She also shined your boots.'

'Please thank her for me. Let's get on with the deposition, then.' Nico's tone was brusque. The maresciallo supposed it was easier to be annoyed with him than with the mutt.

He pointed to a chair on Nico's side of the desk. 'Please, sit.'

Nico sat down, taking care to make sure his feet didn't hit the dog. He heard voices coming from another room. He wondered how many carabinieri worked here. Perillo pulled up a wooden armchair to the other side of the desk and sat down. 'Would you like to dictate to Daniele?'

At the sound of his name, the young man who had been at the wheel of the blue Alfa Romeo appeared from another room in his well-pressed summer uniform – lightweight black slacks and a blue short-sleeved shirt. 'Good day, Maresciallo.' He took his place in front of the computer at the far end of the room.

'He'll transcribe your words directly into the computer. He's very skilled.' It was thanks to Daniele's ability to navigate the mysterious web that Perillo had discovered Conor Domenico Doyle's interesting past. The name Conor was on his birth certificate. But by the time he'd joined the police force, Conor had disappeared from his name. Why erase a name? Daniele had unearthed more. The Venetian police weren't the only ones with a computer expert on staff.

'I would prefer to do my own inputting,' Nico said, his pride kicking in. He was also fast at the computer, having typed countless reports. He welcomed the challenge of writing in Italian.

'You're familiar with the Italian keyboard?' Daniele asked, a Venetian lilt to his words.

He hadn't thought of that. 'Can I write it out in longhand?'

'Certainly.' Perillo held out a hand. Daniele quickly filled it with several sheets of paper and extracted a pen from his front shirt pocket. Perillo handed over the sheets to Nico. 'Please add your phone number and address at the bottom.'

'Of course.'

Daniele stood behind his superior in an at-ease position. Perillo pretended to read a report on the disappearance of ten cases of wine from a Castellina in Chianti vintner. The matter had quickly been solved, thanks to a tip from the vintner's wife. All ten cases were in his mistress's home.

'Done,' Nico said, and handed over a single sheet. Perillo held it back out for Daniele to type up.

While the young man's fingers flew across the keyboard, Nico nudged OneWag with his foot. The dog looked up at him for a moment, then stretched his small body as far as it would go, as if to say he didn't have a care in the world.

In two minutes, Nico's typed deposition was back in Perillo's hands.

'Please reread it.' Perillo slid the paper across the desk after having read it a second time. 'In typing it up, Daniele made a few grammatical corrections.'

'I'm sure there were more than a few.'

'No,' Daniele said. 'Only a few. Your Italian is good.'

Nico knew that was bullshit. 'Thank you.' He had always been lousy at written Italian. It had nothing to do with how people spoke.

Daniele, who looked no older than eighteen, blushed. With his pale skin, rosy cheeks, blue eyes and straight, wheat-coloured hair, he could have been mistaken for a midwestern farm boy. Or a Tuscan nobleman. The portraits in the Uffizi were full of men and women with his fair colouring.

Nico compared his own handwritten deposition with Daniele's typed one. Nothing had been altered except his many mistakes, which he hoped to remember. His life was now a continuing learning process, mastering written Italian being only the first step, and not an easy one at that. He signed the typed version and slid it back across the scratched, ink-stained wooden desk. At his precinct, the desks had all been metal, and the walls filled with details of cases they hadn't solved yet, photographs of the victims and whiteboards covered in the latest rundowns of each case in black Magic Marker, the salient points underlined in red.

In the room he was sitting in now, the pale yellow walls held a large map of the area, a photograph of Greve's famous Piazza Matteotti from the days when wine was sold from horse-drawn carriages. Next to it, an aerial view of tens of stands offering wine tastings, fronted by crowds.

Perillo caught him looking and shook his head. 'Chianti Expo keeps us busy. It's good for the vintners, a headache for us and the idiots who drink too much.' He turned to Daniele. 'Where's the kit?'

Daniele jumped up and rushed out of the room.

'Is he new?' Nico asked, remembering his own anxiety when he'd first joined the homicide squad. After the first week, Joey, his first partner, had presented him with a cigarette box filled with joints. All they did was add five pounds to Nico's girth.

'Six months on the job and his first murder. We don't get too many of those. Fast learner.' They both watched Daniele come back into the room, this time at an intentionally measured pace.

'Now for your DNA,' Perillo said. 'Go on, Daniele. You know how to do it.'

Daniele straightened his shoulders, opened the sealed plastic envelope, took out a large Q-tip. 'Open your mouth, please.'

Nico did as he was asked and had his mouth swabbed. Fingerprinting was next.

When Nico had wiped his fingers clean with the tissues Daniele offered him, Perillo stood up. 'Good. That's done.' He wanted to talk to this man, draw him out, but fair was fair. Conor Domenico Doyle had had a very bad start to his day.

'The rest of the afternoon is all yours now.'

Nico didn't move. Curiosity wound itself around his head like a snake. 'Have you been able to identify the dead man?' Here was Eve, biting into the apple.

Perillo held back a smile of satisfaction. Once a police detective, always a police detective. A cliché. But clichés were just truths made insignificant by too much repetition. 'Not yet. Without a face to show around, it isn't easy. I've contacted all the hotels in the area.'

Daniele's chair squeaked. Perillo waved a hand at him. 'With Daniele's help, of course. He's invaluable.'

Daniele's cheeks reddened again.

'The hotels are going to get back to us if any of their guests don't show up tonight. As for the three families who live near the crime scene, no one heard a thing. Or so they claim.' In truth, he had only spoken to the wives, the men having gone to work for the day. He would need to return there this evening.

'The medical examiner and forensic team came down from Florence and did their work. They combed the area, but the murder weapon, a shotgun, was not found. Nor the casing. Maybe the medical examiner will find the pellet embedded in what was left of the man's face, so we at least know the gauge of the gun.'

'Will that take long?' How fast would Perillo get results from Florence?

'I can assure you it isn't as fast as what you see on *CSI*. By the way, your assumption that the single gunshot you heard killed the victim seems to be correct. At least, the times match. The body's on its way to Careggi as we speak.'

'The hospital in Florence?' Stella had been born there. The eighteenth of August. Every year, Rita sent her a gift.

'That's right. That's where our legal-medical institute is. Oh, we took his fingerprints, of course, and we're having them checked on the national database in Rome and by Interpol. It may be days before we get results. We're not as fast as you Americans.'

'Don't believe what you see on American TV programmes. We take our time too.'

'Glad to hear that.' With a smile on his face, Perillo extended a hand. 'Thank you for coming by, Signor Doyle. I look forward to sharing a coffee. Maybe some morning at Bar All'Angolo?'

This man wanted something from him. Nico could feel it. Maybe it was just the standard Italian curiosity about American life and politics, and Nico was just being paranoid. He shook Perillo's hand. 'I'm there most mornings around nine.' Nico leant down to pick up OneWag from under the desk, but the spot was empty.

'He's by the entrance, ready to go,' Perillo said. As Nico walked to the door, Perillo added, 'I've been wondering how the dead man got to that clearing.'

Nico turned around. 'You didn't find a car?'

'No car, no scooter, no bicycle.'

'Three possibilities. He walked, the killer drove him there or the killer took his car.'

'Perhaps, but we found no tracks. Only some freshly broken twigs. It barely rained on Sunday, so the ground is still hard. What I ask myself is, why did the murder occur at that time? It was still dark when you heard the shot. And why that particular spot?'

'I suppose that's for you to find out.'

'True enough. But please stay in the area for the next few weeks.'

Nico didn't like the sound of that. 'Am I a suspect?'

'No, a witness.'

Nico scooped the dog up, nodded to both men and left.

When the door had closed, Daniele asked, 'Do you want to involve him in the case?' He hoped so. Americans knew how to solve problems. If Steve Jobs were still alive, he'd have figured this out in the blink of an eye.

'The higher-ups in Florence have unfortunately assigned Substitute Prosecutor Riccardo Della Langhe to this case, and I can definitely say that exchanging ideas with an ex-New York City homicide detective will be far more beneficial than listening to Della Langhe's idiotic pronouncements.' He wasn't about to let on to Daniele how unsure he felt about solving this brutal killing. It was complicated. Unknown victim, possibly American, valuables left behind. He had dealt with only one previous murder in his career, easily solved. It didn't help that Della Langhe, prejudiced against anyone from the South, considered him dumb.

Perillo opened his drawer and stared at the messy contents as if they could offer a solution. Eventually slammed the drawer shut.

Behind him, Daniele stood up straighter, steeling himself for an outburst.

'We're going to prove that arrogant jerk wrong,' Perillo said out loud. 'We're going to solve this ugly crime quickly, Daniele. We have to.'

Daniele relaxed his posture. 'Yes, Maresciallo. Maybe we can talk to Signor Doyle, who certainly must have solved many murders in his nineteen-year career?'

'Perhaps, Daniele.' Exactly what he was thinking. 'But right now, it's time for you to go back to calling the Florentine jewellery stores you so expertly unearthed on your computer.'

The list was endless, much to Daniele's dismay. He enjoyed navigating the depths of the Internet to extract the gems Perillo needed. He found talking to people awkward, especially over the phone, without knowing what to expect beforehand. The one advantage, which his mother repeatedly pointed out, was that at least no one could see him blush when shyness made him trip over his words.

'Excuse me, Maresciallo. The dead man was American, so surely the bracelet is American?'

'The technicians did say his *clothes* were American, gold shoes included, but that does not necessarily make *him* an American. New York alone receives millions of foreign tourists a year, and they buy and buy and buy American clothes made in some cheap-labour country by children.' Perillo picked up the suede leather jacket – Italian lambskin, cut and sewn in Florence – he had carefully draped over a chair and flung it over one shoulder. 'No, dear Daniele, be careful of jumping to easy conclusions. The phone awaits you. I'll go and talk to the four jewellers here in town. One of us might get lucky. Ciao.'

Daniele watched his boss saunter to the door on his soft new suede boots and matching jacket. He knew where the maresciallo was going first. The cafe next door, for his tenth or twelfth espresso of the day. How the man didn't have the jitters from all that caffeine was a mystery to him. Daniele looked at his phone, then the screensaver on his computer, a picture of an ascending line of cypress trees silhouetted against a clear blue sky. A picture that had ended up on countless postcards. He loved his job, most of the time. He liked his boss. The world behind the cypress trees would have to wait. Daniele picked up his mobile phone and keyed in the numbers in his notebook.

CHAPTER THREE

Nico and Tilde sat outside at the restaurant, looking out at the dark valley sprinkled with the lights from distant towns. The sky had its own faraway lights and a moon reduced to a smile. The view Sotto Il Fico offered its diners was its biggest drawing card. The food was good, but the view was spectacular. It was now past midnight, and the place was empty. The only nearby sound came from a light breeze teasing the leaves of the fig tree. The tables had been cleared, the dishes and kitchen cleaned. Enzo had taken his mother home. Stella had gone off with Gianni. It was time to relax with a glass of 2013 Sammarco, a 'Super Tuscan' red wine Enzo had introduced him to.

'Looks like Gianni's changed his mind,' Nico said. 'Stella has her smile back.'

'A short-lived smile. I know my daughter. He brought

her flowers. It's a ploy. He has to make her love him again before renewing his demands. She knows that.'

Nico heard anger in her voice. Where was it coming from? He couldn't believe Enzo had ever treated her that way. He was a good man. Un pezzo di pane, Rita had once called him. A piece of bread.

'I'm glad to see my fusilli alla Rita sold out.' He wasn't showing off so much as changing the subject.

'Compliments, Nico. They were delicious. You added just the right amount of garlic, rocket and oil. Did you see Elvira sneaking forkfuls from Enzo's plate when she thought we weren't looking?'

Nico laughed. 'I guess she liked it, not that she'll ever admit it.'

'Not even on her deathbed.'

'I'm sorry we ran out. I would have roasted more tomatoes, if I'd had more. I picked my plants clean.'

'You'll find many more at Sunday's market in Panzano. We can go together if you want.'

'That recipe is yours now,' Nico said. 'I want to offer different dishes.'

'Any recipe of Rita's is welcome here.'

'How about mine?'

Tilde laughed. 'I'll have to taste them first.'

'Done.' They clinked glasses and drank. 'This wine is heaven,' Nico said.

'Yes, it smooths out the wrinkles of the day, and you've had a major one.'

'And your wrinkles?'

Tilde heard the concern behind the question and didn't like that her emotions had been readable. 'They're on my face, but I can only blame them on age, not the day. How did it go with Salvatore? Did he figure out who the dead man is?' Nico could tell she was trying to pivot away from herself.

'Not yet. I believe he's assuming the man wasn't a local, thanks to those shoes, I guess.'

Robi's drunken boast came back: *I'll return covered in gold.* Tilde shook her head to toss the words away. 'A mosquito,' she explained when Nico looked curiously at her.

'Perillo's put the word out to hotels in the area and I guess asked a few real estate agents. A man with that kind of watch might have rented a flat. I wouldn't think he was the Airbnb type, but you never know. It's going to take a while. This whole area is rented out this time of year.'

'Find the unslept bed.'

'It's a start. I imagine there are plenty of guests or renters who find other beds to sleep in while on holiday.'

'I wouldn't limit it to holiday time.' Her voice had gone sharp again.

Nico leant forward, trying to glimpse Tilde's expression in the dim light of the mosquito-repelling candle. Had Enzo cheated on her? Rita had once claimed that cheating was part of an Italian man's DNA.

Tilde caught him peering at her. 'It's not what you think. Enzo has been very good to me.'

'You deserve it.'

She shook her head. 'I wish I did.' She hadn't returned Enzo's love when they'd got married, feeling that she didn't deserve him after what had happened. He had loved her enough for both of them. He still did. She would forever be grateful to him.

Nico didn't know how to respond to the sadness in her voice except by returning to the murder, which seemed to interest her.

'It looks like the shot I heard was what killed the man.'

'Is that significant?' When didn't seem as important as who.

'It establishes time of death. That can be important. Funny thing. Perillo's wife gave OneWag a bath, turned him into a big pom-pom.'

'OneWag?'

'His tail produces one wag at a time. That's it.'

'So you've given him a name. Does that mean you're keeping him?'

'I'm not ready to keep anything besides myself, but I'll feed him and make sure he has water.'

'Help yourself to our scraps.'

He lifted a plastic bag from the floor. 'I have.' Nico finished the wine and leant back in his chair. In the distance, a blinking light moved across the darkness at a steady pace. He watched it move, trying to make out what it was.

'What are you looking at?' Tilde asked.

'That moving light. What is it?'

'When Stella was little, she called it a fairy light.

She wanted to watch it until dawn. I see you're hooked too.' Her beautiful, beloved daughter. She was hiding something from her mother. Something that she suspected had nothing to do with Gianni. Worry about her daughter and the detail of the gold shoes were making her frantic. 'A light blinking in the dark, moving towards some unknown destination. That's what it must feel like when you're trying to solve a murder.'

Nico remembered only too well. 'What is the light, then?'

She laughed. 'It belongs to a rubbish truck making its rounds. I suppose Salvatore will also be picking through a lot of rubbish on his way to a solution. I don't envy him.'

'Neither do I.' He just hoped the maresciallo's light was bright enough.

OneWag was curled up in his usual spot by the vegetable garden gate. Nico spotted him easily, thanks to his torch. 'Hey, brought you something.' He waved the bag in the air, plastic rustling. 'Not that you deserve it after that snub at the station.'

The dog sat up and gave Nico his 'I'm listening' tilt of the head. No wag and no running to the food. It made Nico smile. This mutt was as proud as any Tuscan. The people, at least, had a right to their pride. The Italians owed their beautiful language to the Tuscans, according to Rita. On their honeymoon, she had made sure to point out the greatness of Tuscan art, their architecture, and always Dante's *Divina Commedia*. Endless quotes from the *Inferno*, *Purgatorio*, and *Paradiso*. He understood nothing of the poet's arcane Italian, as he had not understood Chaucer in high school, but loved her, and that was enough reason to listen.

'For you, surviving is enough reason to be proud,' Nico told the dog. 'Okay, you keep your dignity. Here.' He dropped the bag on the ground and opened it. 'Buon appetito.' He walked the thirty steps to the house, unlocked the door, turned on the neon light of the ground floor – one large room where the farmer had once kept his pig, now cleaned up and filled with Aldo's discarded wine barrels – and climbed upstairs.

Nico flicked the switch and watched as the glass bowls of three brass lamps slowly lit up his new home. Brick flooring in both rooms, as well as ceiling beams cut from discarded wooden railroad tracks. In a corner of the main room, a large cast-iron wood stove. In the cold months, the balcony would hold enough wood to get him through the winter. The wall abutting the bedroom and bathroom held a blackened stone fireplace the farmer's wife must have used for cooking. There was no stove when Nico stumbled on the house on one of his long walks. Aldo had planned to demolish the place and build two flats, but he didn't have the money for it, and so they agreed on a five-year lease. Nico had chosen the place not in spite of but because it belonged to another time – and needed a good cleaning, a new bathroom, a brand-new stove. He would fix it up, maybe in the process fixing himself.

The work on the house was almost finished now. He wanted winter to arrive so he could see what more he needed to do. Nico quietly opened the balcony door and checked on his three swallows. They were home, asleep.

All was well, except for a man whose face had been blown off. Lying awake in bed, Nico found himself reliving his discovery. Would the poor man find justice? In his career as a detective, too many crimes had gone unsolved.

In his sleep, Nico dreamt the dog climbed into the bed and slept at his feet, keeping them warm.

Perillo parked the carabinieri's Alfa Romeo in Gravigna's main piazza. He wanted his presence noted. It was his wife who had suggested he wear his uniform to make his visit to the town more official. A murder had been committed nearby, and the townsfolk needed reassurance. The weather helped, with clear skies and a light breeze that would later take the bite out of a hot sun. Perillo checked his watch. Eight forty-five. He'd timed his arrival well. By now, the primary-school children would be in class halfway up the hill, and the older kids in their high school in Greve. Not being a parent, he was awkward at dealing with children. The parents would reassure them far better than he could.

'Buongiorno,' Perillo said, tilting his hat to the foursome of old men sitting on the benches surrounding the fountain. They were typically a happy lot, grateful to be alive, to be able to discuss the Viola, the Florentine football team, their ailments and what they'd eaten the night before.

As soon as he approached them, they crowded around him, assailed him with questions.

'Who was the victim?' 'Was he a local, an Italian tourist, a foreigner?' 'There's a rumour he was a rich American. Is it true?' 'Should we lock our doors at night?' 'Was the dead man robbed?' 'Was it a hunting accident?' 'Are you going to find out who killed him?'

'Of course, I am,' Perillo said, waving down their questions with his arms. 'I assure you, this is not a random killing. Nothing was stolen. You are not in danger. But it's important that if you see something, hear something, know something, please come forward.'

Perillo watched the foursome go back to their benches, shaking their heads and muttering, unconvinced.

Carletta, the lavender-haired waitress of the trattoria facing the piazza, was readying the outside tables for lunch. 'Keep me safe,' she called out as Perillo walked by. If she was afraid, her smile masked it well.

A truck parked on the other side of the street was making its weekly delivery to Luciana's tiny flower shop. Luciana seemed too busy with the delivery of her beloved flowers and plants to worry about murder at the moment.

A few doors down from Luciana, Bar All'Angolo was crowded with locals in a huddle at the far end of the long space, hands gesticulating in the air as they argued, questioned, pontificated about the murder. Perillo walked in. The tourists, seemingly ignorant of the news, sat near the open French doors and enjoyed cappuccinos and hot cornetti. Sandro, the tall, handsome co-owner of the cafe, stood behind the cash register, ringing up orders, dispensing change, selling bus tickets to Florence and the neighbouring towns. Jimmy, the other co-owner and Sandro's husband, manned the espresso machine and the oven.

Perillo went straight to the group of locals at the back of the bar. He knew these men and women had come to the cafe to share their curiosity and their fears. It was his job to make them feel safe again.

Perillo repeated what he'd said to the foursome outside.

A few of his cycling pals contributed their own words. 'Salvatore will find the killer in no time. Let's stay calm. We're in good hands.'

Some nodded. Others looked sceptical.

Perillo raised his hands again. 'I'm sorry, I have no information to give you right now. I can promise you this. I will discover who the murdered man is and find his killer.' *God willing*, he thought as his stomach fluttered with doubt. Why was he so dumb as to ever promise anything? 'What is most important is that if you come to know anything, no matter how trivial it might seem, please let me know. Call me or come by the station if you want privacy. Is that understood?'

Everyone nodded.

'Good. Now go on with your day.'

The group seemed more relaxed as they edged away from him. Perillo thanked his cycling friends for their trust in him. They were all going off to train for the big amateur race at the end of the month. He would have loved to have donned his racing gear and gone off with them, but until this murder was solved, his five-speed Bianchi Vittoria would be staying at the station.

'You've got a big one on your hands this time,' Jimmy said. 'Here, console yourself with this.' Jimmy handed him a sugar-covered ciambella. 'Espresso corrected with grappa, coming up. Breakfast is on us.'

'Thanks.' Perillo took a big bite and let the cream filling ooze down his throat. He needed the consolation after the promise he had just made. Last night's visit to Aldo's three male neighbours had yielded a zero. The search for the jeweller who might have sold the bracelet he'd found in the victim's pocket hadn't yielded any results yet. Two hotels had each reported one missing male guest and three female guests. Perillo didn't worry about the missing women, at least not yet. He hoped, with all his heart, that their absence was due only to the joys of the Chianti vino and the attraction of the Italian male. The two missing men had got his hopes up.

Perillo had sent Daniele on his motorbike to the first hotel in Radda in Chianti. He'd picked the Panzano hotel because it was on the way to Gravigna. While he was en route, both hotels called within ten minutes of each other to say their missing guests had stumbled back in and were fast asleep in their rooms. He immediately called Daniele but got no answer. He blamed it on the young man's motorbike making too much noise and texted him instead: GO BACK TO GREVE. THE FLORENTINE JEWELLERS LIST IS WAITING FOR YOU.

Perillo looked around the room. Could his killer be among the many locals who kept running in for that quick boost of espresso, then back to their jobs? They were good, hard-working people, from what he knew of them. The hunters among them aimed their rifles at boars, shotguns at hares and birds. To blast a man's face off took so much rage. Where could that come from? Greed? Then why leave an expensive watch on the man's wrist? Jealousy? Revenge? No, those gold shoes excluded a local.

Perillo's thoughts were interrupted by Beppe, a slouchy eighteen-year-old, rushing in and shouting, 'Two espressos in paper cups!' like his life depended on it. 'Double the cups, so I don't burn my fingers.'

Sandro took Beppe's five-euro note and gave him change. 'Our espressos taste better with a "please" after the order.'

Beppe pocketed the coins and picked up the cups. 'What century do you live in?' He spotted Perillo. 'Salve, Salvo.' He grinned at his own bad pun.

'Salve to you.' Perillo hated the nickname Salvo but let the kid feel clever. He was sure it didn't happen too often.

'Have you solved that murder yet?' Beppe asked.

'In fact, I'm here to arrest you.'

Beppe's eyes opened wide. The tiny coffee cups in his hands trembled.

Behind the cash register, Sandro laughed. 'Come on, Salvatore's kidding.'

Beppe blinked. The cups steadied. 'That's not funny.'

'Neither are you,' said Jimmy over the sound of steam foaming up milk for a cappuccino.

'I don't try to be,' the young man said in his defence. He turned back to Perillo. 'So who's the dead guy? I bet him and the killer are somebody we know.' Beppe looked around the room, his face flushed with excitement. The bar had thinned out. Only a few tourists remained. 'That would be something, eh?' he said, looking back at Perillo. 'Every newspaper in the country would write about us.'

'*La Nazione* already has.' Nelli, who ran the art centre, was reading about the murder in one of the copies of the Florentine paper the cafe provided for its customers. 'What I don't understand is, why would a grown man wear gold trainers?' A woman in her forties, with pale blue eyes, a welcoming face, and a long braid of greying blonde hair, she favoured muted colours in her wardrobe and her landscapes.

'To hide the grave sin he visited on another,' Gogol announced as he shuffled into the bar, wearing a heavy overcoat and bringing with him the usual overpowering smell of cheap cologne. Luckily, most tourists considered him an added attraction, some asking to take his photo. He was a gentleman somewhere in his seventies who liked to wander through the town, offering to quote any verse from *The Divine Comedy* for a euro. It was the overcoat he could not part with, even in the worst summer heat, that had given him his nickname. Almost no one remembered his real name.

'What sins are you hiding underneath that coat?' Nelli asked. She had offered to buy him a new one countless times and been refused. The one Gogol wore looked as old and wrinkled as he was. At least they were both clean, thanks to the staff at the old-age home on the outskirts of town.

'No sin, gentle lady. It keeps my dreams safe.'

'What dreams can you have?' Beppe asked in a tone Perillo instantly disliked.

'Dreams of a blameless life.'

'Beppe,' the maresciallo called out, 'why don't you bring your mother her espressos before they're too cold to drink?'

Beppe caught the hint with a disgruntled look on his face. As he stepped out of the open door, Gogol quoted his favourite poet. '"I understood that to this punishment are damned the carnal sinners who let pleasure vanquish reason." I offer this verse for no charge except "a resting space bestowed".'

Gogol walked to a table by the open French doors. Some people thought him stupid or mentally disabled, and no, he wasn't as quick as the lizards he'd tried to catch as a boy, but he did know Sandro and Jimmy wanted him to sit near the open air. He sat and took a bite of one of the many crostini he had taken from Sergio Macchi, the butcher, who handed them out to anyone who walked into his shop, along with a glass of red wine. This one was with lard, like the ones Gogol's mother used to make for him. He opened a napkin, placed a salami crostino in the exact centre and pushed it in front of the opposite chair.

Jimmy leant and whispered to Perillo, 'That's for his new friend. Five minutes maximum till Nico walks in.'

'How do you know?' Perillo asked.

'They've bonded. Nico treats him to breakfast every morning. He says Gogol reminds him of his wife.'

'That bad?'

'No, Rita was all of one piece. It's because she liked to quote Dante a lot.'

'I'm glad he's coming. It's time I get better acquainted with Gogol's new friend.' Perillo left the cafe to light a cigarette and wait.

OneWag saw him first. The dog scurried across the piazza on his short legs, fluffy tail high in the air. Nico turned a corner, running after him and yelling.

Perillo laughed as the dog stopped at his feet and sniffed his shoes. Sleek black leather ones this time. The dog licked a drop of cream from the left shoe, then sat down. Perillo bent down and scratched behind the dog's ears.

Nico reached the pavement out of breath. 'That's the first and last time this dog is tricking me.'

'Buongiorno, Nico.' Perillo put out his cigarette against the wall. Americans detested smoking. 'I think you have a rascal on your hands.'

'Sorry. Buongiorno, Maresciallo. I was afraid he'd get run over.'

'Salvatore. The formalities are over. From now on, let's proceed on a first-name basis.'

From now on? Proceed? Nico had the distinct feeling Perillo now knew he'd been a homicide detective – easy enough to find out on the Internet. The good, at least. Maybe not the bad. 'Okay, Salvatore it is.' Maresciallo Perillo was a mouthful.

Perillo saw Nico's recognition. He needed to tread carefully. He wished them to be friends first of all, even though he'd met this ex-homicide detective only the day before. He sensed they shared a love of justice. He didn't know why Nico had been forcibly retired from the police force, but he was convinced that whatever Nico had done had been done for a good reason. Perillo always prided himself on being a strong judge of character. This man was also clearly tutto di un pezzo, all of one piece. To ease the tension, he looked down at the dog, busy gnawing at a paw. 'No lead?'

'I wasn't planning to take him anywhere,' Nico said. 'He slipped into the car without my noticing and jumped out before I had the chance to stop him.'

'He probably doesn't need one. Strays know how to take care of themselves.' The dog stopped gnawing and looked up at him. 'Clever mutt knows he's being talked about.' Perillo bent down, gave the dog another scratch behind his ear and said, 'Sharing a cup of coffee comes with the elimination of formalities.'

Befriend the dog, befriend the owner, was that what Perillo was up to? What Nico wanted was for Maresciallo Perillo to leave him alone.

Gogol waved from the open French door. 'Ciao, amico.'

Nico waved back with a big smile. He'd just been given an excuse. 'Thanks for the offer. Maybe some other time? I don't want to disappoint Gogol.'

'Of course. Some other time.' Perillo held out his hand. Nico shook it and strode inside the cafe, followed by OneWag, his nails clicking against the tile floor. In the States, dogs got kicked out of communal spaces, but this cafe was a free country. 'Buongiorno, Sandro, Jimmy. The usual for both of us.'

'Salve' came from both. He gave Sandro exact change. Jimmy called out, 'One Americano, one doppio espresso corretto and four whole wheat cornetti coming up!'

The few remaining locals in the cafe turned to look at Nico. Stared more than looked. He steeled himself against the questions that he was sure were coming. Tragedy, for most people, was always followed by a nasty, all-consuming curiosity. Murder in a small, quiet village would prompt the ultimate version of this.

A couple of men nodded at him by way of saying hello. After a long minute, they turned back to whatever they were having, murmuring amongst themselves.

Nico relaxed as he realised he'd been wrong. They were certainly curious, but they didn't ask. Maybe out of respect, but probably because he was not one of them.

As Nico walked over to Gogol's table, Perillo made his way to the car park behind Macelleria Macchi. He would try again tomorrow. Maybe by then, he would have some concrete details about the murder to offer the American detective. As Perillo took out his keys, his phone vibrated in his back pocket. Perillo slipped it out and swiped a finger across the screen. 'Yes, Daniele, what is it?'

'I kicked the ball in the net.' The loud excitement in his voice reverberated in Perillo's ear.

'Calm down, I can hear you. You found the jeweller who sold the bracelet?'

'Yes, but not in Florence. Here in Radda. Gioielleria Crisani. It's just past the Fattoria Vignale hotel. I know you told me to go back to the office, but I thought since I was here . . .' Daniele stopped and waited for the reprimand.

Perillo was thrilled but wasn't going to let it show. 'This time you got results. Next time, check with me first. I'm coming to talk to them, but first I have to go back and get the bracelet.'

'I have it with me.'

'Ah.' Perillo held back from saying 'Good.' Daniele was young and needed reining in. Not unlike Nico's stray. 'I'll be there in fifteen minutes.'

Nico sat down across from the old man wrapped in his overcoat. The pungent smell of his cologne was almost gone, thanks to the fresh air coming in from the open doors.

Gogol nudged his chin towards the salami crostino in front of Nico.

'Thank you.' He wrapped the crostino in the napkin. 'I'll eat it later.' He could smell the cornetti coming out of the oven. 'I'm sorry I didn't show up yesterday.'

'We took care of him,' Jimmy called out.

'Thanks. I'll pay.'

'No need,' Sandro said. 'You're a good customer.'

'You did not appear because,' Gogol said, '"the river of blood draws near, wherein are boiling those who harm others by violence".'

Nico picked up the words 'blood' and 'violence.'

'Yes, there was a murder.'

Jimmy carried over a tray with their breakfast, to which he'd added a jar of his home-made raspberry jam. Nico watched Gogol grin with happiness as he slathered jam onto his hot cornetto. It was a sight that started Nico's mornings on good footing. Too bad he'd needed to roast the tomatoes yesterday instead of coming to the bar. He would have made Gogol happy, and someone else would've found the body. He picked up his own cornetto.

Gogol pressed a finger on the back of his friend's hand. Nico understood that he was about to say something he considered important. Two days ago, Gogol had pressed his finger on Nico's forearm before revealing that his mother didn't know who his father was, but God had forgiven her, and she was in Dante's *Paradiso* with the poet.

Nico prepared himself for another quote he would not understand, but this man deserved to be listened to. 'Yes, tell me.'

'The dead man is not a good man,' Gogol said. 'Better dead.'

Nico put his food back on the plate and looked into Gogol's water-blue eyes. People said the old man was simple, but anyone who quoted Dante at will had to have some intelligence. 'You know who he is?'

'Stay away. He will hurt you.' Gogol rubbed his hands over his face as if needing to wipe it clean.

'The dead man will hurt me?'

'Salvatore. Stay away.'

'Why?'

'Bad man.'

'Why is the maresciallo a bad man?'

'No!' Gogol slapped his hand on the table, spilling his coffee. It dripped onto the floor. 'I go now. Tomorrow, if I live.' It was his usual way of signing off.

'You will live, and you will tell me more tomorrow.'

'"Through me is the way to the lost people,"' Gogol quoted, as he tightened his coat around his body and slowly made his way out of the cafe.

'Don't take him seriously. He's the lost one, unfortunately.' Sandro brought over a mop and started wiping the floor. 'You're manna from heaven for him. Not just because you feed him. Not many people really listen to him. They might give him a euro but they don't hear a word. I'm surprised you understand Dante's Italian. I had a tough time with it in school.'

'I only catch words, not whole sentences. I tried to read *The Divine Comedy* in English to make my wife happy, but gave up pretty quickly.'

'And yet you listen. Good for you.'

'The man deserves that much.' What Nico really listened for was the words between the quotes, the man behind the Dante screen. He hadn't found him yet. And what did Gogol have against the maresciallo?

'Has Gogol ever had trouble with the law?' Nico asked Sandro.

'No. We'd know if he had.'

Jimmy, who was washing down the counter with a sponge, joined in. 'In this town, even your farts aren't secret. Not that anyone really cares. Live and let live. You picked a good place to live.'

'I know.' Live and let live was exactly what he needed. Nico stood up, and OneWag followed his lead.

Sandro moved the pail out of Nico's way. 'Don't worry about what Gogol said. He and Salvatore get along fine, but since he really likes you, please do us all the favour of smashing that cologne bottle of his.'

'I can try to talk him out of using it.'

Jimmy laughed. 'You've got as much a chance at that as winning the lottery.'

CHAPTER FOUR

The historical centre of Radda, the medieval heart of Chianti, was a pedestrian-only zone. Perillo drove down one tree-lined viale that skirted the village, then back up the other side. As he expected, no free parking spots. September, with weather that restored the soul after the gagging heat of August, was his favourite month, but also the month the tourists poured in, thanks to the mild sun and all the wine and food festivals. They brought in much-needed money, but Perillo resented their taking over as though the place was theirs. His wife's complaints didn't help. Endless lines at the food shops, crowded cafes, bread selling out early, the best tomatoes gone, restaurants reserved weeks ahead when it had always been possible to reserve the very same day. Not that he ever took his wife out to a restaurant.

Lost in the iniquities brought on by tourists, Perillo

drove right by his uniformed brigadiere standing in front of Gioielleria Crisani.

Daniele waved. 'Maresciallo!'

Perillo saw Daniele in his rear-view mirror and braked. The Fiat behind him swerved to avoid hitting the carabinieri car. Perillo shrugged an apology as the driver passed him, holding back what Perillo knew was a deserved vaffanculo. He turned off the motor, got out and joined Daniele, who was looking at his double-parked car with dismay. Perillo didn't care. Double parking was a privilege that came with the job. It was unfortunate that everyone else thought they had the same privilege.

'We won't be long.' Perillo rang the bell by the door and was buzzed in. The store was a small, narrow room with every available space covered by glass cases displaying glittering and expensive jewellery. He was reminded of the Ponte Vecchio stores he'd seen with his wife in Florence. This one had no view of the Arno in the back, but the young woman behind the display case was just as enticing a sight. Black, wavy hair falling to the shoulders framed a marble-white oval face, full bare lips, large, dark eyes nesting below a thick fringe of black eyelashes and perfectly shaped eyebrows. Perillo took his eyes away to look at the ceiling. The sight of good-looking women lightened his heart, but the sight of the two video cameras, one above the door, the other above the young woman, made it jump.

'Buongiorno, Signorina.' He took out his identification.

73

She held up a graceful hand, devoid of any jewellery. 'No need, Maresciallo Perillo. Daniele told me you were coming.'

Perillo looked at his underling. 'Daniele?'

'I gave her my full name.' Daniele was smiling like someone who'd just found the end of a rainbow.

God, Perillo thought. This woman calls him by his first name and he's already in love! Lovelorn men were useless. Perillo turned back to the woman. 'And your name is?'

She smiled. 'Rosalba Crisani.'

'You are the owner?'

'My mother is.'

Perillo held his hand out behind him. Daniele understood and dropped the bracelet in his palm. Perillo spread the bracelet and its dated charm on the velvet cloth on the counter. 'Now, Signorina Rosalba, I see that you have two video cameras in the store, which is a very good thing for you and I hope for me. Were they running the day someone bought this bracelet?'

'Only the tape from the camera above the door.' She pointed to the video camera on the ceiling behind her. 'This one was being fixed that day. I'm sorry.' She looked chagrined.

'It's not your fault,' Perillo said. There was a sweetness to her that made him want to reassure her, despite cursing his own bad luck. 'It would have been far worse if you had been robbed that day. I hope it's working now.'

'It is.'

'We will want to see the tape from the working camera.'

'I'm sorry. We tape over them at the end of each week.'

Perillo held back a groan. Annoyed, he asked, 'Then why did you tell us about the other camera not working? You would have taped over that one too, correct?'

'Daniele told me I had to tell you everything.' She offered her pretty smile as if it was of help.

'I did, Maresciallo.'

Perillo turned to look at his brigadiere. 'I don't doubt it.' At the same time, Daniele surely asked for her phone number, email, Twitter handle and whatever else young people used to communicate these days. Dio, to be young.

Daniele, who knew to stay in the background when Perillo was questioning witnesses, stepped up to the counter to explain. His face was watermelon-tinged. 'I had a fruit juice at the bar by the hotel, and she was having a coffee next to me. I introduced myself and asked her where I could find a jewellery store.'

Perillo softened, remembering how many times, at Daniele's age, he'd used 'Do you know where I can find . . .' as a pickup line. He turned to Rosalba. 'Please tell me everything you remember about the man who bought this bracelet.'

'There isn't much to tell. He came in last Wednesday, just as I opened the shop at eleven.'

'You open at eleven?'

'Yes. Tuesday to Saturday.'

Perillo pointed to his watch. 'It is now ten to ten. Why did you open so early?'

Rosalba looked at Daniele, then back at the maresciallo, her expression not in the least bit puzzled. 'Daniele asked me to.'

She was either obedient by nature, or Daniele had made quite an impression on her. 'The man came last Wednesday,' Perillo repeated.

'Yes. Daniele said it was important to be exact, so I looked up the sale on the sales log. I'm trying to get Mamma to list our sales and receipts on the computer, but she doesn't trust it, so it took me a while to find it.'

Perillo nodded. It never paid to hurry a witness along. 'Sales have been very good lately.'

'I can see that.' There were quite a few empty spaces in the display cases. 'Can you describe him?'

'Big man. Fat belly,' Rosalba said. 'Dressed in jeans and an old polo shirt with a golf club embroidered on the pocket. Just the golf club, no lettering. I noticed because my mother used to play golf with my stepfather whenever she got the chance. I'd take over here, and off she went. She doesn't do that any more. He died two years ago.' She addressed this personal fact to Daniele, who voiced that he was sorry.

There was no emotion in her tone, Perillo noticed. 'Can you describe the buyer's face?' he asked.

'I didn't look at him really. Old. Maybe fifty?'

Perillo wanted to laugh. Fifty was middle age. He was about to hit that milestone himself in three years, and young women like Rosalba had stopped looking at him long ago. 'Can you go into more detail?'

'He wore a blue baseball cap pulled low in front, so I couldn't really see his eyes. He had a big nose. Dark, leathery skin. Lots of wrinkles.'

'Anything written on the cap?'

'LA Dodgers.'

Perillo let out a sigh of satisfaction. Gold trainers, baseball cap. An American, then, just as he'd thought.

Daniele leant towards Perillo and quietly said, 'The watch.'

Perillo nodded. 'Forgive me, Signorina, one last question. Did you happen to notice what kind of watch your client was wearing?'

'A Swatch, I think. Nothing fancy. He wasn't dressed like a rich man, if that's what you're asking.'

Rosalba's answer didn't surprise Perillo. A foreigner wearing an expensive gold watch would attract muggers. The victim had been prudent enough not to wear it everywhere, yet he'd had it on the morning of his death.

'I'd like to send a sketch artist from Florence to draw his face according to what you remember,' Perillo said. 'She'll show you different lips, eyebrows, eyes, chins. It might jog your memory.'

Rosalba didn't answer right away. Her expression showed she didn't relish the thought of getting more involved. Perillo couldn't blame her. Rosalba, with her perfect diction, hair styled down to the strand, her pretty silk dress, came from a world that shied away from the sordid. 'Has the man done something wrong?'

'He died.'

'Oh.' Rosalba traced her finger over the bracelet. She kept her head down when she spoke. 'I'll try if it will help.'

'Thank you. A few more questions.'

She lifted her head. No smile. 'Please, ask.'

'Did he pay with a credit card?'

'No. All cash, which surprised me. The bracelet and charm cost fourteen hundred euros.'

Daniele whistled and caught Perillo clenching his jaw. He was going to get a good talking-to after they left.

'It's heavy, eighteen-carat gold,' Rosalba said. 'The chain isn't hollowed out. He gave me three five-hundred-euro notes. I don't like holding large amounts of cash. It's dangerous. As soon as he left, I closed the store and ran to the bank. Luckily, it's just around the corner. I was sure he was American, you know, the baseball cap and' – a car honked loudly out on the street – 'he didn't say buongiorno after I buzzed him in, which made me immediately think he was a foreigner, but I was wrong.' She had to raise her voice because of the continued honking. 'He spoke pure Tuscan. You know, how some people substitute their consonants with an "H".' By 'some people', she meant ones outside her social class.

Perillo covered his disappointment with a smile. '"Hasa" instead of "casa".' He'd been so ready to bet the man was American. Hoped for it. They had passports. Their names and passport numbers were recorded in the hotels they slept in or by the real estate agents who rented them fancy villas. They paid with traceable credit cards. A Tuscan could disappear in the crowd more easily. On the other hand, a murdered American would stir up the American press and maybe their police. The botched Amanda Knox case had left a nasty stain on Italian law enforcement.

Rosalba flashed a smile at Daniele for a second, then turned to Perillo. 'Your brigadiere is Venetian. What about you?'

'I'm from Hampagnia.'

She laughed. A light, musical sound that made Perillo's heart jump.

The car on the street kept honking. Perillo took a quick look outside and threw his car keys to Daniele. 'Take that man out of his misery.'

Daniele was happy where he was, but he had no choice. Keys in hand, he gave Rosalba's lovely face another look and left to move the car.

'Did he talk about the date he wanted you to inscribe?' The maresciallo turned over the round charm to show the date – 1/1/97. 'Say anything about what it stood for?'

Rosalba knitted her well-groomed eyebrows together. 'He did say something. What was it? He got very nervous and excited when he talked about the date. He asked to see all the different fonts we had available. It took him a long time to decide on cursive. He was giving it to someone he loved very much, that was clear to me. I hope she gets the bracelet.'

'She will when we find out who she is.' As long as she wasn't the killer. Perillo pocketed the bracelet and gave Rosalba a card with both the station's and his own phone number and email. 'In case something comes to mind.' He suspected she already had Daniele's personal information. Perillo held out his hand. 'Thank you. We'll call you when the sketch artist is ready.'

'All right.' She shook his hand and held on to it. 'I hope you find her.'

'So do I.'

On the street, the car was gone. Daniele, the moralist, had refused to park in the now-empty space because it was in a no-parking zone, which meant he was now circling Radda looking for a spot. Perillo debated between waiting and getting an espresso at the nearest cafe. He opted for the espresso and rang Rosalba's bell. At the buzz, he opened the door and offered to bring her one.

'No, thanks, Maresciallo, but I'm glad you came back. I was about to call your mobile. What the man said popped back into my head. He said it stood for the day he did something both despicable and wonderful.'

'Thank you. That's helpful.' He had no idea what it meant, but it was something to chew on. He started walking in search of a cafe when up ahead he saw the squad car reversing into a legal parking spot. The luck of the young!

Perillo crossed the street and joined Daniele just as he was getting out of the car. 'You and I need to talk.'

'Sorry, I shouldn't have whistled back in the store.'

Perillo got in the driver's seat. 'You showed initiative today, and I like that, but you can't fraternise with anyone involved in this case. Besides, she'd chop you into hamburger meat and feed you to her dog. Now, get on your motorcycle and follow me back to Greve.'

Daniele flushed with anger.

After buying *La Nazione* and yesterday's *New York Times International Edition* from Beppe at the news shop, Nico and the dog strolled up to the castle at the very top of the hill. All that remained was crumbling walls and a restored tower. He liked to take in the clear views of the valley the grounds offered. He could see Aldo's winery spread out mid-valley. He thought he could spot his new home, the dark speck near the Ferriello olive grove. Behind that speck was the wide expanse of woods where he'd found the body. Death was following him around, even now. He whistled to OneWag, who came running. It was time for flowers.

On the way back down, Nico stopped to say hello to Tilde and ask if she needed any help. She was alone in the kitchen, rolling small balls of spinach and ricotta in her palms, which the Tuscans called gnudi, which she would later serve in brown butter and sage. The word meant 'naked'. He found them delicious, but when he tried to make them, they always fell apart.

'That's another secret you're going to have to share,' Nico said.

'No secret. Experience.'

'Okay, I'll try again. How are you?'

'Fine. Busy.'

'Where is everybody?'

'Enzo drove Alba to the Co-op. Elvira is getting her colour touched up, and my daughter is late.'

'Gianni?'

'No, she stayed at a girlfriend's. Or so she said. Not that she has to lie to me. She's very nervous and down. Gianni, the museum exam, who knows? Daughters are impossible. You're lucky you never—' Tilde clasped her hand against her mouth, her eyes wide with regret. 'I'm sorry. Please forgive me.'

He wiped ricotta and spinach from Tilde's chin with his handkerchief. 'There's nothing to forgive.' After Rita miscarried for the third time, they'd locked away their dream of having children. 'Come meet my dog.' He'd ordered OneWag to stay outside, and to his surprise, the dog obeyed.

'Bring him in.'

'Into the restaurant?'

'Why not? My clients' shoes walk the same streets his paws do.'

'Well, look at him,' Tilde exclaimed when Nico carried in a panting OneWag. 'His portrait is in the Uffizi, next to a naked lady. You have to go see it.' She turned on the cold water at the sink and reached for a bowl. 'Put him down. He's thirsty.' She placed the full bowl on the floor. OneWag licked her hand and eagerly lapped up the water. The climb to the castle had been too steep for his short legs.

Tilde picked up the quickly emptied bowl. 'Any news on who the man is?'

'Not that I've heard. You'll have to ask Salvatore.'

'What's taking so long? The whole town is on edge.'

'You certainly are.'

'No. I worry about the poor soul who's waiting for him to come home.'

'Yes, there is that.' How many times had he brought bad news to wives, husbands, mothers, fathers, children? Sometimes their reaction had been a clue that led to the killer.

Tilde waved him away. 'Today's not your day to help out, so go. I'll see you tomorrow at lunchtime. If you want an olive loaf, Enrico, by some miracle, still has a few left.' Enrico had a shop halfway down the hill that supplied the restaurant's bread. The olive loaves usually sold out by nine-thirty. It was now past ten. 'But you'd better hurry.'

'Thanks. See you tomorrow.' Nico kissed her on both cheeks, part of the Italian hello and goodbye.

Halfway down the hill, Nico spotted Gianni trudging up in jeans and the leaf-green and purple Ferriello T-shirt Aldo's employees all wore. He was not a particularly tall young man, with a trim body and a handsome face crowned by a mess of curly dark hair. Gianni waved at him and stopped.

When Nico reached him, Gianni gave him a hug and the double-cheek kiss. A first for Gianni, who usually just said hi and went on his way. 'Ciao, Nico. All is well, I hope?' He was all smiles.

'Everything is fine.'

OneWag ambled over from the gutter, where he'd been

on the lookout for intriguing smells and stopped to sniff Gianni's trainers carefully.

'Glad to hear that after what happened. I've been meaning to tell you, you've been great. You know that?'

'I have?'

'Helping Stella at the restaurant. I can't thank you enough.'

'Stella is family.'

'She's lucky to have you. You're reasonable, not like her mother. I don't know why Tilde dislikes me so much.'

Nico didn't like getting into other people's affairs, but he was on Stella's side. A controlling boyfriend was not good news. 'Stella loves you, Gianni. Be grateful for that. Don't try to control her. Even if she listens and doesn't take the exam, she will end up regretting it and taking it out on you. It's only an exam. She might not win the job, and even if she does get the job, it doesn't mean she'll stop loving you. Have faith in her.'

Gianni laughed and gave him another hug. 'Right you are, Nico. I've been an arsehole. I got her so upset I risked losing her even before she takes that dumb exam. I told Stella she can do whatever she wants. I love her and I'm going to marry her.' He showed off a wide grin.

'Good. And maybe you can come by in the evening and help Stella at the restaurant sometime.'

Gianni dropped his grin. Nico regretted his remark. It was unnecessary and not his place to have said it, but there was a cockiness to Gianni's remarks that had got under his skin. The young man had looked so obviously pleased with his generosity towards Stella.

'Ciao, Gianni. What I do for the family gives me joy. No thanks needed.'

Once back at the main piazza, OneWag ran across the street, aiming straight for Luciana's shop, just two doors down from Bar All'Angolo. Nico yelled his name just as a car rushed past the dog.

New flowerpots the truck had brought that morning lined the outside of the shop. OneWag sniffed the first one, a white cyclamen.

Nico hurried across the street. 'Don't you dare!'

The dog ignored him and sniffed the next plant.

Nico watched, ready to snatch OneWag at the first hint of a raised leg. He would buy the plant, of course, but he'd have a hard time facing Luciana, who was Tilde's good friend. Hers was the only flower shop in the village, and every petal and leaf was her tesoro, her darling. She was capable of banishing him. He'd have to drive to Panzano to find flowers for Rita. It wasn't far, but he owed Luciana his loyalty. She had arranged the wreath of yellow roses he had requested for Rita's burial and refused to accept payment.

Luciana appeared in the doorway. A forty-year-old woman with a wide face, hazel eyes, a chiselled nose and a mass of thick henna-tinted curls that could pass for chrysanthemums. A black tent-like dress covered her large body. 'Buongiorno, Nico, bello.'

He looked up and smiled at her addition of 'bello' to his name. Beautiful or handsome he had never been –

not even as a baby, as his mother liked to remind him. 'Buongiorno, Luciana.'

She looked down at the paper bag on his arm that read DA ENRICO. 'How many did you get?' Enrico was her devoted husband, a man half her size in height and width.

'Two.' The small loaves were made with soft, chewy seven-grain bread dotted with salty black olives. 'I reserved for tomorrow.'

'I should start doing that. You'd think he'd set aside at least one for his wife. Not a chance. His customers come first.' She moved aside to let Nico pass. 'Come and see! The truck brought some lovelies in this morning.'

Nico looked down at OneWag, who was examining his third flowerpot, one crowded with blue asters. Rita would like those. 'I'm worried he'll lift his leg on the flowers.'

Luciana shook her curls. 'Not this one; I already know him. He's a smarty. I give him a treat, he sniffs and leaves his signature somewhere else. Come on, little one. You too. I've got sunflowers that will turn your head. And biscuits for the little one. You can have one too, if you want.'

OneWag scampered inside, followed by Nico. 'No thanks, Luciana.' He looked at the new plants. More cyclamens, mostly red. Small flowers that looked like asters and were called settembrini because of the time they flowered. Early chrysanthemums, the Italians' flower of choice for the Day of the Dead. Rita would never, ever have those on her tomb. For her, only flowers that stood for life. While Nico browsed, OneWag got his biscuit, which he took outside to eat.

'That dog has manners,' Luciana said. 'Someone must have owned him once. Maybe Titian. Have you been to the Uffizi?'

'Years ago, with Rita. I'm clueless about art.'

'Look it up on the Internet. Titian's *Venus of Urbino*. The little one's on the bed, fast asleep. You've got yourself a Renaissance dog.'

'Tilde told me about the painting. What I need to do is take him to a vet.'

'You don't have to. He's had his shots.'

'You took him?'

She nodded. 'I would've brought him home too, but Geisha, my Siamese, would have scratched out my eyes. I'm so glad you've taken him in.' She lunged at Nico and pressed him against her big, soft body. 'You are a good man.'

Nico held his breath, every nerve in his body wanting to squirm free. He hadn't welcomed Rita's hugs either. He hadn't been hugged in his childhood, despite his Italian mother and grandmother. They only hugged their own unhappiness. And his father only liked to use his fists on his wife and his son. At fourteen, Nico had hit him back, and the man had walked out for good.

Luciana must have sensed his discomfort. 'Don't worry. I still love my Enrico.' She let him go. 'I will tell you this. I am relieved you were the one who found that poor man. You are a big-city fellow, more used to violence than us Gravignesi.'

'I suppose that's true.'

'Can you imagine one of us finding him? A child, even? Terrible. Thank you for being the one.'

Nico didn't know how to answer that. 'I'll take the blue aster plant outside.'

'Ah, Nico, you break my heart. Always you pick my darling of the week. I was going to take it home, believe me, but for you and Rita, I give it up gladly.'

She said that every week. Nico thanked her, paid and kissed the cheeks she offered. On the way out, he left one of Enrico's olive loaves next to Luciana's handbag.

Nico was halfway out the parking space in front of the salumeria when the blue Alfa screeched to a halt next to him. 'Ehi, Nico,' Perillo called out from the open window. 'Have you eaten at Da Angela yet?'

Nico's response was a sigh.

'No? I know you're loyal to Sotto Il Fico, but you have to try this place. It's in Lucarelli, twenty minutes from here. My treat. How about tonight?'

Damn! Why couldn't this guy leave him alone? In the back seat, OneWag reached up to the open window and barked a welcome. 'What is it you want, Maresciallo?'

'Salvatore, please.' Perillo left the motor running, got out of his car and leant down to meet Nico's face at the open window. 'I know about your old job and your forced retirement.' His voice was low now. 'Don't worry. That information stays with me.'

Shit, Nico thought.

'I don't—'

'Daniele found the information online. Don't worry, he's as silent as a tomb.'

'So you know. Now what? Are you planning to blackmail me?'

'Dio mio!' Perillo jumped up from the window, hitting his head against the top frame. He rubbed the top of his head. 'How could you think that? Daniele suggested I ask for your help. It was a good idea.'

'No!'

'Why not? You've spent as many years seeking justice as I have. And doubtless with many more cases like this.'

'There's a reason I was fired.'

'That's regrettable for you, but changes nothing for me.'

'It wasn't regrettable. It was deserved.'

'That doesn't change the fact that you have expertise I don't have. I've dealt with only a single murder in my career. Holy heaven, New Yorkers must have murders every day.'

'That's not true by any means.'

'I know. I'm just trying to make a point. Much more than in the villages of Tuscany, you would agree?'

'I don't have the data, but I suppose so.'

'Let's have dinner together. If you don't wish to get involved, we can discuss other things.'

'How can we talk about the murder with other people around?'

This question was good news for Perillo. 'First we eat, drink a good bottle of Chianti Classico, then I drive you home and we strategise like two generals fighting a war. Do you accept?'

'If I don't?'

'I will do the best I can to find who killed this man. He was not American, we discovered this morning from the young woman who sold the man a charm bracelet with a mysterious date on it. He was Tuscan.'

Nico recognised the setup game. His partner had been an ace at it when interrogating suspects. Dangling a new detail in front of them and waiting for them to swallow the bait. No harm in playing along. 'What bracelet?'

'I will tell you this evening.' Perillo reached into the back window and scratched OneWag's head. 'Forza, convince your friend. You can come too. We'll eat in the garden.' He put his scratching hand back in his pocket and turned to face Nico, laughing. 'Asking for a dog's help is the sign of a drowning man.' There was the truth. No more saving face. Honesty was best with the American.

Nico leant over the steering wheel and crossed his arms. He'd heard of Angela's from Tilde, who'd said it was excellent. A good meal, a report on the food for Tilde, maybe discovering a new dish or two to add to Sotto Il Fico's limited menu. And also listening to what Perillo had to say.

He sat back up. 'I don't have any lifesavers to throw at you, but I've been told I'm a good listener. I pay for my own meal.' No way was he going to owe this man.

'As you wish. I'll meet you here in the piazza at eight.' Perillo prayed the restaurant wasn't booked solid, as it was most nights.

As Nico watched Perillo drive away, Gogol's words came back to him. *The maresciallo talk to you. Stay away. A very bad man.*

Tilde had just finished stuffing al dente rigatoni with a veal and broccoli ragout when Stella slipped into the kitchen. As Tilde poured a light tomato sauce over the pasta, she looked at her daughter's unsmiling face. Damn that Gianni. Tilde put the saucepan down and wiped her hands on her apron. It was time to have another conversation with her beautiful, unhappy daughter before Elvira and Enzo came back.

Stella raised a hand in protest. She could tell what was coming. 'Don't, Mamma. I'm sorry I'm late.' She didn't sound sorry. 'What do you want me to do? Set the outside tables?'

'Isn't that what you do every morning?'

Stella sighed loudly and went into the main room to get the cutlery. Tilde followed her. 'Did you get a chance to study for the exam last night?'

Stella opened the heavy drawer of the oak chest that hugged the wall behind Elvira's chair and ran her fingers through the forks, making as much noise as possible.

'There's no need to act like a child. You know I worry.'

'Yes, Mamma, I know you do. And I did study. Not a lot, though. I couldn't stop thinking about the man who had his face blown off.' Stella looked back at her mother, completely pale. 'I'm scared.'

'Oh, Stella, sweetheart.' Tilde enfolded her daughter

in her arms. 'That man's death was terrible, but it has nothing to do with us.'

'Are you sure?'

Tilde cupped Stella's chin and peered into her daughter's green eyes. 'Of course I'm sure.' If only she could believe that. Those damned gold trainers. It was ridiculous to think they had anything to do with Robi. 'Please don't worry.'

Stella pushed herself away from her mother and dropped down in Elvira's chair. She started leafing through her grandmother's *Settimana Enigmistica*. 'I just have the creepy feeling that the man who died was the same man who was following me for a couple of days.'

'What man?' The thought of a strange man following her daughter took the breath from her.

'I don't know. An older guy. I kept running into him in weird places. The first time I saw him, he gaped at me with this stupid grin on his face. He didn't say anything or try to touch me; I would have hit him if he had.'

Tilde felt her knees weaken. She held on to the doorjamb. 'Was it someone who came to the restaurant?'

'I don't think so. I couldn't really tell. He was wearing a baseball cap pulled down low over sunglasses. The first time I noticed him was in Panzano. He was at Dario Cecchini's butcher shop, drinking a glass of wine.' Stella did not add that when the man saw her, he nearly dropped the glass. The next day, when she went to pick up Gianni in her Vespa at the vineyard, she thought she saw the man driving behind her. Gianni told her she was crazy and started to make fun of her. Having her fear dismissed so quickly angered her. She was beginning to think her mother was right about Gianni, but what other man was going to love her as much as he did?

'Why do you think he's the man who got killed?'

'I don't know. He was so creepy.'

Tilde rubbed her stomach to calm herself. Her beloved daughter, prey to men's hunger. She knew where that could lead only too well. She had lived with that fear from the day Stella was conceived. 'Darling, you are beautiful, and men will always look at you, no matter how old they are. Maybe you made him remember when he was young and in love, or maybe he just wanted to fall in love one more time.'

Stella looked at her mother in amazement. 'Since when were you a romantic? Feet on the ground, Mamma, please. I don't want you getting sappy on me. He was probably looking at my breasts.'

Tilde laughed in relief. This was the daughter she knew. Sassy and down-to-earth. 'You do have to get used to men staring at you. There's no need to be scared.' She too had to stop being scared. She had let her imagination run away with her. 'Just be careful.'

'Yes, Mamma. I've heard it all before.' It was her eyes the man had liked. She'd bumped into him again at the big Co-op in Greve. He'd bared his teeth at her, like he was ready to bite into her. 'You cannot imagine how happy you make me,' he whispered. Gianni was with her and threatened the man with his fist. She dragged Gianni out of the supermarket as fast as she could, the shopping she needed to do completely forgotten.

'You know that old turd,' Gianni accused when they were out on the street. He seemed not to believe her when she said she didn't. His ridiculous jealousy was one of the reasons her feelings for him were cooling.

She kissed Tilde's cheek to reassure her. 'I'm not stupid. I can take care of myself.'

'But you were scared of this man. Did you think he might hurt you?'

'No. It's just the way he kept staring at me like we knew each other. Then the murder happened, and for some reason I linked the two.' Stella stood up and grabbed a handful of forks. 'Come on, Mamma. Time to work.'

'Right you are.' Tilde pushed the old memory back into the hidden recess of her mind where she had kept it for twenty-two years and went back to the kitchen to toast the breadcrumbs she would sprinkle over the rigatoni before putting them in the oven.

The small cemetery was on a hill behind the town, enclosed by a high stone wall and the stately cypress trees that acted as a cemetery's logo throughout Italy. It was a modest place. The one mausoleum, a sixteenth-century marble temple edged with Doric columns, had belonged to a humbler branch of the Medici family whose villa now housed Gogol's old-age home on the outskirts of town. The rest of the grounds were covered with stone and marble gravestones neatly divided by narrow dirt aisles, many with enamelled photos of the dead. Only a few embellishments. A two-foot-high marble angel wept over a child's nineteenth-century grave. A stone basket filled with meticulously carved grapes sat atop the grave of a man who had died the year before. A faithful stone dog lay atop another grave. Flowers real and fake graced every grave, even the ones from past centuries. The Gravignesi cared for their dead.

Nico and OneWag passed through the open wrought-iron gate and walked to the water fountain in the corner. Nico picked up one of the empty plastic water bottles left there by other visitors for anyone to use and filled it. Water gurgled from the old spout. OneWag, thirsty again, sat up on his hind legs, a trick he'd picked up watching fancy dogs beg for a treat. Nico lifted him up and let him catch as much water as he could. With the full bottle in one hand and the dog under his arm, he walked to where Rita rested next to her parents. He watered the cyclamens he knew Tilde had brought for all three, then placed his own aster plant over Rita. He straightened up and stood, looking at the neatly carved letters of his wife's name, the numbers that marked the years of her life, at the bottom, the words BELLA, DOLCE DONNA E MOGLIE, 'beautiful sweet woman and wife', words he had thought of in English, but had wanted in Italian so that all who came here would know how wonderful she was.

She had died fourteen months ago, and her face, her voice were beginning to fade. He missed them both.

OneWag sniffed the air loudly and dropped into a crouch with a low growl. Nico heard footsteps and tucked OneWag under his arm. 'Shh. No acting out on holy ground.'

'"Bella, dolce donna." A beautiful inscription.'

Nico turned around to see who had spoken.

The woman noticed the startled look on his face. 'Please forgive me.' She offered her smile. 'I didn't mean to interrupt your thoughts. I simply want to thank you for giving me a much-needed ride on Monday. Remember?' She held out her hand. 'Maria Dorsetti.'

He shook the offered hand. 'Nico Doyle.' He didn't mumble this time. 'Yes, I do remember. You gave me directions to the carabinieri station in Greve.' She had a pleasant face and large, rich brown eyes that kept a steady gaze on him. Today, she was wearing a perfectly ironed pale blue short-sleeved linen suit that showed off her good figure. Nico shifted OneWag to his other arm. Making conversation with this attractive woman in front of Rita's grave embarrassed him.

'The meeting went well, I hope.'

Was she just making conversation, Nico wondered, or was she the meddling kind? 'The maresciallo is a very nice man,' he offered as an answer as he nervously stroked OneWag.

'Of course he is. We depend on him and his men to keep us safe. I'm sorry we are meeting again in such a sad place.' Actually, though, she considered it a happy event. There was a gentleness, a childlike lost quality to this man that had attracted her right away. American men had a reputation for being kind, she'd read somewhere. She'd been foolish enough to hope she would spot him over the weekend among the hundreds of people at the

Chianti Expo, perhaps share an espresso with him later to counter all that wine tasting. Or even a meal. Her other widowed friends had told her often enough that she was foolish to hope their lives would change, but as Ungaretti concluded in a sad poem she studied in school, she had never been so coupled to life.

'I buried my husband here four years ago.' Maria waved to the wall of tombs at the upper end of the cemetery. Four rows of loculi that looked like filing cabinets. 'My inscription isn't as loving as yours. Just his name and the years he lived.'

OneWag squirmed against Nico's grip.

'I see your dog has got impatient. I'm sorry to have disturbed you.' She stepped closer. He inhaled her scent and recognised it as sandalwood mixed with something else. Tilde had given him a box of sandalwood soap at Christmas. He found the smell comforting.

'Goodbye, Signor Doyle. Maybe we will meet at one of the wine stands this weekend. I'm going on Friday when it opens at eleven. I like to watch the people flowing eagerly into the piazza.' The crowd's chatter and laughter getting louder with one wine tasting following another lifted her spirits. 'Podere San Cresci offers very good wine.'

'Thank you for the tip,' Nico said. He understood that she was giving him the opportunity for a date. Maybe after four years, she had put grief aside.

Maria hesitated for a moment. When Nico added nothing, she lowered her head and walked away.

OneWag yelped. Nico had been holding him too tight. 'Stop it!' He loosened his grip and bent down on one knee. With his free hand, he fidgeted with the aster plant. Months after it had become clear that he and Rita would never have children, he'd brought home a hairy ragamuffin of a mutt from the ASPCA, a dog he'd instantly taken to. Rita had burst into tears and asked him to take it back. She couldn't accept a substitute for the child they could not have. And she wouldn't adopt a child, for reasons he was never able to understand.

He held up OneWag close to the gravestone. 'Look what found me, Rita. He needs a home.'

CHAPTER FIVE

Daniele's motorbike zoomed into the car park at the station just as Perillo got out of the Alfa Romeo. He acknowledged his superior with a curt nod. Perillo supposed his words about Rosalba turning him into hamburger meat still stung.

'Ehi, Dani, I'm going for a coffee.' He knew he'd been a little rough. 'Come on, my treat.' When he'd been stationed in Naples, he'd never had to pay. Cafes and restaurants were only too glad to see him scare the pickpockets away. Tuscans weren't as generous. They also didn't have as many pickpockets.

Daniele shook his head. A coffee or a fruit juice wasn't going to do it. 'I'd better see if any messages have come in. We've been gone a while.'

Perillo pointed a finger at him. 'Good thinking. I'll be fast.'

When Perillo walked into the bar next to the station, he was greeted by the grumpy bartender with a torn rotator cuff thanks to thirty years of making espressos. 'What's the count so far?'

'Eight, maybe.'

'How about a glass of milk?'

Perillo snorted. 'You want to kill me?'

'Caffeine will kill, not milk. Caffeine and cigarettes.'

'If everyone stopped drinking coffee, you'd be out of a job. I need the jolt. I've got a big one on my hands.'

The bartender put the espresso cup on the counter and took the euro Perillo gave him. 'This isn't like the last one, eh?'

'Nothing like it.' He'd solved the other murder in two days. An Albanian had stabbed another Albanian to death over a woman. Back in the late nineties, the Albanians had poured into Italy, fleeing the war in their homeland. Most had come with good intentions. A few less so. An Italian thief Perillo had sent to jail several times had come into the office to announce he was changing careers because the Albanians had taken over his territory. There was nothing politically incorrect about admitting it was a fact. People stole when they couldn't find work. There was work here in the vineyards, in construction. They were hard workers. The Africans were still coming too, but too many drowned en route. Now the government wasn't allowing them in. How could anyone turn desperate people away?

Perillo drank his espresso in one gulp, raised his hand in salute to the bartender and walked out, jabbing a cigarette in his mouth. He was about to light it when his phone rang.

'Are you coming back?' Daniele asked.

'After I smoke a cigarette.' The carabinieri stations were now smoke-free by order of some high-ranking health nut. 'Why?'

'There's news.'

'I'll be there.' He shoved the cigarette back in the pack and hurried back to his office.

Daniele sat by the phone at his desk, next to his computer, his face beaming with excitement.

Good news, then, Perillo sensed, and felt his stomach do a tarantella step. 'Yes?'

'The Avis car rental company from Florence just called and said one of their cars was supposed to have been returned yesterday. The employee remembered that the man who rented it said he was going to Radda in Chianti.'

'Did you get the name?'

'Yes, and the make and number plate.' Daniele took his time looking over his own note. 'A metal-grey Fiat Panda, number plate SI 182144.'

Daniele was certainly getting back at him. 'Name, please.'

'Robert Garrett.'

Mother of God and all the saints! An American. Not their dead man. Perillo threw down his car keys on the desk and sat down. He turned to face Daniele, whose desk was in the back of the room, where his keyboard tapping was less noisy, allowing for Perillo to think, which he felt compelled to do at times. 'What do they want from us? To look for their car when we've got a murder on our hands and the substitute prosecutor calling any minute to ask why we haven't solved the case yet? Tell Avis they're going to have to send their own people looking.'

'Substitute Prosecutor Della Langhe called while we were in Radda. Do you want to hear the message?'

'Not on an empty stomach. Give me the short version.'

'He expects you to call him first thing tomorrow morning. Tonight he has a gala at Palazzo Vecchio and can't be disturbed.'

Perillo looked up at the ceiling and silently asked if a kind God would send him some good luck for once. 'How long has it been since we found the man? Twenty-eight hours?'

Daniele looked at his watch.

'Stop that, I don't need to know. It's been no time at all, and already Count Roberto Della Langhe or whatever his title is wants results. All we've got is how much the bracelet cost and that a Tuscan with a weathered face bought it.'

'A Tuscan who wasn't wearing an expensive watch. Maybe he bought the bracelet for somebody else?'

'What are you saying?'

'Fourteen hundred euros is a lot of money. Maybe the dead man hired this man to buy the bracelet for him because he didn't want anyone to know about it. It could also explain what he was doing in the woods so early in the morning.'

'And what was that?'

'Maybe he was meeting someone and didn't want to be seen.'

That made sense. 'Wait a minute. Are you saying this Robert Garrett who was going to Radda in Chianti and didn't return his car might be our dead man?'

'The technicians confirmed that the victim's clothes were American brands. According to Avis, Garrett's passport said he'd come from California.'

AP, the only legible letters on the blood-soaked T-shirt. 'Napa Valley is in California,' Perillo exclaimed with a quick burst of excitement.

'Exactly! The "AP" on his T-shirt. And gold shoes. Maybe he was from Hollywood. I've read that movie people love glitter.'

Whether the man was from Hollywood or not, his brigadiere, who'd been on the job only six months, was possibly onto something. Why hadn't he considered that the Tuscan might be a go-between? 'I'll send Dino and Vince to look for the car. Call the other carabinieri stations from Florence to Siena and ask them to help.'

'I think we should try the roads surrounding Gravigna first.'

'You think so?' Perillo asked sarcastically.

Daniele felt his cheeks go hot. 'Yes, Maresciallo. He died there.'

'Indeed he did,' Perillo said. He knew he was being a resentful idiot. 'Good thinking, Brigadiere Donato. When you're finished, come upstairs and we can have lunch together.'

Daniele shot out of his chair so quickly his chair almost overturned. An invitation to share a meal with his superior upstairs was a first. An honour. Every day, the smells of Signora Perillo's cooking wafted downstairs to tease his nostrils and make him salivate. 'Thank you, Maresciallo.'

Perillo walked to the door, opened it and waited for Daniele to follow him. 'My wife's made veal involtini stuffed with mushrooms and spinach.'

Daniele still stood by his chair, his face pale.

'What's the problem? You're not hungry?'

'I am, but I'm a vegetarian, Maresciallo.'

Perillo lifted his arms in a sign of resignation. Of course, Daniele the moralist! 'So my wife will heat up what's left of last night's aubergine parmigiana. No dead animal in that. Now get going. The day won't last forever.'

At eight that evening, Nico sat on a bench in the main piazza of Gravigna while OneWag circled the area in search of new scents and what tourist titbits the pigeons and sparrows hadn't got to yet. The sun had fallen below the hills, but the day's light seemed reluctant to cede its place to darkness. The old men had gone home. At one end of the piazza, the trattoria was filled with locals and tourists. Lavender-haired Carletta with nails to match was serving the few intrepid tourists who preferred the outside tables despite the cool air. The florist and newspaper shop had closed. Behind the closed glass doors of Bar All'Angolo, Jimmy was mopping the floor while Sandro buffed the long steel counter. The glass balls of old cast-iron street lamps burst into life just as Perillo stopped in front of the cafe.

After his visit to Rita, Nico had gone to Panzano to do some shopping at the small Co-op, the nearest supermarket, then gone home and eaten lunch. OneWag got half a can of dog food he barely touched, preferring Nico's salami. After lunch, Nico had settled on the balcony with the Italian translation of Jo Nesbø's latest thriller. The dog preferred the sofa.

Maresciallo Perillo's request for help kept interrupting Nico's reading. It left a mark he recognised. The one left by a man in need. A need far lighter than the one the murder suspect in his last case had left on his conscience. Responding to that woman's need had cost him his job. But he had no regrets. He would do it again. And tonight, he would listen to the maresciallo, even if Gogol thought the man was bad. Maybe because of it. Finding out made life interesting. Besides, Nico was willing to bet Perillo didn't hold a candle to some of the men he'd met in his line of work. And if he could help solve the case, why not? He had nothing to lose except boredom.

'We're in luck. I nabbed the last table in the garden,' Perillo announced as soon as OneWag settled in the back seat of the Panda and Nico buckled his seat belt. He shifted into first gear. He swung the car onto Route 222, which would take them towards the village of Lucarelli and Da Angela's restaurant.

Nico inhaled deeply and was relieved the car did not smell of cigarette smoke.

Perillo heard the intake of breath. 'Ah, no, my wife would divorce me if I smoked in our car.'

Nico smiled. 'Mine was the same. No smoking in the house, either.'

'We have a balcony.'

'We didn't. It was just easier to give it up. Now I've gone back to having one or two a day.'

'I admire your restraint. I love it too much.'

They both knew they were exchanging easy talk, a warm-up.

They climbed up a winding road. Perillo drove fast, cutting the curves. It wasn't dark enough to see oncoming headlights yet, and Nico chose to keep his eyes on the wall of trees whisking by, then the suddenly revealed scenery below.

'We've made some progress. First, the jeweller.' Perillo went into detail about his visit.

'Do you believe her?'

'That she sold the bracelet to this man? Yes.' He turned to look at Nico just as the Panda approached another sharp curve. Nico held his breath. 'Why would she make that up?'

'Your brigadiere is very handsome.'

'Well, I suppose he is,' Perillo conceded, 'but with her looks, she wouldn't have to make up lies, I assure you.'

It was clear to Nico that Daniele wasn't the only man smitten by this Rosalba, which didn't make for clear thinking. 'Maybe I'm too cynical.'

'I didn't think cynicism was an American trait. It's an Italian speciality.'

'It comes with police work. If she's detail-oriented, a sketch artist will help.'

'I thought of that, although we may not need one.' Perillo told him about the missing car rented to an American. He was about to go into Daniele's theory of a go-between when, just before the umpteenth curve, a car barrelled past them with only a few inches to spare.

Nico's heart missed a few beats, or so it felt. He'd always been a careful driver. 'Stodgy,' according to Rita. 'Slowpoke Doyle' in the squad room. 'Let's continue this conversation when we're not in motion.'

Perillo laughed. 'As you wish. Just remind me never to give you a ride in our Alfa. That one can do two hundred and fifty-seven kilometres per hour. I think that's about a hundred and sixty of your miles.'

'I'll be sure to remind you.'

Rosalba looked up from setting the table when she heard the front door. 'Ciao, Mamma, I'm in the dining room.'

'What's for dinner?' Irene called out as she walked down the hall. The flat was large and crammed with the heavy, dark furniture Rosalba's great-grandfather had chosen when he'd bought the building that housed his jewellery shop. The other three flats had been sold to keep the business going during the lean years. The furniture stayed. Rosalba's mother had tried to sell it, but no one wanted antiques any more. Italy was going modern.

'Pina made stuffed courgette. They're warming in the oven. How did it go?' Rosalba prayed the trip to Florence had been successful. She needed her mother in a good mood.

'Florence was a nightmare. I had to elbow my way through Piazza Signorina just to sit down and have a lemonade at Rivoire.'

'Will he design for us?'

'It depends on how much I'm willing to pay him.' Irene clicked across the marble pavement in her heels, impeccably dressed in a red silk Valentino dress she'd bought at the Barberino Designer Outlet three years ago. 'He showed me some lovely designs he can make in gold, silver and even steel. I don't see the purpose of having steel jewellery. You might as well put a series of paper clips around your neck and call that jewellery.' She pecked at her daughter's cheeks. 'But *de gustibus non disputandum est*.' She stepped back and surveyed the T-shirt and pants Rosalba had changed into after closing up the store. 'Not attractive.'

Rosalba puffed out a sigh. She wasn't in the mood for this. 'I was tired. It hasn't been a good day.'

Irene's hand reached down to realign a knife and spoon. Now they lay in perfect parallel. 'You didn't sell anything.'

'I did. Six hundred and twenty-three euros in cash with a fifteen per cent discount. Eight twenty in credit cards, full price.' Proving her mother wrong gave her the boost she needed. 'The carabinieri came by this morning.'

Irene raised an eyebrow, waiting for more.

'They showed me the bracelet and asked if it came from our store. They said he was dead and they wanted to know what he looked like. He must be the man they found dead in Gravigna.'

'Of course. His face was shot off.'

'I expected you to be upset.' Her mother's face had gone white when she'd told her that the man who bought the expensive bracelet had asked if Irene Crisani was now the owner of the shop, claiming he was an old friend of hers. Rosalba has answered with a simple 'Yes.'

'People get killed all the time for one stupid reason or another.' Irene refolded a napkin. 'Did they ask about the video cameras?' She had pressed the delete button on both tapes with a stomach-wrenching combination of joy and anguish.

'Yes.'

'And what did you tell them?'

'That one was being fixed and we'd erased the tape in the working camera at the end of last week. They're bringing in an artist from Florence to make a sketch of what I remember of his face. What should I remember?'

'Whatever you want. He's dead.'

As soon as Nico and the maresciallo entered the restaurant, they were greeted by a woman in a flowered dress and espadrilles. 'Ciao, Salvatore. It's been forever.'

'I know, Angela, I regret. Too much work.' He kissed her cheeks and introduced Nico.

'Piacere.' Angela shook hands with Nico. She was in her forties, with a fleshy, round face and smiling grey eyes. A frown appeared on her face when she noticed OneWag looking up at her. He had no collar, no lead.

'He's an angel of obedience,' Perillo said.

'We have a cat.'

Nico had forgotten that every Italian restaurant had at least one cat. 'I'm sorry.' He picked up the dog. 'I'll leave him in the car.'

Perillo stopped him. 'Rocco eats with us. Don't worry, Angela. He's under my tutelage.'

'But my cat isn't. If he gets his eyes scratched out—'

'I'll arrest her.'

Angela's smile came back. 'Good idea. She can have her kittens in jail.'

'Again?'

Angela shrugged. 'What can I do? Romilda is a nymphomaniac, and my mother refuses to have her fixed.' She picked up two menus and led them to the garden. 'Take that last table in the far corner. I'll take Romilda upstairs.'

Perillo took the menus. 'Thank you, Angela, you are indeed an angel.'

Nico and Perillo sat down facing each other. A baffled Nico held on to OneWag. 'Why did you insist on the dog? And his name isn't Rocco.'

'He is an Italian dog. He should have an Italian name. The one you chose is also impossible for us to pronounce properly. Call him what you wish, of course, but for me he is Rocco. I insisted he stay with us because he needs reassurance you will not abandon him.' Perillo had taken care of many street dogs as a kid. He had identified with their need to be loved. 'It is clear to me that he is a wise dog. If he disobeys, you may put him back on the street. He knows this. Put him down and command him to stay. See if I'm wrong.'

Curious, Nico put the dog down on the dirt floor. 'Stay here.'

OneWag looked up at the man, undecided on what to do. The words were new to him, and so many different smells and bits of food on the ground called to him. But the low voice called too. This man who fed him and did not kick him wanted him to do what?

Nico leant down and patted the ground. 'Stay.'

OneWag curled up underneath the chair. Gestures, he understood. And now the word 'stay'.

Nico sat up, surprised. 'You're a dog expert.'

'No, just on strays.'

'You've owned many?'

The American was looking at him with an honest, unsuspecting face. He was waiting for an answer. Perillo looked down at the menu. Good, Angela was serving la peposa tonight. Domenico Doyle, a man whose help he sought. Should he tell him? 'No,' he said out loud in answer to Nico's question and his own. 'I never owned one, but there was an abundance of strays back in Pozzuoli.' He did not add that this meant both dogs and humans, sleeping on the streets, eating food from rubbish

111

bins, stealing anything they could get their filthy hands on. Years of it. He could still pick a wallet from a pocket without being caught. He'd tried it just a few weeks ago, to see if he still had that ability, and put the wallet right back without Daniele noticing.

The angry edge in Perillo's voice made Nico curious. 'Why did you choose to become part of the carabinieri?'

'Where I come from, I had three choices. I could be a man of the cloth, a man of the Camorra or a man of the law. I don't believe in God. I don't believe in killing people. I didn't believe in the law back then, either, but it was by far the better choice. Besides' – Perillo's face broke out in a grin – 'I liked the uniform.'

Nico recognised the pat answer. 'Do you believe in the law now?'

'Do you?' Perillo asked, wondering how Nico had lost his job.

'I took an oath to uphold the law, but sometimes the law as we have worded it is imperfect.' He had indeed broken the law and been fired for it. The law had deemed his actions wrong, but in his mind, what he had done was right. 'Sometimes, the law does not take into account the despair suffering can bring. Sending a guilty person to jail isn't always the right answer, and too many times, the innocent end up there.'

'Good. I see we think alike. The real reason I became a carabiniere? The jokes. There are thousands of them. A ship goes down at sea and the entire crew drowns. Surprisingly, two carabinieri survive. "How come you didn't drown like the rest?" the rescue crew asks. One answers, "We're not allowed to drink on the job."'

Nico laughed.

'One more for you. Why do the carabinieri smile during storms?' Perillo waited. Nico shrugged. 'Because they think the lightning is a series of camera flashes. Now, let's order before I tell any more dumb jokes.'

Nico sighed. 'When I was growing up in the States, we had Polish jokes. Sometimes, you need a little laughter.'

Perillo raised his arm and called Angela. 'Nico, you trust me to order for you?'

'Please do.'

Angela strolled over, her eyes on OneWag asleep under the chair. 'You were right. He's the picture of obedience. Bravo, Rocco. Now then, gentlemen, what do your stomachs desire tonight?'

'A bottle of your house red—'

Nico lifted a forefinger. 'Excuse me, but I'd like to start with a glass of white wine first.'

Perillo looked at Angela apologetically. Asking for white wine in Chianti was almost an insult.

Nico noticed the look. 'I'll switch to red for the main course.'

'Good.' Perillo continued his order. 'A platter of your crostini – you pick the tastiest ones – and la peposa for both of us. We'll see if we have room for dessert later.'

'What's la peposa?' Nico asked.

'Ah,' Angela said, 'you're in for a delight.' She pulled out a chair and sat down.

Perillo sat back, satisfied. He had ordered the dish for a specific reason. One of many admirable traits he had discovered in Americans was their curiosity about his country, and Angela never missed a chance to tell the story of la peposa.

'It's a historic meat dish,' she began. 'Chianina beef cooked in red wine with lots of pepper kernels, garlic, rosemary and sage, served on toasted bread to soak up the sauce. It was invented in my home town, L'Imprunéta, where we have been making the best terracotta tiles in the world since the Middle Ages. The work was hard, and the men had to stay by the burning furnace all day, so they came up with the idea of cooking their lunch next to the tiles. Not only will it fortify you, but you will be eating an exquisite dish that fed the men who built Brunelleschi's cupola for the Duomo of Florence. Without la peposa, who knows if the cupola would still be with us after almost seven centuries?'

'Thank you, Angela,' Nico said. A fun story with perhaps some truth to it. 'I look forward to eating history.'

'And we both need fortification,' Perillo said. 'You've heard about the murder?'

Angela's hands clasped her cheeks and she stared at Nico with wide eyes. 'Oh, holy Jesus, are you the one who found him?' Her voice was loud, and some diners turned to look at Nico.

'It was the dog who found him first,' said Nico quietly, not enjoying the attention.

'But I have to find out who killed him,' Perillo said.

'Of course you do,' Angela snapped. 'It's your job.'

Perillo laughed. He could always count on Angela for a put-down. And he always deserved it.

Angela stood up and put the chair back in place. 'No house wine for you tonight. I'll open up a bottle of Brunello di Montalcino. It's on us. I'll bring it right away, plus some scraps for Rocco.'

'Thank you,' Nico called after her, 'but his name isn't Rocco.'

'Resign yourself, friend.' Perillo leant forward and said in a low voice, 'Now, let me tell you about Daniele's theory and what the substitute prosecutor thinks.'

'After dinner,' Nico said. A few diners were still openly staring and muttering to each other. 'Let's discuss the case on my balcony with a bottle of duty-free Johnnie Walker Black that's been waiting to be opened since May.'

Perillo grinned. 'Excellent whisky, excellent idea. A judicious amount of alcohol will illuminate the brain and further cement collaboration.'

For the next two hours, they shared opinions on the latest news from both countries while polishing off all the crostini, wiping the peposa plates clean, and draining their bottle of 2010 Brunello di Montalcino.

CHAPTER SIX

Daniele was in the barrack's kitchen filling a plate with freshly drained bigoli and thinking of Rosalba. He dressed the thick noodles with olive oil, capers, a couple of smashed anchovies, pitted green olives and a coating of toasted breadcrumbs. It was a dish his mother had made for as long as he could remember, a dish that had become his go-to whenever he was down. The maresciallo's remark still stung. Rosalba might be rich, better schooled than he was, but he'd felt something special pass between them. He knew her smile had been for him, not the maresciallo. How old was his superior? Forty-five? Maybe beyond that. He was getting old. Daniele plunged his fork into the heaped mound of thick pasta strands and twisted. The maresciallo was jealous, that was it. Even before taking his first bite of the pasta, Daniele felt better.

After his meal, Daniele went downstairs to the

computer in the maresciallo's office that only he used and now considered his. He knew he had to stay away from Rosalba until they had closed the case, but there was no harm in looking her up. He went to Google and typed in her full name. To his surprise, there was no trace of her on the Internet. Not on Facebook, Instagram, Pinterest or Twitter. Only Gioielleria Crisani showed up on a dull website with shots of the store's display cases filled with jewellery and no one behind them. Had he designed the website, Rosalba would have been front and centre, her smile bidding online searchers to walk into the store. The 'About' page told him the store was run by Irene Castaldi, née Crisani, third-generation owner of Gioielleria Crisani, started in 1952 by her grandfather Tuccio Crisani.

No wonder he couldn't find her. Her last name was Castaldi, not Crisani. He went back to look for her on social media. Still nothing.

Why was a beautiful girl like Rosalba trying to stay hidden? Maybe her parents were old-fashioned, afraid their beautiful girl might be found by sex-hungry men. Well, it wasn't sex he was looking for – not right away, at least. A connection would be nice. He'd been assigned to Greve six months ago, and he still hadn't found a girl he wanted to be with for more than five minutes. He would turn twenty in January. It was time he got a girlfriend.

Daniele's fingers flew over the keyboard to find Rosalba's parents in the Radda in Chianti registrar's office.

Irene Crisani, born in 1975 and married Giorgio Castaldi in 1999 in the Basilica of Santa Croce.

Rosalba Crisani, born in Milano in 1997.

Damn! Rosalba was two years older. She'd never consider him.

The night air had turned chilly, but Perillo wanted to smoke, and so the two men, stomachs full of excellent food, settled out on the balcony on two uncomfortable metal chairs. The three swallows were asleep, tucked in their usual spot between the beam and ceiling. OneWag was curled up at Nico's feet, thanks to Perillo's insistence that the dog deserved a roof over his head.

Nico poured the whisky into two glasses, handed one to Perillo and placed the bottle on the small table between them. 'You had two theories for me.'

'First the more probable one. It's about the Tuscan who bought the bracelet. Daniele thinks he might have been a go-between.'

'Possible, although why would the victim feel he needed a go-between? How much did the bracelet cost?'

'Fourteen hundred. He paid with three five-hundred-euro notes.'

'That's a lot of money. If the Tuscan was a go-between, he must have been a friend of the victim.'

'Maybe even the one who killed him.'

'Possible. As for why hire a go-between, our dead man might not have wanted to be seen. It would explain why he was out in the woods so early.' Perillo took a sip of his whisky and smacked his lips with approval. 'What's the first thing you did when you were assigned a case?'

'I always made my own list of the facts I had at that moment. Facts, no opinions or conjecture. They were written on the whiteboard, of course, but I liked to have the list with me at all times. When new facts came in, I'd add them to my list and tuck it in my pocket.'

Perillo lit a cigarette. 'You're a methodical man.'

Nico lifted the small pot of geraniums on the table and handed Perillo the under-dish to use as an ashtray. He laughed as he said, 'I guess I thought that the facts in my pocket would eventually make their way to my head and illuminate me.'

'The only facts I have are: A dead man's face was blown off at close range. The pellets we found tell us the weapon was a twelve-gauge shotgun, manufacturer unknown since the killer took the casing with him. It's the type of gun that's probably owned by every hunter in Tuscany, which means most of the male population. Next up, a tanned Tuscan bought a bracelet with a mysterious date on it. And finally, a missing grey Panda that may or may not have been rented by our dead man. Every dumpster in the vicinity is being checked for bloody clothes, and so far, nothing. No autopsy report yet. No news about the fingerprints. This wealth of information I can certainly keep in my head.'

'The killer must have been covered in blood. The best way to get rid of bloody clothes would be to burn them. Have you looked into unexplained bonfires in the area?'

Perillo raised his arms in a gesture of despair. 'Every day a farmer or a vintner is burning something, even if the wind is high and they risk burning acres of surrounding land. I have to call the prosecutor assigned to this case tomorrow morning. I dealt with him once before, when his seventeen-year-old daughter claimed her Morris Mini had been stolen while at a party in Greve. We found the car after two days, parked in the garage of the boy she had spent the night with. Della Langhe wanted the boy arrested for theft, but I spoke to his daughter, a nice girl, not one of those spoilt, the-world-owes-me-deference types like her father, and suggested that she would feel better about herself if she told Pappa the truth. She did, and Della Langhe has never forgiven me for knowing she slept with a boy she'd just met. He will not take kindly to my not having much to report. Besides, he thinks all Southerners are slow.'

Perillo liked to talk. Nico was grateful for it, after so many evenings on the balcony with only sleeping swallows for company. 'I had a few difficult district attorneys in my day. Beware of ones running for political office. If it's a front-page kind of case, they won't let the truth get in their way.'

'Ah, then America is not so different.'

Nico thought his country was very different – ninety-nine per cent of its citizens paid their taxes, for one thing, but he went back to the subject that had brought them together. 'Your case raises many questions.'

'Too many.' Perillo flicked ash over the balcony railing. Nico's vegetable garden was below. He didn't like the idea of finding ash on his courgette and pushed the terracotta dish closer to the maresciallo. 'Please use this, if you don't mind.' He leant back in his chair and took a sip of his whisky. 'In your office, you wondered why the victim was in the woods so early in the morning. Now you think it might be because he didn't want to be seen, but what was he doing there? Was he meeting someone? Perhaps the person he was going to give the bracelet to? Or was the bracelet incidental? Who could it have been for?'

'A woman, of course.'

'Nowadays not necessarily, but probably a woman. Someone who lives here, presumably. The date, a New Year's Day twenty-two years ago, what does it stand for? The new year? A wedding? A birthday? Why give this as a gift so many years later?'

Perillo dutifully flicked his ash in the dish as a smile of relief crossed his face. His American friend was hooked on the investigation. 'If he was meeting someone, the logical explanation for the place and time is that he didn't want to be seen. But what if the person who was meeting him also wanted secrecy?'

'Or maybe he wasn't meeting anyone. Maybe he was hiding because he knew he was in danger.'

'Too many questions for one maresciallo and a young brigadiere.' Perillo leant back in his chair and hugged his elbows. 'You will help, yes?'

Nico had to admit he was intrigued, but he still had no interest in becoming involved with an official case. 'As I said, I'll listen.'

'Your ears are good, Nico, but I need your New York

mind.' Perillo lifted his glass. 'Let us toast to America and Italy, Salvatore and Nico, with your excellent whisky.'

Nico raised his glass.

'Cin-cin, amico,' Perillo said.

'To your health.'

'And Rocco's.'

'OneWag's.'

They clinked glasses.

It was a few minutes past midnight when Perillo got home; Daniele was waiting for him outside the carabinieri station.

'Why still awake, Dani?'

'The substitute prosecutor wants you to call him immediately.'

'At Palazzo Vecchio?'

'He's in his office. I guess the gala was a bore. He didn't sound happy.'

'Mother of God and all the saints!'

'Sorry, Maresciallo.'

'"Sorry, Salvatore," and you don't need to apologise. You should have just left a note.'

'I was afraid you wouldn't see it.'

'You're right. There's been too much food, wine and whisky tonight, but an important connection has been forged.'

'I'm glad. Shall I put the moka on?'

'No, thanks. Go to sleep, Dani. I'll go face my penance in the office.'

'I was hoping to listen in.'

'I like your enthusiasm, although you might regret it.'

Before calling Della Langhe, Perillo made himself a drink with bicarbonate of soda and water. It would stave off the hangover that was sure to come. There was nothing he could drink, unfortunately, to stave off Della Langhe.

The prosecutor answered on the first ring. 'Perillo, your report is unacceptable.'

'It has only been two days.'

'I am perfectly aware of how long it's been since that poor devil was atrociously murdered. The idea of having a man's face blasted to pieces no bigger than confetti' – *There he goes with his florid imagination*, Perillo thought as he stirred his awful drink with his finger – 'is repugnant to me. A man's face is the mirror to his soul.' Della Langhe was both handsome and vain, and Perillo had often caught the procuratore looking into whatever reflective surface he passed. Perillo was guilty of stealing glances of himself here and there, as his wife occasionally pointed out. In his case, it had nothing to do with being handsome, which he was not. His vanity came from having survived.

'We will find the man who did this. But there are quite a few questions in this case that will take time to answer. Would you like to hear them?'

'I'm a busy man. I am only interested in answers.' Busy, but he had time, as always, for his closing speech about the evil of today's youth, how the rejection of sound Christian values was leading the world to utter chaos. He was probably thinking of his daughter.

'I am in perfect agreement with you.' The last time Perillo had gone to church was for his own wedding twelve years ago. 'Let us hope this new Pope will bring our young ones back to the church. As soon as I have some news, I'll let you know. I am not, may I point out, the only slow one. I haven't been sent the autopsy report yet.'

'Ah, yes. The autopsy report. I have it here.'

'I should have been sent a copy.'

'I'm sure you were. Ah, no, I have the second copy here. Yet another clerical error. Let me see.'

Perillo slurped the last of his drink, not caring if the man heard him. Merda, how long had that autopsy been sitting on Della Langhe's desk?

'Ah, Perillo,' Della Langhe exclaimed smugly. 'This could change everything.'

Perillo did not rise to the bait.

'Your silence makes me wonder if you are interested.'

With this man in his ear, his headache was only getting worse. 'It is my duty to be interested. I did not wish to interrupt.'

'I did not think you capable of such thoughtfulness. This man's death, as horrid as it was, may have been a mercy killing. Dr Rotunno has written here that the man had at the most six months left to live. His body was riddled with metastasised cancer. The possibility of a mercy killing lifts my heart. Finding the perpetrator may turn out not to be so urgent.'

Perillo was tempted to remind the substitute prosecutor that mercy killings were still considered murder by Italian law. He controlled himself. 'Difficult to establish whether it was a mercy killing.'

'I speak of it as a possibility, not fact. I will have my secretary fax you your copy of the autopsy. Urgent or not, keep me informed, Perillo. We're in full-blown tourist season. The Chianti Expo starts tomorrow. We want our wine drinkers to be happy, not fearful.'

Keep me informed. Six months to live. Mercy killing. Perillo's head couldn't make sense of it, not without another espresso. A double, corrected with grappa.

At nine forty-five that morning, the local coffee and cornetti crush had abated at Bar All'Angolo. Now it was the tourists' turn. Nico had come earlier and had been lucky enough to snag a table by the open French doors. He was happy to sit. His legs ached after running an extra two miles to fend off last night's food and drink. His Dante-quoting friend was very late. Nico yearned for a whole wheat cornetto, but he didn't want to offend Gogol by not waiting for him. He whiled away the time reading *La Nazione*, skipping the crime section. He wasn't avoiding the paper's account of the murder, although he was sure it wouldn't tell him anything he didn't already know from Perillo. He was avoiding the cruel, sometimes petty crimes that filled this section every day. An elderly lady robbed by two men pretending to be carabinieri. A metal donation bin that collected clothes for the poor, broken into and ransacked. Teenagers beating up a sleeping immigrant who had survived the boat crossing from Africa. Because of Rita, he had always held Italy to a higher standard than the States. She believed Italy was a fairyland, and therefore so did he. Even now. It was why he wanted to help Perillo, despite his reservations. Solve the murder and wipe this corner of the world clean again.

Nico stretched his legs in front of him and looked out onto the piazza. It was another clear day with a breeze that would later keep heat at bay. The week's only rain had been on Sunday, just enough to wash dust from the vines and his vegetable garden. The retired men were sitting on their usual benches chatting, one of them smoking a Toscano cigar. No Carletta with her lavender hair setting up the trattoria tables outside today. The restaurant was closed on Wednesday. On the far end of the piazza, the weekly fish truck was doing brisk business. Were its goods frozen? The Mediterranean was at least forty-five miles away. Many restaurants, even those close to the sea, served frozen fish, but there was always an asterisk that warned the customer. Nico constantly marvelled at how a peninsula surrounded by the sea had the most incredible selection of frozen fish in its supermarkets. He preferred his fish fresh.

Nico looked at his watch as Sandro walked over with a small tray. Where was Gogol? Before he worked any further with Perillo, he wanted to know why Gogol thought the maresciallo was a bad man.

'It's time to eat,' Sandro said as he slid the tray on the metal table. 'This is Jimmy's last whole wheat cornetto, just out of the oven, your Americano and yesterday's cornetto for the dog. You've been stood up, amico.'

Nico dropped the stale cornetto into OneWag's open mouth. 'Maybe he's sick.'

'In all the years I've known him,' Jimmy said, 'he hasn't missed a day of spewing Dante to the tourists. My bet is he's pissed with you.'

Nico waited until he'd swallowed a bite of his cornetto before asking, 'About what?'

'Something to do with Salvatore, probably,' Jimmy said. 'You might have misunderstood him.'

'Jimmy has sharp ears,' Sandro said.

'I can see that.'

Jimmy leant over the counter. 'Like I said, you fart and the whole town knows about it, me included. You'll have to forgive me.'

'What did I misunderstand?'

'Salvatore's a good man, and Gogol knows it. He must've been talking about someone else.'

'According to town gossip,' Sandro added, tugging at the earring on his left ear, 'Gogol hasn't had a friend since his mother died. We put up with him. We give him money every once in a while. The kids make fun of him. We make sure no one hurts him, but that's all. It doesn't necessarily make us feel good about ourselves, but it's good to know someone cares.'

'I do.' Nico finished his cornetto and Americano and got up. He wasn't quite sure what it was that had made him latch on to Gogol. Yes, Rita and Dante had to do with it, but there was more. He saw Gogol as a lost man, maybe one who reminded him of himself. 'I'll stop by the butcher's to see if he's there.'

'If he's not,' Jimmy said, 'come back. I'll give you a thermos full of coffee and a ciambella. You'll find him somewhere.'

'Who was it who didn't care?'

Jimmy shrugged. Sandro busied himself counting change for a customer.

Luciana peeked out of her shop as Nico and OneWag walked by. 'Ciao, Nico. Thank you for the olive loaf. You're a dear. Enrico couldn't figure out how I got it. It's our little secret! Are you going to visit Rita? I've got some pretty daisies today.'

'Thanks. I'll be going later.'

'Well, stop by. I'll be happy to give them to you.'

He lifted his hand in a salute and turned the corner. Sergio, the butcher, was a few shops up the road to the cemetery. Nico walked in. On one side, a long refrigerated counter held beautiful cuts of meat that Sergio, following Dario Cecchini's lead, imported from Spain. There wasn't enough pasture in Italy to meet the demand, Sergio had told him on one of his shopping trips for Tilde. There was no sign of Gogol, but against the wall on one side of the shop, a long marble table held plates of crostini topped with lard or salami. Nico picked one of each and wrapped them in a napkin. He turned down the plastic cup of red wine an aproned young man offered him.

Sergio was behind the counter, weighing a mound of bright-red beef diced in quarter-inch pieces to be used for beef tartar. He was big, handsome, all muscle, with a large steak tattooed on one of his biceps. On the wall behind him was a sign celebrating the rebirth of the great bistecca alla fiorentina, the thick, delicious Florentine T-bone steak that had been banned during the mad cow disease scare. Luckily for Sergio and his far more famous rival Dario Cecchini in Panzano, the ban had lasted only a year.

Nico lifted the napkin holding the crostini. 'Thanks. I'll come back and pick up a chicken later.'

'Anytime,' Sergio answered without turning his head.

Wednesday morning, Daniele left his room in the barracks at six ten. He had slept badly, thanks to Rosalba. Something was bothering him, but he couldn't pin down what. It wasn't just that she was older than he was. Maybe it was the man without a face who kept intruding on his dreams, frightening him. He went downstairs and peeked into the back office to exchange a few words with the brigadiere on night duty. Vince was slumped over his desk, fast asleep. Daniele woke him up.

'Go to bed. I'll take over.'

'Thanks,' Vince mumbled. 'Nothing came in.'

'Too bad. We could use some news.'

Daniele went to the maresciallo's office, turned on the computer and started searching for a pirated download of *Wonder Woman*. He'd seen pictures of the Israeli actress playing Wonder Woman. She looked a lot like Rosalba.

The call from the carabinieri station in San Gimignano came through at six twenty. They had spotted the missing Avis car being driven on the outskirts of the town by a kid and his girlfriend. The carabiniere on night duty asked whether Maresciallo Perillo wanted to pick up the car and the kids or if the San Gimignano station should take over.

'I'll let you know,' Daniele said, and hung up. Should he wake the maresciallo? He'd gone to bed late last night and was sure to have a hangover. Besides, he never came down before eight. Could it wait? *Wonder Woman* was ready for download.

No. Duty came first, even if the maresciallo's mood would be black for the rest of the day.

Daniele picked up the phone and called upstairs.

Nico followed OneWag, who had picked up the scent of Gogol's cologne and was scurrying down the road that led out of town. They found him sunning himself on the stone bench in the Medici garden behind the old-age home. His overcoat was open. Underneath, he was wearing pyjamas. His feet were bare.

'I brought you breakfast.' Nico sat beside Gogol and placed the thermos and the crostini between them.

Gogol snatched the lard one without looking at Nico. OneWag sat at the old man's feet, looking up with hope. '"I craved for peace with God on the last shore of life."'

'You're nowhere near the last shore yet,' Nico said. He understood this quote. Gogol didn't want him there. 'I am sorry I made you angry yesterday.'

Gogol chewed on his crostino.

Nico unscrewed the thermos top and poured Gogol some coffee. The old man ignored the offer. 'I don't blame you for not coming to the cafe.' Nico held on to the cup. 'This sun feels good.' The garden, a large, elegant space with winding paths and arched stone niches at one end, was now in a sorry state. A carpet of weeds covered the gravel paths. The boxwood hedges had dried out. The few mouldy rosebushes that had survived desperately needed pruning.

'I misunderstood you,' Nico said. 'The maresciallo isn't a bad man, is he? You were trying to tell me something else.'

Gogol leant down and gave the dog what little was left of the crostino. '"If to thy mind I show a truth . . ."' He grabbed the thermos cup from Nico and drank. 'Jimmy is a coffee artist. His brew brings happiness.'

Nico leant forward and turned his head. He wanted Gogol to look him in the eye. 'What truth were you trying to tell me?'

The old man shook his head and bit into the salami.

'Gogol, do you know who the dead man is?'

'Dead is good.'

'You do know. Who is he?'

'You are my friend. Stay away.'

'If we are friends, tell me why I should stay away.'

Gogol wrapped his arms around himself as though a cold wind were sweeping right through him. 'Because your heart no peace will claim.' He started rocking back and forth. 'There will be much weeping and no singing. Your wife is a good woman. She knows.'

'My wife is dead.'

Gogol stopped rocking and wrapped his arms around Nico. 'I go now.' He rose from the bench and waved. 'Tomorrow, if I live.'

Nico and OneWag both stood up. 'We'll walk you back to the villa.'

'I am in no danger of straying into a dark forest. *You* are the one who must be careful. Part of your wife lives on.'

Gogol had already strayed from a normal life, Nico thought as he watched the man shuffle up the incline that led to the old Medici villa, now a place for the infirm. What did his friend mean by part of Rita living on? Was it her memory? And what had she known?

CHAPTER SEVEN

On the way to San Gimignano, Perillo called Nico and filled him in on the latest. 'Garrett's car's been found. We're on our way to pick it up and interrogate the two kids who stole it. And listen to this. When I got home last night, Della Langhe was waiting for me to call him. It made me sober up pretty quickly. The autopsy showed Garrett was in the late stages of cancer. He had only a few months left. Della Langhe thinks it's a mercy killing.'

The phone call had come in as Nico was getting into his car with OneWag. He took a long breath to think over the possibility, then said, 'The prosecutor thinks the victim hired a man to kill him by shooting his face off? And after being paid to kill him, he takes his wallet and credit cards but walks away leaving a five-thousand-dollar watch and fourteen-hundred-euro charm bracelet?' He shook his head. 'No.'

He heard a loud noise. Perillo hitting something. 'No was my thought exactly. Murder it is. Ciao, Nico.' He clicked off. 'Caro Daniele, today is going to be a very good day.'

Daniele smiled with relief.

A tall, good-looking carabiniere in uniform greeted them outside the San Gimignano station. Perillo and Daniele were in jeans. 'We've got the two kids inside. We fingerprinted them, but that's it. I thought you might want to be the one to question them.'

'Thanks,' Perillo said after he introduced himself and Daniele to Maresciallo Second Grade Davide Serroni. 'The kids can stare at the walls for a while. Car keys?'

Serroni handed them over. 'The car's in the back.'

'That's good,' Perillo said when he spotted the Avis Panda.

Daniele hitched his thumbs into his jean belt loops and looked to the fourteen towers that gave San Gimignano its fame. Once, the town had boasted seventy-two towers. One day soon he'd visit. 'It's good that the car was found.'

'That too, but what's also good is that it's still covered in dust and bird droppings, which means the kid who stole it didn't bother to clean it up. I'm hoping he didn't bother with the inside, either. If the car belongs to the victim, we should find some useful information.' Perillo slipped on rubber gloves and opened the boot. An expensive-looking tan leather suitcase took up most of the space. On top of the suitcase, a set of spread-out keys, looking like they'd been tossed carelessly there. Perillo picked them up. A brass ring held five different keys and an inch-long enamelled wine bottle key chain. Three of them were stamped star, MADE IN THE USA and seemed to be house or office keys, while the other two were small. He picked the longer of the small keys and tried the lock on the suitcase. It fit. Perillo looked into the side pockets first and found neatly folded white sport socks. He lifted the clothes. Two pairs of tan slacks, one dress shirt, several polo shirts, T-shirts. No pyjamas. No shirt with an embroidered golf club on the pocket. Underwear. A swimsuit. Blue New Balance trainers.

While Perillo rummaged through the suitcase, Daniele was looking through the window on the passenger side, wondering if he'd ever love a girl so much he'd steal a car just to take her to see another town. He didn't have gloves with him, and not wanting to erase any possible evidence, he just stared at the inside, entranced.

A terry cloth towel lay bunched up in the well below the passenger seat next to a half-empty plastic litre bottle of water and three empty bottles of Peroni beer. A torn package of condoms was wedged between the front seats, making Daniele think they had been too much in a hurry to open it properly. The ashtray was full; all the butts had traces of lipstick on them. His eyes travelled to the driver's seat, which had a whitish smear on it. Daniele felt his cheeks get hot and looked away, spotting a blue fold of paper jutting out over the edge of the side compartment of the driver's door.

'Mother of God!' Perillo slammed the lid of the suitcase shut. 'Where the hell is his passport?'

Daniele pointed at the driver's door, even though Perillo couldn't see him. 'Over there, maybe?'

Perillo appeared from behind the boot of the car like a Pamplona bull ready to trample anyone who got in his way.

Daniele took a step back, still pointing. 'In the driver's-side compartment. Something blue is sticking out. Aren't American passports blue?'

'Right you are.' Perillo unlocked the door on the driver's side and stuck his gloved hand in the side pocket. 'Got it!' He held up the passport like a goalie showing off the football he'd just intercepted. 'Bravo, Dani.'

Daniele felt as tall as one of those towers in the distance.

Perillo opened the passport. The colour photo showed a man with a wide face, chiselled nose, full lips and the usual expressionless gaze people adopt for passport photos. Handsome. Not many wrinkles. He looked much younger than fifty. The picture had probably been taken years ago.

'Surname,' Perillo read out loud for Dani's sake. 'Garrett. Given name: Robert. Nationality: United States of America. Date of Birth: The twenty-ninth of November 1974.' That made him only forty-four years old. Perillo looked under Place of Birth and whistled.

'Is it our man?' Daniele hurried past the car hood to see for himself what made the maresciallo whistle.

'Unless you believe in such coincidences.' Perillo held up the open passport for Daniele.

'Don't touch it. Just look under Place of Birth.'

'Good God, and his mother,' he said instead. 'He's a local!'

'And not just from the region, but our very own Gravigna, Italy.' Perillo flipped the page over. The bearer's address was listed as Delizioso Wine Company, Route 29, Napa, California, 94581. The foreign address and emergency contact had both been left blank. Perillo extracted a plastic bag from his back pocket, slipped the passport inside and locked the bag in the leather suitcase. With boot and car doors locked, he said, 'Let's go inside and interview those two idiots.'

'It's thanks to them that we have the car,' Daniele reminded him. He hoped they wouldn't be in too much trouble.

'They will get no thanks from me. Or you.'

'Of course not, Maresciallo.' But he *was* grateful. Now he had an excuse to see Rosalba again, to tell her she wouldn't need to see a sketch artist.

In the entrance hall of the station, the two teens sat on a wooden bench holding hands. The boy, with a chunk of hair falling over his eyes and both sides of his head shaved off, stood as soon as he saw Perillo. 'I didn't know the car belonged to the murdered guy. I swear I didn't.'

The girl stayed seated, tossing her long chestnut hair to one side. She smiled at Daniele. He did not smile back. 'It was just sitting there,' she said. 'For two nights.'

The carabiniere at the front desk pointed to the first door along the corridor. 'Maresciallo, you can take them in there.'

The boy grabbed the girl's hand and followed Perillo into a small, windowless room with a wooden table and four metal chairs. They sat down next to each other at the far side of the table. The girl was short and 'in flesh', as Italians liked to say about someone chubby, wearing cutoff jeans and a spaghetti-strap top that showed off her abundant breasts. Her face might be pretty if she weren't sulking. The boy was tall, strongly built. He had on jeans and a sleeveless T-shirt that showed his deep tan ended mid-bicep. A boy who worked outdoors.

Perillo and Daniele sat down opposite them. Daniele took out his notebook and pen.

'Your names?' Perillo asked.

'We gave them to the fat guy at the desk,' the girl said. 'And where's your tape recorder?'

Perillo nodded his head towards Daniele. 'He's my tape recorder, and an excellent one too. Please tell him your name, address and birthdate.'

The boy leant forward with an apologetic look on his young face. 'We don't want to get into trouble. I'm Bruno Dini, and she's Katia Paccini. We both live on Via della Conca D'Oro in Panzano. She's at Thirty-One, I'm down the street at Fourteen. I was born the sixth of February, 2002.'

'Too young to have a driver's licence,' Perillo said.

'I've been driving my uncle's harvester since I was twelve.'

Perillo turned to the girl. 'Your age, Signorina Paccini?'

'A woman should never reveal her age.'

Bruno kicked her under the table. She kicked him back.

Perillo said, 'You're not a woman yet.'

Katia stuck out her lower lip in a pout.

'She was born on the seventh of July, 2003.' Bruno joined his hands together as if in prayer. 'We're really sorry we did this, Maresciallo. We just wanted to have some fun. Katia's never been to San Gimignano. We were going to spend the day here, then drive the car back where we found it.'

'And where was that?' Perillo asked.

'The San Eufrosino sanctuary. We both live with our families and go there at night sometimes to get some privacy. You must remember how it is for young people, Maresciallo.'

Perillo wanted to kick the kid for that remark. Instead, he nodded.

'Only if the weather is good,' Bruno said, looking at Katia. 'We don't have a car, which I guess is obvious.'

Daniele lowered his head to hide his smile. If you had a girl and lived with your family, the car became the bedroom. In Venice, the only place cars were allowed was in Piazzale Roma. His friends used to make out in gondolas. He'd tried it once, but the rocking made him seasick.

'Some important information for you, tape recorder.' Katia eyed Daniele while she tugged at her top to reveal more of her breasts. 'The car wasn't there Sunday night. Monday, it was parked behind the sanctuary. I was cold and we tried the door. No luck and no keys on the ground till last night. How they got there, I have no idea. I looked everywhere the night before. Even got down on my hands and knees. It was freezing, and I wasn't wearing much.' She dropped her elbows on the table. 'Got all that?'

Daniele kept his head down and wrote, praying he wasn't blushing. Of course he was.

Katia laughed.

Perillo stood up. He had the information he needed and had had enough of Katia Paccini. 'Let's go, Daniele.'

Daniele closed his notebook, slipped his pen in his pocket and followed Perillo without looking at the teenagers.

'What about us?' Bruno asked.

Perillo left the room without answering.

Katie wiggled her fingers like a two-year-old. 'Bye, tape recorder. Don't let the battery run out.'

As Daniele closed the door, he overheard Bruno whisper angrily, 'Why do you always have to be such a bitch?'

'It's fun,' was Katia's answer.

The carabiniere stopped Perillo as he headed for the exit. 'What do you want us to do with those two?'

'Let them sit there for a bit and enjoy the San Gimignano air.'

Once they were outside, Daniele asked, 'You don't think they're involved with the murder?'

'They're dumb kids, but not quite dumb enough to kill a man and go joyriding in his car two days later.'

'Kids do a lot of stupid things, though,' Daniele said in a tone that indicated he'd passed that stage long ago.

Perillo lit up a much-yearned-for cigarette. 'Of course. I did some pretty crazy stuff myself, but these two didn't blow our victim's face off with a shotgun.'

'How can you be sure?'

'When I was a kid, I lived in a bad area and had to watch out for myself. After I was beaten up too many times to count, I developed an itch in my fingers whenever I met up with a bad one. Those two aren't bad. Just dumb.'

Weird, Daniele thought, not sure whether to believe

the maresciallo's fingers could serve psychic purposes.

Perillo was watching him. 'Okay, I'll give you a more concrete reason. The killer clearly went through the victim's pockets. There's not a chance that besotted kid or his nightmare girlfriend would have left that watch and the bracelet.'

Daniele rubbed his neck, as if that would hide the creeping redness. 'What do we do now?'

'We need a tow truck to pick up the car and take it to Florence. Maybe we'll get lucky and the forensic technicians will get us some useful information about the killer before Father Christmas comes calling. We're taking the luggage with us. It should tell us more about our victim. And we'll take those kids home.' Perillo took a long drag. 'That girl really took to you.'

Daniele found a pebble to kick. He knew she was just toying with him to make Bruno jealous.

'Rosalba and now Katia. You've got a way with women. Enjoy it.'

There was nothing to enjoy. He hadn't been with a girl since he'd moved into the barracks in Greve.

Perillo stubbed out his cigarette on the sole of his shoe. 'Dani, tell me the truth. How old do I look?'

Daniele stood at attention. This was a serious question. Age was the maresciallo's Achilles' heel. 'Thirty-seven, Maresciallo. Thirty-eight at most.'

Perillo laughed and slapped him on the back. 'You're a good liar, Dani. That is an asset in our business.' He tossed the cigarette on the ground and headed to the victim's car. 'I want you to find out if those two kids ever got into serious trouble. Itch or no itch, it's always best to turn over every stone.'

Nico watered the aster plant and placed the fruit-juice bottle with Luciana's daisies in it under Rita's photo. He was relieved to be alone. The white of the flowers added a brighter sheen to the greyness of the picture. He resolved to bring more white flowers next time. He stood awkwardly, hands folded over his stomach, with OneWag curled at his feet. Gogol's parting words had left a stone of guilt in his heart, one he needed to dislodge.

You still live, Rita mia. In me, in Tilde, in Stella. You are unforgettable. Gogol, who shares your love for Dante, remembers you too. He thinks you know a gravely upsetting truth. I only know two truths. That you're gone, which still brings tears, and that I love you.

Nico leant down, kissed Rita's photo and slowly walked down the path to the gate. The stone in his heart was still there, but it felt lighter now. He trusted somehow that Rita heard him. It was true that he had trouble summoning her face now when he woke in the morning. Her voice had retreated to a distance he could barely reach, but he would fight to keep her with him. Letting her go was like letting go of the beauty in his life.

OneWag trotted ahead of the man who cared for him, head and tail held high, eager to find somewhere smellier.

Back down in the piazza, the dog stopped by Luciana's

flower shop to make a show of sniffing the flowers she kept outside. Luciana had cookies.

'No begging,' Nico ordered as he walked past and waved. 'Thanks for the daisies, Luciana.' He was thankful she was waiting on a customer, which meant he wouldn't get one of her suffocating, breast-filled hugs.

OneWag assessed the situation with one glance. He ran across the piazza and aimed his small body towards the steep road that led to Sotto Il Fico. Nico followed the dog up the street and allowed himself a smile when OneWag stopped in front of Enrico's food shop. Yesterday, Nico had reserved two olive loaves for today. Had the dog stopped for the salty-sweet smell of the prosciutti hanging from the ceiling of the shop? Probably. Or was it the instinctual understanding some dogs had of their owner's next move?

There was a customer in the small shop. Behind the counter, Enrico was carving into a giant Parmigiano Reggiano wheel. After he'd extracted a chunk and wrapped it in butcher paper, Enrico dropped a round of mortadella on the slicing machine and worked his arm back and forth until five hundred grams of paper-thin slices sat neatly piled on oiled paper. Outside, OneWag gave a bark of protest. The smells had prompted a growl in Nico's own stomach. He'd already gained six pounds since coming here. Best to distract himself with something else. Had any new evidence appeared in the murder case? Was Perillo – fine, Salvatore – any closer to knowing the dead man's identity?

The Parmigiano and mortadella customer brushed past Nico, bringing him right back to the matter at hand. Food.

'Buongiorno, Enrico. Your arm must be aching after all that slicing.'

'Salve, Nico.' He was a short, slight man with a pale face and a half-crown of thinning hair hugging his head. 'I started slicing as soon as I was tall enough to reach the handle. After forty years, I'm used to it. I've got your two olive loaves. And here's a slice of mortadella for you, and one for your dog.'

'You'll have him at your doorstep every morning now.' Nico stepped outside to give the dog his slice and got the usual one-wag response. Nico went back inside to taste his own slice. The meat was so soft and luscious he barely had to use his teeth. 'Thank you. Delicious! I'll take a hundred grams of it. And some ricotta. Just enough for two people. I was thinking of trying my hand at making a ricotta tart.'

Enrico sliced some more mortadella. 'Ask Luciana for her recipe. She makes a good one.'

'Thanks, I will if my attempt fails.'

'Don't stint on the nutmeg.' Enrico weighed the food, wrapped it in two separate parcels and rang up the amount on an old cash register. Nico paid him.

As Enrico handed over the change, he asked, 'Any news about the dead man?'

The question surprised Nico, and it showed.

Enrico looked embarrassed. 'You found the body and you've been seen with Salvatore, so some of us thought you were working together. You used to be a policeman, no?'

So that wasn't a secret any more either. 'I patrolled the streets, but I had nothing to do with murder.' Why was he still lying? Rita was gone. At least Tilde deserved to know what his job had really been. The forced retirement he would keep to himself. Himself, Salvatore and Daniele.

Nico took the slim packages and the change. 'For news, you'll have to ask the maresciallo. See you tomorrow.' Nico pulled aside the beaded curtain that kept the flies out. 'Come on, OneWag. Time to go to work.'

Stella's boyfriend blocked his path halfway up the hill to the restaurant. 'Can I talk to you, Nico?' Today, Gianni's face was darkened by a deep frown.

'Is something wrong?' Nico asked.

'No.' Gianni's fingers nervously combed through his curls. 'Well, yes. I need your advice. Let me.' Gianni reached for Nico's bag. It made Nico feel like an old man, but he released his hold on the bag. Gianni was only being polite.

'Maybe we can sit on the church steps?' Gianni asked. 'Out of sight of the restaurant?'

Nico nodded with what he hoped was an encouraging smile. If Gianni was having romantic problems again, he could listen for a few minutes. Tilde was expecting him to help with lunch. He followed Gianni the fifty uphill metres to Sant'Agnese, a largely restructured church dating back to the fourteenth century. If consolation was what Gianni was looking for, this would be the right spot.

Gianni didn't wait to sit. 'Stella is pulling away from me, and it's tearing me apart. What makes it worse is, I have no idea why.'

Nico welcomed the sit-down. He picked the third step and stretched out his legs. Gianni loomed over him, his hands stuffed in his jeans pockets. OneWag went exploring their surroundings.

'Sit,' Nico said gently. 'Did you tell her taking the museum exam was okay with you?'

'Yeah, if that's what she wants.' Gianni dropped down next to him. 'She talks about the museum job as her future, but I mean, is sitting in a chair for eight hours looking at old paintings and answering stupid questions a future? "Hey, miss, where's the john?"' He imitated an American accent. '"I can't find the Botticelli, whadja do with it?"'

'There's no need for that,' Nico said curtly.

Gianni looked at him in surprise. 'Oh, sure. I forget you're American.'

An apology would have been nice, Nico thought. 'Maybe she doesn't believe you.'

'Why wouldn't she? Tilde is getting to her. Stella has changed. I'm treating her like a princess. I tell her I'm going to marry her even if she ends up working in Florence. I'll get a job there too. What more does the girl want?'

'I'm afraid I can't answer that for you. I do think, though, that it would help if you treated Stella as a woman, rather than a princess. My wife taught me that what women want is respect first. It keeps the door open to love.'

'Respect?' Coming from Gianni, it sounded like a foreign word. 'What more do I have to do?'

'Ask Stella.' Nico stood up. 'Now, forgive me, Tilde is waiting for me.'

'Of course. Put in a good word for me, will you? Tell

her Stella's future is maybe with the job, but it's also with me. You can tell Stella that too.'

Nico bent down to hide the disappointment in his face. He picked up his bag. Gianni persisted in being cocky and possessive, a bad combination. Nico straightened himself up and whistled. OneWag came running with a small red rubber ball in his mouth.

'No.' Nico did not pronounce the word with any force, but OneWag took it as a command and let go of the ball. The three of them watched it stumble down the slope. Later, OneWag would retrieve it in the piazza below, and Nico would let him keep it. His no had been for Gianni.

Sotto Il Fico did brisk business at lunchtime, selling out of the courgette lasagne, the stuffed rigatoni au gratin and the pappa al pomodoro. Nico gulped down the last portion of navy bean and kale soup served at room temperature. At three o'clock, the terrace had emptied except for two older Englishmen who were finishing the last drops of their 2013 Castello di Rampolla, a renowned vineyard they could spot in the distance. In the front room, Elvira napped in her armchair with the completed front-page crossword of the *Settimana Enigmistica* on her lap. Her pen had fallen to the floor. Enzo stood at his perch behind the bar, catching up on football news in the *Gazzetta dello Sport*. Stella was supposedly at home studying for the museum guard exam. Tilde and Alba, the Albanian helper, were wiping the kitchen. Nico finished loading the dishwasher. They had been too busy cooking, plating and serving to say more than two words to each other until now.

Tilde asked as she hung up the scrubbed skillets on the brick wall, 'Did Salvatore find out the dead man's identity?'

'Not yet. Look, there's something I need to tell you,' Nico said.

'Ah, yes. Enzo saw you talking to Gianni up at the church. What did he have to say for himself?'

'Nothing interesting.' Nico did not want to add to Tilde's bad opinion of Gianni. It was up to Stella to decide whether to keep him in her life or not.

'All right.' It was clear she didn't believe him. 'How was your dinner at Da Angela? I want to hear about every crumb you ate and every word you and Salvatore said to each other. You talked about the murder, yes?' The man's death and his gold trainers still haunted her. Shooting his face off, erasing his identity struck her as an act of rage. It brought back the memory of her own rage from years ago. That was what scared her. That rage was still inside her. 'Start with what the two of you ate. Anything we should be serving here?'

'Can we take a walk?'

Tilde took in Nico's serious expression. A walk meant he wanted privacy. Whatever he needed to tell her had nothing to do with food. 'I've been on my feet since six o'clock this morning. I'm ready for a sit-down.' She took off her apron, hung it on a nail by the kitchen door and walked out of the restaurant. Nico retrieved his package of food from the refrigerator and followed. OneWag trailed them both to the steps of the church, where he had sat with Gianni. From this vantage point, they had a good view of the medieval town. The new houses had been built on the other side, below the hill.

Tilde sat on one of the steps and offered her face to the sun, eyes closed. Nico lowered himself down next to her, and she sensed how tense he was. 'Let me guess what you ate,' she said to make the moment easier for him. Nico's dinner with Salvatore made her think she knew what he wanted to say. 'A plate of the usual antipasto, salami, prosciutto, grilled aubergine, yellow and red peppers, courgette. Pecorino cheese with a sweet onion marmalade from Certosa.' She turned to face Nico, locking arms with him. 'Then what? Pasta or risotto?'

Nico nudged her shoulder. He knew what she was up to, and it was working. 'We had a historic meat course. La peposa. It was very good, although I would have liked a little less pepper. You should put it on the menu.'

'We do on occasion. And Salvatore, what did he tell you about the murder? You're conspiring together to solve it, aren't you?'

Nico took a deep breath. 'Rita will have to forgive me. But before I get into that, there's something you should know, something Rita asked me not to tell anyone here. I was a homicide detective in New York City for nineteen years before I left the force. Salvatore knows. That's why he wants me to help him. I'm sorry I didn't tell you earlier. I wanted to honour Rita's wishes.'

'Bravo. I'm impressed.' Tilde feigned surprise. Her aunt had told her the truth in that terrible last letter. A letter that had also told her Rita had stage-four cancer; a letter that had asked her to welcome and care for Nico once she was gone. Rita had correctly guessed Nico would move to Gravigna after her death.

Tilde took his hand in hers and squeezed. 'Thank you for telling me. It must have been a very difficult job, and I'm proud of you.'

'I'm not sure Rita felt the same.'

'Of course she did. You were the earth and the sky to her. I imagine she was afraid for you. Not telling anyone meant you were safe. We women have funny ways of dealing with our fear. I worry that Stella won't get the museum guard job she wants, so I spend half the night on the Internet, memorising the art in that museum. It's my good-luck charm for her.'

Nico kissed Tilde's forehead. 'I thought you would be angry.'

Tilde let go of Nico's hand and stood up. 'I think I used up my anger long ago. At least most of it.' She looked back at the church, hoping Nico wouldn't see that she was lying. 'I'm going back to work on dinner. You've done enough for today. I don't want to see you tonight.'

'What about feeding me?'

'I don't trust you. You'll eat a single bite, then start serving on tables. Come up with a great recipe to feed yourself. Our menu could use another of your ideas. And don't let Salvatore take over your life. He's got bored with being married, and any excuse to stay out at night is good. Although I'll admit murder is an excellent one.'

Nico was reminded of Gogol's words that morning. 'You know Gogol, don't you?'

'Of course. He's one of our village landmarks. The castle, the church and Gogol. I've heard you've become fast friends.'

'He got all worked up when he saw me talking to Salvatore. He said something odd. That there would be much weeping and no singing. That my wife is a good woman who knows the truth. What do you think he meant by that?'

Tilde felt a chill in her heart. 'He's probably misquoting Dante. Or letting his imagination fly in the wind.'

Nico lifted himself slowly. The church's steps were low, and he was still feeling the morning's run in his knees. 'Maybe, but he was trying to warn me off something. I'd like to know what.' OneWag, who had curled himself in the shade of a potted hibiscus, stood up, stretched and sauntered over to Nico.

Tilde hastily kissed Nico on both cheeks. She was eager to reach the safety of her kitchen, a place she considered her own, where she felt empowered. 'Find a good recipe,' she said simply, and walked away.

'I do have an idea. Easy, inexpensive. I just have to play around with it first.' By the time his final sentence had ended, only OneWag was listening.

CHAPTER EIGHT

Daniele and Perillo had delivered Katia and Bruno to their homes, warning them to stay in town. The tow truck was on its way to San Gimignano to pick up the Avis Panda. On its way back to Florence, it would stop by the Greve station to collect Robert Garrett's suitcase, which had been carefully emptied by Daniele, its contents neatly laid out on two tables in Perillo's office.

'Make a list,' Perillo said.

'Aren't we sending everything to Florence?'

'Yes, but the dead man is an American. I wish to be prudent. The Florence lab will make its own list. We will have ours, witnessed by – who's on duty today?'

'Dino and Vince.'

'Witnessed by Dino and Vince. Go ahead, don't leave anything out. Toothpicks included.' He caught Daniele hungrily eyeing his computer in the back of the room. 'A handwritten list first, Dani.' He opened his desk drawer, took out pen and paper and handed them over. 'These are good items. They've been used for centuries. With these, no hacking, no computer malfunctions.'

'Paper gets lost.'

'Files get erased. You'll type it into your machine later.'

A reluctant Daniele went back to the two tables and started writing. He listed the three most important items first. As soon as Daniele had written them down, Perillo slipped on a new pair of rubber gloves and transferred the listed items to his desk, where he could sit down and think about them. He had already read the information on the American passport back in the carabinieri car park in San Gimignano. Now he examined the hotel receipt that had been stuffed in a trouser pocket. Hotel Bella Vista, seven nights at 160 euros a night. No credit card numbers.

'He told Avis he was going to Radda in Chianti,' Perillo muttered to himself. 'Instead, he stayed in Panzano. Why not Gravigna, his home town?'

Daniele always listened to Perillo's mutterings, hoping to learn something and also to have answers for him. 'Judging from the other receipts we found, he was a Dario Cecchini fan. He ate at his top restaurant five of the seven nights he was here. Paid with cash every time.'

'Maybe Garrett didn't believe in credit cards,' Perillo muttered to himself. He'd paid for the bracelet in cash too. There was no cash in his pockets when he was found. The killer must have taken it. Maybe the dog's barks scared him off before he could grab the watch and the bracelet.

'Even kept the menu.' Daniele waved the large sheet in the air. '"Leave all hope, ye who enter here. You're in the hands of a butcher." I say, leave all your money ye who enter here. Fifty euros a meal. That's crazy.'

'If we find the killer, I'll take you there.'

'I'm a vegetarian, Maresciallo.'

'That's right.' Why did he keep forgetting things like this? Was he already going senile? 'You liked the leftover aubergine parmigiana.' He did remember the look of joy on Dani's face as he stuffed himself. 'I'm sure they'd have something for you too. And don't "Maresciallo" me.'

'Signora Perillo is a very good cook.'

'Yes, she is. Excellent, in fact.' And a lovely woman. If only the fire between them hadn't flickered down to the strength of a single candle. 'We have more important things to worry about here than my wife's cooking skills. Get back to your list.'

'I never stopped, Maresciallo. Sorry, Ma—Salvatore. I can write and speak at the same time.'

Something Perillo had never mastered. 'Good for you.' He picked up the third item on his desk. Another passport, Italian this time. He opened it. The photograph was of a much younger Garrett, the name different: Roberto Gerardi. This passport had been issued twenty-three years ago. The tax had been paid only that once, which allowed Roberto Gerardi to use his Italian passport for one year. Perillo slapped the passport down on the desk. 'Why did Roberto Gerardi become Robert Garrett?'

'He became an American citizen.'

'But why change his name?' Perillo said, more to himself than to Daniele. 'Your given name is who you are. It represents you.' He was proud of the name he'd been given by the Perillos, the couple who had opened up their home to him. On the streets of Pozzuoli, he'd been known as Sbriga because he was always hustling. He knew no other name until he was given the name Salvatore, 'the one who saves'. It should have been Salvato, 'saved', but that was not a name anyone used. Salvatore replaced Sbriga. 'You don't just throw your name away like it's rubbish.' And yet, ashamed of what he had been, he had done exactly that with Sbriga.

'Maybe that's what he wanted to do. I'll see if he had a criminal record here.'

'Don't bother. You can't become an American citizen with a record. Or get a resident alien card.'

'What a terrible name, alien. As if immigrants come from Mars.'

'We're all aliens to each other, I think.' Perillo watched Daniele write for a moment and remembered what Nico had said about making a list. Not a bad idea. He felt like he'd just been dropped into a high-walled maze where the exit would always be hidden. A list might help clear his head, arm him for the inevitable phone call to Della Langhe. He took out another sheet of paper and a pencil from his drawer. He'd always preferred pencil to pen. Mistakes were easily erased with a pencil, unlike in real life. He'd been lucky. He'd been given a choice and had the good sense to seize it.

Perillo bent over his desk and began in his best grammar-school handwriting. Signorina Bianchi, his teacher, had praised him for his neat, rounded letters. He chuckled as he remembered it was the only praise he'd received on starting school. Once he was done writing, Perillo folded the sheet of paper twice and started to tuck it in his pocket. A thought came to him and he unfolded it and added:

6. *Remember to buy flowers for your wife. Just because.*

List refolded and safely in his pocket, Perillo reached for the phone.

Nico's phone rang just as he was slurping water from the tap to cool his mouth. He'd been too eager to taste the ricotta tart he'd just plucked out of the oven. 'Nico here.'

'We've identified the victim.' Perillo's voice sounded triumphant. 'The dead man was Roberto Gerardi, a Gravignese, and also Robert Garrett, an American owner of a vineyard in Napa Valley called Delizioso.'

'Good.' He was happy for Perillo, but half his mind was concentrated on what he had just cooked. Nico's forefinger pressed gently on the surface of the tart. Still too hot. OneWag sat at his feet, hungrily gazing at Nico.

'His being American complicates things,' Perillo said. 'Your people will want to take charge, send a detective or two.'

'They're not my people any more.' Nico walked away

from the oven. 'And they won't take charge. It's your jurisdiction. They might put some pressure on the embassy in Rome, but if they took charge, would it matter to you?'

Perillo thought over the question for a moment. If the Americans took over, they'd be the ones to have to deal with Della Langhe's arrogance. That would be a relief. He and his men would go back to worrying about the pickpockets at the Expo del Vino opening tomorrow. Last year, more than twenty thousand people had shown up during the four-day festival. Only two wallets had been lost, one retrieved still full of money. A boring job.

'Yes, I would care,' Perillo said. He wanted to rise to the challenge of this difficult case, prove to the procuratore that he had a brain, that he wasn't Southern Italian scum. 'This is my case. Our case.'

At the other end of the line, Nico felt an unexpected thrum in his chest. He had both loved and hated his job in New York. Loved it when justice was found for the victim and their grieving family. Hated it for the ugliness he faced with each murder. In his last case, the ugliness had been the victim's. He sighed loudly. Maybe with luck and some smart work, they could clean up the mess. 'When you're done with everything you have to do today and your wife doesn't mind, come for dinner and we'll go over the new details. Bring Daniele. He's got some good gears in his head.'

'Thank you. It's a welcome invitation. My wife is bringing dinner to a friend who's fallen ill. I have two bottles of wine to make our minds and a moonless sky shine with light.' Never mind that the moon was almost full. Nico's willingness to collaborate thrilled Perillo. Maybe their minestrone of backgrounds – American, Venetian and Neapolitan – had a chance of cracking the case. He started to add *I made a list,* but stopped himself. Nico's suggestion had helped to clear his thoughts, but as a maresciallo of the carabinieri, he needed to maintain some dignity. 'Daniele is a vegetarian,' he said instead.

Too bad, Nico thought. He'd found a loose brick downstairs, which had given him the idea to make one of his favourites – pollo alla diavola, the devil's chicken. An easy recipe. All it took was a hot grill, a chicken split in two, well seasoned and brushed with olive oil, and a heavy brick to weigh it down and give it a crisp skin. 'What about gluten?'

Perillo turned to Daniele. 'Nico's invited us to dinner. I warned him you only eat sheep and cow fodder. Any gluten problems to add to that?'

'No, none at all. Tested negative when I was a baby.' Daniele felt his chest warm, bringing a smile. He was being treated as an equal.

Perillo spoke into the phone. 'We're fine with gluten.'

'So I can serve pasta?'

'You can. We should be done here by eight, eight-thirty.'

'Call me when you're on your way.' Nico hung up. Perillo followed suit.

Daniele had just finished listing all the items in Gerardi's suitcase. He turned to look at his boss with a puzzled look.

'What, Dani?'

'I was wondering what happened to Gerardi's mobile phone.'

'Ah, that's right. It's missing.' Perillo tried to keep the annoyance from his voice. He had overlooked that. He was getting duller.

'I bet it was a new iPhone and the murderer pocketed it. With what they cost here, I don't blame him.' Daniele's face instantly reddened. 'I mean, I don't condone—'

Perillo dismissed his brigadiere's embarrassment with the flick of a hand. 'You're speculating again. Gerardi could have lost the phone. My wife is always losing hers, buying a new one and then finding the old one weeks later.' He'd finally bought her a traded-in iPhone and activated the Find My iPhone feature. 'The murderer could have taken the phone to cover their tracks.'

'They communicated?'

'Maybe.' Perillo sighed. *Maybe, could have, might have, what if.* Everything in the case was speculation. He'd put Daniele down out of pique, but now they needed to find the phone.

Noticing the maresciallo's dark face, Daniele regretted having brought up the missing phone. It was all about timing with his boss. He should have remembered that Perillo was tired. 'I'll bring something typically Venetian tonight.'

'Bravo. Nice idea.' Perillo handed over the two passports. 'Get Vince or Dino to make photocopies of the American picture – it's more recent – and get it faxed over to *La Nazione* and *Chianti Sette*. Put everything back in the suitcase and make sure someone sticks around to hand over the suitcase when the tow truck arrives. Then you can play with your computer. Don't forget to get the typed copy witnessed. Then scrounge around and see what you can come up with for Bruno and Katia. If Della Langhe calls, stall. Not a word about the victim being American.'

'I'll do my best, Maresciallo.'

'I know I can count on you, and as a reward, tomorrow morning you can take a copy of the victim's older photo up to Radda to see if he's the man who bought that bracelet from the beautiful Rosalba.' They had not found a receipt for the bracelet among Garrett's belongings. Too often a cash payment meant no receipt. That was the finance police's problem, not his.

As expected, Daniele blushed. 'I'll go first thing in the morning, Maresciallo.'

'The store doesn't open until eleven, but you might find her again at the cafe.' Perillo slipped on his leather jacket. 'On my birth certificate, the name Maresciallo does not appear.'

'Yes, Maresciallo.'

'Yes, Salvatore,' Perillo corrected. Daniele was turning purple now. It was time to leave. 'I'm off to Hotel Bella Vista. Who knows what hidden nuggets of information I might find there.'

With OneWag following, head and tail held high, Nico took the plate with the cooling tart out on the balcony and sat behind the small round metal table that must have once belonged to a cafe. The centre held a fading painted ad for Lavazza Coffee. He plunged a fork into the now-cooled tart and tasted.

What a disappointment! The tart was much too bland. And here he had thought it would make a nice appetiser for the restaurant. For a toddler, maybe. Nico lowered the plate to the floor. 'All yours, OneWag.'

The dog approached the plate and sniffed. After one lick, he padded back inside to sleep on the sofa. Nico went inside and threw the tart in the bin. 'Come on, off to shop for food,' he told the dog. 'We have guests tonight.'

OneWag jumped off the sofa and scrambled to the door with a small pink tongue protruding from his dog smile.

Nico smiled back.

The well-named Hotel Bella Vista sat on the crest of a hill facing away from Panzano. The wide stone building was embraced by a semicircle of tall chestnut trees. The front side faced a garden filled with late summer flowers, which ended with a descending slope marked by slanting lines of young grapevines. In the distance, a perfect view of Vigna Maggio.

'It has been a working farm since the early fifteenth century,' said the woman, who had been pointed out to Perillo as being the manager of the hotel. A hotel guest listened by her side. 'The original Vigna Maggio was built by relatives of the Mona Lisa Gherardini, rendered famous by Leonardo Da Vinci. It's perhaps the most renowned hotel in the Chianti region.'

Perillo listened patiently, not wanting to interrupt with his sordid business. The manager, somewhere in her twenties, had a caressingly soft lilt in her voice, a lovely face with rounded cheeks, a pale complexion and long, blonde wavy hair that fell loosely down her back and glinted pink in the sun, features he always associated with Tuscan women. She wore a long, loose skirt of deep blue cotton with a white scoop-neck blouse trimmed with lace. Perillo thought she could have walked out of an eighteenth-century portrait hanging in the Uffizi.

The manager sensed a movement behind her and turned to face the man. 'Oh!' She seemed startled. As this was official business, Perillo was in uniform. 'I'm sorry. I didn't see you.'

'I just need a minute of your time, when you've finished.'

'I need to be off,' said the guest, an older woman whose face had surely been tightened by a surgeon's hand. 'Thank you so much,' the guest said. 'I'm sure our stay here will be a delight.'

The manager smiled. 'My pleasure.' She turned to Perillo and held out her hand. 'Laura Benati. I'm the manager here. How can I help you?'

He shook her hand, introduced himself, and showed her the hotel bill. 'Your guest Robert Garrett is the man we found murdered in the woods.'

Laura's only reaction was to study the hotel bill more closely, as if it could tell her that Perillo was mistaken. 'You found him on Monday morning, didn't you?'

'Yes.'

'He paid the bill Sunday night in cash. He said he had to leave very early Monday. He seemed very excited, and had a lot to drink at the bar that night, which he hadn't done the other nights he stayed here. I thought he was just nervous about flying back home to the States.'

'Did he only speak English to you?'

'Yes, although he did have an accent, and quite a strong one. Spanish, I thought.'

'He was Italian.' No harm in revealing that much, even if Della Langhe hadn't been informed yet.

'Odd, I didn't spot it. Are you sure the dead man is Garrett?'

'I am. I won't go into how we know, but there is no doubt that the murdered man was Robert Garrett. Has his room been cleaned out?'

'Yes, and rented to the signora you just saw. He did leave a dirty polo shirt in one of the drawers. I was going to mail it to him.'

'Did you by any chance find a mobile phone? His is missing.'

'No, I'm sorry.'

Perillo had no doubt Garrett/Gerardi had a mobile phone – everyone and their grandmother did, but it was best to ask anyway. 'Did you ever see him use a mobile phone?'

'The guests aren't allowed to use their mobile phones in the hotel's public spaces. Some naturally pay no attention, but if they're quiet, I let them be. If he did, I didn't notice. My job keeps me rather busy.'

'Did he have visitors or anyone asking for him? Phone calls?'

'Not while I was at the front desk. I'll have to ask the two girls who take over from me. Why don't you come inside while I fetch the shirt and call them?'

Perillo followed Laura to the hotel. The wide front hall had a beamed ceiling, old tapestries on the walls and dark furniture scattered here and there. On the floor, a gleaming expanse of old terracotta floor tiles for which Tuscany was famous.

Laura suddenly twirled to face him. 'One odd thing did happen. You must know the man everyone calls Gogol?'

'Who doesn't. What did he do?'

'Tuesday, the day after the man you say is Garrett was killed, Gogol walked into the front garden laughing loudly and clapping his hands. He had never come here before. He was making a lot of noise, and I had a hard time getting him to leave.' She put on a smile she didn't mean. 'I'll get the shirt for you and make those calls. While you wait, can I offer you a coffee?'

'Thank you. A coffee is always welcome.' Perillo followed Laura to the bar at the back of the hotel, a small room with wooden bookcases filled with books in various languages covering three sides of the room. Perillo had to weave his way between two small leather sofas and armchairs to reach the bar. Behind it, a man who looked to be on the wrong side of eighty was drying a glass.

Laura flung her arm towards the bartender. 'Meet Cesare, the man who holds this place together. Cesare, this is Maresciallo Perillo of the Greve Carabinieri. Cesare has been working here since the dinosaur age. We can't live without him.'

Cesare grinned, all his teeth still in place. 'I'm really the ghost of the original owner, who died in 1891. I was a bad one in my day and am paying my dues by humbly bartending until the end of time.'

'Cesare likes to tease, and the foreign guests eat it up. The maresciallo would like a coffee. Excuse me, I'll be right back with the shirt.'

Cesare shrugged and put the dry glass away. 'I guess I have to be serious with you. Anything stronger than coffee?'

'No, thank you. An espresso will be fine.'

'So I finally get to meet the man who keeps order in these parts. What has kept you away from this nice hotel and our bar?'

'You haven't needed me.'

'But now you're looking into the death of that man found in the woods.'

'Yes, I am.'

'The look on Laura's face told me. Her face was a burst of sunshine before you showed up. Now she's a storm cloud. And she's gone to get a shirt – perhaps the shirt one of our guests left in his room?'

'You would have made a good carabiniere.'

Cesare turned to the large shiny espresso machine, filled the holder with fresh coffee and fitted it into the machine. 'All it takes is knowing how to add. I learnt that in Year 4.' After less than a minute, Cesare placed the espresso on the wooden counter in front of Perillo.

'Addition with calculus thrown in, I think.' Perillo took a sip. Cesare went back to picking up glasses from the mini dishwasher behind the counter and drying them. 'How long have you worked here?'

'I've been behind this bar since I was eighteen.'

Two sips and the cup was empty.

'Did you ever serve a guest who called himself Mr Garrett?'

'He was a strange one. Liked an Aperol Spritz every night. I can make you one now, if you want. On the house. It's refreshing.'

'I don't go for orange drinks. Did he look familiar?'

'Never seen him before. Aperol Spritz is the latest craze from Venice. Prosecco, Aperol, soda water. Three, two, one is the formula. Signor Garrett would have just one and take it to his room.'

'Was that what made him strange?'

'What was strange was that he kept to himself for five days and on the sixth, Sunday night, open sesame, the cave opened and he couldn't stop talking. Like he knew he wasn't going to get another chance. He boasted a lot about his success in America. Repeated himself. It sounded to me like he was the one who needed convincing that he'd done all right with his life. His American had an accent. Italian, I thought.'

'You thought right.'

'I wanted to ask him, but I've learnt that asking isn't always welcome. Listening is the most important part of my job.'

'And what did you hear?'

'That for all his bragging about being rich, he was very nervous about something. Insecure. He said he had an important meeting in the morning that was going to make things better. I wanted to ask, what things? He had all the money he could want, according to him, a great big house overlooking the Pacific. He showed me a picture. Again, asking isn't part of my job.'

'He was dying of cancer,' Perillo said, divulging a fact that was going to be in the papers tomorrow.

'That might explain it, I guess. He did mention that the purpose of his trip here was to heal. Maybe he was meeting up with a doctor, maybe one who was going to sell him some crazy cure. When people are desperate, they'll believe anything.'

Was it his cancer that had brought Garrett home? Perillo wondered. The man had booked a flight back to California, which meant he hadn't planned to die here. Maybe the fact that he was dying had prompted him to come back. To do what, heal somehow? The cancer had been too far along to hope for a recovery. Perhaps to take care of something?

Cesare noticed the maresciallo was lost in thought. 'Maresciallo, yours is a tough job. You need a break from murder. A glass of 2013 Panzanello Riserva on the house?'

'Did Garrett mention anything about a gold bracelet he'd just bought?'

The bartender was about to answer when Laura walked into the room. 'I'm sorry I took so long,' she said. 'The housekeeper had locked the shirt up in the linen closets. I had to track her down for the key.'

'I know nothing about a gold bracelet,' Cesare said after a look at Laura.

'Neither do I,' Laura said, holding out the shirt, seemingly eager to get rid of what had belonged to a murdered man. 'The girls said no one called or asked for Signor Garrett.' Tucked in the pocket of the shirt was a piece of paper. 'I wrote down their numbers in case you want to ask them yourself.'

'Thank you. Not that I don't believe you.'

She nodded. 'Do have a glass of wine.' What she meant was, *Take this and leave.*

Perillo responded to Laura's words at face value. 'Thank you, I'll pass on the glass, but how much is the bottle? I'll take two.' It would save him a trip to the wine store. He couldn't show up at Nico's empty-handed.

'Consider them a welcoming present from us,' Laura said.

'Too kind, thank you, but I must decline.' Daniele would be proud of him. His wife less so. She wasn't happy about his pay.

'We're not trying to bribe you,' Laura said with an annoyed look on her face.

'I know, but it's policy,' a policy to which Perillo suspected too few colleagues paid attention.

Laura placed the shirt in his hands with determination. 'I understand.'

Perillo noticed the golf club embroidered in red on the

pocket of the blue shirt. This was the shirt Rosalba had mentioned, the one Garrett had worn to buy the bracelet. He was glad it was now accounted for, but it would tell him nothing more. 'Thank you for the coffee and the shirt. If you ever need help, let me know.'

'I hope you'll come back without us needing your help,' Laura said, playing the welcoming manager with clear insincerity. He didn't blame her – a carabiniere on-site in uniform wasn't the best for business.

'Come back for another espresso anytime,' Cesare said, tossing a wet dish towel over his shoulder. 'I hope I was of some help.'

'You were. Your last name, please? For the report.'

'Cesare Giovanni Rinaldi.'

'Thank you. Thank you both.'

Laura accompanied Perillo to the entrance of the hotel.

'If you think of anything that might help with the investigation, please call me.' He wished he had a business card to give her as he'd seen the TV detectives do, but he'd never had the need for one. 'I can give you the number if you have something for me to write it on.'

'I don't think anything else will come up, but if it does' – if it did, she wasn't sure she would tell him; she hated the thought of the hotel's name being connected to the gruesome murder – 'I can easily look up the number. Here's my card.'

Perillo took the card and they shook hands. Laura stood at the entrance and watched as Perillo stopped and took in the view, then walked down the gravel path to the carabinieri car he'd parked just outside the gate for all the guests to see. Tomorrow, even if they didn't read Italian newspapers, her guests would discover that a fellow guest had been murdered. How many visitors would she lose? She had nothing against Perillo. He was a nice man just doing his job, but she hoped to never see him again. He brought trouble with him. No, she was wrong. He *followed* trouble and she didn't like trouble. No one did.

'What did the maresciallo ask you?' Laura asked when she walked back into the bar.

Cesare sipped the Panzanello Riserva wine he had offered Perillo. 'It's what he told me that's interesting. Gerardi was dying of cancer. That explains why it took me a while to realise who he was. It's been decades, and he was all swollen, I guess with steroids.'

'Why didn't you tell the maresciallo you recognised him?'

'Sixty years a bartender, I know when to keep my mouth shut.'

CHAPTER NINE

Nico had just finished the pasta sauce when Perillo called to say they were leaving Greve.

'Good. I've left the downstairs door open.' The two carabinieri were his first dinner guests. Tilde never had a free evening. The one night of the week the restaurant was closed, she inevitably wanted to stay home. He'd put on clean khakis and a dark green polyester short-sleeved shirt. Both needed 'a touch of the iron', as Rita used to say, but sweeping a hot gadget back and forth without burning anything was a skill Nico had yet to master. At least cooking was easier. Nico dipped a coffee spoon into the sauce and tasted, a hungry OneWag watching closely.

'Sorry, you'll have to wait. Guests come first.' Nico added a pinch of salt and pepper, used the wooden spoon to mix it all up. It was a nice sauce, nothing to be ashamed of. Thinly sliced leeks, broccoletti and mushrooms browned in butter, then wetted with a little white wine. Once the wine had almost evaporated he'd added vegetable broth, salt and pepper and let it simmer until slightly thickened. The last touch was whisking in a few tablespoons of mascarpone. Tonight he was going to serve it with penne, although any pasta would do the sauce honour. If Daniele and Perillo liked the dish, Nico would suggest it to Tilde. While cooking, he'd even come up with a name: Pasta Nico's Way. He was getting arrogant in his old age. Well, at least he was trying to make a mark in the kitchen, if not at solving crimes.

He filled the large pot with water, put it on the gas flame and placed the sea salt next to the pot as a reminder. Rita had taught him he had to wait until the water boiled to add the salt, otherwise the water would take forever to boil. In his zeal to eat, often he'd toss in the pasta and forget the salt.

Nico filled a small bowl with Castelvetrano olives from Sicily and chunks of Parmigiano Reggiano. He poured himself a glass of Aldo's white wine and took the bowl and his glass out onto the terrace. Clouds had slipped in and darkened the sky. The air was cooling. Dinner would have to be inside. He had no tablecloth or place mats, just cheap plates and cutlery he'd bought at the big Co-op in Greve. As he went back inside and set the table he could hear Rita clucking her tongue. All the stuff in their Bronx home, he'd given to the Salvation Army. He didn't need to take any more weight with him.

* * *

Despite the cooling evening, the three men sat on Nico's balcony, listening to the crickets. Perillo had shown up wearing jeans, a blindingly white starched linen shirt, his leather jacket and his new suede ankle boots. Daniele had tried on two pairs of slacks and the three dress shirts his mother had given him before he left. After long minutes of uncertainty, he'd decided on black trousers and his favourite dress shirt, a striped blue one. Seeing him in the car park, Perillo had whistled his approval. The 'Dani bloom', as Perillo had dubbed it, followed.

Nico and Perillo smoked, wine glasses in hand. Nico stuck to his white, Daniele and the maresciallo with the first bottle of Villa Antinori Toscana. As the breeze shifted and smoke came his way, Daniele pushed his chair a little farther and tried to ignore the smell. The sky was dark early tonight, the moon having disappeared behind a thick screen of clouds. The swallows were safely asleep in the balcony rafters. The bottle of red was half-empty. The only thing left in the small bowl of olives and Parmigiano Reggiano was a thin sheen of oil.

The pasta timer rang, calling for the cigarettes to be put out, the glasses gathered and the three men and one dog moved inside.

Perillo poured a glass of red and handed it to Nico. 'Time to switch colour. You're in the land of the Super Chianti, Nico, not at some fancy New York cocktail party.'

'How do you know anything about New York cocktail parties?' Nico asked as he drained the penne.

'Television, where else?'

'I planned to switch for the pasta course.' He had always preferred red, but its high tannin levels upset Rita's stomach, and so white wine was all they drank on Saturday nights when he wasn't on a case. Now in the evenings, his first glass was always white, a tribute of sorts. Nico poured the penne back into the pot, added the hot sauce, mixed well, and let the pasta cook in the sauce for a couple of minutes. After placing a mug filled with freshly grated Parmigiano Reggiano on the table, he served his guests directly from the pot.

'Buon appetito.'

'Bravo,' Perillo said, after taking a couple of bites. 'This is tasty.' He managed to keep the surprise out of his voice. He lifted his glass in a toast. 'To Italian American cooking.'

Daniele lifted his glass. 'Very good, Signor Nico.'

'Cut the Signor. My name's Nico.'

Perillo winked at Daniele, who dropped his head to hide his cheeks. All three dug their forks into the penne. The smell wafting down from the table had OneWag's stomach turning somersaults, but in the past few days he had learnt optimism. Something was likely to come his way, and so he curled himself at Nico's feet. With optimism came patience.

The three men ate in silence for a few minutes, too hungry to interrupt their enjoyment of good food with talk of murder.

'His picture will be in the paper tomorrow,' Perillo said finally, his plate empty. 'I put in an appeal for people who knew him to come forward. So far, I've got nothing from the Gravignesi, but maybe people in the nearby towns know something.'

'Won't people be too scared to talk?' Daniele asked. His plate was empty too and he looked longingly at the pot that still had some pasta in it. 'They might be worried about becoming implicated in the murder.'

'Maybe, but some are going to want to show off what they know,' Perillo said. 'They'll start talking amongst each other, and someone will be happy to bring the information to us. I'm friendly with the locals, thanks to my Sunday cycling jaunts. People don't see me as a menace. I've shut my eyes to a few things, which always pays off. Information will eventually come to us – if not directly, indirectly.'

Nico tore off a piece of olive loaf and gathered up what was left of the sauce on his plate. 'Maybe we'll find out what enemies Gerardi left behind when he took off for the US.'

Daniele watched Nico's swiping with envy. His plate still had sauce waiting to be scooped up, but his mother had insisted it was impolite. 'Did you know that's called "making the little shoe"?'

'Thank you, no, I didn't.' Nico had known that, but why disappoint? He pushed the olive loaf towards Daniele. 'Help yourself, and there's plenty more pasta in the pot. There's only salad and fruit after that.' He waited until Daniele and Perillo had refilled their plates to ask, 'Did you get hold of the prosecutor?'

'He was off to a reunion of the Five Star Party, probably kissing ass. I spoke to Barbara, his secretary, a woman I admire and respect. She knows how to listen, often makes good suggestions. I asked her to advise the American embassy in Rome that we had a murdered Italian American on our hands.'

Nico clinked his wine glass against Perillo's. 'I hope you kept me out of it.'

Perillo wiped his lips with a paper towel. 'I thought it best.' Nico was now a friend. He didn't want to embarrass him by having the embassy look into his career. 'Barbara will hold off telling Della Langhe until the morning, since he told her he could be disturbed only if it was a national emergency, and in her opinion the Garrett/Gerardi murder is only an international blemish.'

'And so it is.' A grateful Nico poured more wine into their glasses. 'Let's drink to the three of us finding the murderer.'

Daniele raised his glass, happy to be part of the three, but worried about the consequences of not calling Della Langhe. 'Won't we get into trouble?'

Perillo drained his glass. 'Oh, tomorrow he'll call screaming. I might have to temporarily lose my phone.'

Nico picked up the empty pasta plates and, followed by OneWag, put them in the sink. What little was left in the pot he scraped into the dog's bowl, which earned him a grateful tail swish. 'I hope the American embassy won't start breathing down your neck.'

'I think the Americans have bigger problems than

one murdered dual citizen to deal with these days.' Perillo opened the second bottle of wine. 'By the way, we didn't find a computer or a mobile phone among Gerardi's possessions.'

'He must have had at least a phone. You need to find that.'

'I am certainly aware of that.'

'Sorry, you're right. Old habits.' His partner had always complained he liked to state the obvious. Nico dressed the salad of fennel, olives, rocket and slivers of aged Asiago cheese with lemon juice and Aldo's olive oil.

Perillo did his dismissive hand wave. 'I'm not going to waste my time – our time,' he corrected, 'guessing whether the phone was lost or stolen. We have to find it. The murderer must have communicated with him.'

'Even if we find the phone, it'll have a password,' Daniele pointed out.

Perillo shot him down with a look. 'Pessimism gets us nowhere.'

Daniele said nothing. Perillo obviously had no idea how long finding the password would take.

'I went to the hotel and got the missing shirt back,' Perillo said. 'The manager is too young to have known Gerardi, but Cesare Rinaldi, the hotel bartender, is a local in his eighties. He certainly could have. I asked him if he'd ever seen Gerardi before his stay at the hotel. He said no, but he could be lying. When I confirmed Garrett was Italian, Rinaldi didn't even ask his name, which I find odd.'

'Listening and not asking is part of a bartender's trade,' Nico said.

'Rinaldi did also make that point.'

'And he might not have wanted to get involved,' Nico washed his hands and tossed the salad with his fingers. It was the best way to ensure all the ingredients were mixed well.

'Could be,' Perillo admitted.

Nico washed his hands again and dried them. 'I looked up Gerardi and his wine company on the Internet.'

'I was planning to go online after dinner tonight,' Daniele said through teeth he realised were clenched. The Internet was his domain. 'I had too many things to take care of.' He stole an accusatory glance at his boss.

Perillo ignored him and poured more wine into each glass. 'What did you find out?'

'The company's website shows pictures of its buildings, its vineyards, the list of its wines, the usual stuff, but no history of the place, which is unusual. The other winery websites I took a quick glance at all had founding histories.' Nico brought clean plates and the salad bowl over to the table. 'Luckily, he was written up several times in the California newspapers. Serve yourself, please.' He sat down. 'Gerardi's story is one everyone likes, especially in the States. According to the articles I found, he arrived in Napa with very little money. After a few months working part-time with other immigrants at various vineyards, he was hired full-time by a small Italian American vintner, John Delizioso.'

'Delicious.' Perillo savoured the English word. Repeated it. 'An improbable name,' he added in Italian.

'A good name for a wine company. The two men became very close, and the vintner sponsored Gerardi's American citizenship. He was a good worker, and when Delizioso wanted to retire, he sold Gerardi the vineyard at a very good price. Gerardi expanded it, added different varieties of grapes and became rich. How rich, the Internet didn't tell me. I did come across a speech he gave to the Napa Chamber of Commerce about a year ago. He was going to expand his company by buying land near Gravigna. He'd found an ideal plot and claimed he made a bid on it. We need to look into that.'

'I'll look in the land register,' Daniele immediately offered, 'and see if any empty plots are for sale.'

Perillo served himself a few slices of fennel. Salad, even with cheese added, was for rabbits. 'Go ahead and look, but I haven't heard of any land available for wine-making. The only land up for sale is the fifteen-some hectares that include the wood where Gerardi was killed. Aldo had the soil tested, and it's not good wine-growing land.'

Daniele drew the salad bowl close. 'You could build a huge hotel on it.'

Perillo shook his head. 'Can't. It's marked for farming.'

Daniele refused to give up. He'd been invited to dinner to put forward his opinions, and he would keep doing so. 'I still think he could have been killed in that wood because he was trying to buy the land and someone else wanted it.'

Perillo heard the anger in Daniele's voice and softened his tone. 'No, Dani. The experts who tested the soil decreed that it's only good for hunting and picking mushrooms. No one is going to buy it to grow grapes.'

'Experts can be bought,' Daniele countered. He didn't enjoy the maresciallo's condescension and hated the fact that any so-called experts would lie for money.

'In his speech,' Nico said, changing the subject, 'Gerardi made a big deal about how he missed Italy and his home town, missed what he had given up by leaving. He was nostalgic, and yet he never came back until now. What kept him away?'

'There's not much holiday time when you're running a vineyard,' Perillo said. 'Just ask Aldo. You're right, though. We need to find out what made him leave Gravigna, and what brought him back.'

'Maybe the same thing that made him leave brought him back,' Nico said.

'Could be.' Perillo refilled Nico's glass. 'The bartender at the Bella Vista said Gerardi talked a great deal about needing to heal here.'

'That makes sense. He was riddled with cancer and wanted to live.' Daniele covered his glass with his hand. He wished the maresciallo hadn't opened the second bottle. Too much red wine would affect Nico's taste buds and maybe change the taste of the Venetian surprise he had in store. Plus, he needed to keep his own head clear and not make any dumb remarks.

'You're right,' Nico said, 'but he must have known his cancer was too far gone for it to heal.'

'Hope doesn't give up that easily, does it?' Daniele asked.

'No, it doesn't.' Rita had held on to hope. Nico had steeled himself for the inevitable and only pretended he still had hope. 'There are other ways of healing. Making peace with yourself is one. Asking forgiveness of someone you have hurt is another. Maybe that's why Gerardi came back. He must have relatives here.'

'If he does' – Daniele could feel his heart beat a little faster – 'the registrar's office will tell us.' The office was in Radda in Chianti. He would go there first, phone in whatever he found out, then stop by Rosalba's shop. His thumbs started flying over his phone. Seconds later, he looked up with disappointment etched on his face. 'They're closed tomorrow. I could try getting into their files.'

'Don't,' Perillo said. 'That's illegal, and I don't want to be responsible for leading you down the crooked path. Not everything gets resolved by using a computer. I'll make a few phone calls in the morning and find an employee to open up for you. I'm also counting on the article in *La Nazione* to bring people to the office.'

'Unless, as Daniele mentioned, they don't want to get involved with the police,' Nico said. 'I was always surprised at how many friends and relatives of the victim didn't come forward voluntarily. They had done things that had nothing to do with the murder – most times not very bad things – but if any of that guilt was involved, they stayed away or lied.'

'We also need to know if he had any family in the States. I couldn't find any mention of a wife or children in the articles I read,' Nico said. 'And if he wrote a will, we should find out what's in it. If he did, it's probably with a lawyer in Napa. The Napa police need to be told. His house and office have to be searched for links to anyone here. That goes for his computer too. Gerardi might have corresponded with his killer here. Someone needs to go to his house and office, get into his computer. That's something for Della Langhe to ask the American embassy. That and how much money he had.'

Perillo filled his wine glass again and took a long drink. 'Unfortunately, that will take time. You think this murder was motivated by money?'

'Money, hate, unrequited love, revenge. All motivators. It's good to rule them out one by one.'

Daniele cleaned out the salad bowl with the last of the bread. 'There's something that's bothering me.'

Perillo snorted. 'You're lucky it's only one thing. I'm bothered about everything in this case.' He drained his wine. 'Go ahead, Dani. What is it?'

'Why did Gerardi tell the Avis people he was going to Radda in Chianti, but then not stay there? It's like he knew he was going to buy the bracelet in that town.'

Nico took the empty salad bowl and the plates to the sink. 'Could be he remembered the jeweller from the old days. I wonder how long that store has been around.'

Daniele stood up. It was time to serve his Venetian surprise. 'It was founded by Rosalba's great-grandfather in 1952.'

'So, you've been looking up Rosalba on that lump of plastic you love so much,' Perillo teased.

Daniele would have blushed if his face weren't already red from the wine. 'I wanted to know how old she was.'

'And?'

'Two years older, unfortunately.'

Nico gave Daniele's sagging shoulders a pat. 'It's not a death sentence. Today, young people don't care as much about age. Charm, looks and sexiness are what counts.'

'And from the way Rosalba reacted to you,' Perillo added, 'I'd say she thinks you've got all three. Now that we have two dead on the table, what's the Venetian dish you've brought?'

'What do you mean, two dead?' Nico asked.

'That's what we call empty wine bottles. We also say there's a hole in the bottle. Come on, Dani, tell us what's next.'

Daniele took his bag to the small counter next to the sink. 'Not a dish. A digestivo. Un sgroppino.'

'That's a new one to me,' Nico said with an edge in his voice. Every Italian after-dinner drink he'd ever been offered – Fernet-Branca, grappa, limoncello, sambuca – had all tasted like cough medicine. But he didn't want to upset Daniele by not drinking. 'What's it made of?'

'You'll see.' Daniele unwrapped the three flutes he'd borrowed from the maresciallo's wife. He'd promised he would replace them if they broke, but she'd waved him away, too happy arranging the yellow roses the maresciallo had bought her.

Perillo hoped whatever it was had plenty of grappa in it. The day had been intense. He needed the jolt grappa

183

always gave him. Grappa or the whisky Nico had shared with him earlier.

Both men and the dog – the men anxiously, the dog calmly – watched as Daniele dropped six tablespoons of lemon sorbet into a bowl. He popped open a bottle of prosecco and poured two-thirds of a cup of the sparkling wine into the bowl. 'Some people add an equal amount of vodka, but my mother was always afraid I'd get drunk, so we make it this way.' With a whisk he used to foam up the milk for his morning cappuccino in the barracks, he blended the prosecco and sorbet together and filled the flutes. For that extra touch his mother insisted on, he wedged a slice of lemon onto the rim of each glass. 'Ecco fatto!' He handed out the drinks and sat down.

Nico raised his glass. 'Thank you.'

'To our health.' Perillo took a sip. Refreshing, but vodka would have made it a lot better.

'A real treat,' Nico said after drinking. OneWag lay down on the floor, dropping his snout heavily on Nico's foot. Dogs had a language all their own. 'Anything left in that bowl?'

Daniele had seen the dog's move. 'Enough for a lick or two.' He got up and placed the bowl on the floor. OneWag pattered over to the bowl.

The opening notes of 'O Sole Mio' broke the quiet. Perillo muttered, 'Shit.' Daniele stiffened in his seat. Perillo took his time digging out the phone from his pants pocket. He squinted to check the number. Double fuck. He needed glasses.

'Della Langhe?' Daniele whispered.

Perillo shook his head. 'Ehi, what's up? Is somebody making off with your beautiful wife?'

Excited words rumbled out of Perillo's phone. That the caller was a man was all Nico could make out.

'Who told you?' Perillo asked. He didn't think Laura or Cesare would be eager to spread the word about their murdered guest.

'Ah, Bruno.' Perillo pressed a cigarette between his lips. He'd have to be satisfied with the pretence of smoking while he listened to the anxious sputterings. 'The very same Bruno who stole our poor murdered man's car to take his girlfriend for a dawn joyride to the town of many towers and Vernaccia wine. The only good thing I can say about him is that he has good taste in locations.'

While Perillo sucked on his cigarette and listened, Nico took the flutes to the sink. There was no point to eavesdropping on someone else's phone conversation if you didn't know who was on the other end of the line. OneWag gave one last sweeping lick of his bowl and scampered to the sofa to sleep. Daniele, more concerned about the glasses he might have to replace, joined Nico at the sink and took over washing them. The American's big hands didn't look like they were used to handling delicate things.

'Yes, I agree with you, Aldo,' Perillo said, the jocular tone gone. 'Your nephew is a jerk. And yes, I'm sure it's all his mother's fault, and no, I'm not going to tell you who our victim is.'

'The news will be out in the morning,' Nico said. 'Tell him to come over now. We offer whisky and the man's identity.'

Perillo relayed the invitation to Aldo and clicked off. 'He'll probably fly over. You think he might be involved?'

'Too soon to know, but I bet he can tell us something about Roberto Gerardi. It's a small town. He's bound to have known him.'

CHAPTER TEN

While waiting for Aldo, Nico put out a bowl of fruit salad. He added a mug filled with sugar next to it on the table. As heavy footsteps made the stairs creak, OneWag jumped off the sofa, parked himself in front of the door and barked his head off.

Nico barked back. 'OneWag!'

The dog turned to look up at Nico, understood he meant business and with a huff went down on all fours, ready to jump at the intruder if the situation called for it.

Aldo burst into the room with his face flushed from the effort of the stairs. He was wearing his usual entertain-the-tourists uniform: jeans and the bright leaf-green and purple Ferriello T-shirt. He waved a bottle like a man who'd found a lost treasure. Aldo had told Nico he was in love with every single bottle of wine he produced, a love he was always eager to sell.

'I thought vin santo, the wine of hospitality and friendship, was just the thing to keep us safe from murder. It's new this year. Wait until you taste it. Made with half merlot grapes, half cabernet.'

'Stop selling it and uncork it.'

Aldo dropped his full weight onto the chair Nico had vacated and handed the bottle and corkscrew to Daniele. 'Sorry, they ate all my cantuccini.' He shifted position to face Perillo. 'So tell me. Who is it?'

'First, let's have a taste of this holy wine. We could all use some of that, right, Dani?'

Daniele turned his back to Perillo as he uncorked the bottle.

Aldo clasped his knees and tried to lean forward, but his belly got in the way. 'Come on, tell me.'

Perillo enjoyed keeping Aldo in suspense, his revenge for the measly discounts the vintner had given him last year when he'd treated his wife to a Super Chianti for her birthday. 'Tell us how you make it. Does a priest bless it?'

'Stop it, Salvatore.' Aldo, who loved to expound on his own wines and his olives, was in no mood for games now. 'Christ, tell me who it is.'

Was it simple curiosity, Nico asked himself, or was he afraid?

Daniele sat down in his chair and poured the wine into the three flutes he had just washed. He would abstain. Mixing red wine, prosecco and sweet wine would hammer nails into his head.

'No, I'm sure Nico and Daniele want to know about

188

the production of this special wine,' Salvatore replied. 'I hear it's expensive and takes a long time to make. We'll enjoy it more if we know the process. You tell me, then I'll tell you. It's only fair.'

Nico stayed by the sink, flute in hand, and wondered if keeping Aldo on tenterhooks had another purpose besides annoying him.

Perillo lifted his flute. The wine's amber colour turned gold in the light. 'Just pretend we're foreigners.'

Aldo resigned himself with a loud exhale. 'One: you need perfect grapes. No rot. Two: they're dried until they shrivel like raisins.' He spoke quickly. 'Three: they get pressed. Four: into oak barrels they go. Five: I wait from three to seven years, depending on how intense I'd like the wine. It is very costly and time-consuming.' Aldo pressed against the back of his chair, which creaked in protest. 'Your turn.'

Perillo complied. 'Roberto Gerardi.'

The flush on Aldo's face disappeared, and his expression went dead for a moment. He stared at Perillo. 'Are you sure?'

Perillo nodded while Daniele quietly spooned fruit salad into his dish.

After what seemed like a full minute, Aldo let out a laugh from the bottom of his stomach.

From the sofa, a disturbed OneWag sleepily lifted his head.

The blood rushed back to Aldo's face. 'That's a good one. So Roberto Gerardi got his comeuppance. Never thought I'd see that! He left years ago. No one around here has heard news of him since. Why the hell did he come back?'

'That's what we need to find out.' Perillo forked a pineapple piece and put it in his mouth. 'You knew him. What can you tell us?'

Daniele followed Perillo's cue and started eating, careful not to make a sound. He didn't want to miss anything. OneWag settled back to continue his slumber.

Aldo wiped his large hand over his face. When it came down, all trace of laughter was gone. 'I guess you'd find out anyway, so I might as well tell you. I don't want you to think I'm the one who killed him, though, because I'm not.'

Nico leant against the narrow kitchen counter. He liked watching, getting a first impression from a distance. It was something he'd picked up from Rita when she took him to see his first abstract art show at MoMA, back when he was still a patrol officer. The paintings were just a jumble of coloured splotches and lines to him. She told him to step back to see the whole and allow the painting to speak to him. He did step back, and just sometimes, he saw something that he maybe understood. Oddly, Rita's advice about viewing art stuck with him once he made detective. When he needed to interrogate a suspect, he would let his partner do it first as he stepped back to watch. Watch the body, the twitches, the shifting, the breathing. Hear the words last.

Perillo took a sip of vin santo. 'Why would we think you killed him?' He raised the flute. 'This is good, by the way.' Far too sweet for his taste, but Aldo only ever wanted praise.

'Gerardi worked for me for a couple of years.'

'When was that?' Perillo asked casually, wanting Aldo to

think they were just having a conversation between friends.

'I hired him to work at the winery twenty-four years ago. The first year Ferriello Wines made a profit. A small one, but still, not a year I'm likely to forget.' Aldo's stomach started shaking with breathy laughter. 'You know what's funny? I'm not making this up. Last time I saw Roberto, I told him I never wanted to see his face again. And now he's got his face blown off. Cinzia will get the shivers when I tell her.'

'What did Gerardi do for you?' Perillo was willing to wait to see what was so funny.

'It was Cinzia's idea to hire him. He was working at a hotel in Panzano. Roberto was good-looking, well spoken. He knew a little English and French, enough to show tourists how we make wine, walk them around the vineyard. He could charm them into buying more than they'd planned on. He was a real asset.' Aldo paused, his eyes on some distant point beyond the room.

Perillo waited, plucking another piece of fruit from the bowl, playing the disinterested listener.

Daniele had cleaned his plate and sat still, his stomach muscles clenched in anticipation.

Nico leant against the kitchen counter and sipped the sweet wine. The murdered man had been important to Aldo. So something had soured.

'But he stopped being an asset?'

Nico regretted the question as soon as he asked it. This was Perillo's case. He was just a bystander.

Aldo lifted his head slowly. Anger burnt in his eyes

now. 'Roberto was someone I trusted completely. I was still learning the wine and olive oil business. I needed help, and he gave it to me.'

Perillo could repeat Nico's question, but he preferred approaching this from another angle. As the Tuscans said, with patience, you won everything. 'Do you know anything about his life outside of work? Any relatives?'

'A lot of time has passed. His parents were dead. I think he had a married sister somewhere, but they weren't close. I don't know her name.'

'Did you two socialise outside of work? Ever meet any of his friends?'

'If he had friends, I didn't know them. The two of us went out for pizza occasionally when Cinzia was off somewhere. Sometimes we drank too much.'

'What did you talk about?'

'Just gripes about too much work, too much rain, not enough sun, lazy workers, women troubles. His, not mine. Look, I wish you'd stop interrogating me. I told you, I didn't kill him.' Aldo was quickly clenching and unclenching his hands now.

Perillo straightened his back, aware of the impatience flickering across his face. 'I'm not interrogating you, at least not while we are in Nico's home and sharing the wine you've brought. I'm asking questions because we're dealing with a very ugly murder, and I'm hoping you know something about Gerardi that could help us. *You* are the one who's said we might think you killed him.'

Nico opened the kitchen cabinet to get the bottle of whisky.

There was one glass left, and it looked like Aldo needed it.

Aldo stretched his fingers. 'One night, Roberto got very drunk and confessed he was very much in love with someone. Wanted to marry her. There was some kind of trouble with her though, something about her family being against it. He did have a reputation for womanising, which might be the reason he was having trouble with the family. He wouldn't tell me who she was.'

Nico filled a glass, walked slowly to the table and placed it in front of Aldo.

Perillo looked at the half-filled glass of whisky with great envy. 'Anything else you can think of that might help us get a sense of the kind of man he was?'

Aldo downed the whisky in one go. 'Well, the bastard stole from me.'

From me were the key words there, Nico noted. Aldo could have said *from the winery* or simply called him a thief, but it was the personal affront that mattered, not the action itself.

'I even loaned him some money, idiot that I am.'

'What did he steal?' Perillo asked, wondering if there had ever been rough patches in Aldo's relationship with Cinzia. She'd been the one to bring Gerardi in. Men couldn't stop looking at Cinzia. Even he'd had his own inappropriate thoughts there.

Aldo leant back in his chair and fixed his eyes on the now-empty whisky bottle. 'It was Arben who figured it out. He was the most ambitious of my Albanian employees, and at first I thought he was just smearing dirt on Roberto because

193

he was after his job. Well, he got it. It took a few years, and now he can run the place without me. Arben's a very good man.' Aldo looked up. 'I'm the godfather of his first child,' he said proudly. 'Our families get together a lot. You know, I hired quite a lot of Albanians and Kosovians after they fled their countries and came here. Sure, they were hungry, but I discovered they were good workers, and cheap.'

Perillo let Aldo ramble. He always talked too much.

'I'm ashamed to say, though, I haven't always trusted them. They get into fights with each other, don't they, Salvatore?'

'So do Tuscans.'

'Yes, yes, of course, but I was just trying to explain why I didn't listen to Arben. Roberto was Tuscan, and I trusted him. Arben was a foreigner, and therefore I didn't believe him. Arben understood that and was too proud to insist. That's how stupid I was. When I found out Arben had told me the truth, I punched Roberto in the face. He punched me right back. Arben and the others had to separate us. That's when I fired him and told him I never wanted to see his face again.'

'What did he steal?' Perillo asked again.

Aldo looked surprised. 'My wine, of course. What else could he steal? That's all I've got.'

What about a wife? asked Nico silently.

'He stole straight from the barrels. Siphoned off the wine just before we bottled it. A bottle or two at a time, not so much that we'd notice.'

Nico asked, sitting with the others at the table, 'How did Arben find out?'

'One night, we had a big group of Americans here. Arben was upstairs helping with the dinner because Cinzia wasn't feeling well. She's in charge of feeding the guests. We always serve a dinner or lunch with the tour, and once it was over, it was part of Roberto's job to escort the group across the courtyard to the dining room in the other building and eat with them. The guests came, but Roberto showed up late. I was too busy talking about the wines they were drinking to notice anything. After everyone had left, Roberto included, Arben went down to the basement and checked the barrels. He noticed wine on the floor under several of the taps. He'd made sure the floor was spotless before the guests came. Arben went back upstairs to the bottling and labelling room and noticed a few empty bottles were missing. He'd noticed missing empties before and told me about it, but a missing empty or two went with the territory, I told him. That night, after everyone left, he told me he thought Roberto was siphoning off wine. I accused him of being jealous. It's a miracle Arben didn't walk off the job that very night. I know I hurt his pride, and maybe he decided to stay to prove me wrong. After that night, whenever we had an evening tour, Arben would offer to help Cinzia. She couldn't have been happier. What we didn't know is that he'd set up a camera in the barrel rooms that he turned on just before the guests went down there. Early the next morning, he'd go back to turn it off. He gathered three months' worth of stealing before he showed me the videos. I had, thank God, the good grace not to ask him why he waited so long.'

'Thank you, Aldo. For the moment, I don't believe you shot Gerardi's face off, but tomorrow, who knows?'

Aldo flung his arms in the air. 'Good God. You're joking, right?'

Perillo clinked his empty flute against Aldo's empty whisky glass. 'Don't I always?'

Aldo let out a grunt that might have been a laugh. 'You do, and I put up with it.' He stood up. 'Thank you for the hospitality. By now, Cinzia must be jumping out of her skin to know who it is.'

'I'll have to talk to Cinzia too,' Perillo said. 'She might know more about his love life.'

Aldo scowled. 'What are you implying?'

'Sometimes men confide in women.'

'He didn't get anywhere near her.'

'I'm not saying he did, but she's the one who pointed him out to you. She might know something you don't.'

Aldo seemed mollified. 'All right, I'll tell her.'

Perillo stood up and the four of them shook hands.

After the door closed and Aldo's footsteps disappeared, Perillo asked Nico, 'What do you think?'

'After twenty-two years, he might still carry a grudge against Gerardi, but not one major enough to kill him.'

'Unless he didn't tell us the whole story,' Daniele added. This job was making him cynical.

Perillo picked up his leather jacket. 'We'll find out. But for now, I think it's time to bid our host goodnight. Pack up the flutes, Dani, and we'll go. Goodnight, Rocco.'

OneWag lifted his head, wagged once and went back

to sleep. Nico was surprised the dog reacted to the name. 'You'll turn him into a schizophrenic.'

'Italian dog, Italian name. Anything else is against nature.' At the door, Perillo remembered and turned around. 'Your friend Gogol made a first-time appearance at the local hotel yesterday, laughing loudly and clapping. Laura, the manager, had a difficult time convincing him to leave. Maybe you can find out why?'

'I can try.'

Once the maresciallo and his bridgadiere were gone, Nico washed the pots, dishes and tableware, dumped the empty wine bottles in the recycling basket and sponged the table and the sink clean. He dried his hands and walked over to the sofa. 'Bedtime, OneWag.'

The dog uncurled himself and waited.

'No dice.' Nico walked to his bedroom. 'You've got four legs. Use them.'

OneWag turned over and began scratching his ear, which didn't itch. Next, he busied himself with gnawing his front paws, which were perfectly clean. After what the dog considered a suitable amount of time, he jumped off the sofa and, tail held high, slowly made his way to the bedroom.

The next morning, Thursday, the sky was a thick grey cap leaking heavy rain. With OneWag still nestled between the sheets, Nico took his espresso out on the balcony. A flutter of wings brushed his face as the swallows left their sleeping quarters to swoop through the curtain of rain, not caring if they got soaked. The vegetable garden would be grateful – Nico had forgotten to water it last night – but he knew Aldo and the other local vintners wouldn't be happy to see the rain dilute the sweetness and strength of their grapes. Enough water had fallen during the summer to satisfy the humidity required by the vines. With the grape harvesting only five or six weeks away, heat was needed to produce a good year.

Aldo. Had he told Perillo everything he knew about Gerardi? Perillo seemed confident that they would find out more, but unpleasant actions and events often managed to stay buried.

Nico brushed his teeth, washed his face and, after peering at himself in the cracked mirror, decided to forgo shaving. After last night's drinking, what he really needed was a long, brain-clearing run. He'd gone out in far worse weather, but this morning he had work to do. Perillo was going to be dealing with Della Langhe and whoever showed up in his office to tell him what they knew about Gerardi. Daniele had to reach into the annals of his computer to dig out what he could about Gerardi and the land Aldo had wanted to buy. Nico had assigned himself the job of eavesdropping and questioning Gogol. Roberto Gerardi's photo was in the paper this morning, and the sooner he got to Bar All'Angolo, the better.

OneWag lifted his head from the bedsheets and watched as Nico dressed quickly in jeans and a long-sleeved polo shirt. 'Come on, you lazy mutt. We're off.' The dog jumped from the bed and scampered over to the adjoining room. He sat at attention in front of his empty food bowl.

'It's whole wheat cornetti this morning.' Nico slipped on his parka and opened the door. A blur of orange and white streaked by him.

The Ferriello wine shop/dining room was a large, handsome beamed room that gave out to a sprawling covered terrace facing a well-tended lawn and, beyond that, an olive grove. Perillo's shoes squished – he had managed to step into a puddle as he'd got out of his car – across the smooth, polished floor, leaving a trail of wet footprints. He had come alone in civilian clothes, although this was an official call that technically required a uniform and another carabiniere to act as a witness. Throughout the years, he had learnt to bend the rules. He also wanted Aldo's wife to feel his was a friendly visit.

On the terrace, a couple was seated at a table well away from the dripping awning edges. Above them was the drumming sound of rain. Perillo watched as Cinzia poured them two generous glasses of a Ferriello red. What had brought these two foreigners here for a wine tasting at nine o'clock in the morning, and in this weather, was beyond his comprehension.

Cinzia walked towards him with a teasing smile on her face. 'Ciao, Salvatore.' She was a petite, slender brunette originally from Rome, with sparkling eyes and a pretty face. She stepped inside the room and Perillo followed.

'Here for a wine tasting?' She waved the open bottle. 'They're having a Chianti '15 vintage.'

'Too early for me.'

'An espresso, then?'

'Gladly.' He sat on a barstool in front of the counter at the far end of the room. Cinzia went behind the counter and into a small kitchen partially hidden by a wall of shelves filled with photo albums of the wine dinners they'd hosted for scores of tourists throughout the years. Perillo peered. The older ones showed a thin, eager-looking Aldo, a long-haired Cinzia by his side.

'Aldo hired Gerardi twenty-four years ago, at your suggestion. Is that right?' Perillo asked, remembering what Aldo had said the previous night.

'Wrong.' Cinzia lowered the flame on the stove and placed a small moka over it. 'I hired Robi.'

Perillo noted the more intimate name, Aldo having called him Roberto.

She came back to stand behind the counter, the sparkle in her eye gone. 'I can't stomach Robi's death. And the way he was killed. Shooting his face off like that, wiping out his identity. That's pure hate.'

'Maybe. It could also have been to serve the killer, gain him time while we blundered about trying to find out who the victim was.'

'I'm sure you didn't blunder.'

'We don't usually, but this time . . .' Perillo shook his head. 'How did you meet him?'

'I was having lunch with a friend from Rome at Hotel Bella Vista in Panzano, where she was staying. Robi was our waiter. The only one in the place, and most of the tables were taken. He handled the crush beautifully. And the women were lapping him up. That was important. My friend was so smitten, she ate every meal at the hotel during her week's stay.'

'You must have been smitten too, if you hired him.'

The moka stopped gurgling. Cinzia slipped back into the kitchen. 'Sugar?'

'No, thanks. I've had my limit today.'

She poured two cups and set them on the counter. 'I enjoy looking at a handsome man. No sin in that. I convinced Aldo to hire him because men like to be the wine buyers, but women have veto power. We were also both exhausted. I'd come up with the idea of hosting lunches and dinners for tourists. We started offering simple Tuscan specialties – a platter of salami, crostini, then panzanella or ribollita. But the main attraction still had to be our wines.' She drank down her coffee and wiped her mouth with a napkin. Perillo did the same. 'The idea really took off. There were only four of us at the vineyard. We needed extra help just for the events. Buses were bringing people in droves from Siena and Florence.'

'Did you know anything about his love life?'

'Robi liked to brag a lot about his conquests, but I didn't believe him. I think he was just a lost soul who needed to feel important. He loved the attention the tourists gave him, which worked well for us.'

'Did he talk about anyone in particular that you can remember? Parents, friends, a girlfriend?'

'When I hired him, he told me both his parents were dead, and that he had a sister he wasn't close to. A few weeks before we found out he'd been siphoning off our wine, he said he was getting engaged and showed me a pair of earrings he had bought in Florence – two coiled silver snakes with tiny green eyes. I guess they were pretty, but snakes give me the shivers. I asked who she was. He wouldn't tell me because her parents didn't know yet. I wondered if he was making the whole thing up. For all I know, those earrings could have been his sister's.'

'You weren't curious?' His wife wouldn't have let the matter go until she'd found out who the girl was. He often thought she'd have made a very good carabiniere. He'd once been tempted to enlist her help but stopped himself in time.

'I didn't ask questions. My only interest was that he show up on time and do his job well, which he did until he got it into his head to start stealing from us. If I come up with anything that might help, I'll call you. Now I have to get back to those two Belgians and try to unload a case of Ferriello Chianti '15 vintage.'

Perillo got off his barstool. His shoes had stopped squishing. The damp was all in his socks now. 'Thanks, Cinzia. I appreciate it. And thanks for the coffee.'

The cafe was noisy and crowded, with no seats available. The doors were shut to keep out the slanting rain. The smell of coffee, hot butter and damp clothing filled the room. Nico opened his rain jacket and, after lowering a dry OneWag to the floor, raised a hand in salute to Sandro and Jimmy. They were too busy behind the counter to look up. Breakfast was going to have to wait.

OneWag went off on a hunt of his own, sniffing between legs to find choice titbits of flaky cornetti, fallen sugar from the ciambelle. Paper napkins with drops of spilt jams or custard he licked carefully. Paper was not part of his diet.

Nico leant against the wall and scanned the bar for signs of Gogol, just in case the news had brought him out before his usual time. It hadn't. The place notably was filled with locals this morning. It was either too early for the tourists or they had shown up and left, finding Bar All'Angolo already packed with locals. Nico knew only a few of them by name. Luciana the florist was standing next to the counter with her Enrico, master of the olive loaves. Sergio the butcher, who looked at least forty, was telling the couple he was too young to have known Gerardi. Enrico gently reminded him that twenty-two years ago, Sergio was twenty years old.

Sergio was quick to rebound with a smile. 'I thought he had left town thirty-two years ago!'

Beppe, the son of the newspaper vendor, was in a corner nearby, telling a small pack of students that he had known right from the start the dead man was a Gravignese.

'Why were you so sure?' asked a pretty girl with tiger-striped leggings that matched her backpack. 'Are you psychic?'

The attention made Beppe stand taller. 'I guess I am.'

'Is the killer here now?'

Beppe shifted his weight back and forth as he glanced around, unsure of what to say. 'I can't tell. It's too crowded.' He smiled at the girl, hoping she accepted the excuse. 'Maybe he is.'

'Maybe he's up your ass!' The girl and her companions laughed loudly.

Beppe's eyes went wide with surprise and hurt. The girl started to say something else, surely something equally mean, but a distant honking of the bus sent the students running en masse out of the cafe. Beppe retreated into a corner and started playing with his phone.

Not a fighter, Nico thought. An assessment, not a criticism. He'd only learnt to fight back bullies thanks to his fist-happy father, the only good lesson he'd ever got from the man.

Some locals he didn't recognise huddled together over the tables, pointing to the two copies of *La Nazione* that the cafe provided. Others clasped tiny espresso cups, their free hands either placing food in their mouths or dancing in the air to emphasise a point. The voices were subdued rather than excited. No one seemed terribly sad or shocked by the brutal murder of one of their own.

'I knew his father,' said one of the old men who, in good weather, always sat on the piazza benches. Somewhere in his eighties, he had a long, thin face with an equally long prominent nose and a surprisingly full head of fluffy white hair. Now, he sat at the centre table holding the newspaper close to his chest. Nico changed position against the wall to hear the group better.

Ettore, a fellow pensioner sitting next to him, reached for the paper. 'Gustavo, let me see, let me see.'

Gustavo held on. 'He ran the gas station outside of Radda. A good man. Can't say as much for the son.'

'You shouldn't speak ill of the dead,' objected Nelli as she walked in, arms filled with posters for the

204

children's art show next week. 'Hi, Nico.'

Nico nodded in greeting. He didn't want to call attention to himself, aware he was still considered an outsider.

'You're wrong, Nelli,' Gustavo said. 'Once they're dead, that's the only time you can speak the truth. They can't get back at you.'

'Where's the rest of the gang?' Nelli asked. Gustavo and Ettore were always with two fellow pensioners.

'It's raining,' Ettore offered.

'They're afraid of shrinking,' Gustavo said. 'Ehi!' Ettore had grabbed the paper away.

'I paid for that, so don't mess it up.' Gustavo looked up at Nico. 'I like a neat paper.'

'So do I,' Nico answered. So much for remaining unnoticed.

Ettore stared at the two photos: Gerardi twenty-two years ago and Gerardi now. 'Poor Robi. He didn't age so well.'

'Can't you read?' Gustavo pressed his finger at the article below the photos. 'Cancer all over. Six months to live. Why kill him, I say.'

'Maybe he didn't tell his killer he was sick. I barely recognise him in the second photo.'

Nelli dropped her pile of posters on the table, accidentally tearing a page of the paper. Gustavo let out a yelp.

'Don't worry. I'll buy you another one.' She called out to Beppe, who was still in the corner entrance by his phone. 'Do me a favour and get another copy of *La Nazione*. Tell your mother it's for Gustavo. She'll understand. And don't get it wet. I'll pay later.'

Beppe rushed out, happy to have a task.

Gustavo looked placated. 'My wife used to iron the paper when it got wrinkled.'

'Your wife should have been locked up in a madhouse.'

'*His* house was the madhouse,' Ettore said. 'Robi was a looker. Thought he was a rooster in a henhouse. I say a jealous husband killed him.'

'Twenty-two years later, with him looking like that?' Nelli turned to Nico, who was still leaning against the wall like the proverbial fly. 'That couple behind the column are getting up. Grab their chairs. I need to sit, and I bet so do you.'

Nico had been too busy eavesdropping to notice. As he walked over to the chairs at the other side of the room, he wondered if Nelli wanted him out of earshot for a moment, then quickly dismissed the thought. He hurried, though.

As they sat, Ettore peered at Nelli above his glasses. He was also somewhere in his eighties, with a shiny bald scalp, jowled cheeks and kind eyes. 'Now, I recall that when you were a pretty girl of eighteen or so, handsome Robi conquered a corner of your heart, and maybe something more.'

'You recall incorrectly. All of my heart was taken when I was sixteen by the man who became my husband – now ex-husband, thank the heavens. I will admit to not minding looking at Robi when the occasion presented itself, which wasn't often. He was always off somewhere with his fiancée.'

Gustavo grunted. 'What fiancée?'

'I never met her.'

Gustavo looked around the room. 'Did this fiancée have a name? Did anyone ever see her?'

'I didn't,' Nelli said.

No one else answered.

'If no one saw her, she didn't exist.' A mischievous grin added more wrinkles to Gustavo's cheeks. 'It's an old ploy to make women want you more. Used it myself in my younger days.'

Ettore laughed, showing off all his gold crowns. 'No woman wanted you.'

Curious about the mysterious fiancée, Nico interrupted from his seat behind the pillar. 'I heard Gerardi was madly in love.'

At that moment, Beppe darted in and dropped a plastic bag on Gustavo's lap. Just as quickly, he darted back out.

Nelli stood up and gathered her posters. 'Maybe he was, maybe he wasn't. Robi was a slippery man.'

'Who, then?' Ettore asked, perking up at the possibility of learning a gossipy titbit he could take back to his wife. 'Who was Robi in love with?'

Gustavo took out the pristine newspaper from the bag and spread it out on the emptied table. 'Himself.' He turned to the sports section. 'Who else?'

Nelli hugged her posters against her chest. 'You're turning into a nasty old man, Gustavo.'

Gustavo shooed her away with his hand. 'Always was.'

'How about a cappuccino, just the two of us?' Nico suggested to Nelli.

'Excellent idea,' Nelli said. 'As far away from this meanie as we can get.' She kissed Gustavo on top of his head, then pecked Ettore on the cheek. 'How you put up with him is beyond me.'

Ettore shrugged as though it was beyond him too.

Nelli walked to the table where Nico was sitting, dropped her posters on a nearby table and sat down. The rain had let up, and the place was now almost empty. The people who had gathered early at the cafe were now taking their talk of the murdered to homes, offices, shops, workstations and all the vineyards of the golden valley.

Nico went to the counter and ordered two cappuccinos from Sandro. 'Did you know this Robi?' he asked casually as Sandro handed out his change.

Sandro shook his head. 'I'm thirty-two.'

'But recently? Did he ever come in here?'

'Not that I noticed. Jimmy, did you see him in here?'

'Who knows? I don't look at faces when I hand out coffee.'

'Stop talking to Nico,' Nelli called out to Jimmy, 'and I'll take a ciambella with my cappuccino, please. Nico, you might as well order your cornetti. Gogol won't show up today.'

'Coming up,' Jimmy called. 'But since when is Gogol afraid of a little rain?'

'He isn't. He's gone mushroom hunting.'

Nico brought the cappuccinos and the ciambella to the table. Two whole wheat cornetti were in the oven.

'Do mushrooms pop out that fast when it rains?' Nico asked as he sat down.

'Depends.' Nelli leant over the table. 'I made that up.' Her voice was low. 'I think Gogol will probably be hiding in his room for a few days.'

Nico lowered his voice too. 'Why?'

'I imagine he's scared, now that he knows who the dead man is. He attacked Robi once. By the tower behind the church. It must have been a Sunday, because I was walking to church. Robi was a few feet in front of me, and yes, I was taking a good look at his nice ass and having impure thoughts I wasn't about to confess in church. Just as Robi reached the tower, Gogol pounced on him, swinging a thick tree branch. I screamed. Of course. Robi easily stopped him. He wrenched the branch out of Gogol's hand and threw him on the ground with a single punch to his chest. I asked Robi if he was going to call the carabinieri, begged him not to. He walked away without answering. He must not have said anything, because nothing came of it.'

'Were there other witnesses?'

'Not that I noticed. I was on my knees, trying to help Gogol stand up. The poor man was crying, hiding his face in his hands, shaking his head. He was very upset.' She would discover the reason days later.

It was hard for Nico to think of Gogol as violent. He did live in a world all his own, but Nico had always instinctively sensed that violence did not enter into it. And yet, it had. The smell of warm cornetti hit his nose. He waited until Jimmy had placed them in front of him and walked off to ask, 'Did Gogol offer any explanation?' He remembered what the manager of the hotel had told

209

Perillo. Gogol, for the first time, appearing in front of the hotel where Gerardi had stayed, laughing loudly.

'I asked him why he was angry with Robi,' Nelli said. 'He wouldn't answer. After I got him on his feet, I asked him again. All he said was "a river of blood". I suppose that's what he was hoping for, a river of Robi's blood.' There was no reason for anyone else to know, she thought.

'"A river of blood". Gogol quoted that to me yesterday. A line from *The Divine Comedy*, I think. Did you ask Gerardi about the attack?'

'I never saw him again. A few weeks later, I found out he'd left town shortly after the incident.'

'I'll talk to Gogol. Try to reassure him. I know he's not the killer.' Nico's heart told him that, though his head had room for doubt.

'Of course not. He's petrified of guns. Gustavo told me the kids used to shoot at him with BB guns when he was young. Gustavo was probably one of them.'

'You don't think Gerardi was in love with anyone?'

Nelli leant back and bit into her ciambella. She took a sip of her cappuccino, then looked at Nico with an indecipherable expression. 'If he was, it wasn't me, although back then, I wished it with all my heart.'

CHAPTER ELEVEN

Perillo held the phone away from his ear as Della Langhe went on one of his tirades. After a few minutes of being told he was incompetent, that he was unnecessarily complicating Della Langhe's life, that if the case wasn't solved quickly his career would be in jeopardy, Perillo tried to interject with, 'It's not my fault Gerardi became an American citizen.'

The substitute prosecutor seemed to grasp this, because his tone changed. 'My secretary has already contacted the American embassy. As soon as they inform us of the name of his lawyer and whether he had any family there, she will inform you.'

'We also need to know if he corresponded with anyone in Italy.'

'Whatever information the Americans give us, I trust you will then act quickly.'

'I assure you that I don't waste time. As we say back home, the rooster crows in the morning.'

Della Langhe sniffed over the phone. 'I wouldn't know about roosters, and Southerners do not have a reputation for haste. Keep me informed.' The line went dead.

Perillo slammed down the phone and made for the door of his office. 'I need a cigarette.' Daniele followed.

Outside, the rain was coming down in thick sheets. Perillo stood under the eaves and took drag after drag. Why was he saddled with a pompous ass like Della Langhe for this case? Why not a reasonable substitute prosecutor? Maybe there weren't any reasonable ones. He'd heard Della Langhe had got his job because he was in deep with the conservative party, who was now in control. But in Italy, no party stayed in control for long. Elections were coming up in March. There was hope. This time, he'd vote against Della Langhe's party. In the past, he had left the ballot blank in protest. Politicians were all liars.

Daniele stayed on the other side of the entrance. Rain splattered on his shoes. 'Do you think it will let up soon?' He was hoping the maresciallo would calm down and find a registrar's office employee so he could ride his motorbike up to Radda, get the name and address of Gerardi's sister and finally tell Rosalba she wouldn't have to deal with the Florentine sketch artist. By now, she must know they'd discovered the identity of the man who'd purchased the bracelet. He didn't have to go, but he wanted to see her, and he was more comfortable armed with an excuse. He had dreamt about her early that morning. The two of them were holding hands, their faces close. He'd leant in to kiss her just as his alarm went off.

Perillo finished his cigarette in silence and tossed the butt into a wide puddle at the bottom of the stairs.

Daniele winced. He would pick that up later and throw it in the bin.

Perillo ignored the wince and asked, 'Did you look into the records for those kids?'

'I did. Bruno Dini and Katia Galli. No arrests. Same for the bartender at Hotel Bella Vista. I also checked to see whether there was any land for sale in the area. I came up with nothing.'

Perillo nodded and lit another cigarette. Daniele hovered. 'What is it?'

Daniele hugged the wall, trying to protect his shoes. He had spit-shined them late last night in anticipation of his trip to Radda. 'The registrar's office is closed.'

Della Langhe's words were burning a hole in his stomach. 'Yes, you told me. I'll get on the phone and see if I can find someone to open up for you.'

Daniele nodded. Waiting was good. The rain might stop.

'I just need a few minutes, Dani.'

'Yes, Maresciallo.' Daniele retreated backward through the open door.

'Yes, Salvatore!' Perillo yelled after him and took out his phone.

Nico was putting a wet OneWag into the 500 when his phone rang.

'No need to come at lunch,' Tilde said. 'With this rain, very few people are going to show up.' Sotto Il Fico had only five indoor tables.

He dropped into the driver's seat. 'I'll come by anyway. You've seen the paper?'

'Heard it thanks to Elvira, who read the article out loud over breakfast like I was illiterate.'

'Did you look at the photograph?'

'No need.'

'Then you knew Gerardi?' He heard Tilde's intake of breath.

'In Gravigna, everyone thinks they know everyone. That doesn't mean they do.' Her voice had turned steely.

'And you?'

'I saw him around.'

'I'd like to find out whatever you, Enzo and Elvira know about him.'

'I thought you weren't getting involved.'

Nico didn't remind Tilde that she had been the first to suggest it. 'Perillo asked for my help. I reluctantly agreed.' During last night's dinner, as Perillo, Daniele and Nico talked about the murder, his reluctance had melted away. He was working on something important again. Something that needed resolution. Being part of a team, puzzling things out together was what he most missed about his years as a homicide detective. 'Anything you can tell me will help.'

'You should be looking at his life in America.'

'He was killed here.' The phone beeped again.

214

'That doesn't mean a local killed him,' she insisted. 'The wine festival in Greve brings Americans in by the dozens. The opening is tonight. Go look for your killer there.'

That was Tilde's local pride talking. 'I'm sure Perillo and the substitute prosecutor in Florence will look into the American angle. So will the American police. Can I come talk to you about him?'

'I don't have that much to tell. I'll feed you lunch if you want. We'll talk afterwards.'

'When Elvira has gone off to take her nap.' He'd said it to make Tilde laugh but was met with silence.

Nico's phone rang as soon as he clicked off.

'I'm afraid we'll have to wait a few days to know about Gerardi's American life. And no one is around to open up the registrar's office,' Perillo announced. 'According to a grandmother I got hold of, the whole group went off in this rain to the castle of Meleto to celebrate a birthday. They'll be back in the late afternoon. I'll get someone to open up the office then. Della Langhe can't blame this delay on me. The employees are all Tuscan.'

'What did he say?'

'He yelled for a bit, then insulted me by saying Southerners are not known for their haste. Is that something you believe?'

'I've heard that said about all Italians.' Nico wasn't about to say that the reputation was worse from Rome on southward.

'Yes, yes, I know. You Americans want to fly through your lives, then end up with a heart attack. "Who goes slowly goes far and stays healthy", is the saying here. Not so today for Daniele. He was like a racehorse at the starting gate, pawing at the ground and waiting for that whistle.'

Nico laughed. 'That's called love.'

Perillo remembered how love had made him crazy for a while. Four women he had loved; only one endured. The craziness of it had now been replaced by comfortable habit, warmth and a hint of boredom. 'With that beauty, good luck to Dani.'

'Did anyone answer your appeal for information?'

'A lot of people came in, worried about their safety. I assured them that they had nothing to worry about. It wasn't a random murder, and we're not dealing with a serial killer.'

'What about a murderer who's lost his mind?'

'I wasn't about to point out that possibility. I don't believe it, anyway.'

'Don't rule it out. In my experience, you have to keep every possibility on the table.'

Perillo nodded. 'A few men came in to offer information, which amounted to nothing. They didn't know him well, didn't like him, saying Gerardi thought himself the only rooster in the henhouse. They didn't know anything about a girlfriend or even his sister's name. Arben, the Albanian who works for Aldo, confirmed Aldo's story about Gerardi stealing from him. He just flew back yesterday from two weeks in Tirana. He offered to come in and show me the boarding passes. I told him not to bother. I did get one phone call that sounded interesting. A woman, says she knew Gerardi very well. She wouldn't give her name, but she's coming in after she's done shopping. Anything on your end?'

'I was about to call you. Nelli, the art centre director here, told me that Gogol attacked Gerardi with a tree branch here in the piazza right before Gerardi left town. She asked him why. Gogol's only response was, "A river of blood". That could be one of his usual Dante quotes, but it could be that he wanted actual blood. I'm on my way to the home to see if he'll talk to me. I'm also going to ask Tilde and her family if they know anything about Gerardi that might be useful.' Twenty-two years ago, Tilde was in her early twenties. If Gerardi was as handsome as Nelli said, Tilde would have at least noticed him, and Elvira would have known what gossip there was about him.

'See if you can find out who he was in love with. If he walked out on her, whoever it is could still be carrying a grudge.'

'Nelli didn't know. Neither did Ettore and Gustavo. Do you know them?'

'Sure I do. Half of the Bench Boys. I gave them that name because I can't keep their names straight. Thanks, Nico. I appreciate your help. Ciao for now.'

'Ciao.' At the sound of the phone's click, OneWag jumped onto Nico's lap and pawed at the window.

'You're not going anywhere.'

OneWag dropped his head between his paws and whimpered his protest.

'Don't try that on me. Be reasonable. You'd get soaked.'

OneWag looked up at Nico's determined face. After a few seconds, the dog dropped his head back down and closed his eyes. At least he had the comfort of knowing this man would never abandon his car.

Nico got out of the car, shut the door and unfurled his umbrella. There was no place to park near the 'house of rest', as Italians called an old-age home. As Nico walked the five hundred metres to the home, he hoped his own old age would be filled with much more than rest.

The woman at the front desk raised an eye in Nico's direction and went back to crocheting her yellow wool and reading the newspaper. He noticed it was open to the page with Gerardi's two passport photos. 'Gogol's gone. Who knows when he'll be back.' She kept her head down, showing a scalp covered by thin, short, curly white hair. He could see through to the pink skin beneath. Nico didn't know her name, though Gogol had once referred to her as Cerberus, the three-headed dog guarding hell.

'How did you know I was going to ask for him?'

'You're Gogol's friend.'

Nico held out his hand and introduced himself.

She reluctantly set down her crocheting, shook his hand quickly and went back to her work. 'Lucia,' she muttered, keeping her last name to herself.

'Do you know where he went?'

'Mushroom picking. What else can you do in this weather?' She raised her eyes for a moment with a look that questioned his mental capacity.

He knew that many of the guests at the home had mental disabilities. 'One could stay dry at home.'

'Gogol was too happy for that. Took one look at Robi's photos and laughed his head off.'

'He was happy Gerardi was dead?'

'Seems so to me. It didn't surprise me.' She looked at the strip of yellow wool and started counting loops. 'Whatever happened between those two must have been nasty. Gogol has always been a good man. No trouble at all, if you don't mind his Dante gibberish.'

'Are you referring to the time Gogol went after Robi with a big tree branch?'

'Robi was able to stop him and no one got hurt, God be praised.' She crossed herself and brought the gold crucifix that rested on her chest to her lips.

'You have no idea why?'

She was back to swinging the crochet hook in and out with a twist of her wrist. 'No one does. Robi said they'd never even spoken to each other. Gogol must have just been seized by some anger from his childhood. He's never been a hundred per cent, and the kids used to bully him mercilessly.'

'Could Gogol have killed Robi?' Nico asked just to see her reaction.

'May God forgive me for saying this,' she said, kissing the crucifix again, 'but humans are basically cruel. Cain killed his brother. From then on, we have been killing each other. God isn't even trying to stop it. The world turned away from God from the moment Eve stuck her teeth in that apple. We do not merit the life He gave us.'

'Did Robi merit death?'

'I would say he was not a God-fearing man, but I'm sorry

Robi had to die in that terrible way. To think that he would have died naturally six months later in his own bed. Only God knows why this happened to him. As for Gogol, God's light shines on him. He cherishes all life. Gogol promised to make me a potato and mushroom omelette if he found enough porcini. He'll be back by dinnertime.'

'Gogol cooks?'

'When something makes him happy, he stirs it up in the kitchen. There's nothing wrong in his head when he's cooking.'

'You wouldn't know where Gogol went mushroom picking, would you?'

'The woods behind the Ferriello Vineyard is his favourite spot, but he could be anywhere. I'll tell him you stopped by.'

The woods behind the Ferriello Vineyard had been where Gerardi was killed. He needed to find Gogol. 'Thank you, Signora Lucia.'

'Signorina, and proud of it. As a young girl, I suffered men's ways and promised myself to keep them at a distance. My life couldn't have been more pleasant.' Her head stayed bent over her work. 'I won't forget.'

Nico walked away, wondering if 'I won't forget' meant telling Gogol he had been by or her suffering of men's ways.

Daniele parked the bike, took off his helmet, removed his plastic poncho and spied himself in the door of the ceramic shop next to Gioielleria Crisani. Wanting Rosalba to forget he was a carabiniere, he had dressed in newly laundered jeans and a striped red and purple birthday present from his mother. As he looked at his reflection, his hopes of making a good impression on Rosalba sank to nothing. His boots, the bottom of his jeans and the lower half of his face were dark with mud. He unlocked his motorcycle seat and took out a towel. He wiped down his face, put the towel and the helmet under the seat, locked the bike and filled his lungs with air, then pressed the buzzer.

The door opened. Daniele looked up to see an older replica of Rosalba standing behind the counter. The same round face, large dark eyes, full lips, long black hair coiled back in a loose bun reflected in the mirror behind her.

Irene Crisani eyed the boy with his cheap shirt and his muddy boots dirtying the floor. At the most, he could afford a small silver trinket for his girlfriend or his mother. 'Can I help you?'

Not an exact copy of Rosalba, Daniele decided. Her warmth was missing.

'Good morning.' He tried to imitate the maresciallo's officious tone. 'I need to speak with Rosalba Crisani.'

Irene looked at Daniele with renewed interest. What need did this boy have to see her daughter? Was he another one of Rosalba's strays? She often wondered where Rosalba had got her overfriendly genes. Certainly not from the Crisani side of the family. Maybe from her charmer of a father.

'She's not coming in today.' A lie. Rosalba was taking over after the lunch break. 'I'm her mother.' She didn't bother to give her name. 'You can tell me.'

He took out his carabinieri identity card. 'Brigadiere Daniele Donato. Maresciallo Perillo and I are looking into the murder of Roberto Gerardi.' The shine in her eyes disappeared, Daniele noticed. Or perhaps it had never been there. It was just that the rest of her had so instantly recalled Rosalba. He explained his previous visit to the store.

'Yes, you asked about a bracelet my daughter sold to a man. She told you all she knew. What is it that you want from my daughter now?'

Irene's condescending tone didn't sting Daniele. He disliked her for it but was grateful. Disliking someone always made him feel as though he had the upper hand. It stopped him from blushing. 'I wanted to show her the picture of Gerardi, to see if he was the man who bought the bracelet.'

'She saw the photo in the paper and told me she was almost certain he was the same man.'

'Almost certain?'

'The man wore a baseball cap pulled low. I will ask her to call the maresciallo if you don't believe me.'

'I believe you, and please thank her for her cooperation.'

Irene nodded. She had no intention of mentioning this brigadiere.

'Rosalba is too young, but perhaps you knew Roberto Gerardi?'

Irene fiddled with the gold bands on her wrist. 'I doubt my age is reason enough to assume I knew him.'

The bracelets kept clinking. For a moment, Daniele felt bad about her discomfort. 'I'm sorry, Signora Crisani. I'm not very good at explaining myself. Your age has nothing to do with it. It's the fact that Gerardi knew this shop. If not you, maybe your husband or your father knew him?' Daniele was aware he was going out on a limb. Gerardi could have just as easily found the shop by chance, but he had told Avis he was coming to Radda. Why say that and end up in Panzano? Maybe because he knew he would buy his bracelet here, the only jewellery shop that had existed here twenty-two years ago. Daniele had double-checked that last night.

Irene placed both her hands flat on the glass counter. Below the glass, the display of glittering jewellery seemed to smile back at her. Looking at the necklaces, bracelets and rings always calmed her down. They were her riches, her strength. The shop had thrived under her ownership. She didn't miss her father, a cruel man who had stunted her life. Her husband, whom she'd met only after her father's death, had loved her, and in return she'd given him what little love she had left. 'I'm afraid I can't answer for them. My father and husband are both dead, and whether they knew that man or not is buried with them.'

'Thank you, Signora. Please do tell Rosalba I stopped by.' Daniele suspected she wouldn't, but for some reason his questions had made Rosalba's mother sad. For that he was sorry, even if he disliked her. Sorry, but curious.

Outside, the rain had stopped.

Sitting at his desk, Perillo glanced at his watch as his stomach growled. One o'clock on the dot. Lunchtime. His mobile phone rang. Punctual as ever, Signora Perillo informed him she'd just thrown the pasta into boiling water and he should come up. Today, she was offering spaghetti loaded with roasted yellow peppers and Parmigiano

Reggiano, a dish he cherished. Since he'd given her those flowers, she'd been as sweet as those yellow peppers she was about to serve. The main course was breaded chicken breast and fennel and olive salad. As always, an espresso would be his only dessert.

As Perillo hung up, his mouth already watering, the office phone rang. He let out a long sigh and for a second or two thought of letting the call go unanswered. No, spaghetti took nine minutes to cook al dente. Whatever it was, he'd make it brief.

'Yes?'

'There's a woman to see you,' said Vince from the front desk. 'She's got information on the dead man. She said she called earlier. Should I tell her to come back?' Vince knew how Perillo felt about his lunch break.

'No, send her in.' Perillo understood that people who had information, or thought they did, wanted to be treated with importance. Making him wait until she had finished shopping was a clear indication that the woman felt very important. If he didn't see her now, she might not offer any information. 'Please call upstairs and tell my wife to keep the plate warm for me. That I'll come up as soon as I can.'

The woman walked in through the door Vince had opened for her, burdened by two large shopping bags from the Co-op. 'Here I am at last.'

A pleasant-looking woman in her late forties, Perillo guessed, dressed in a beige ruffled blouse and matching skirt that showed off a good figure. She looked familiar, but he couldn't place her.

She lifted her heavy shopping bags as though she was ready to do some bodybuilding. 'I should have brought these home first, but I knew you were anxious to know more about Robi.'

Then you could have done your shopping afterwards, Perillo thought as he stood up and said, 'Very kind of you.' He extended his hand. 'Maresciallo Salvatore Perillo. And you are?' Still holding on to the bags, she shook the tips of his fingers. 'Roberto Gerardi's sister.'

His hunger pangs disappeared. 'Very good. Please, have a seat.' He waited for her to settle her bags onto the floor and sit before sitting down himself.

Her light brown eyes didn't blink. 'There's nothing good about it.'

'I'm sorry. That was insensitive of me.'

She waved his words away. 'Oh, you can be as insensitive as you like. Robi was not a very nice man to me – or my husband, for that matter. We already know each other, by the way, although it's clear you don't remember me. Too old to leave an impression, I guess.' It wasn't a lament. She sounded very matter-of-fact about it. 'When I was young, it was different.' She smiled, reminiscing. The smile made her more attractive.

'I'm sorry. I'm so focused on your brother's murder, everything else has ended up locked away in some cubicle in my head. Please tell me about him.'

'I take care of the Boldini villa, just down the road from here. They spend most of the year in Milan. We had a theft there two years ago. You came over with another carabiniere. You never did find the thief. Whoever it was stole my mobile phone and laptop. Do you remember now?'

'Yes, of course. You're Maria Dorsetti.' He also remembered being suspicious when he'd discovered that the Boldinis' expensive objects and silverware had been untouched, only Maria's things having been taken. Nothing else in the villa had been disturbed. No locks broken, no windows smashed. No other thefts in the neighbourhood. She'd kept calling him for news, wanting him to come and check the villa again. After a few weeks, he'd filed the case away, judging her a lonely woman needing attention. 'I'm sorry we didn't find the thief.'

She shrugged. 'I'm the one who should be sorry. I was wasting my time.' Maria Dorsetti sat back in her chair and crossed her arms below her chest. It would muss up her blouse, but the weight of her arms gave her comfort. 'I didn't know Robi was here. I have no idea why he came back, unless he wanted to settle an old score, but he could have at least come over. He knew where I lived.

'I didn't hear from him at all, not even when my husband died four years ago. When I let him know, he sent a five-thousand-dollar cheque and not a word of condolence. I guess he thought money spoke for itself. Five thousand dollars certainly wasn't going to replace my husband, but it did help.' Her words flowed like water from an open tap. A lonely woman who had found her audience. 'After that cheque, nothing. I did write from time to time, giving him titbits of gossip. What was going on in Gravigna. Who got married, who had children, who did what.' The truth was, he'd been the one who kept writing, asking all sorts of questions about one woman in particular. 'Gravigna's our home town. I was too proud to ask outright for money. I hear he was wearing a very expensive watch when he died. Does that mean he was rich?' She gave her cheek a gentle slap. 'How greedy of me. I apologise, but I am, after all, his only living relative.'

Ah, so that was it, Perillo thought. This was all for show.

'Oh, but maybe not. He could have a family in America. Do you know if he did? It would be nice. Maybe I could fly over and meet them.' She stopped again and this time patted her chest. 'I'm sorry, I'm nervous. I wish I could have loved him.' She pulled down on her blouse to smooth out the wrinkles that had formed. 'When I was a young girl, I envied his good looks. He had such beautiful green eyes. Mine are the colour of mud.' She gave a flirtatious, girlish laugh, perhaps hoping Perillo would contradict her.

'The American embassy in Rome is looking into his life in America,' Perillo said. 'As soon as I have information, I'll let you know. You mentioned he might have come back to settle old scores. Did he have enemies here?'

'I imagine a lot of husbands were mighty relieved when he took off.'

'Any specific husband?'

She straightened her back as if offended by the question. 'I don't know anything about the women who threw themselves at him.' He claimed not to have bedded any of them, but he had always liked to boast about his affairs around town. It had been a way to keep his great love secret, she'd decided. 'Who I love is no one's business,' he'd replied when she'd pressed him for the name. Calling his sister 'no one' was insulting, she'd told him. He didn't budge.

'Do you know of anyone who might have wanted your brother dead?'

'I just told you, I don't. I'm so angry at him for not giving a damn about me.' She started to cry and reached for a tissue in her purse. 'I'm sorry. He died in such a horrible way, could've lived a full life.'

'He was very sick. Cancer. It was in the newspaper article. The medical examiner thinks he only had about six months to live.'

'Oh. I didn't read to the end. It was too upsetting.' Maria wiped her eyes and looked at Perillo, her eyes softening. The news seemed to give her some relief. 'Maybe that's why he didn't get in touch. Didn't want me to see him so sick. Poor Robi.' She moved to the edge of her chair to be closer to Perillo. 'That explains his coming back here, then, doesn't it? He was making amends and saying goodbye. If he hadn't been killed, he would have come to me. I know he would have.'

'Making amends to whom?'

Why had she used that word? Foolish. 'I don't know.' To the nameless woman. Something had gone wrong between them. It had been what drove him to leave. 'I'm not a good man,' Robi told her a few days before he left. 'I don't deserve any love. Not even yours.' There was good reason not to reveal her name to the maresciallo, a name she had discovered only by the questions Robi asked in his letters.

Perillo's mobile phone started to belt 'O Sole Mio'. He glanced at it. His wife, probably furious. He cut off the ringer. 'You are his only relative?'

'Yes. It was just the two of us.'

'Do you have children?'

'I am not blessed.' The expression on her face was noncommittal.

'Your brother worked for Aldo Ferri for a while.'

'He loved that job. Robi told me he liked Aldo so much, he left his wife alone. That's my Robi, his bird always ready to fly into a new nest. At least towards Aldo, he showed some respect.'

'Wasn't he in love with someone then?'

'Well, isn't that what you tell a girl when you want to get her between the sheets?'

'Do you have any idea who the girl was?'

'He never told me about his personal affairs. We weren't close, you know. My husband disliked my brother, and I didn't much like him myself. He was arrogant. Why would he stick with one woman when he could have any girl he wanted?' She looked straight at Perillo. He wouldn't guess she was lying. Liars turned their eyes away, she learnt from the police shows.

'You can't think of anyone who had a vendetta against him?'

'Not from here. He left twenty-two years ago. Who holds on to hate that long? Besides, all he did was fool around. We're not in Sicily. We don't have honour killings in Tuscany. Maybe someone from America.'

'Maybe. I do have to ask you this.'

Maria eagerly leant towards the desk.

'Can you tell me where you were Monday morning between five and seven in the morning?'

Of course, Maria thought. Just like on TV. She smiled at Perillo to show she understood he was only doing his job. 'I was in bed, of course. I sleep at the Boldinis' villa when they're away. No witnesses, though, alas.' A smirk this time.

'Do you own a shotgun?'

'My father did. He went hunting every Sunday. That he would kill on the Lord's day infuriated my mother. She always refused to cook his kill.'

'Do you still have it?'

'No. He loved that shotgun so much, we buried it with him. A year later, Mamma was dead too. Then my husband. Now my brother.'

She looked crestfallen, but Perillo wasn't sure if that was genuine. 'When you're not at the villa, where do you live?'

'The new development in Gravigna, via Moro Twelve. I've rented it to an English couple for the month.' She reached over the desk and took the maresciallo's pen and a Post-it and wrote down her address and mobile phone number.

Perillo took the Post-it and stood up. 'Thank you. If you think of anything else that might help, please call. I'll get one of my men to drive you home.'

She laughed. 'How kind of you.' She leant over the desk and gave him an awkward hug. 'You'll let me know what the embassy says? And if there is a will. I know I sound crass, but if I inherit even a little money, it will be like winning the lottery.'

'I understand. I'll let you know as soon as I know. I have to ask you to make an official statement and sign it.' He picked up her shopping bags and walked her to the door. 'Vince in the front room will take it down.' He would have preferred to have Daniele take the statement – Vince always insisted on writing in long hand to show off his meticulous handwriting. There was a chance Vince would still be writing when he came back down from lunch.

'I do have to ask you not to take any trips until your brother's death has been cleared up.'

Her expression brightened. 'Am I a suspect?'

'I may have more questions.' Certainly she was a possible suspect. The only one he had so far. 'Vince!'

Vince showed his round, curly-haired head in the doorway, his mouth working on a focaccia sandwich. 'Please take Signora Dorsetti's statement, then get Dino to take her home.'

Maria blew Perillo a kiss he did not acknowledge.

Upstairs, in his one-bedroom flat, part of the barracks, the kitchen clock showed it was 1.52 p.m. He called to his wife. She didn't answer. Neither did the cat. The bedroom door was closed. The table was now set for one. He found his meal in the warm oven. As he slipped his hand into an oven mitt, he made a mental note to get her a box of chocolates.

CHAPTER TWELVE

Nico parked the 500 on the bald patch of earth that had once been for farming equipment behind his new home. He held the door open and OneWag, who'd been fast asleep, took his time to stretch and examine what might need cleaning or scratching.

'Come on, mutt. You've got a job.'

OneWag's ears perked up. He understood that something was required of him, which was much better than being locked away upstairs. The dog jumped out of the car and looked up at Nico. Expectation made him wag his tail – once.

'We have to find Gogol.' Nico started walking towards the path edging the olive grove, the path he had taken on Monday morning looking for a hurt dog.

OneWag followed, nose in the air, taking in the smells. Olives ripening, their green tartness softening, the dark richness of wet earth. Pine sap. From far away wood burning. Nearby, his master's sweat and his own damp fur. Nothing that didn't belong in their surroundings.

They reached the woods. Birds stopped singing and the light became a lacy pattern of sun and shadow. Gogol was somewhere in here, Nico was convinced, but not because it was his favourite spot. Twenty-two years ago, Gogol had attacked Gerardi with a tree branch. The other day, he had shown up at Gerardi's hotel for the first time, laughing his heart out. He was happy the man was dead. And now, Gogol could be laughing where Gerardi had been killed. Maybe where he'd killed him?

OneWag scrambled to keep up with Nico's fast-scissoring legs, his own panting tongue bobbing to the rhythm of his shorter steps.

As Nico got closer to the site, he was purposefully loud as he walked, crushing twigs. He didn't want his presence to be a complete surprise.

A thick oak loomed in front of Nico and the dog, its branches twisted with old age. Stepping to one side, Nico walked past it. OneWag instead stopped and stood still, swivelling his snout from left to right like a periscope. The dog turned his small body to the right. He whimpered a warning to Nico and took off.

Nico heard only the sudden rush of crackling twigs. OneWag had picked up Gogol's scent! He ran after him.

A hundred yards farther, underneath another old oak, Nico found OneWag with his head deep in a wicker basket. 'What are you doing?'

OneWag retrieved his head from the powerful-smelling mushrooms, lay down and stretched his hind legs behind him, looking very pleased with himself. He had found food. Far more important than a smelly old man.

Gogol had to be nearby. 'Gogol, it's Nico. Where are you?'

'"Turn your eyes to the valley,"' Gogol quoted.

There was no valley to turn to, but Nico followed the voice.

Ten feet deeper into the woods, Nico found Gogol rocking on his knees in front of the clearing where Gerardi had been killed. A forgotten strand of police tape hung limply from a branch. Raindrops dripped from the tree leaves onto his face.

Nico knelt next to him. 'Come with me. This is no place for you.'

Gogol pushed him away. 'His is the place of justified violence.' He laughed, a raucous sound like rock rubbed against rock that seemed to come from the bottom of his soul. 'Roberto Gerardi boils in hell.' He stopped rocking and turned to Nico. 'I burn too. I saw it and did nothing.'

'You saw the murder?'

'The murder of a heart. Her body twisting, turning, his body a weight to carry for a lifetime. I heard the moans, mournful sounds escaping through fingers set on silence.'

Nico assumed Gogol was quoting Dante again until he heard him say, 'I drown in shame, friend. You understand?' Tears mixed with raindrops.

'You witnessed a rape?'

'Carnal violence. And did nothing.' His body shook with sobs now.

Nico held him. 'You were scared.'

'He died for the grave sin he visited on another. I breathe, I eat, I shit, but I too have died. When I quote the great poet, I quote from hell.'

OneWag nudged his head against Gogol's thigh. The old man picked up the dog and held him under his coat.

'Who was raped?' Nico asked.

'You will not know from my mouth. At least I can keep silent.'

More questions would come only after Gogol calmed down. Part of Nico hoped Gogol had only imagined this terrible thing. 'Let me take you home.'

Gogol lifted one of OneWag's long, furry ears and dried his eyes with it. In response, OneWag licked his face. 'My mushrooms.' He scrambled to his feet with Nico's help, holding the dog tight. 'I must gather my mushrooms. Thank you, friend. I go now. Hell's gatekeeper is waiting for me to make dinner.'

'I'll take you home.'

Gogol gave one last look at the clearing where Nico had found Gerardi. 'He left in shame. He came back to die for it.' He handed the dog to Nico and they set off for his old-age home.

Perillo was at the cafe next to the station, having his mid-afternoon espresso, when Nico called and related what Gogol had said.

'That's all I could get out of him.' Gogol hadn't spoken a word during the ride back. On seeing Lucia at the front desk, he'd proudly shown off his basket of precious mushrooms and hurried off to the kitchen.

Perillo paid for his espresso and walked out, not to be overheard. His stomach tightened into a fist. 'Do you believe him? I mean, his circuits are a little jammed up, aren't they?'

'Gogol's not crazy. I want to believe him. He was overwhelmed with pain and shame. He must have witnessed a rape, and that could be the killer's motive.'

Perillo tried to release his muscles by letting out a long, silent breath. 'Maybe he just saw heavy-handed sex. People get off on being rough sometimes.'

Nico walked out onto his balcony, needing to rest his eyes on the soaked colours of nature. 'We have to at least consider that a rape may have occurred and look into it.'

'How?' Perillo stood rooted in place, his stomach still tight. 'Even if the victim went to a doctor, her files will be private.'

'Asking around. Jimmy at the cafe says you can't fart without the whole town knowing about it.'

'And yet no one knows who Gerardi's love was. Besides, there's no shame involved in farting. Embarrassment at most, which is not the case with rape. And how the hell would you ask someone if they've been raped?' Perillo searched his jeans pocket for his cigarettes. 'Mother of God and all the saints!' He'd left them on his desk. 'When did this supposedly happen?' He started walking to the station. 'Did he at least tell you that?'

'Gogol said, "He left in shame." I take that to mean it happened not long before Gerardi took off. It might even be the incident that prompted him to leave. It could also explain why Gogol attacked the man with that tree branch.'

'That's one supposition after another grounded on very threadbare fact.' Perillo spoke sharply and instantly regretted it. He needed to calm down, and a dose of nicotine was exactly what he needed. 'Let me get to the office.'

Nico waited on the phone, surprised by Perillo's resistance to the news. The possibility that a woman had once been raped by Gerardi was tragic and a very strong motive for murder, even after all this time. He'd expected the maresciallo to want to look into it immediately.

Perillo walked into the station, nodded as he hurried past Vince, who quickly stood and shoved his mortadella sandwich into a drawer – there was no eating allowed on front-desk duty. In his office, he put the phone back to his ear. 'I have a possible suspect.'

'That's good news.'

'Remember when I told you that a woman had called with news?' He wiped his face with his handkerchief. 'Well, she took her time showing up, but it turns out she's Gerardi's sister – younger, by the looks of her. She didn't seem in the least bit upset that he was dead. She was upfront about them not getting along, angry that he hadn't been helping her financially.' The maresciallo grabbed his cigarettes and walked back out. The mortadella sandwich was back in Vince's mouth. Perillo ignored him and parked himself under the eave of the entrance to smoke. 'She's hungry for his money, that's clear. Immediately asked about his will. A strong-willed woman is the impression I got. And not a very nice one. I know that doesn't make her a killer, but she has an obvious motive. She has no one to corroborate that she was sleeping in the villa she works at early on Monday morning. I'll call her back for more questioning once we hear from the police in California. We can't move forward until they answer our questions. Did Gerardi have a family there? Did he have a will? Who benefits from it? Was he in contact with anyone here? We have to wait, that's all.'

'I hope you're not going to ignore what Gogol said.'

'I won't. We'll talk about it some more face-to-face, and I hope to come up with some delicate way of asking around that won't get me kicked out of town. Not tonight, though. We've got the Chianti Expo opening in a few hours, and I have to show up with my men armed and in uniform to reassure the crowd that we'll protect them.' He looked up at the now-clear sky. Good. No hint of more rain. 'Come hear the band play. They're pretty good.'

'I do miss the old days when people didn't show up wielding AK-47s,' Nico said, 'but I'm sure you and your men will do a wonderful job.'

'Thank you. I'll be in touch as soon as Della Langhe has news for us.' Perillo headed back to the cafe for a shot of grappa. The cigarette hadn't helped. Gogol's revelation had brought back the violence of his childhood – he could feel it in the pit of his stomach. He didn't even taste the grappa.

Nico showed up at Sotto Il Fico near the end of the lunch hour. He was hungry and hoping to catch Enzo and Elvira so he could ask them about Gerardi. Enzo was at his usual post behind the bar, making two espressos. Elvira commanded the small room from her rickety gilded armchair in one of her seven housedresses, this one dark grey with pale flowers, matching the grey light of the day. Her hair, freshly dyed, sat like a matte black cap on her head. She didn't look up from her weekly crossword magazine. Of the five tables in the room, only one was taken, by a German couple, judging by Elvira's shoe classification. Sandals with socks, soaked through.

'Sit, Nico, sit,' said Enzo as he brought the espressos over to the couple.

Nico leant his umbrella in a corner by the door and wiped his shoes on the doormat. 'Let me say hello to Tilde. She was expecting me later.'

'I hear you,' Tilde called out from the kitchen. 'You couldn't wait, could you?' She sounded angry.

'Sorry. Hunger got the best of me.'

'Is the dog with you?'

'Left him at home. I was afraid it was going to rain again.'

Tilde popped her head out of the door that led to the kitchen. She had wrapped her hair in a blue bandana, and her face was sprinkled with flour. 'Too bad. I had some good titbits for him.'

'I'll take them home. You're making pasta?'

'Olive oil cake,' Tilde snapped, and withdrew her head.

'She's nervous today,' Enzo said apologetically. 'Stella's taking her museum exam on Monday afternoon in Florence.'

'Wonderful,' Nico said. 'Does she need a ride? I'll happily drive her there.'

'I wish you could. Gianni's taking her on his motorbike. He's suddenly discovered being nice to her pays off.' Enzo leant over the bar and lowered his voice. 'He says he has you to thank. Don't tell Tilde.'

Nico laughed. 'I won't.'

'Stop muttering, you two, and you, Nico, shouldn't settle for dog food,' Elvira said. 'Tell her to give you the chicken rags.' Her voice was loud enough for Tilde to hear. 'It's an old recipe of mine.'

'It was your mother's, not yours,' came from the kitchen.

'My mother was *mine*, therefore the recipe is mine. My cranky daughter-in-law has finally deigned to offer it to our patrons.'

Nico sat down. He knew the chicken would appear without his asking for it. One did not deny Elvira without good reason. Enzo poured him a glass of the house red, an unlabelled Sangiovese that came straight from a barrel. 'Now we know who it is. Poor Robi. I knew him. He used to eat here a lot. Mamma had a soft spot for him. Gave him extra portions. Tilde wasn't in the kitchen then.'

Elvira looked up at her son. 'But she was here every day. I was convinced she came here looking for Robi.'

Enzo lifted his arms in exasperation. 'Mamma! Stop it. We were engaged already.'

'Well, women often change their minds. In my heart, you are the handsomest son a mother could have, but Robi, well, "la donna è mobile", as Signor Verdi puts it.' She closed her eyes as if to summon the past. 'An Adonis with charm, Robi could inflame any heart, even mine, which as you know is diamond-hard.' She lifted her chin with unabashed pride.

Nico laughed. 'Elvira, yours is all an act.'

'It isn't in the least.' This time all of Tilde appeared at the door, her face now clean of flour. Underneath a long, white chef's apron, she wore a burgundy dress with ruffled sleeves. 'Tell the truth, Elvira. You were hoping I'd fall in love with that horrible man so I wouldn't marry your son.'

Elvira went back to her crossword magazine.

'Chicken rags coming in a minute.' Tilde disappeared again.

Nico waited while the Germans settled the bill with Enzo. Once they'd left, he asked Enzo to sit with him. Enzo obliged.

'Was Gerardi horrible?' Nico asked.

'No, the opposite in my view. He boasted about his conquests, which is what turned Tilde off, but it was just talk. He was in love with someone.'

'Did he tell you that?'

'No, not in words. I'd known him since we were kids. He was older, and I used to look up to him. He was nice to the younger kids. He gave us football lessons, refereed

241

our games. He brought us cookies his sister made. He was always kind of serious, but once in a while, all he would do was smile. I thought he was getting high. I got up the courage to ask him if he was doing marijuana or something. He laughed. "No, a much stronger drug. The strongest drug there is." I assumed he was talking about love.'

'Or heroin,' Tilde chimed in from the kitchen.

Elvira looked up from her crossword. 'Robi was clean. A good man.'

Nico asked Enzo, 'When was this? How long before he left?'

'At least two years. I hadn't fallen in love yet, and I wanted to ask him questions, but he never spoke about it again after that once. Said I'd find out soon enough. And I did, when I met Tilde.'

'Love was no drug for you,' Elvira remarked. 'You burn a low flame.'

'Which lasts much longer than a bonfire.' Tilde placed the chicken rags plate in front of Nico and kissed her husband's head. 'I love that low flame and always will. It kept me sane. Still does.'

Nico thought of Rita. She had kept him sane too, but her love had been strong. He took a bite of the chicken. 'It's very good.'

Elvira puffed up her chest. 'Of course it is.'

'Why the name "chicken rags"?'

'The chicken breast is sliced very thin and sautéed with radicchio, cut into strips. A little olive oil, salt and pepper, a dose of balsamic vinegar, push it around the hot skillet and serve. It ends up looking like rags. There's a beef dish with rocket that's done the same way, but without the vinegar. Simple, easy to eat and good for you.'

'Thank you. It's delicious. I'll try making this at home, and if I ever write a cookbook, I'll call it "Elvira's chicken rags".'

'No, "Elvira's mother's chicken rags". Give credit where it's due.'

'What was your mother's name?'

'Giuseppina Gioia Maria Consolazione. But stick to "Elvira's mother".'

Nico drank the wine and finished the rags. While Enzo made him a coffee, Nico turned to Elvira. 'What was Robi like, besides being clean and good.'

'Why?'

'Curiosity.'

Elvira crossed her arms over her chest. 'Don't lie to me, Nico. The whole town knows you're helping that idiot Perillo. He needs all the help he can get, and if you want my opinion, find the woman Robi loved and you might have your killer.'

'Why do you think that?'

'Enzo is right. Robi was very much in love. He told me so himself, but when I asked who she was, I got the silence of a tomb. Why not tell me?'

'Maybe she was married.'

'Or engaged.'

Tilde strode out of the kitchen. 'Are you implying' –

she stopped at Elvira's feet, towering over her – 'what I think you're implying?' Her voice was knife-sharp.

Elvira stiffened and looked up at her daughter-in-law. 'Well, we don't know who this great love was, do we? And Robi did come here a lot.'

'He came here for good inexpensive food and to chat with his childhood friend, your *son*.' Tilde dropped down on her haunches. 'Elvira, why do you hate me so much?' Her voice was soft now.

Elvira riffled through the pages of her magazine.

Tilde put her hands on Elvira's lap. 'I have a heart as hard as yours. The only person you're hurting by hating me is your son.'

Elvira looked up with wet eyes. 'I miss my husband. He won't be coming back. I miss my son even more.'

Enzo walked over to his mother and squeezed her shoulder. 'Mamma, we spend most of every day together.'

'You go home with her.'

Tilde stood up and retreated to the kitchen. Nico followed her. 'I'm sorry you had to witness that,' she said, slipping the olive oil cake into the oven.

'I wanted to give the three of you some privacy, but I didn't want to leave without saying goodbye.' He'd hated every moment of the exchange. It brought back the memory of the conflicts between his own parents, which had always ended the same way.

Tilde wiped the counter clean of flour. 'Italian mothers and sons can never be separated. She still insists on doing his laundry and ironing his shirts, which is fine with me. Less housework.' With the counter cleaned, she untied her apron. 'I've set the oven alarm for the cake. Let's go outside. It's cooler and out of earshot.'

'Enzo won't mind?'

'He doesn't need me. We have this confrontation three or four times a year. She makes some especially nasty remark, I ask her why she hates me, she goes into her "My son no longer loves me" nonsense. Enzo reassures her of his undying devotion, and for a month or so, she's nice to me. Then it starts again. My husband has the patience of Sisyphus.'

Nico laughed. 'Rita liked to claim that for herself whenever I left a mess.'

'I know full well my lovely aunt was a neat freak. Remember the time she came in here at dawn and scrubbed down the already perfectly clean kitchen? I'll admit, the pots gleamed for months.'

They walked outside. The storm clouds had floated away. The leaves of the fig tree still drooped, dripping their morning's load of rain onto the metal tables and chairs, making soothing *plink* sounds.

'Wasn't Sisyphus punished for testing his wife's love?' Nico asked.

'I don't know, but Enzo's mother certainly tests mine.' She opened the small window that allowed whoever was in the kitchen to see the tables. Now she would be able to hear the oven alarm. 'Enzo told you about Stella?'

'Yes. She's taking the exam on Monday.'

'God, I pray she gets in. It's not a great job, but it's a start. If you still lived in America, I would have asked you to sponsor her. She's such a bright girl, and I don't want her stuck with a self-serving jerk like Gianni. He has no ambition, perfectly happy to label wine bottles for the rest of his life.'

'If Stella loves him, though, that's what matters, isn't it?'

'That's the thing. I'm not sure she does. And he's noticed it. That's why he's being so nice to her.' She leant her head against Nico's shoulder. 'I know, enough. Stella will have to sort out her life by herself, but that doesn't mean I don't have jellyfish in my stomach.' She straightened her back and met Nico's gaze. 'You're here for a reason that has little to do with hunger. I'm ready for the interrogation now.'

'I won't ask any questions if you don't want me to.'

She tapped her shoulder against his arm. 'Ehi, what kind of detective are you?'

'A lousy one.' He'd always been diligent at his job, but never a star. He didn't have the necessary ambition or hardness. 'You're family. I don't want to pry.'

'If you don't, Salvatore will. I'd prefer it be you. Ask away. I have nothing to hide.'

'Elvira implied—'

Tilde finished the sentence for him: 'That I was Robi's secret lover. I wasn't.'

'Do you know who was?'

Tilde stretched out her arm and held her palm up to catch a raindrop from the tree. 'I don't.'

246

Nico suspected Tilde was lying. Her posture had gone completely rigid, the outstretched arm trembling. If she did know, Tilde must have her reasons for not telling him. He wouldn't push her for the name. Not today, at least. 'Gerardi had a gold bracelet in his pocket when he died, a bracelet he'd bought a few days earlier in Radda. It had a charm with the date the first of January, 1997, engraved on it.'

Tilde withdrew her arm and looked at the one drop that had fallen in her palm. She could see a fraction of her life line through it. She blew on the drop, and it broke apart. That date explained why – no, it had to be a simple coincidence. 1st January, 1997, was a date she would never forget. 'That's the day I told Enzo I would leave him if he didn't marry me. I gave him a month.'

'Weren't you engaged already?'

'A we'll-get-married-someday kind of engagement. Mamma Elvira was holding on tight. I finally got fed up. We got married three weeks later. Elvira has never forgiven me for strong-arming her precious son.'

'No regrets?'

'I've got a good husband and a wonderful stubborn daughter, what else could I wish for? I ignore Elvira. So, what else do you want to ask me?'

'I heard some disturbing news from Gogol that might be able to help us with the case. He says he witnessed Gerardi raping a woman.'

Tilde's face blanched. 'A rape? Did he say who she was?'

'No. He was completely silent after that. He was upset he didn't do anything to help her.'

'No.' Tilde's hand swiped the air in front of her. 'No, I don't believe it. Gogol gets confused. His mind doesn't work properly. I refuse to believe a woman was raped. It's too ugly, too cruel. Let's not talk about it any more, please.' Tilde walked back inside, Nico right behind her. 'Let me deal just with chicken rags, olive oil cakes and tonight's dinner menu. I don't want your help tonight. Go to Greve and taste all the wines at the Chianti Expo. No more talk of hideous crimes, please.'

The delicious smell of cake wafted through the kitchen doorway. 'I'm sorry I upset you.'

'You're only doing your job. Before Salvatore comes around asking, tell him I don't know of anyone getting raped in this town. Ever. Now take the scraps for the dog and let me do my work.'

Enzo was still reassuring his mother of his undying filial love when Nico left the restaurant. The wet greyness of the day clung to the old stones of the church and the buildings that led down to the main piazza, matching Nico's mood. The encounter with Tilde and her family had left him sad. He had no desire to go to the Chianti Expo, to hear the Friends of Chianti's band play or listen to eight mayors of the Chianti Classico municipalities go on and on about how flawless their wines were. He certainly didn't want to see Perillo or Daniele. His questions had clearly upset Tilde, his wife's closest family and a woman he respected and loved. He regretted getting involved with Gerardi's murder. He would go to the Expo tomorrow when the booths opened, he decided. Tonight, he would taste his own perfectly good wine at home with dinner.

Walking down the hill to his car, he passed Enrico's shop. Its grate was down, but the shop door was open. Food shops in Italy closed from one to five in the afternoon, sometimes five-thirty.

Nico stopped and looked at his watch. It was three o'clock. 'Hey, Enrico, no siesta for you?'

'Doing a little clean-up.'

Enrico's shop was always spotless. Nico suspected the shopkeeper was taking a break from Luciana's hugs – and her cat.

'Need anything?' Enrico stepped out of the darkness of the shop and lifted the grate halfway. 'You look like you need something.'

An astute man, Signor Enrico. But his need had little to do with food.

'It's all right. You can't sell me anything now, and I'm too lazy to come back later.' He had every intention of parking himself in his chair on the balcony and sitting there until the swallows came home.

'You are right. I can't sell to you now. I'll sell to you tomorrow when the shop is open and you pay me. I give to you today.'

That was the Italian way, the law only serving as suggestion. Nico was tempted. He slipped under the grate and entered the shop. 'Thank you, Enrico. I'll take fifty grams of finocchiona and a chunk of Parmigiano Reggiano.'

It would be his dinner. He wasn't in the mood to cook.

Enrico sliced the salami, cut a chunk of cheese from the Parmigiano wheel, added a thick slice of cooked ham on the house for OneWag and handed Nico the package. 'Two olive loaves tomorrow?'

'Two olive loaves tomorrow and today's bill,' Nico said. 'A domani.'

'A domani,' Enrico repeated to Nico's back.

The afternoon hours went by, Nico sitting on his balcony with OneWag. First, they watched the swallows flutter in short loops over the neat rows of vines and the grove of olive trees under a now bright, sunny sky. Swallows represented loyalty, freedom, hope, he had read somewhere, and finally the three of them came to sleep on his balcony. Their presence gave him a sense of home. Rita would have been 'tickled pink', an expression she'd fallen in love with when she'd first immigrated to the States as a teenager.

As the afternoon glided on, Nico's sadness wore off, replaced by questions. Why would Tilde have reason to lie about the identity of Gerardi's great love? Her body language, the complete stillness of her expression told him she knew. Why was she protecting this mystery woman? Didn't she realise that woman could be the killer? Or did Tilde know the woman was innocent, meaning to protect her from a painful interrogation and town gossip? With OneWag asleep, Nico let the questions swirl in his head unanswered, and after a while, he nodded off too.

What seemed only minutes later, he awoke to the sound of the dog scratching at the front door. 'Coming.' Nico stood up stiffly and was surprised to see a dipping red sun leak its pink-orange light down the length of the horizon. He let OneWag out and followed. The vegetable garden needed to be checked after a hard rain. An earthworm wiggled past his foot. He hoped there were many more to aerate the soil. As always, a few snails were gathered by his salad patch. He picked them up and put them in the pail he kept for weeds. Later, he would drop the snails on the grass behind the house – a great distance away for a snail, but he suspected he would find the very same ones in the garden a few days later. He picked a small bunch of string beans and a head of lettuce for tonight's salad and whistled to OneWag for them to go back inside.

Nico poured himself a glass of red wine. He was beginning to sag again. The change from day to night always brought him down. It was when he missed Rita the most. Best to concentrate on dinner. He put a small pot of water on the stove to cook the string beans. As he waited for it to start boiling, he cut up Tilde's scraps and Enrico's ham gift, and mixed them in with OneWag's dry food. OneWag skittered over on nails that needed cutting, too hungry to bother with his usual one wag of thanks.

Washing the lettuce was next. The leaves were a beautiful light green. The colour made him think of Stella's eyes. The same translucent colour. Gerardi's passport photo flashed through his mind. Green eyes. And Elvira had implied . . . Was it possible Stella was Gerardi's daughter? Stella had been born prematurely.

Nico turned off the stove, his appetite gone. He went out on the balcony with his glass and lit a cigarette. His swallows had flown off again, but he would wait for them to come home. The pieces fit together. Stella could very well be Gerardi's child, but he wished with all his heart it wasn't so.

CHAPTER THIRTEEN

At ten o'clock on Friday morning, a small crowd was already lining up at the Chianti Expo cashier's booth. Most of the guests bought their tickets and immediately wandered off to have breakfast at one of the cafe porticoes. The Expo didn't open until eleven. Foreign wine buyers and tourists had already shown up for what was considered the most important Chianti Classico showcase in Tuscany. A week later, Panzano would have her own smaller showcase, Vino al Vino, but this one was the oldest and the biggest. Sixty-six producers of Chianti Classico, a wine marked by the Gallo Nero black rooster insignia, were here.

Daniele strutted up and down the four aisles between the booths in his summer uniform: short-sleeved blue shirt, dark blue trousers with bright red bands running down the sides. A white bandolier crossed his chest. Last-minute preparations were still being made at many of the booths. Wine bottles wiped clean and displayed according to vintage year and importance, wooden crates stacked neatly, signs with the vineyard logos pinned across the backs of the booths.

After his second go-round, Daniele made his way to the Ferriello Wine booth at the north end of Piazza Matteotti. He was hoping to catch Arben, Aldo's Albanian assistant, during a break, which didn't look like it would be anytime soon. Arben and Gianni were still unloading crates from a large handcart parked in front of the bronze statue of Giovanni da Verrazzano, the Greve native who explored North America. Aldo's wife, Cinzia, was lining up bottles on a shelf below a map depicting the Chianti Classico region, while Aldo uncorked some bottles. All four wore Ferriello T-shirts.

'Ehi, Carabiniere, keep us safe, eh?' Cinzia said, with a wink and a smile.

He looked down at his feet. 'Yes, Signora.'

'Welcome,' Aldo said. 'Cinzia, meet Daniele. He's Salvatore's right hand and makes a great sgroppino. Come by when there aren't too many people and taste some wine.'

Being called Salvatore's right-hand man made Daniele find the courage to look up. 'I can't afford your wines, I'm afraid,' he said, taking off his hat. Oblique rays of sun were already heating up the piazza. His head needed cooling in more ways than one – Aldo's wife's breasts looked like they might tear through the T-shirt.

'For free, Daniele,' Aldo said. 'You keep us safe, we thank you. Tell Salvatore too. He hasn't been around.'

'I will. Thank you.' The last he'd seen of the maresciallo, he was back in the office calling Substitute Prosecutor Della Langhe to see if any information had come in from California. He was glad he wouldn't have to listen to the curses that came afterwards, information or no information. The man brought out the worst in the maresciallo. 'Good luck with sales today.'

'Thanks.' Cinzia flashed her smile.

Feeling his cheeks burn, Daniele put his hat back on and approached the handcart behind the booth. Gianni was lifting the last crate. Daniele had seen him here and in Gravigna, usually with his arm around the same pretty woman. He envied his having a girlfriend.

'You can't leave that here,' he said to Gianni, hoping Gianni would take the handcart and leave him alone with Arben.

Gianni, his arms around the heavy crate, stopped to look down at him, a full head taller than Daniele. 'Like I don't know that? That uniform has gone to your head.'

Arben elbowed Gianni. 'He's just doing his job.' He extended a hand towards Daniele. 'Arben Kazim.' He was a short man with a torso rippled with muscle, full dark hair and eyebrows, a strong nose and chin.

Daniele happily shook his hand and introduced himself. 'Daniele Donato.'

'I'll take the cart back to the van.' Arben started pushing it across the wide piazza. He was headed for the car park across the main street, Daniele guessed. His patrol territory was technically within the piazza, but he needed to ask Arben a question. He scanned the area. Vince and the other men were walking the aisles, eyes peeled for trouble. Five minutes was all he needed.

Daniele hurried to catch up with Arben. 'I need to ask you a question about Roberto Gerardi.'

'I don't have anything good to say about the man.' Arben's Italian was fluent; his accent was detectable only on the vowels. He had lived in Italy twenty-four years, one of the eight hundred thousand Albanians who had reached the eastern coast by sea.

'Being around him so much, two years, I thought—' Daniele stopped to catch his breath. Arben was walking so fast.

'Yes, two years.'

'Maybe you knew something about the woman he was in love with.'

'I know where he fucked her.'

Daniele clasped his bandolier to control his excitement at the lead. 'Where?'

Arben didn't answer until they reached the covered car park, opened the back of the van, hauled the cart inside, locked the door and lit a Toscano cigar.

Daniele stepped away. The smell was vile. 'A Toscano isn't really Tuscan,' Daniele said, repeating what the maresciallo had once told him. 'The tobacco is from Kentucky.'

'Where's that?'

'America.'

Arben smiled. He had incredibly white teeth for a smoker, Daniele thought.

'Marlboro Man country.'

'Where did Gerardi take the woman?'

'Oh, he took her all right. And from the floor creaking and both their moaning and groaning, she knew how to give back. It was upstairs in the abandoned farmhouse Aldo owns, the one where the American lives now. We used to store our old barrels on the ground floor, where the farmer who'd been there before had kept his animals. One day Aldo told me to grab one of the barrels. That's when I heard them.'

'Did you ever go upstairs when they weren't there?' He would have wanted to. Maybe.

'Only once. It was clean up there, just a big bed with fancy sheets and a cashmere blanket. A table, two broken chairs. I guess they weren't interested in sitting.'

'No personal belongings besides the bedding?'

'Towels in the bathroom, nothing more. I didn't search the place, I just wanted a look. I'll tell you, that blanket was just asking to be swiped. That would have shaken up that thieving turd, but then I figured he couldn't afford a blanket like that. I'd be stealing from her, whoever she was. Maybe she could afford ten cashmere blankets, but I don't steal from women. I give.' He winked at Daniele and took a long drag of his Toscano.

'You never saw her?'

'No. Sorry.'

'After Gerardi left town, did you go back to the house?'

'I confess I did. Maybe whoever she was was going to entertain other men in there. I was going to leave my phone number, but the place had been totally cleared out. I did find an earring stuck between the floorboards. A curled silver snake with green stones for eyes.'

Daniele's heart skipped. Gerardi had shown Cinzia Ferri the snake earrings he was going to give to his lover. 'Did you keep it?'

'Dreaming of a snake can have many different, powerful meanings in Islam, mostly bad. I keep it under my pillow to keep me from dreaming snakes.'

Daniele's heart was drumming so fast now it hurt. 'Fantastic! The maresciallo will need to take it.'

'Only if he gives it back at night.'

'Yes, yes, he'll understand about the dreams.'

'No, he'll think all Muslims are stupidly superstitious. We're not! Just me.'

'He won't think that. Italians have countless superstitions.'

Arben threw his Toscano on the concrete floor and stepped on it. 'I have to get back. We open in thirty minutes.'

Daniele straightened his bandolier and readjusted his hat in an attempt to calm down. The maresciallo would be proud of his detecting skills. Daniele thanked Arben as he followed him out of the car park.

'What made you think I might know something?'

They wove their way between cars stuck in gridlock on the main street. 'You were competitors, from what Signor Aldo told us. That means you watched Gerardi, hoping to catch him in a mistake. You caught him stealing, so I asked myself what else you might have observed.'

Arben slapped him on his back. 'Good thinking.'

Daniele wiped his cheeks with his hands as if getting rid of sweat. It was a new ploy he'd discovered to hide his exaggerated blushing. 'Did you tell Signor Aldo what you heard in the farmhouse?'

'I don't interfere with anyone's fucking. It's a right given to man and woman by Allah.'

They shook hands when they reached the piazza. There was now a long line at the two ticket booths. Ten euros for a wine glass embossed with the Chianti Expo logo, a red cloth holder and six tasting pours of wine.

It was almost lunchtime when Nico parked the 500 a good distance from Greve. With the Expo in full swing, he was lucky to find a spot just off the main road. He welcomed the walk, despite the hot sun and OneWag pulling back against his unfamiliar and unwelcome lead. He replayed the morning in his head, what had been said and not.

Anxious to get to the cafe in case Gogol had shown up early in order to avoid him, Nico had skipped his morning run. When he walked in with OneWag, Nico said hello to Jimmy and Sandro. They waved back. He looked around. A few students with bulging backpacks were already there, stuffing themselves with ciambelle and cornetti. No Gogol, but Nelli was sitting by the open French doors, reading the paper, a cappuccino raised to her lips. His first lucky break. Nelli was Gogol's friend.

Nelli looked up as OneWag ran to her. She'd conquered his heart by stooping down and rubbing his ears whenever they met. The dog leapt onto her lap and licked her chin. Nelli smiled as Nico approached. He admired how easily smiles came to her. And there was nothing fake about them.

'I'm glad you came in early,' Nelli said. 'I can give you this in person.' She handed over something wrapped in the paper. 'OneWag will never forgive me' – she kissed the top of the dog's head – 'but I think it's best for him.'

Nico sat down next to her and opened the package. A red harness collar with a tag engraved with Nico's name and phone number and a matching lead. 'I hope you don't mind, they're old. My dog was about the same size as yours.'

'How nice of you. Thank you, but don't you want to get another dog?'

'No. Too painful.' As soon as the words were out, she apologised, putting a hand on Nico's arm. 'She was just a dog. I know her death doesn't compare to—'

'Please, don't apologise.' Nico clasped her hand. 'Pain is pain, for the loss of any loved one.'

'Thank you.' She looked up at Nico with her welcoming face and warm smile.

Nico felt a rush of emotion that, seconds later, made him uncomfortable. He took back his hand. 'How did you get my phone number?'

'I had to convince Tilde I only needed it for the dog tag.' Despite being aware of Nico's discomfort, Nelli kept her smile as her rejected hand kneaded OneWag's ear. She resented Tilde's assumption that she was out to snare Nico. He was a nice man with good looks and kindness to spare, but she wasn't looking for a relationship. Friendship would be nice, though. 'She's very protective of you.' She'd almost said 'possessive'.

'Tilde has been very good to me. She, Enzo and Stella are the only family I have left.'

Nelli changed the subject, asking, 'Is Salvatore any closer to finding out who killed Robi? I know you two are friends.'

'Even if I knew I couldn't tell you, but I'm glad you brought it up. How well do you know Gogol?'

'Pretty well. Why?'

'Is he crazy?' He'd denied the possibility to Perillo, but maybe he was wrong. 'Does he ever make things up?'

'I'm not a doctor, but we've been friends since I was a little girl. He would come by the house and give me *Divine Comedy* lessons I wasn't the least bit interested in. Georgio, that's his real name, lost his mother when he was maybe nine or ten. Father unknown. The old townspeople say he was pretty normal until she died. I think he just couldn't accept a reality that included his mother's death, and so he made up his own. His mother became Beatrice, Dante's great love, who also died young. By spouting Dante, he keeps his mother alive. The coat he refuses to take off? That's his mamma hugging him.' Nelli put OneWag on the floor and sat back in her chair. 'Now you're going to think *I'm* the crazy one.'

'Not at all.'

Sandro came by the table to deliver Nico's breakfast.

Nico thanked him and waited until he was back behind the counter. OneWag was busy wandering the cafe, licking up crumbs. Nico leant over the small table and in a low voice told Nelli what Gogol had said at the murder site.

Nelli pressed her hand against her mouth and closed her eyes.

'Could he have made that up?'

'No.'

'How can you be sure?'

She opened her eyes filled with tears. 'Because he asked me back then if I was the woman Robi had raped. He was pretty sure it had been someone else, but he wanted to be certain it wasn't me. This was after Robi had left.'

'Why didn't you give this information to Perillo once you found out the murdered man was Gerardi?'

Nelli pulled her hands over her face. 'I was going to. But then I thought he'd try to find out who'd been raped and accuse her of killing Robi.' Nelli dropped her hands on the table. They were spotted with grey and yellow paint. 'I couldn't do it. Whoever she is, she's suffered enough. I don't know if you can understand.'

'I do understand what abuse can do to any human being.' His mother had certainly suffered enough of it. And his understanding of another woman's suffering had ended his career. He and his partner had been first to the murder scene. A man, shot multiple times, lay on his back by the entrance. A woman was on her knees still holding the phone, trembling. A very slight woman, much younger than she looked, he would discover. An intruder had shot her husband, she said in a thin whisper. He walked over to her, helped her up and sat her on a nearby armchair. She explained that she was in the bathroom when she'd heard the shots. She'd rushed out, but the man was gone. He owed money, she said. She didn't know how much. He loved to gamble.

And loved to hit her, Nico suspected. July. No air-conditioning. Despite the heat in the room, her legs were covered in dark stockings, arms hidden by long sleeves. He remembered how carefully his mother would hide her bruises. When his partner walked into another room, he lifted one of the woman's sleeves and saw the burn marks.

She pushed the sleeve down quickly. 'I bruise easily.'

'I understand that oil splatters when you cook.' He realised he was feeding her a more believable answer. He was going to help her. Gently, he asked where the gun was.

She shook her head. 'No gun.' Her eyes darted to a full rubbish bag by the door.

'Your husband was going to take out the rubbish,' Nico said.

She clutched his hand. 'Yes, yes. You see, I forgot to do it.'

And he was going to make her pay for forgetting. 'Let me take it out for you.'

'Thank you,' she said in her meek voice.

His partner was back in the room and nodded, understanding he was going to look for the gun. When he found it, he slipped it inside his jacket without giving it a thought. 'No gun,' he told his partner, hauling the rubbish bag back in. He still remembers the stink on his hands from the rotting rubbish. 'Maybe the others will find it in there.'

That night, he wiped the gun clean and threw it in the Gowanus Canal. The woman got off on reasonable doubt. A few weeks later, Rita died. Nico went bar crawling with his partner shortly afterwards. In a drunken stupor, he'd confessed about the gun.

'When did Robi leave?' Nico asked Nelli.

'Sometime in January.'

'Did Gogol tell you who he thought the woman was?'

'No. I didn't want to know. I was actually jealous of that woman for a disgusting minute or two. Afterwards, I was so ashamed of myself, I sent half my savings to a centre for abused women in Florence.'

'And yet you really have no idea who Gerardi was in love with? Please forgive me, but I find that odd. Women in love usually know who their competition is.'

'You think he raped his girlfriend?'

'If he did rape her, that would give her a motive, but even if she wasn't raped, she might have useful information. I can't believe no one knows who she is.'

'I followed him once. I could tell he was going to see her by the way he was dressed. Pressed trousers, new shirt, polished shoes. I got on my Vespa and followed him up to Radda. He went into a jewellery store there. Crisani's. Before Robi went in, he combed his hair with his fingers, tucked in his shirt. I just knew she was in there, but I didn't have the courage to follow him inside. I hid behind a car across the street and waited to see if they'd come out together. Instead, an older man followed him out, screaming at him. I jumped onto my scooter and swung away, not wanting Robi to see me. I went back a few days later and walked into the store, and there was this stunning girl behind the counter. About eighteen. The man who had shouted at Robi came out from a door in the back as soon as I stepped in. I pretended I was looking for a charm for my mother's bracelet. He dealt with me, she only watched. My mother doesn't own a bracelet. I muttered something stupid and left, convinced I'd found Robi's great doomed love. At least, that's what I hoped. I was twenty at the time, and all I read was romance novels. What else was I supposed to think?'

'Why doomed?'

'Crisani is a well-known jeweller, and Robi came from nothing. Not the ideal husband for a rich girl. I told myself that was the reason for the secrecy.'

'The girl might have been an employee, but you could be right. Why didn't you tell Perillo?'

Nelli sighed. Men really didn't understand, not even nice ones like Nico. 'For the same reason I didn't tell him what Gogol had asked me way back.'

Nico nodded. 'Of course. This girl could have been the rape victim.'

'That's right. Besides, that the Crisani girl was Robi's beloved is just another one of my theories, not fact.'

Nico remembered Aldo's comment while explaining his relationship to the victim. Gerardi had told him he wanted to marry a woman, but the family was opposed. 'You've been a great help, Nelli. Thank you for telling me.'

'I trust you.'

A smile came to his lips, unbidden. 'Now let's enjoy our breakfast.'

'I've already had mine.'

'If you keep me company, I'll treat you to another cappuccino.'

'Add a custard-filled cornetto and I'm in.' Her wonderful smile came back.

By the time Nico reached Greve's Piazza Matteotti, he was carrying an exhausted OneWag. He stopped and let a sudden breeze cool his face. It was just past eleven o'clock; the Expo had opened. Nico hated crowds, but he had to speak to Perillo.

Nico walked to the first restaurant under the portico and asked the waiter setting up for lunch for a glass of water. He poured the water into a clean ashtray and put it on the floor. OneWag lapped it up happily. The waiter, a young, skinny black man in jeans and a colourful tie-dyed shirt, brought another full glass. 'This one for you. Still, not sparkling,' he said with a strong accent. A man who knew the value of water and compassion. One of thousands who were still crossing the sea from

Africa, blessed not to have drowned and lucky enough to have found a job.

Nico drank the water and held out the glass and a five euro note. The waiter took only the glass. 'Water is free. Come eat, then leave money.'

Nico nodded, thanked him and returned the now-empty ashtray to its original place. He looked above the door and made a mental note of the restaurant's name. He would come back and eat here, maybe invite Nelli.

'Signor Doyle!'

Nico didn't need to turn around to know who it was. 'Signora Dorsetti.' This time she was wearing something fancy, a shiny apricot-coloured dress with ruffles at the hem and sleeves.

'How wonderful that you're here. And your sweet dog.'

'It's nice to meet you again.' Nico picked up OneWag. 'I hope you'll excuse me, but I need to see Maresciallo Perillo.'

'Something to do with the murder?' She gave him no time to answer. 'Robi was my brother, you see. As I told the maresciallo, I know nothing about his new life or his old loves. Nothing at all. I think the maresciallo doesn't believe me. I can't blame him. Brothers and sisters should be close, confide in each other.' She smoothed her dress. 'Robi was a complicated man. Very proud, quick to anger when he didn't get his way. But I can't think of why anyone would want to kill him. Maybe for money, but that can't be, because whoever it was didn't take his watch. I hope he left me something. If it's a great deal of money, though, then I'll be a suspect, won't I?' She laughed as though the mere thought was ridiculous. 'Please, come have an espresso with me. Three minutes and you're free. Surely you have three minutes to give a grieving sister?'

Nico let out a long internal sigh. 'Of course, Signora.'

'Please, call me Maria. When we were children, Robi used to call me Marimia. How would you say that in English?'

'My Maria.'

'Not as pretty. Robi adored me then. I'm ten years younger than him. I was his pet.' She sat down at the nearest table, already set for lunch. 'Do sit. I think he stopped loving me when I got married. He was such a jealous man.'

Nico obliged and placed OneWag on his lap as insurance. He felt assaulted by this woman's unwanted speech.

The African waiter appeared, then smiled at both of them. 'Good day, Signora. The usual?'

'Too early for my beer, Yunas. Two espressos.'

That he might want something else was clearly a possibility that hadn't occurred to her. 'No coffee for me, please,' Nico said. 'But another glass of water would be welcome.'

Yunas smiled. 'Still. Not sparkling.'

'Thank you.'

'Yunas is from Ethiopia. Italy is full of Africans now. We'll soon have only cappuccino-coloured children. Some people get very upset at the thought. I don't.' She smiled proudly.

Nico wondered if she expected a compliment for her tolerance.

'Now, tell me about you, Nico.'

'There isn't much to say.' Before he was forced to supply information he had no desire to give, Yunas appeared with their order. Nico seized the glass and gulped down the water.

Maria realised he was going to rush off. 'My brother's death must have greatly upset Tilde Morelli.' Nico froze. 'You're related, I hear.'

'Yes, she and my wife are cousins.' What was this woman getting at? Nico put his glass down and reached into his pocket to pay the waiter. 'I think his death upset many people,' he said curtly.

Maria tilted her head. She'd been very circumspect with the maresciallo, but this man was being rude. She wanted him to regret that. 'They were very close, you know.'

Her words felt like a punch to the stomach. Nico stood up, dropped a ten-euro note on the table. 'I'm sorry. I really do have to go.'

Maria felt something bubble inside her. Rejection in any form made her seethe. Americans had a reputation for being nice, even gullible. Who did Nico Doyle think he was? She'd only been trying to help, thinking he must be lonely.

'I'm sorry, Maria.'

She acknowledged his apology with her sweetest smile. She was good at hiding her feelings, always had been. She had her pride to think of. This was a stupid man who deserved to have his face slapped.

Nico tucked OneWag under his arm again. 'You caught me at a bad time.'

She flicked her wrist in the air. 'I'm afraid the good times are gone for everyone.'

'I hope not for you,' he said, and walked away.

'I'll have my beer now,' she called out to Yunas when Nico was out of earshot. She thought of poor dead Robi, her only sibling, coming back without planning to see her, not even calling. He'd left her to lick his own wounds on another continent. Made himself rich too.

Maria crunched on the chocolate square that came with her coffee. *I hope not for you.* Well, that was unexpected. Maybe even sweet. As the chocolate melted in her mouth, so did her anger. There was yet still a chance at good times.

Daniele saw Nico making his way to the northern end of the piazza and met him halfway.

'Where's your wine glass?' Daniele asked Nico after they greeted each other.

'It's a little early for that. I'm here to talk to the maresciallo.'

There was urgency in the American's voice. Something new had come up. Well, he had something new too. 'I left him in his office, calling Della Langhe. I don't know if he's still there.' He started to pet OneWag. It helped slow his racing heart. 'I have something I need to tell him too, something that could be important, something Arben told me.'

Nico could see that Daniele was dying to tell him

whatever it was. Daniele kept absentmindedly petting the dog, who surprised him with a lick on the wrist.

Deep in thought, Daniele didn't notice. Would the maresciallo mind if he told Nico what Arben had said? After all, he'd enlisted Nico to help them. He mulled the possibility over for a minute, then let out a sigh. No. After dealing with Della Langhe, his boss would be furious. He gave Nico his full attention. 'I'd come with you to the station, but I'm on duty.'

Nico saw Daniele's disappointment and said, 'We'll wait for him then.'

Some twenty minutes later, Nico stood in the shade behind the statue of Verrazzano and finally saw Perillo stride into the piazza in full uniform, hat slightly askew on his head and boots shined to a gleam. He looked taller, handsome, important. Relieved to see him, Nico waved. He was eager to share Nelli's information. Maria Dorsetti's comment about Tilde he intended to keep to himself for now.

Daniele, who had just patrolled the piazza, spotted the maresciallo and stood up straighter. To his surprise, his boss was in full uniform, which had been required only at last night's opening. Well, the maresciallo could be a bit vain. The men at the station sometimes made fun of him for it behind his back. Daniele thought it was disloyal and never joined in. His boss did look good in full uniform, except for the dark expression on his face. 'Good news?' Daniele asked, knowing the answer.

'News. But not good. Gerardi wasn't married. The police finally got a subpoena to search his home and office. They took his laptop but haven't looked through it yet. The computer at the winery only had production and client lists. So for now, no copy of the will and no personal correspondence.'

'He didn't have a safe in the house?' Nico asked.

'No. He did have a safe deposit box, and according to the Delizioso manager, before Gerardi left for Italy, he added his lawyer's name for it at the bank and left him the key. The lawyer's secretary claims she knows nothing about a key, and the lawyer's on holiday, not responding to calls or email.'

'The police can get a subpoena to open it.'

'They're trying, but Gerardi's bank demanded a death certificate first, which then had to be translated into English and notarised. The American embassy in Rome took care of that yesterday, but so far no news.'

Daniele asked, 'What about the manager? Are the police looking into him?'

'He's been with Gerardi since he took over the Delizioso. According to all the employees there, he was devoted to his boss. Plus, he knew Gerardi was dying. They all knew. Why have someone kill him?' Perillo spread his arms in protest. 'We've got nothing.'

Nico gave Perillo a pat on the shoulder, relieved that nothing involving Tilde had come out. 'Murder cases require patience.'

Perillo shook his head. 'What they don't need

is Della Langhe. He broke my eardrum with this information, then threatened to send down some "experienced men" from Florence, as if it were my fault we're still in the dark. I told him to go ahead and send. Of course, he's not actually sending a goddamn soul, because in about an hour, he'll calm down and realise what an idiot he is.' Perillo turned to Daniele. 'Are you religious?'

'I go to church on Sundays.' He'd done so since birth. His mother made sure no Sunday Mass was missed. He used to fall asleep as a child. Now he found it restful.

Perillo reached into his trouser pocket and slipped a ten-euro note into Daniele's hand. 'If that lawyer isn't found by Sunday morning, go light some candles for us. If he is, give it back. It will be the seed for a Dario Cecchini meal.'

'I don't eat meat.'

'Ah, right.'

Daniele stuffed the money into his pocket. He would add five euros of his own, even though he didn't actually believe the candles would help.

Cinzia spotted Perillo and wiggled fingers at him. Their booth was only a few feet away. Perillo waved back. Aldo shot him a glance and went back to pouring wine into several raised glasses.

'Salvatore, Nico,' Cinzia called out. 'When this is over, you're all coming to our house for our best wine and my cacio e pepe spaghetti.'

'You mean the Expo?'

'No, the murder investigation. Hope it's soon.'

'It will be,' Perillo answered with false confidence.

'We have things to tell you too,' Daniele said loudly, his eagerness taking over.

Perillo looked at Nico.

'Yes, I have something new.'

'Very good. The more information, the better. But this isn't exactly a good spot to discuss anything except wine. Let's go to the pharmacy instead of the station. It's just around the corner. The pharmacist is a friend of mine, and he'll give us his back room while we talk.'

In a small, hot room filled with unopened cartons of medicines, shampoos and creams but no chairs, Daniele told Perillo and Nico about the love nest, the snake earring Arben had found and kept. He didn't mention why.

'Bravo, Dani. Get the earring from Arben tomorrow morning. Unless it has the jeweller's markings on it, I'm not sure it will be of much help. But whether it is or not, excellent thinking on your part.'

Daniele felt his cheeks get hot. Was he supposed to be proud? Disappointed? Both, maybe. But he was still convinced the forgotten snake earring would help to solve the puzzle of the mystery lady.

Perillo leant back against a wall of well-stocked shelves. 'Now you, Nico.'

Nico told him what he had learnt from Nelli.

'So you think Gogol really witnessed a rape?'

'Nelli believes him.' Nico noticed Perillo go pale.

'For now, let's concentrate on the earring,' Perillo said, pulling himself together. 'Maybe it's one of Crisani's. Thanks to you two, we have a new lead. We're already short-staffed at the Expo, so pursuing it will have to wait until tomorrow morning. I'm sorry, Nico. I would love to have you come with us to Crisani's, but I'm afraid it's not possible.'

'Of course.' Nico was just as happy not to go. He had Tilde to worry about. Tonight, after dinner, he had more questions for her, unsure he wanted to know the answers.

CHAPTER FOURTEEN

At eleven at night, the downhill slope that led to the main piazza was empty and dark. Tilde lowered herself onto one of the church steps just above Sotto Il Fico and placed the bowl of string beans on her lap. On each side of her, a line of terracotta pots filled with pink geraniums disappeared up the dark stairs. She reached into her apron pocket and took out a cigarette, lit it, took two puffs and placed the lit cigarette carefully on the step. Her fingers started snapping one end of the string beans. The lamp outside the restaurant barely gave her enough light, but after years of experience, Tilde could have snapped those string beans in pitch black.

Nico sat down next to her. 'I didn't know you smoked.'

'I don't.' She avoided looking at Nico. Instead, she looked straight ahead, the snapping mechanical.

'Rita used to snap both ends,' Nico said as a warm-up.

'Italian string beans are thin, they don't need it.'

'How are you cooking them?'

'In tomato sauce, but I know you're not here for cooking tips. Go ahead, ask your questions.' Her tone was angry.

Nico reached for her hand. She pulled away, picked up her cigarette and took a deep drag. 'I gave up smoking when I was pregnant.'

Nico leant in, his voice low. 'Tilde, I don't want to pry in your affairs, but I'm worried you're not telling me the truth about Gerardi, and if Perillo decides to question you . . .'

'I don't remember what I told you.'

'If you don't, that means you were making it up.'

'No, it means I am very tired, Nico, so let's get this over with. I'm not Robi's mystery woman. I knew Robi the way I know most of the people who live here. We were friendly in a "hi, how are you" sort of way, whenever we happened to run into each other.'

'His sister says you and Gerardi were very close.'

'She can say whatever she wants.'

Nico put his hand on her arm. This time, she let it stay. 'He didn't harm you, did he?'

Tilde looked at her half-smoked cigarette. 'Why? Am I trying to kill myself?' She stubbed it out on the stair, put the butt in her pocket and turned to face Nico. In a perfectly level voice, she repeated his question, adding, 'Why would you ask me that?'

Nico softened his expression. Even in the semidarkness, he could see that her face was wiped clean of emotion.

He wished he could hold her, as Rita would have done. 'Because of what Gogol witnessed.'

'If you insist on talking about it, I'll ask you a question. Did he see who she was?'

'Does that mean you believe him?'

'Why shouldn't I? If Gogol saw a rape, he saw a rape. I just don't want to talk about it. I already told you that.'

'If Gogol did see who the woman was, he won't say. That's why I brought it up again. I'm sorry, but after what Maria said . . .' He let the rest of the sentence drop.

She started snapping peas again. 'How awful for Gogol.'

'Worse for the woman.'

'Yes, much, much worse.' She snapped faster.

'It wasn't you?'

'If it were, I wouldn't kill him for it. I'd have erased it from my mind by now. I'm sure whoever it was has dealt with it.' Tilde stood up with the bowl in the crook of her arm. 'Women are much more resilient than you think.'

Nico got on his feet. 'Rita showed me that every day.'

Tilde stood on her toes and kissed both his cheeks. 'Thanks for worrying about me, Nico. I'm fine. I really am.'

Nico very much wanted to believe her.

At nine sharp the next morning, the Crisanis' seventy-year-old housekeeper, Pina, answered the door. Seeing Maresciallo Salvatore Perillo and Brigadiere Daniele Donato standing on the landing in their well-pressed uniforms, she let out a small cry.

278

Perillo smiled to reassure her. 'Nothing to be afraid of. We're only here to have a word with Signora Crisani.'

Pina straightened her back to cover her embarrassment. 'There is no Signora Crisani here. Maybe you mean Signora Castaldi?'

Perillo cast a look of reproach in Daniele's direction. He should have been told of the married name. 'Yes. Signora Castaldi.'

'Good. If you wanted Signorina Crisani, you'd be out of luck. She's at the seashore.'

Daniele's shoulders slumped. Expecting to see Rosalba, he'd dreamt of her all night.

'Who is it?' asked a woman's voice from the flat.

'Two carabinieri, Signora. They want to speak to you.'

'Then let them in.'

Pina stepped back and, with a grim expression, opened the door wide.

Irene Crisani Castaldi appeared in the large, dark foyer, wearing a long, red kaftan made of a light material that billowed as she walked on bare feet. Her nails, toes and lips all matched the rich red of the kaftan. Long, black hair hung over her shoulders. A stunning woman, thought Perillo. She barely looked older than her daughter.

'Come in.' Irene had a deep, harsh voice that seemed to contradict her beauty. 'Pina, make us some coffee and bring your lemon pound cake.' She turned to Perillo and said in a flat tone, 'She's a wonderful baker.' From her lips, it didn't sound like a compliment.

Perillo introduced himself and Daniele. With a nod of acknowledgement, Irene led them into a large room overstuffed with heavy furniture and dark oil paintings. 'Forgive my attire. I wasn't expecting anyone at this hour.' In truth, she never expected anyone at any hour, except for her daughter and faithful Pina, who had brought her and then Rosalba up. They were the only people she loved. The rest of her heart was reserved for her grandfather's jewellery store. Would these two men understand that devotion? She doubted it.

'Please sit down.' She floated down into a brocaded armchair and arranged the kaftan around her legs. Perillo watched her as he undid the bottom button of his jacket in order to sit on the sofa. The sofa was a deep one, and Perillo was now on edge. Either his wife had moved the button or he had to go on a diet, a prospect he'd planned to avoid. What he found more interesting was the fact that Irene Castaldi wasn't in the least nervous or intimidated. They were either wasting time, or she was a very good actress. But Pina, the maid, had cried out on seeing two carabinieri at the door. For Perillo, that was a first.

Irene sat back in her armchair. 'How can I help you, Maresciallo?'

Daniele took out his notebook and sat at the far end of the sofa. Perillo leant forward, elbows on knees. 'I'm hoping you can help us with information about the murder victim, Roberto Gerardi. I believe you knew him before he left for the United States.'

She frowned as if trying to place the name. 'If I did, I don't remember. Twenty-two years is a long time.'

Daniele looked up in surprise.

Irene noticed and smiled at him. 'I know he left twenty-two years ago because I read it in the paper.'

Perillo kept his eyes on Irene. Daniele really did need to learn to keep a straight face.

'Robi, as everyone in Gravigna calls him' – had her eyes just widened at the nickname, or was it wishful thinking on his part? – 'had told a friend he was very much in love with a woman and wanted to marry her.'

Irene reached for a cigarette and was about to light it when Pina came in with a silver tray holding a silver coffee service, delicate cups, a stack of small plates and a large one with sliced lemon pound cake. Pina kept her eyes on the shaking tray. Perillo wondered if his presence had anything to do with that shaking.

'Thank you, Pina.' Irene put her cigarette and lighter down and indicated the wide wooden bench in front of the sofa. 'Just set it there. We'll serve ourselves.'

Rosalba is rich, Daniele thought sadly as he eyed the moist, pale yellow slices of pound cake. They smelt of lemon and vanilla. He would never be able to afford her.

Perillo accepted the coffee, added three sugar cubes and stirred for a long time. 'No cake for me, thank you.' Accepting coffee from an interviewee was perfectly fine. A cup of coffee was like a glass of water. Accepting food placed them at a disadvantage, made them indebted to her. 'Gerardi used to meet this woman in a small abandoned farmhouse belonging to Aldo Ferri. Gerardi worked for him then.'

Irene picked at the pound cake slice. 'A place filled with mice.'

Perillo leant forward, almost hitting the coffee cup with his knee. 'Was it?'

Irene put the plate back on the bench and lit her cigarette. 'Aren't all abandoned houses filled with mice?'

Perillo scanned her face. Her cool control had changed. To what? Defiance? Anger? Not at him. At something, someone more distant.

'Your father was a difficult man,' Perillo ventured.

'Yes, he was.' Pina had begged her to walk away, make her own life, but her father made it clear that he would disinherit her if she did. She had promised her grandfather, who had no love for his son, that she would one day take care of the business, that it would always belong to a Crisani.

'That must have been hard for you.'

'No more than for most children who lose their mothers early.'

'Gerardi mentioned that there were problems with the relationship. It seems her family didn't approve.'

'I suppose that's sad for him, but why are you telling me this?'

'Gerardi was seen entering your jewellery store a few weeks before he left.'

'Not mine back then. My father's. It became mine on his death fifteen years ago.' His death had brought her a joy she was no longer ashamed of. 'Many people went into Crisani's.'

'But I imagine not many were kicked out of the store by your screaming father.'

'Any little thing set my father off.' She took a deep drag of her cigarette. On the exhale, she did her best to wipe her thoughts clean.

Perillo noticed the change. She was once again controlled, calm. He had no evidence she was the mystery woman except for the discovery of the earring – a coiled silver snake with tiny green eyes. Maybe it was the same pair Gerardi had shown Cinzia, an engagement present for the woman he loved.

'Please tell me the truth, Signora Castaldi.'

'What truth? There are always many versions, don't you think? My truth is that I didn't kill Gerardi.'

'Were you Roberto Gerardi's lover?'

'No.' Irene stood up abruptly. 'If you have nothing else to ask me, I really must get dressed and get to work. I open at eleven.'

Perillo and Daniele stood. 'Thank you for your time.' Perillo planned to come back when Irene Castaldi was in the shop and talk to the housekeeper. Pina had been genuinely frightened at seeing them. Either she had been up to no good or she was frightened for her employer.

Irene walked the two carabinieri to the door. 'I'm sorry to have disappointed you, Maresciallo.'

'Don't be. Being disappointed is part of our job. As is being persistent.'

As Irene lowered her head to turn the lock, several strands of her long hair fell over one side of her face.

'Thank you for your time,' Perillo said as she opened the door. As he stepped across the threshold, Irene's fingers tucked the fallen strands behind her ear.

Daniele stared, inhaled deeply and said, 'What a beautiful earring, Signora.'

Irene quickly covered her ear with her hair. 'Thank you,' she said with a stiff voice.

Perillo stepped back into the foyer. 'Let me see?'

'An unusual design,' Daniele said, eager to keep this part of the interrogation on his plate.

She didn't uncover her ear. 'A present from a friend, nothing special. I have far more beautiful earrings in the store.'

Daniele reached into his pocket and took out the earring Arben had given him that morning. 'Did your friend give you this one too?'

As Irene's eyes dropped to the silver snake earring, its sheen tarnished by twenty-two years of neglect, a tidal wave of pent-up emotion washed over her. Irene stared so intently that Daniele closed his fist over the earring, afraid she might try to snatch it.

Irene took her eyes away. She had turned ashen.

Daniele asked, 'Do you need to sit down?'

She nodded. He took her arm, walked her back into the living room and sat her back in the armchair. Perillo followed.

'A glass of water?'

'Yes,' she said in a threadbare voice. 'Tell Pina it's for you. Keep her in the kitchen, please.'

Perillo sat down on the sofa, impressed by Daniele's initiative. His young brigadiere had pinned Signora Castaldi into a corner.

A minute later, Daniele came back from the kitchen with an apologetic face. Behind him came Pina carrying another silver tray, this time with the glass of water on a doily. She took one look at Irene and turned to glower at Perillo. 'What have you done to her?'

Irene waved Pina away. 'It's nothing, Pina. Please leave us alone.'

Pina put the tray with the glass of water on the bench, then straightened up to her full five feet two inches. Her anger seemed to turn into stone. In a glacial voice, she said, 'As you wish, Signora,' and retreated on slippered feet.

While Irene drank the water, Daniele eyed his boss. Perillo nodded. Daniele sat at the other end of the sofa as before and took out his notebook. He understood that his time with Signora Castaldi was over.

Irene put her glass down and sat back in the armchair. Some of her colour had returned. 'Where did you find it?' Her voice was still weak.

'In your love nest. The abandoned farm.'

'When?'

'Shortly after Gerardi left town.'

'Who?'

'That is of no concern to you.'

She looked at Daniele and held out her hand. 'Please?'

'I'm sorry, Signora,' Perillo said. 'You will get it back

when we have found his killer. Now, I think it's time you told us the truth.'

Irene reached for the ear that hadn't been exposed and removed an earring identical to her other earring and to the one Daniele had in his pocket. She held it out for them to see. 'I kept the box, you see. When I couldn't find it, I went to a jeweller in Florence and had a copy made.'

'The eyes are different,' Daniele said.

'They're onyx. I didn't want them to be identical, and black seemed appropriate. I turned down his marriage proposal, you see. I loved him very much, but my father made it very clear that he would have nothing to do with me ever again. He was a widower, and I was his only child. Once he died, there would have been no more Crisani Jewellery. I couldn't accept that.' She sat up. The wave had receded. The strength that had allowed her to carry on without regret all these years was back. 'It was a painful decision, but the best one under those circumstances.'

Perillo leant forward. 'What circumstances?'

'He'd stolen from Aldo Ferri. He was fired.'

Before Daniele could control himself, the words slipped out. 'Maybe he needed the money to pay for these earrings.'

Perillo shot out a curt 'Daniele!'

'That was the problem. I was rich, and he was poor and probably always would be.' She had loved him in spite of that, or because of it. She no longer remembered. What she did remember was the pain of that decision. Irene looked down at the coiled black-eyed snake in her hand.

She had always liked money too much. It was that simple.

'Gerardi became a successful owner of a California winery.' How successful, Perillo hoped to discover over the weekend.

'I likely helped with that,' Irene said. 'Anger is an excellent motivator. I knew it was Robi when I read about the gold trainers. When I told him it was over between us, he was furious, spat out insults. His last words to me were, "I'll show you, you bitch. When I come back, I'll be wearing gold shoes, that's how rich I'll be."'

'But he didn't come here to show you how rich he had become?'

'No. After I broke up with him, I never heard from him again. I guessed that the dead man was Robi from the description of the shoes, but once the newspaper confirmed his identity, I was surprised he hadn't got in touch to show me how wrong I'd been to leave him.'

'He bought a bracelet in your store and he didn't ask about you? That's hard to believe.'

'He did. He asked my daughter if I owned the store.'

'You recognised him from the tape. That's why one camera supposedly didn't work and the tape of the other had been wiped clean.'

'Yes, I'm afraid so.'

He could have her arrested for tampering with evidence, but to what purpose?

'It must have given him perverse pleasure to buy such an expensive bracelet from my store, and in cash.'

'As you know, the charm on the bracelet was engraved

with the date January first, 1997. Does that mean anything to you?'

'No. We broke up a week before Christmas, and I spent the holidays out of town. My father thought it prudent to send me on a ski trip to Switzerland, in case I changed my mind about Robi.'

'Where were you between five and seven o'clock Monday morning?'

'Why would I kill Robi? If anything, Robi might have wanted to kill me.'

'I have to ask the question, and I need you to answer it.'

'I was asleep in my bed until seven-thirty, when Pina brought me a coffee. She arrives at six and won't be able to corroborate my being in bed before that.'

'Was your daughter here?'

'No. She came home from Siena, where she was visiting friends, later in the day.' She looked at Perillo with a defiant expression. 'I didn't kill Robi, but I'm afraid I have no alibi. Even if Rosalba had been here, she would've been fast asleep.'

'You don't love him any more?'

'You can't love a dead man, only your memory of him. Did he ever marry?'

'No.'

'I see.' She had made up a whole life for him in her mind. A wife and three boys and a wooden house with a nice garden, like the American homes she had seen in the movies. He owned a pizza restaurant – all he'd ever wanted to eat was pizza. Sometimes she'd imagined him owning an auto repair shop. He was good with his hands.

Irene stood up. It was time to let the past go. 'I think I've answered enough questions. I really need to get dressed.'

Daniele and Perillo got up awkwardly, the sofa being very deep. They both shook down their trouser legs. Perillo followed Irene to the front door. He had one last question for her. One he had held off on for a purpose.

Daniele went back into the kitchen to thank Pina for the coffee and her lemon pound cake. She was rolling a sheet of pasta on a marble-topped table. 'Signora wouldn't listen to me. Her father would have come around and forgiven her.' She lifted her head to look at Daniele. 'You're too thin. There's more pound cake in that bundle over there. Take it and enjoy, but don't go around saying I bribed you.'

Daniele grabbed the bundle and planted a kiss on her cheek.

In the foyer, as Irene was about to open the door, Perillo said, 'Just one more question, Signora. Forgive my crudeness, but I need to ask. Did Gerardi force himself on you or anyone you knew of after you turned him down?'

Irene clasped her throat. 'God no! Did someone accuse him of that?'

'It seems so.'

'When?'

Perillo studied Irene's blanched face, her widened eyes, the shock in them. She wasn't the one. 'It happened between your break-up and his departure.'

'I don't believe it.'

'If you have to leave town for any reason, please let me know first.'

Daniele slipped behind Perillo, holding the pound cake bundle so Irene wouldn't see it. He wasn't sure she'd approve of Pina's generosity.

Perillo extended his hand. Irene took it gingerly, still shocked by the news. 'Thank you for your time, Signora Castaldi. Goodbye.'

Irene stood at the door as they walked down the stairs. 'I don't believe it,' she repeated in a voice too low for them to hear.

CHAPTER FIFTEEN

Lucia, Gogol's gatekeeper of hell, looked up from her crocheting as Nico approached the front desk of the hospice. Her expression was grim.

'He's waiting for you in the garden, God knows why. I don't know what you did to him, but that poor man has barely eaten since you brought him back. He burnt the mushroom omelette for the first time ever. He's still asking me to forgive him.' She pointed the crochet hook at him. 'You upset Gogol again, and you'll answer to me.'

'Right you are,' Nico said, and pulled a growling OneWag out the back door.

Gogol was raking the leaves on the winding gravel path of the garden. His coat lay neatly folded on the bench where they had sat together before. The morning was sunny but still had a night's edge of coolness. Nelli had told Nico that Gogol never took off his coat. Something had changed.

'Good morning,' Nico called out as he undid OneWag's lead. The dog scurried over to the old man and waited for a head pat. Gogol obliged. 'Good. We're friends now, yes?'

OneWag licked his hand. Gogol laughed.

Nico realised he had never heard Gogol laugh before. It was a beautiful sound. He walked over to where the old man had amassed a small pile of fallen leaves. It was too early for the big shedding of trees. 'I have breakfast for us. The usual salami and lard crostini.' Nico waved the bag. Gogol's head stayed bent down, laugh gone. He swept his rake back and forth, raising dust.

'Your gatekeeper said you were waiting for me.'

The rake kept grating against the gravel. OneWag barked, but Gogol didn't stop.

'Do you want me to leave?'

'"The tangle of pathways contain my blindness." I woke up with Ungaretti this morning. Dante will forgive me, I think.'

'Is that why you're raking the path? To see again?'

'Not the woman. As the poet said of himself, I am a man of sorrow. All I need is an illusion to give me courage.'

'What illusion will help you to tell me what you know?'

Gogol dropped the rake, walked to the bench and put his coat back on. Nico and OneWag followed. Once seated, Gogol held out his hand for the bag of crostini.

'I woke up hungry this morning.'

'Good. Take all of them. Lucia told me you haven't eaten much lately, for which she blames me.'

'She's angry because I burnt the omelette and didn't go back for more mushrooms.'

Nico opened the bag, placed a paper napkin on the bench and lined up the four crostini on it. 'Lucia is angry with me because she cares about you.'

Gogol's fingers went from salami to lard and back again, undecided which to take first.

'You usually go for the lard right away.'

Gogol grabbed the salami crostino and bit into it. 'My mother was the one who loved me,' he said with his mouth full. 'She took most of me with her.' He swallowed, then took another bite. 'A little bit of me must be coming back now. I haven't remembered Ungaretti since my school days.'

'A few days ago,' Nico said, 'you told me to stay away from the maresciallo. I think I understand why now. You saw who the woman was. I remember your words. That my heart would claim no peace if I didn't stay away. You wanted me not to get involved with the murder investigation, because you were afraid it would lead to the rape. You said my wife—'

Gogol squeezed Nico's arm, his eyes on his face. 'The illusion I need to give me courage?' He looked down and held out what was left of his crostino for OneWag. 'The impossible illusion that what I saw will not hurt a beautiful woman and her child.'

'Tilde and Stella. Stella a child of the rape.'

'Stella is good and beautiful. She is a child of love, not carnal violence.'

Nico knew there were thousands of beautiful, good children born after their mothers had been raped, but he let Gogol keep this illusion. He was angry with himself for having told Perillo about the rape. Tilde would become a suspect. Maybe even Stella. He knew in his blood that Tilde could not have killed Gerardi, as sure as his heart was beating. But what could he do to protect them?

Gogol had looked up at his pained face and understood. 'Let us both have the courage of silence.'

Perillo's phone rang just as Daniele drove out of the parking space a few doors away from the shuttered jewellery store.

Perillo listened for what Daniele thought was a long time. He couldn't understand the words, but the voice on the other end of the line was female. The maresciallo's wife, maybe. Today was Saturday, market day in Greve. It wasn't the first time she'd given him a list of vegetables to bring home for the night's dinner. Daniele loved going to the market and feasting his eyes on shiny red, orange and yellow peppers in a basket, opened heads of escarole that could be mistaken for enormous flowers, the red sweet onions from Certosa, and deep orange apricots, dark purple plums.

'The station or the market first?' Daniele asked after Perillo hung up.

Perillo slapped his thigh and grinned. 'You can give me my ten euros back. That was Della Langhe's secretary, the wonderful Barbara. Gerardi's computer is now an open book. Any content that might shed light on the case will be sent to the American embassy today. We should receive it by tomorrow. And the good news doesn't end there. Gerardi's lawyer has finally returned. He was off scuba diving in the coral reefs in Australia, and here I was thinking there weren't any left. What's important is, he's getting on a plane to Los Angeles in a couple of hours. He's already instructed his secretary to scan Gerardi's will and relevant papers. We'll get them by email soon.'

'What about the papers in the safe deposit box?' Daniele asked.

'That'll be next, unless the police get to the bank first. By the time the lawyer gets home, the banks will be closed. Whatever's in the safe deposit box will have to wait until Monday. The best part is, Della Langhe will be in Capri for the weekend, which means I get to keep dealing with Barbara.'

Perillo picked up his phone again and pressed Nico's number. 'Our first lady has been found, thanks to Daniele here.'

'The owner of the jewellery store?'

'She was wearing the matching earring. She says she's the one who left him, and I believe her. She chose money over love. She was asleep at the time of the murder, has no alibi, and she was truly horrified when I asked her about the rape. She's not the one.'

'She might be a very good actress.'

'I consider that a very small possibility. There's more.' Perillo relayed the information he'd got from Della Langhe's secretary. 'I'm feeling good. Finally we have information to work with.'

Information that might hurt the people Nico loved. He asked, 'Do you know who the beneficiary is?'

'The lawyer didn't remember, as the will was prepared four years ago, but he thinks Gerardi might have wanted to update it. They had an appointment set for this Monday.'

'I see.'

'You don't sound as excited as I am.'

Nico tried to put more energy behind his voice. 'You're getting closer to a solution, and that's good news.'

'*We* are getting closer. This is a team effort, don't forget that.'

'I haven't.' That was the trouble. How could he be loyal and honest at the same time?

'I'm feeling good, Nico. So should you. Come by the station after the Expo closes for the day. We need to drink to continued health and safe travels for Gerardi's lawyer.'

'I can't,' Nico lied. 'I'm helping Tilde at the restaurant.' He wasn't needed at Sotto Il Fico thanks to Gianni, who'd taken his advice and was helping Stella wait on tables. Nico planned to show up for dinner anyway, but he wasn't going to say anything to Tilde. She had denied the rape. He could only respect her need for privacy. As Gogol had said, part of his wife lived on in Tilde and

296

Stella. His ardent hope was that Gerardi's papers made no mention of them.

'Too bad,' Perillo said. 'I'll call you as soon as something comes in. Ciao, Nico.' Perillo pressed to end the call and turned to Daniele. 'Come on, Dani, let's go grocery shopping and make you and the wife happy. She gave me a long list of vegetables. You're having dinner with us tonight.'

Daniele blushed, with happiness this time.

Before going home, Nico stopped by Luciana's shop and picked a small pot of pink baby roses. Luciana was too busy with three different customers to give him her usual hug, one he would strangely have welcomed today. He paid and made his way up to the cemetery with OneWag at his side. He followed his usual ritual of filling a watering can and watering Rita's old flowerpot, which was still in bloom, and added the roses. He then watered her parents' boxwoods. OneWag dropped down by Rita's tomb, head between his paws. With a faithful dog's instinct for his master's mood, he understood these visits were sad ones.

Nico sat down on the grass beside him and silently spoke to his wife. *Gogol told me you were a good woman. I think he meant because you didn't tell me what happened to Tilde. I would have liked to know the truth because I'm sure you suffered. Maybe I could have helped. I'm not angry or disappointed. Your loyalty was to the women of your family. You were always a good woman, the best. I promise to do my best to protect them.*

Nico leant in and kissed Rita's photo. OneWag licked his hand.

'We've got a full house tonight,' Elvira declared from her chair as Nico walked into the restaurant. 'We could have used your help a little earlier.'

'Sorry, I'm not on duty tonight. It's Gianni's turn.'

Elvira huffed. 'He's useless. Too taken by his good looks, in my opinion. He goes on and on with the clients, trying to show off the very little English and German he knows, and ends up getting their orders wrong. Poor Enzo and Stella are constantly scrambling to set things straight. I won't tell you the mood Tilde is in. I would help, but my sciatica is in full furore.'

Nico kept a straight face. Elvira had been soldered to that armchair since Nico had first seen her years before. She gestured towards the terrace. 'Go out there and help, for God's sake, and get rid of that sad face.'

Nico faked a smile. 'At your service, ma'am.'

Elvira let out a raucous laugh, strongly resembling a donkey braying. 'You've got that right. I'm the general here. Now get going.'

Nico passed the kitchen. 'Ciao, Tilde. I'm in.'

Without looking up, Tilde squeezed a double ring of chocolate sauce over two plates of panna cotta and handed them over. 'Table six, left corner.'

'I know where table six is. I'm not new.'

She looked up, saw who it was. 'Sorry. It's a little hectic tonight.'

'What's Stella doing here? Shouldn't she be studying?'

'You tell her that.'

Nico delivered the panna cotta to table six, where a young couple was too busy gazing at each other to notice the incredible view or the food. Honeymooners, he decided. Gianni passed by him and flashed a smile. 'See, I listened.'

'Bravo.'

Behind Gianni, Stella made an exasperated face.

Nico made the rounds, taking orders. Panzanella, aubergine parmigiana, rigatoni with mushrooms and sausage. As he worked, weaving in between Enzo, Gianni and Stella, his mood lifted. When Nico got a chance to pass by Stella, he whispered, 'I meant well.'

She squeezed his hand.

'Shouldn't you be studying for Monday's exam?' he asked.

'My head needs breathing space. It's turned into Google for art. All you have to do is click, I've got the answer. The photographic memory helps.'

'Good for you.'

The evening cooled and daylight dimmed. Only two tables were still occupied.

'So you were telling the truth,' Perillo announced as he strode out from behind the huge fig tree in jeans, a short-sleeved shirt and his precious suede ankle boots. 'You're working tonight.'

Nico looked up from clearing a table at one end of the restaurant. He waited until Perillo was close to say, 'Why would I have lied?'

'May I steal you away from your duties?'

'Please do,' Stella said as she gave table two their bill. 'He deserves jail time for enlisting Gianni to help me.'

Perillo was stopped short by her deep green eyes. He'd seen and admired them many times, but they now reminded him of something they hadn't before.

'Stella doesn't appreciate excellence,' Gianni said from somewhere behind the tree. 'She'll learn.'

Stella stomped over to where a seemingly exhausted Gianni was leaning against the kitchen wall, sneaking a cigarette.

'What I appreciate is humility and honesty.' She snatched the cigarette out of Gianni's mouth and crushed it underfoot. 'Restaurant staff are not allowed to smoke.'

Nico couldn't see Gianni's expression, but didn't want to stay for the fight that was sure to come. Luckily, Stella knew how to take care of herself, and Tilde was in the kitchen, ready to step in even when she shouldn't.

'Let's go,' Nico said, and walked the dirty dishes to the kitchen. Perillo followed, carrying two water glasses from another table.

Tilde was cleaning the counter with watered-down bleach. 'Thanks for stepping in and helping at the last minute.' Enzo looked up from stacking the dishwasher. 'Ehi, Salvatore, we've missed you. Help yourself to a drink at the bar.'

'Thanks, next time.' Perillo gave Nico's arm a light punch. 'Last minute, eh?'

Nico shrugged. So the lie was out. 'Goodnight. See

you at the Panzano market tomorrow? Nine o'clock.'

Tilde nodded, her ear tuned to the ominous silence coming from the terrace. Nico helped himself to the leftover bag of meat Tilde always reserved for OneWag. He and Perillo passed a sleeping Elvira on the way out.

Perillo stood under the restaurant lamp and lit a cigarette. The rest of the street was dark, windows shuttered for the night. Perillo offered his pack to Nico.

'No, thanks.'

'Where's Rocco?'

Nico shifted weight from one foot to the other. He had the feeling this wasn't a friendly visit. 'I left OneWag home. Why did you come here? You have news?'

'No. I was hoping you had something to tell me.'

Nico stopped himself from speaking. It was impossible to remain loyal to Tilde and be truthful with Perillo.

Noticing how tense Nico was, Perillo put a hand on his shoulder. 'Halfway down the hill, there's a side street that leads to a terrace with benches. A good place to talk, unless couples have got there first.'

The terrace was empty. They sat on the bench closest to the railing. In front of them was a sea of black, dotted with a few distant lights. Crickets made their usual racket.

'You once asked me why I became a carabiniere,' Perillo said in a low, soft voice. 'I gave you an incomplete answer.'

'I don't need to know.' One intimate revelation would demand another.

'I want you to know. You noticed a reaction of mine when you told me about Gogol witnessing a rape. I heard the surprise in your voice, just as I heard the lie when you said you were working at the restaurant tonight. I'm certain you have the same ability. It's a skill that comes with our work, from years of watching reactions, listening to lies.'

'Yes, I've counted on that ability, but I've made a lot of mistakes.'

'Don't we all? I felt like one big mistake as a kid. I had a mother who didn't give a damn and no idea who my father was. So I lived on the streets, grabbing food from rubbish bins, stealing whatever I could get away with. When I was eleven, I got caught with my hand in a woman's handbag by a carabiniere, Maresciallo Francesco Perillo. Instead of dragging me to the station, he took me home to his wife. He cleaned me up, fed me and told me what I made of my life was up to me, that I had choices. "Stay with us for a month, follow our way of life and see if you like it. If not, you're free to leave."'

'That's a pretty easy choice.'

'Yes, if you have at least a shadow of common sense. I ran away after two nights. I missed my street friends, especially this wonderful girl, Ginetta. She was older, thirteen or fourteen, and always looked after me. If she had food or money, she shared it with me. And I did the same with her. I went looking for her and didn't find her. My street pals avoided me. I thought it was because I'd stayed with the maresciallo for two nights.'

'They saw that as a betrayal?'

'That's what I thought, but I kept asking where Ginetta was, and finally Mimmo – he was the oldest of the group – told me the truth. Ginetta had gone looking for me in another part of town. The carabinieri found her hanging from a tree wearing only her bra. She'd been gang raped. Afterwards, she tore her dress into strips to commit suicide.' Perillo leant back on the bench and pressed a hand against his eyes.

Nico had no words.

Perillo slowly took another cigarette from his pack and lit it. 'I was ready to kill. I wanted to find whoever they were, smash their heads in, slash them to pieces. I wandered all over Pozzuoli, asking questions armed with a knife. I got beaten up for it more than once, but finally I remembered the man who took me in. A week later, I was at his door. If anyone was going to find Ginetta's rapists, it was his people. He took me back in and promised the carabinieri would look for them.'

'Were they ever found?'

Perillo shook his head and took a long drag of his cigarette. 'Ginetta, Francesco and his wife, Bice, made me a carabiniere. I still miss all three of them.'

'Francesco and his wife died?'

'Yes, nine years later. One after the other in a matter of weeks. Cancer.'

Nico eyed Perillo's cigarette pack. Perillo handed it over. Nico took a cigarette and lit it. 'Thanks.' They leant back on the bench and listened to the crickets for a few moments.

'As you know, I was kicked out of the police force,' Nico said.

'The reason for that is yours to keep.'

'One confession merits another. Rita was dying when I did what I did. My captain found out from my partner and offered me a deal. Instead of publicly denouncing me, which could have got me a two-year jail stint and given his leadership a bad name, he officially kicked me out of the force for some trumped-up infraction.'

'And the deal?'

'Keep my mouth shut.'

'Fair enough. Any regrets?'

'I miss some of the men I worked with. I miss not helping to find justice, but what I did was right, so no, no regrets.'

'I'm glad,' Perillo said. 'And now, to our problem at hand. I've been trying to understand the reason for the date on the charm bracelet. Could it have to do with the rape Gogol witnessed? I thought it was perhaps a birthday instead, but Daniele's checked the birth records of Gravigna and nearby towns. Gravigna, zero births. In nearby towns, seven boys. I doubt the bracelet's for them. Have you spoken to Gogol again?'

'I have.'

'Did he tell you when he witnessed the assault?'

'I didn't ask. I should have, but I didn't want to upset him again. I'm sorry.'

'Please talk to him if you can – the information he has is very likely what we need to solve this case. I should be the one to ask, but I'm not his friend. I'd get Dante for an answer, and I don't believe *The Divine Comedy* talks of dates.' Perillo noticed Nico had withdrawn, become a reluctant investigative partner, and after seeing Stella tonight, Perillo thought he knew why. 'Gogol knows who the woman is, then.'

'If he does, he didn't tell me.'

'No, he wouldn't.'

Nico said nothing.

'I understand,' Perillo said. Family came first. 'You're under no obligation to tell me anything.' And maybe he was wrong. Stella's green eyes weren't necessarily proof. Perillo put out his cigarette and stood up. 'Goodnight, Nico. Tomorrow or Monday, we'll know more. I'll call you as soon as that information comes in.'

Nico looked up. It was too dark for Perillo to see if there was surprise on his face. 'We're still in this together, yes?' Perillo asked.

Nico slowly nodded, a gesture Perillo guessed at rather than saw.

Late Sunday night in Greve in Chianti, the madhouse of the Chianti Classico Expo was over for another year. How many tickets and wine had been sold would be tallied Monday and bragged about Friday in the regional paper. The sixty-one exhibitors were gone, their stands dismantled. The carabinieri had gone home as well. A tired sanitation crew was busy putting Piazza Matteotti back to its pristine condition. Under one of the arches, Maria Dorsetti sat at a cafe table. The cafe was closed, but she had convinced Yunas to leave one table out for her. On the spur of the moment, she had splurged on a bottle of Fontalloro. At home, she would have been alone. Here she watched the crew working and the people sauntering home. The wine was an extravagance, but money was coming her way. Robi had no one but her. She knew he hadn't married. He'd told her as much in one of his emails after she'd asked. She deserved this money. She deserved this superb wine. It was her time to get.

At the farmhouse, Nico roasted the red, yellow and orange peppers he'd bought that morning at the Panzano market. He was discovering that cooking absorbed him and pushed any other thoughts, pleasant or not, away. He wanted to offer Tilde a new recipe. It was time-consuming but worth it, he hoped.

Once the skins had blackened, Nico removed the peppers from the oven and sealed them in a sturdy paper bag to let them steam. It made it easier to remove the skin. Once cleaned of skin and seeds, each half was laid out on a cutting board and joined by some crumbled sausage meat and onion Nico had sautéed earlier. He carefully attempted to roll the pepper half around the meat, but the filling kept falling out or the pepper tearing. Another fiasco. Nico washed his hands, poured himself half a glass of wine and went out to sit on the terrace. OneWag followed.

Nico lifted the dog onto his lap. He needed to think how he could protect Tilde and Stella once Perillo figured it out. It was clear he was already suspicious. All he could do was stand by them and beg the maresciallo to be discreet.

At eleven o'clock that Sunday night, Daniele and Perillo were still in the maresciallo's office. To pass the time, Perillo was teaching Daniele how to play Scopa, a card game Neapolitans loved. Emptied dishes sat piled on the maresciallo's desk. His wife had sent down dinner, a dish called 'stingy spaghetti' because it had no meat, just garlic, oil, pecorino, potatoes and string beans. Perillo was too anxious for news to care what he ate, but Daniele happily cleaned his plate. He was now beginning to figure out how to use the strange-looking cards when Perillo's phone rang. The maresciallo rushed to answer, scattering his cards on the floor.

Barbara from Della Langhe's office in Florence was on the phone. Gerardi's lawyer hadn't sent anything yet, and she was going home. 'I'm sorry, Salvatore, but you have to remember that California is nine hours behind Italian time. The chances of anything coming through tonight are very slim. Unfortunately, tomorrow Della Langhe will be back, and I'll have to show whatever information comes in to him first. I can't sneak anything to you.'

A tired and frustrated Perillo let out a string of obscenities.

'Salvatore, please understand, it's too big a risk,' Barbara protested. 'That man is waiting for the chance to get rid of me and replace me with some young busty blonde.' Barbara was fifty-two and liked to boast an airplane could land on her chest.

'Forgive me, Barbara. Of course I understand. Thank you for giving up your Sunday.'

'Glad to. Gave me a chance to read a good book in holy peace. Let's keep our fingers crossed the information comes in overnight. The boss never gets to the office before ten. I'll get in at eight, and if anything has come through during the night, I'll send it over directly.'

'Good idea, thanks.'

'Goodnight, Salvatore. Golden dreams. Give a kiss to Dani.'

'You too. Goodnight.' Perillo put the receiver down and stood up.

Daniele handed him the cards he'd picked up from the floor. 'Tomorrow's the day, then.' He was unable to hide the relief in his voice. They could quit waiting. He was having a hard time keeping his eyes open, and he had never liked playing cards. He always lost.

'Tomorrow, the next day, who the hell knows.' Perillo threw the collected cards on his desk. 'Our beds are calling. Check your machine by eight tomorrow morning, in case Barbara has sent something. By the way, she sends you a kiss.'

Daniele's eyebrows swept up. 'Why? She doesn't know me.'

'She thinks you have a sexy voice.'

Daniele's cheeks responded for him.

'Goodnight, Dani.'

In a dream that night, it was Rosalba who thought Daniele's voice was sexy. Even in sleep, he blushed.

CHAPTER SIXTEEN

At eight-fifteen Monday morning, chewing on a ciambella filled with strawberry jam, Daniele turned on his computer. He was able to take two more bites before the desktop came on. Jam dribbled on his chin as he clicked on Barbara's email. 'Good morning,' followed by two emojis – a thumbs-up and a kiss. She had included an email from the lawyer with an attachment labelled 'The Last Will and Testament of Robert Garrett.'

Daniele's stomach did a flip as he knuckled the jam off his chin, put what was left of the ciambella aside and sat down. The lawyer's email had come in on Monday, 5.15 a.m. Italian time. In his email, the lawyer explained that the banks were closed Sundays, and so he was unable to access the safe deposit box. He planned to go to the bank on Monday afternoon after taking care of some urgent matters regarding other clients. He left his phone number in case there were any questions.

After taking a deep breath, Daniele clicked download and called the maresciallo.

At Bar All'Angolo, Nico was having his usual breakfast with one eye on the door, hoping to see Gogol shuffle in with his overcoat and overpowering cologne. Instead, Nelli walked in, bringing with her the smell of oil paints and Marseille soap. Not an unpleasant combination, thought Nico as he pulled out a chair for her. He was glad to see her, and Gogol would be too, were he to come by.

'Sorry, I've been working,' Nelli said as OneWag jumped onto her lap. An orange streak adorned her cheek. Multicoloured dabs covered her T-shirt. She wore no make up. 'I have a small show at the art centre next week. I hope you'll come?'

'I'll be glad to, though I don't know much about painting.'

'In my case, that's good. I did a small portrait of this little guy – it didn't come out too badly. I see he's wearing his collar today.'

'He took to it right away but not the lead. Whenever I attach it, he lies down and refuses to budge.'

'He wants to maintain the freedom of being a stray.' Nelli's wide eyes, a light, transparent brown flecked with black, rested on Nico's face for a moment. 'You look a little glum. I hope it's not because of Gogol. You have to give him time. He knows you're a friend.'

How to answer. He couldn't tell her what made him sad. He took a bite of his cornetto, chewed slowly and swallowed. An idea came to him. 'I failed at cooking a dish. More than one, in fact. My last attempt was roasted peppers rollatini stuffed with sausage and onions.'

'Sounds delicious.'

'It sounded delicious to me too. I wanted to surprise Tilde and offer it to the restaurant. It's labour-intensive but relaxing. I was so sure it would work out, which shows how arrogant I am.'

'Mix everything together and add some Parmigiano Reggiano, and you've got a wonderful sauce for any pasta.'

Nico smiled at Nelli. 'Fantastic. Why didn't I think of that?'

'Because you were so focused on one thing, you didn't consider the other possibilities. It's a male weakness, I think.'

'Not this male.' Perillo suddenly appeared behind Nelli. He was dressed in a freshly pressed plaid shirt, pressed jeans and his usual suede boots. 'A one-track mind wouldn't get me far in my job. Good morning to the two of you.'

'Ciao, Salvatore,' Nelli said. 'You look sleepy.' She looked at both the men and sensed she was now a third wheel. She put the dog down and started to stand. Perillo stopped her with a hand on her shoulder.

'No need to leave. I just need Nico to translate something into English for me. I'll bring him back.'

Nelli got up anyway. 'I have work to do.' She resented Salvatore's assumption that she wanted Nico to come back, even if it was true.

As Nico went to pay for his breakfast, Perillo said, 'I have a question for you, Nelli. Nico told me what Gogol asked you.' He didn't want to utter the word 'rape' in front of a woman. 'It makes me think Gogol really did witness the violence.'

Nelli gripped his arm. 'You have to believe him. He doesn't invent things.'

'Did he tell you when it happened?'

She let go of his arm. 'Nothing specific that I remember. He asked me about it maybe three weeks or a month before Robi left.'

'Thank you.'

Nico came back. 'Ciao, Nelli. Thanks for the cooking tip. I'll try to keep my mind open to all the possibilities.'

'I'm counting on it,' Perillo said as Nelli watched them walk out. She realised that she was counting on it too.

'You have news?' Nico asked, feeling his stomach clench.

Perillo nodded and kept walking until the two men and the dog reached the terrace where they had spoken last night. Luckily, it was still empty.

They sat on the same bench, which in daylight offered a view of the rooftops of the newer part of town. Beyond them, a distant patchwork of vineyards, each one going in a different direction. OneWag scouted the area for interesting titbits, found none and wandered off.

'The lawyer scanned the will over,' Perillo said. 'We got it this morning. The sister inherits seven hundred and fifty thousand dollars, which sounds like a good motive to me. Gerardi's manager and three employees get the winery and vineyards and three million dollars to run it. They all knew Gerardi was dying, which removes any reason to have him killed.'

Greed wasn't the only reason people killed, but Nico wasn't going to point that out. 'Didn't Maria Dorsetti know he was dying?'

'Not according to her statement. She said she hadn't been in contact with her brother in four years, since her husband died.'

'You only have her word for that.'

'That's true. There are generous bequests to the gardener, the housekeeper, other employees. Our victim was a very generous man. Even Aldo gets something. I guess it's penance money for the wine Gerardi siphoned off and the loan.'

'How much?'

'Ten thousand dollars. Not enough to kill for.'

'Thank God. I like my landlord.'

'There's more. Remember the piece of land next to Aldo's property? Where Gerardi got killed?'

'The one Aldo had tested for planting vines?'

'Yes, where the ground was decreed too loamy for wine making. Gerardi bought it eighteen months ago. Maybe Daniele was right to suggest the people who tested the ground were paid to declare the land wasn't wine-friendly.'

'If so, that puts Aldo back on the suspect list.'

'Daniele is getting another tester to check the ground.'

Nico stood up and walked the perimeter of the terrace.

'Need to stretch my legs. I ran too far this morning.' What might come next was getting to him. There was nothing wrong with his knees. 'So,' he said, on his second round. 'Who gets the land?'

'The will predates Gerardi acquiring the land. The lawyer added the information because he thought it might be connected to the murder.'

One down, Nico thought. How many more to go? He sat back on the bench, willing his stomach to relax. 'Anyone else get anything?'

'Oh, yes. Five million dollars' worth. Five million dollars that corroborate Gogol's story.'

Stomach clenching, Nico reached for one of Perillo's cigarettes. 'How so?'

Perillo flipped opened his Zippo and offered a light. 'The money goes to three different organisations that deal with rape and domestic violence. To me, that says Gerardi was making amends. Maybe his success changed him, or the cancer, but the will shows he regretted what he'd done.' He was still holding up his Zippo. 'Do you want to light that cigarette?'

'No.' Nico removed the cigarette from his mouth and looked at it. The wet filter showed teeth marks. 'Sorry. I took it without even asking.'

'Friends don't have to ask, and there's more where that came from.'

'Anything from Gerardi's computer yet?' There was a good chance he had written to his victim. Maybe even asking forgiveness.

'No, it should have come in yesterday. Somebody's sleeping on the job. I asked Barbara to give the embassy a nudge. Actually, I said a kick in the ass, but that's not very diplomatic.' A clickety-click sound made Perillo turn around. OneWag's long nails tapped the tiles of the terrace floor. He stopped at Nico's feet and looked up.

'Good timing, Rocco,' Perillo said. 'We're done.'

The dog jumped up onto his owner's lap. His breath smelt of mortadella. Nico started kneading his ear and felt his own body ease. The only Italian woman in the will, then, was Maria Dorsetti.

Perillo stood up. 'I'll call you when more news comes in. Ciao.'

Nico smiled for the first time that day. 'Thanks for letting me know.'

'We're still partners.' Perillo gave OneWag a scratch on his back and walked away.

Nico stayed seated and let his mind turn to Stella. Her exam was in the afternoon. He called her. 'When are you leaving?'

'At eleven-thirty. I don't have to be there until three.'

He looked at his watch. It was just past nine. 'Can I see you before you go?' There was something he wanted to give her.

'Sure. Gianni and I are having an early lunch. We'll be there in an hour or so. Come by and wish me luck.'

Good. That gave him some time to go home and work on Nelli's suggestion.

* * *

When Nico came back to Sotto Il Fico, Elvira was napping and Enzo was in the kitchen with Tilde, checking what to write on the day's menu. Nico uncovered the large bowl of sauce he was carrying. 'Add this too?'

Tilde looked down at the jumble of peppers, onions, sausage meat and Parmigiano Reggiano. She slowly inhaled its perfume. 'Good with rigatoni. Thanks. Write it in, Enzo. I've already got the water boiling for Stella. She gets the first portion.'

'I added some dried hot pepper.'

'Bravo. A little heat activates the brain. She'll need it today.'

Nico looked out the kitchen window. The terrace was set up for lunch, but no diners yet. 'Is she here?'

'At the corner table, her favourite. Where I can't see her from here. Gianni's with her.'

He had hoped to catch her alone. 'I want to give her my old rabbit's foot for luck, but not in front of Gianni.' He'd only make fun of it. 'Where's her purse?'

'That's nice. Thank you.' She was also going to slip something inside Stella's bag. 'Her bag's hanging behind the kitchen door.'

The only thing hanging on the peg was a worn black backpack. Nico stuck his head back into the kitchen.

'A backpack?'

'Her bag's in there.'

Nico unzipped it and dropped the small package into Stella's handbag.

'Do you think you can stay?' Tilde asked from the

kitchen. 'With Stella gone, I could use your help.'

'Of course.' He welcomed the idea. It would keep his mind off worrying. He went out on the terrace and kissed Stella's cheeks. 'In the mouth of the wolf, my dear.'

'Shit' was her answer. It was the obligatory one, but Nico still didn't understand what one had to do with the other.

While Nico was wishing Stella good luck, Tilde dug into her apron pocket and fished out the rosary she had bought after she gave birth. Stella had given her back her belief in God. He would watch over her baby. She went behind the kitchen door and pushed the rosary deep into the backpack, where her atheist daughter wouldn't find it and have a fit.

Gerardi's emails started coming in while Daniele sat in front of his computer, eating his share of the casserole Perillo's wife had prepared: fettuccine with courgette and string beans, coated with a tomato and béchamel sauce. As his loaded fork made its way to his mouth, Daniele read the first one. His fork crashed on the plate. They had their murderer.

Perillo picked up his phone from the kitchen table. Across from him, Signora Perillo crossed her arms on her chest and gave her husband a don't-you-dare look.

'Are they in English?' Perillo asked with a full mouth.

'Italian. I'll read the first one. It's dated the twenty-ninth of August. It must be the last one he wrote.'

'Go on.'

Daniele cleared his throat. '*Ciao, Maria. I have not written often and you know why. Your incessant requests for money were not met for a reason, which you very well know. You and your husband turned your back on me twenty-two years ago when I needed it most. I left Italy for various reasons, you being one of them. However, that's in the past. Now it's time to make amends. I have cancer and do not expect to live very long. You will receive money when I die. How substantial that amount is will depend on how my trip back home goes. I'll text you once I'm there. I do not have your telephone number. Robi.*'

'Get hold of Maria Dorsetti now.'

'I'm scheduled to take over for Vince at the front office in fifteen minutes.'

'He'll have to wait.'

'I'll bring him a sandwich.'

'Better make it two.' Perillo clicked off and plunged his fork into the fettuccine. He had plenty of time to finish lunch, maybe even a coffee at the bar.

Seeing her husband eat with such gusto, Signora Perillo unfolded her arms and went back to eating.

Elvira sat in her armchair folding napkins, looking extremely annoyed. 'If you're going to cook for a restaurant, you have to make more,' she said as Nico walked by to receive a well-earned espresso from Enzo. At three-thirty, the few diners still on the terrace were having their coffees. Nico was eager to gather OneWag from wherever he'd wandered and go home.

'The amount you brought was ridiculous,' Elvira complained. 'What was it? Eight portions? They were gone in the blink of an eye.'

'It was my first attempt at this sauce.' Nico wasn't about to mention that it was the result of a failure. He'd never hear the end of it. 'I wasn't going to make a huge batch and then have Tilde reject it.'

Elvira straightened her neck as far as it would go. 'I do think I should be able to give my approval or disapproval of the food that is served in *my* restaurant.'

Enzo handed Nico his coffee. 'Mamma, you should thank Nico. He wasn't even supposed to work today.'

'He's helping Tilde and getting some very strange ideas in his head.'

Nico laughed and sat on the barstool to drink his three sips of espresso. 'I'm not trying to take over the restaurant.'

'Not while I'm alive.' Elvira put the napkins on the side table and slowly stood. 'It's time for my nap.'

Enzo rushed out from behind the bar. 'I'll bring the car around.'

'No, I need a walk, and as punishment for not allowing me to taste what several guests told me was a delicious pasta dish, Nico will accompany me home.'

Enzo looked at his mother with disbelief. 'Mamma, you asked them if it was good?'

'Of course. Don't look so aghast. How else was I going to know what it tasted like?'

Nico walked to her and offered her his arm. They made

their way slowly to the door. 'They would never tell you if it was bad. You're the owner.'

'I'm perfectly aware of that. I asked them what dish was their favourite.' She turned to her son. 'Don't pick me up tonight. I feel a cold coming on.'

Enzo shook his head. His mother felt a cold coming on every Sunday. 'Rest up and drink lots of liquids.' Her favourite TV programme would be on.

Elvira lived a short walk away, in a ground-floor flat behind the church. Nico followed her past a narrow kitchen into a living room overstuffed with dark furniture. The only bright spots came from the white crocheted doilies on the armchair and sofa and two narrow windows that overlooked a large courtyard lined with blue hydrangeas.

'That's part of the castle,' she said when Nico walked to the window to look out. 'I like to say I live between God and royalty, although the royals are long gone and God with them.' She settled herself in the worn velvet armchair. 'Sit.' She indicated a spindly-legged settee opposite her. Nico doubted it would hold his weight and chose the sofa. As soon as he sat down, his rear end was welcomed by a sharp spring. He winced.

Elvira nodded with satisfaction. 'Men always think they know better. It's an old home. My husband grew up here. When his parents died, my husband was only too happy to come back to what he considered his real home.'

'Did you mind?'

'I did, but said nothing. Men were obeyed in my youth. I've made up for it since. I'd offer you coffee, a must when you enter an Italian home, but you've already had yours at the restaurant. I've brought you here to set you straight.'

'About what?' He had no idea where this was going.

'You're wrong about Stella.'

'What do you mean?'

'Stella was born early and, like all newborns, her eyes were blue. The village tongues started flapping. A small town breeds gossip. Enzo getting Tilde pregnant before marriage wasn't shocking, so the tongues decided Enzo was forced to marry Tilde. My daughter-in-law has always been a strong, outspoken woman, which many women don't like, and which is the very reason I like her.'

Nico tried to keep a straight face, but she saw through it. 'I know. I'm not always nice to her. Showing affection was not something I was taught. I do care for her. It's that sometimes I want to roll back time, have my husband and my son still with me. I shouldn't complain. I have a sweet, loving son with a backbone that Tilde holds up nicely. That was my job once.' She looked down at her lap, smoothed her blue housedress over her knees.

Nico moved to another part of the sofa. He sank. No springs at all.

Elvira looked up. 'Where was I?'

'Tongues flapping.'

She sucked in her lips, took a deep breath, exhaled. What she was about to say clearly pained her. 'When

Stella was six or seven months old, her blue eyes became the beautiful green you see now. The minute those eyes went public, the flapping tongues retreated behind closed doors. Walking on the street with the baby, we got silence. It meant their thoughts had turned uglier. To them, it was clear that Tilde was Robi's mystery woman and Stella was his child.'

Nico wanted to point out that Elvira herself had implied that Tilde was that woman just the other day. Instead, he said, 'The maresciallo has been asking about this woman. No one pointed to Tilde or to anyone else.'

'Because green eyes are proof of nothing, and they know it. Besides, the women in this town don't betray each other.' Elvira looked at Nico with reproach in her eyes. 'You also think Stella is Robi's child.'

'What makes you think that?'

'You've been asking Tilde questions, and she's upset. She's good at keeping a tight grip on her feelings, but I've known her a long time. She's kept her jaw clenched since you spoke to her on the church steps.' She unclasped her pocketbook next to her, fished out a small iron key and waved it at a heavy dark bureau wedged between the two windows. 'Please unlock the second drawer and bring me the photo album.'

Nico did as he was asked. There was a knot of expectation in his stomach. He gave Elvira the album and went back to the sunken spot on the sofa.

Elvira carefully wiped the embossed leather cover with her handkerchief and placed the album on her lap. 'I will show you why you and those tongues are wrong.' She slowly leafed through the crumbling pages. Each page was covered in small black and white photos with wavy white edges. As she leafed through, many photos fell out of their corner holders. Elvira let out a loud satisfied breath. 'Here she is.' She held out the album. 'Be careful, or we'll have photos all over the floor.'

Nico carefully took the album and put it on his own lap.

'On the right-side page.' The pitch of Elvira's voice rose. 'Can you spot her? She has green eyes and is the very image of Stella.'

Nico saw several close-ups of a beautiful smiling girl with big clear eyes. They may have been green or blue, though the photo was in black and white.

'She was christened Anna, but when the colour of her eyes turned jade, they started calling her Giada. She was Enzo's paternal grandmother, Stella's great-grandmother. I met her, and her eyes were as green as Stella's. I am witness to that.' There was great conviction in Elvira's voice. 'You see, Nico? Stella's green eyes have nothing to do with Robi.'

'Yes, I do.' He only hoped it was true.

Maria Dorsetti settled herself in the hard wooden chair, smoothed out the wrinkles of her beige linen skirt and looked up at Perillo with a smile on her face. She was nervous and trying hard not to show it. 'I agree,' she said in answer to the maresciallo's accusation. 'The statement I signed the other day was incorrect. I knew Robi was coming, but what was the point of telling you? He died before he could get in touch with me.'

'I have only your word for that, which isn't worth much now.' Perillo ruffled the papers on his desk, looking for copies of the emails Maria Dorsetti had sent her brother. One was particularly interesting. He looked back up at Maria. Her smile was still there.

'In his last email, your brother makes it clear that the size of your inheritance depends on his trip here. Do you have any idea why?'

She shrugged. 'A while back, he mentioned that he was buying some property here. Maybe he needed to pay for it, which meant less for me. How much do I inherit, by the way?'

Perillo ignored her question. 'Gerardi had an appointment with his lawyer today. The lawyer believes he wanted to change his will, which is something he implies in his last email to you. His being killed before going home lets the old will stand. That benefits you directly.'

Visible fear gripped her face. 'You think I killed him.'

'Did you?'

'No.' Her chin started trembling.

'I have one more question.' With the palm of his hand Perillo spread out the emails, found the one he wanted and slipped it across the desk. 'The email you're looking at, dated in August of last year, seems to be in answer to some questions your brother asked you.'

She held the copy in front of her face and squinted. She was too upset to reach in her handbag and take out her glasses. 'Yes, I sent that.'

'You tell him Tilde and Enzo are still married, that Stella has grown into a real Tuscan beauty. You add that her green eyes are the envy of all the girls in Gravigna.'

'I was answering his questions.'

'Why did you think he asked them?'

'It's obvious. He was still in love with Tilde. You obviously haven't figured it out yet, have you?' A flash of smugness crossed her face. 'She was his mystery lady, and her daughter is the result.' She smirked.

'When I asked you at our first meeting if you knew who his mystery lady was, you said you didn't.'

'Of course I said that. Women honour each other's secrets.'

As long as it's convenient, Perillo thought. 'You've made two false statements, which is a violation of the penal code. You will be tried. Go home, call your lawyer and don't even contemplate leaving the area.' He was glad to be rid of her for now, but he would need to search her home and the villa she took care of. She had raised a few questions that needed answering. He sat back, satisfied not only by his wife's delicious fettuccine casserole but by the conviction that he was so near to the end of the case.

CHAPTER SEVENTEEN

The sky was fading to a grey-blue, and the birds had started their evening racket. OneWag was stretched out on the grass next to the rudimentary fence Nico had put up around his vegetable garden. Perillo stood behind the chicken wire, held up by dried branches of varying lengths as he watched Nico weed his courgette patch. He had just finished telling him about the emails and the Maria Dorsetti interrogation.

'She's the one, then.'

'Everything points to her. Tomorrow I should have the warrant to search her home and the villa she works at. I can search for arms and drugs on my own, but I want to get into her laptop and phone, and that requires Della Langhe's approval.' He took hold of one of the branches and shook it gently. The chicken wire danced with the movement. 'You need to get yourself a real fence. Any rabbit can break right through here.'

'I'll get to it this winter. I was in too much of a hurry to start planting. It's been a dream of mine. For now, let the rabbits in. Look at this.' He held up a courgette the size of a pineapple.

'Good for soup.'

'You think?'

'With lots of leeks, shallots, carrots, celery. No tomato paste.'

'Do all Italian men cook?'

'In my household, the wife reigns in the kitchen. Sometimes after work, I read the newspaper in the kitchen and watch her with one eye. When she goes back to Pozzuoli to visit her mother, I put what I've observed to some use.' Perillo shook his head. 'Doesn't compare.'

Nico stood up and brushed the dirt from his pants. 'I know what you mean.' He looked around the small garden, at what had once been, before the murder, a neat garden with neat rows of plants. Bamboo sticks held up the coiling branches of string beans. Some of the string beans were as thick as thumbs. In another row, bamboo sticks kept tomato plants erect. A few small tomatoes peeked out from their leaves. The lettuce was overgrown. Something was eating the aubergine leaves. At the four corners, he had planted climbing red roses. The roses were now gone, and the leaves of one plant had started shrivelling. 'I've been neglecting this place.'

'But you've been helping me.'

'Have I?' Nico walked out of the garden with two

courgettes and tied a string to lock the gate. 'I don't think I've been helpful to you. I should have told you from the start I was never a very good homicide detective. I'm not sure why you wanted me involved.'

'I've had to deal with only one murder, easily and quickly solved. You, how many?'

'I didn't count.'

'There's your answer. Are you on waiter duty tonight?'

'No, Alba and Enzo are taking over.'

'My wife has abandoned me tonight. She's playing bingo at the church.' Perillo lifted his arm to show Nico a wine bottle. 'What do you think?'

Nico looked up. 'Not a bad idea.' Certainly better than drinking alone. 'I'll throw in a courgette frittata and another bottle of whisky.'

All through the afternoon, Tilde worked mechanically, her head and heart focused on what she had inadvertently found in Stella's bag. She kept her phone by her side, looking at it every five minutes, hoping, praying Stella would get in touch. She forced herself not to be the one who called. She wouldn't be able to hold back. *Come home, Stella, call, Stella, come home* became a refrain swirling in her head for hours.

At 8.10 p.m., as Tilde was dishing out the last of the ribollita, her phone rang. 'Hi, Mamma, I just got out. I think I did all right.'

Tilde held her breath. Not now. 'Good,' she managed to say.

'It wasn't half as hard as I expected. Really. Of course, I won't know for a few months, but I think I did really well.'

Tilde was silent.

'Mamma, are you there?'

A quick intake of breath, and Tilde was back in the moment. 'Yes, of course. I was so nervous for you. I'm glad it went well. When are you coming home?'

'Tomorrow morning. The last bus is at ten, and we want to celebrate my getting through this. Here comes Gianni. Bye, Mamma. Keep your fingers crossed for me!'

'Of course. See you in the morning.' Tilde would need far more than crossed fingers to help her daughter.

Nico and Perillo were out on the balcony. The swallows had returned and settled in for the night. The frittata was eaten, the Panzanello Riserva bottle empty. They'd moved on to whisky and were watching the sunset when 'O Sole Mio' rang out from Perillo's phone.

'The lawyer got to Gerardi's safe deposit box,' Daniele said. 'He found a revised handwritten will, which he's scanned and sent over.'

'Hold it.' Perillo reached for a cigarette, lit it. 'Go on.' He was a little fuzzy right now. Smoking helped him concentrate. 'How is it different?'

Daniele told him.

Perillo clicked off and met Nico's anxious eyes. 'Gerardi wrote out a new will.' Nico wasn't going to like it.

'What's it say?'

330

'That green eyes don't lie.'

Nico closed his eyes and emptied his glass.

Daniele was sitting in front of the computer in the maresciallo's office when Perillo came back from dinner with Nico.

'What are you still doing here? Frying your brains on that computer?'

Daniele turned off the screen before anyone saw it and managed not to blush. 'The printout is on your desk. It's incredible that he had nothing to do with her for twenty-two years and then he gets sick and leaves not only the land, but enough money to build a palace on it, if she wants. If we can prove Signora Dorsetti knew about this will, she's finished.'

Perillo glanced over the handwritten sheet. The letters wavered. Nico's frittata was good, but too light a dish to absorb the drinking they'd done. 'I'm off to sleep. Get to bed, Dani. We're going to need sharp brains tomorrow.'

Daniele reluctantly turned the screen back on, put the computer to sleep and promised himself he'd wake up very early to pursue the idea that had popped into his head that morning.

Stella was in the kitchen in her bathrobe, dipping a slice of pandolce in her caffelatte when her mother walked in.

Tilde's heart jumped. 'Oh, good morning.' She thought she'd have more time before facing Stella.

'Ciao.' There was no enthusiasm in Stella's voice.

'I didn't expect you this early. When did you get in?'

'I took the ten o'clock bus last night. You were still at the restaurant, so I just went up to my room to sleep.'

'What happened to your celebration with Gianni?'

'I realised that the exam had drained all the energy out of me. I just wanted my bed.' She wasn't about to tell her mother that Gianni had been horrible to her.

Stella's eyes were glued to her coffee cup, Tilde noticed. Why wouldn't her daughter look at her? What was she hiding? *I took the ten o'clock bus*, she'd said. *I*, not *we*. Another fight with Gianni? Far better that possibility than . . .

Tilde interrupted her own ugly thought by pouring what was left of the coffee into a cup.

Stella stole a glance at her mother. Stone face, rigid shoulders. 'I found the rosary. That was sweet, Mamma.' She didn't believe there was a God looking after anyone, but on the bus home, she'd been surprised at how fingering the beads comforted her. 'Can I keep it?'

Tilde kept the surprise off her face. 'Of course. It's yours.'

Stella told herself to keep talking. 'Did Nico show you what he gave me? A rabbit's foot key chain.' Stella got up and went to the counter to cut herself another slice of pandolce. 'I know he meant well, but I found it a little creepy. Please don't tell him.'

Tilde drank the tepid coffee in one gulp. 'Sit down, Stella.'

Stella raised her eyebrows at her mother's harsh tone. 'That's what I was planning to do, Mamma. Sit and eat my second slice of cake and wait for you to ask me all about the exam.' She walked back to the table, sat, placed the slice directly on the table and waited. A lecture was coming. About Gianni still being in her life, not that he would be any more. But Mamma didn't know that. Or maybe it was about not telling her she'd be home last night, or not coming home right after the exam to share her excitement with the people who really loved her, or not putting the slice of cake on a plate. Or who knew what else it could be? She loved her mother so much, but recently, ever since that man had been killed out in the woods, she sometimes found it hard to breathe near her.

Once Stella was seated, Tilde reached into her pocket, took out a handkerchief and slowly unfolded it.

'Where did you get this?'

Stella gasped and tried to grab it back.

'Don't touch it!' Tilde yelled.

'It's not yours.'

'What was it doing in your backpack?'

For several minutes, mother stared at daughter, and daughter stared at the object in mother's hand. Then Stella told her.

Shortly before eleven, Nico was watering the vegetable garden before going to the restaurant. Gogol hadn't shown up for breakfast again. Neither had Nelli. He missed them both.

OneWag waited by the open gate until Nico's back was turned to sneak into the garden, which had become forbidden territory ever since he was caught scratching at the dirt under one of the roses. He planned to scratch some more dirt, even make a hole.

Nico's phone rang. He turned to reach his back pocket and out of the corner of his eye caught OneWag pushing himself forward on his stomach. 'Out you go,' he said, and turned the hose on him for a few seconds. A wet OneWag quickly rolled over and offered his dirt-covered belly as a peace offering. The phone kept ringing.

'Forget it!' Nico freed his phone from his pocket. 'Out!'

OneWag rolled back over, got on his feet, shook himself violently and, with tail held high, trotted out as if that had been his intention all along.

Nico pressed the green button and put the phone to his ear. 'Hi, Tilde. How did Stella do yesterday?' He'd called last night to ask, but Tilde hadn't answered.

'I need you to meet me at the carabinieri station in Greve in half an hour.'

'What happened? Is Stella okay?'

'I'm not going to explain over the phone. Be there, please.'

'Of course.'

'Half an hour.' The line went dead.

Nico called Perillo and told him about Tilde's request. 'What's going on? Did she find out about the second will?'

'There's no way she could have. I'm in the dark too – she called the station right after we got back from searching Maria Dorsetti's home and the Boldini villa. Tilde called and said she had something important to show me. Her tone could have melted Antarctica. Whatever it is, we'll find out soon enough. I came down hard on the sister, but she insists she's innocent. Claims she would've been happy even if Gerardi had left her only a thousand dollars. That all that matters to her is that her brother remembered her. We found no traces of a shotgun, and Daniele's checking her computer now. Maybe Tilde will surprise us and confess.'

'That's not funny.'

'I'm sorry, Nico. It's possible that she killed him. She had a motive and a gun—'

Nico said, 'No,' and clicked off. It was not a possibility.

Nico was already there when Tilde marched into the maresciallo's office, followed by an angry-looking Stella. Two empty chairs were waiting for them in front of Perillo's desk. Nico sat to one side. Daniele stood by his computer, ready to sit and start transcribing if needed. As soon as Stella sat, one of her legs started jittering rapidly. Tilde remained standing and opened her handbag. She took out tweezers and carefully clasped a hundred-dollar bill, which she dropped on Perillo's desk.

Both Nico and Perillo peered at it. The bill was strangely smooth, even though it was clearly old. In one corner was a series of brown smudges.

Tilde hovered over the desk. 'That money has been washed and ironed, but you can still see the bloodstains.'

'Thank you, Tilde.' Perillo could observe that for himself. He wasn't sure about the smudges being bloodstains. 'Now, please sit. Let's have this conversation without me craning my neck, shall we?' The two aspirins this morning hadn't helped much. He'd just taken another two.

Tilde sat down and reached over to clasp Stella's hand. Stella's other hand became a fist pressed against her lips. Nico could see she was fighting tears. His own body was stiff with dread. Gerardi's pockets had been emptied of money, and here was a hundred-dollar bill with what looked like dried blood on it. And Stella . . . he wanted to hug her, to tell her it would be all right. But he couldn't bear to look at her.

'Where did you get this?' Perillo addressed the question to Tilde, although Stella's clenched jaw told him she had the answer. There was no need to rush things – the truth liked to take its time.

Tilde explained that Stella had gone to Florence yesterday to take the museum exam. 'I wanted her to have a rosary for protection. I didn't want her to find it because she thinks that's all mumbo jumbo. So I tried to hide it at the bottom of her bag, and my fingers found what I thought was a piece of paper.'

In the far corner of the room, Daniele took notes. Nico could hear the clicks of his keyboard.

'Why did you take it out?' Perillo asked.

'I was going to use it to wrap the rosary. When I saw what it was, I kept it.'

'It's the only bill you found?'

'I was so shocked when I saw it that I didn't look to see if there were more.'

'Why did you wait until this morning to show this to me?'

'Like any mother, I wanted to talk to Stella first. I

didn't expect her until this morning, and wasn't aware she'd already come back last night.'

Perillo turned to Stella and, in a gentler voice, asked, 'Can you explain this hundred-dollar bill?'

'It's not mine!' The words came out as a bark.

Perillo's tone remained level. 'Why was it in your bag, then?'

'It wasn't.' Stella's leg stopped bouncing, and she leant forward in her chair. 'It was in my backpack with my overnight stuff and Gianni's.' Her face was now a startling white. 'That money is his. Don't ask me how I know because I'll tell you, and it's not a nice story.' Stella stopped to swallow.

Nico swiped the plastic water bottle from Perillo's desk and offered it to her. He could see tears welling up in her eyes.

Stella grabbed the bottle and gulped half of it down. She clutched it to her chest and sat up tall. The tears stayed floating in her eyes. 'I walked out of a gruelling three-hour exam feeling like I'd just won my future, and my boyfriend, instead of congratulating me, accused me of stealing his money. He wouldn't let up. He was sure I'd taken it. He grabbed my bag and threw everything out on the street.' She turned towards her mother. 'That's how I found the rosary and the rabbit's foot.' She looked over her shoulder. 'Thanks, Zio Nico.' She turned back to Tilde. 'I told you the exam was easy so you wouldn't worry, but I know I did very well. I know I'm going to get that job, and Gianni can drop off the edge of the earth for all I care. I'll never forgive him for treating me like a thief.' Her tears finally fell. 'How could he do that? When he claims to love me more than anything in the world. How could he? You'll be happy, Mamma. It's over between us. I told him I never want to see him again. I took the bus home early.'

Tilde, demeanour completely changed, reached over to hug her daughter. Nico wanted to do the same. Stella backed away. 'Mamma, I'm fine. I really am.' She wiped her eyes and gave a throaty laugh. 'I just had to get my anger off my chest, even in front of a maresciallo of the carabinieri.'

'Thank you for being so honest.' Perillo picked up the office phone and asked Vince to call the cafe next door for five espressos and more water. He smiled at Stella. 'I think we need refuelling before we go on. If you need a cigarette break' – he was badly in need of one – 'please feel free.'

Tilde shook her head. Stella said, 'I don't smoke.'

Perillo closed his eyes in resignation. One day, caffeine would be enough, but it wasn't yet.

'Do you have more questions?' Stella asked, turning back to him. 'I'd like to get this over with.'

'I understand. Did Gianni explain how he happened to have this American money?'

'He says he found it on the floor of the Co-op in Panzano.'

'Do you know why he didn't convert it into euros?'

'He said he was going to do it in Florence. The streets are full of exchange booths, and he could shop a better deal. He was going to use it to pay for some of the hotel.'

Perillo shot a questioning look at Nico, who said, 'The banks give you the best rate. I always used the ATM in Gravigna.'

'But Gravigna is the town where a bloody murder occurred,' Perillo added, forgetting for a moment Nico wasn't the only one listening. 'A bank clerk might wonder about a hundred-dollar bill with suspicious brown smudges on it.'

Stella frowned. 'What are you saying? You think that money has the dead man's blood on it?'

'Or the blood of someone who cut his finger,' Perillo said with a reassuring smile. 'Or melted chocolate.' Borrowing Tilde's tweezers, he slipped the hundred-dollar bill into a clean envelope and dropped it in his drawer. 'Does Gianni know your mother found the money?'

'She forbade me to tell him.'

'She did well. Please don't let him know.'

'I never want to speak to him again, but why shouldn't he know?'

Perillo's smile reappeared. 'I think it's best for your mother's sake that I let him know *we* have it.'

Stella looked at Tilde, who nodded. 'I guess you're right. They've never got along.'

'Thank you for coming in, Stella.'

In one graceful movement, Stella was on her feet. 'I didn't want to.'

'Still, thank you.' Perillo stood and extended his hand. She shook it reluctantly. 'You can go home now.'

Tilde got up from her chair.

'No, Tilde, please stay. Something has come up, and I need your help with it.'

Tilde looked at her watch. Ten past twelve. 'I have a kitchen to run.'

'This is important. Nico, can I ask you to take Stella home?' Talking to Tilde with Nico present would be awkward. His American friend was too emotionally involved.

Nico understood and shook his head. 'Tilde asked me to be here.'

Tilde understood that Salvatore's 'something has come up' meant he was going to question her about Gerardi. Nico would try to defend her and make the situation even more painful. Tilde reached for Nico's hand and squeezed it. 'Go, please. Stella needs company right now. Take her home.'

'Don't worry, Mamma.' Stella wrapped her arm around the man she'd thought of as her uncle since she'd been a little girl. 'The two of us will take over in the kitchen until you're back. Ciao, Maresciallo. Ciao to you too.' She waved at Daniele in the far corner.

Caught off guard, he waved, cheeks flaring. It wasn't dignified brigadiere behaviour, but she had smiled at him despite what had to be a broken heart.

Daniele was wrong. Stella felt much better now that she'd got Gianni off her chest and her heart. She had the urge to skip out of the carabinieri station, do cartwheels in the park out front. She'd done the right thing. Where there was love, there was trust. Watching her parents had taught her that. Her love for Gianni had been dwindling for some time, and now it was over. Finished. Later on she might cry a little, or even a lot, because she'd be alone. Right now, she was her strongest self.

As Stella walked towards the door, she asked Nico, 'Why is a poor rabbit's foot lucky?'

'I wish I knew.'

Tilde waited until the door had closed to sit down again. With arms folded, she gazed at the man she knew not as a maresciallo of the carabinieri, but as Salvatore, who loved her pappa al pomodoro and argued about Sunday football moves on Mondays with Enzo. He was fumbling with a sheet of paper, clearly uncomfortable. She was about to put him out of his misery when the bar boy walked in carrying a tray with a water bottle, an empty plastic cup filled with sugar packets and five plastic cups of coffee.

'The espressos, Maresciallo.'

'You took your time,' Perillo grumbled, eyes still on his desk. He didn't know the best way to start with Tilde. With the dead man's crime? With the hastily drafted new will? The will, yes. It would naturally segue to the rest.

'Sorry, Maresciallo. Where shall I put them?'

Perillo looked up. 'Renzino!' He raised his eyebrows, held them high, exaggerating his shock. 'What the hell have you done to yourself?' The boy's appearance was a welcome distraction. 'You used to be a handsome kid.' He had completely shaved both sides of his head. The top boasted a mop of fire-truck-red hair.

Renzino's deep laugh wobbled the tray, almost spilling the coffees.

Tilde quickly took the tray from him and placed it on one side of Perillo's desk.

Perillo's eyebrows relaxed. 'What did your mother say?'

Another rumble of laughter from Renzino's nearly sumo-sized belly. 'This was her doing.'

'She must love you very much. Close the door behind you, and have Vince pay you from the petty cash fund. I'll bring the tray back later.' Perillo looked at the five espressos at his elbow and offered Tilde a smile. 'Two each. That's good.'

'None for me.' Tilde uncapped the water, emptied the cup with sugar packets, poured from the bottle and drank.

In the far corner, Daniele did not move to pick up his espresso. He knew what was coming was embarrassingly private and hoped Tilde would forget his presence.

Silence followed while Perillo drank the first coffee, then the second. 'Did you have any contact with Gerardi after he left Italy?'

'No.'

'He never wrote to ask how you were?'

'No.'

'It seems he got that information from his sister. Gerardi discovered he had a short time to live and came home. But he didn't come here to die. He was flying back to California the day he was killed. I need to know what brought him back after twenty-two years if I am to solve his murder.'

'He didn't come back for me.'

Perillo knew he was talking in circles, but he couldn't bring himself to ask the question. 'Did you have any reason to hate him?'

'Not one enough to kill him.'

Perillo stood up. 'Excuse me. I'll be right back.' He took the evidence bag with the hundred-dollar bill and quickly walked to the door. In the corridor, he signalled Vince, who came forward with his heavy, rocking gait. 'Get in the car and rush this to the lab in Florence. Have them check for blood and fingerprints. Tell them we need the results yesterday.' That message delivered, Perillo stepped outside to light a cigarette. This time, he needed strength more than concentration. After two long drags, he put the cigarette out under his heel and went back in.

'Sorry,' Perillo said, sitting back down behind his desk.

Tilde closed her eyes. 'Why don't I just tell you what you want to know?'

After a moment, she reopened them and wet her lips. 'In 1996, I went to a New Year's Eve party that Nelli Corsi was throwing.' She spoke with no inflection in her voice, as if she was telling a story she had no interest in. 'I was supposed to go with Enzo. I was engaged to him by then, but he came down with the flu.'

Tilde took another sip of water. Why not just say it in three words? She looked down at her cup. It was empty now.

'I wanted to ring in the new year with him anyway,' she continued, 'but his mother wouldn't let me, so I went to the party by myself. There were about twenty of us.

Sandro and Jimmy from the cafe. Luciana, Enrico. Robi, who looked miserable. Nelli was in love with him then and tried to cheer him up. We drank, ate, danced to records. It was fun. The new year came, we all kissed each other and it was over. Outside, it had started snowing lightly. I'd come on foot, and my family lived on the outskirts of town. It was a twenty-minute walk. Friends offered me a ride, but I said no. I've always liked walking, even in bad weather, and I'd had too much to drink. The walk would clear my head. I'd just passed Aldo's winery when Robi came up beside me in his car.'

Listening to her, Perillo thought of Ginetta. If she were still alive, would she be telling her story years later in the same mechanical way? Would she still be screaming?

'He offered to take me home. I told him I was enjoying myself, that I was nearly there already. "Please," he said. "I need someone to talk to."' She could still hear his soft, pleading voice. 'He'd seemed so down at the party, I couldn't say no.'

'He drove for a minute or two and stopped the car next to the small chapel at the edge of the road. He said he knew Enzo's parents owned Sotto Il Fico and asked me if I was marrying Enzo for money. No, I said. Would I marry him if he was dirt poor, he asked. No, I would wait until we both had good jobs. I wanted to have children. He told me I was a liar, that all women wanted was money. I argued with him. He called me a whore and slapped me, then dragged me out of the car. I was screaming and fighting, but Robi was very strong.

344

Yes, Roberto Gerardi raped me. That's all you wanted to know, isn't it?'

Perillo looked down at his papers, feeling shame.

'He raped me, but I didn't kill him.'

Perillo held out the sheet he'd been fumbling with earlier. 'This was found in Gerardi's safe deposit box in California.'

Tilde put the empty water cup on the desk and took the sheet. It was a printout of a handwritten letter. She read it twice before putting the paper down. 'He wanted to leave three million dollars and ninety acres of land in the town of Gravigna to his daughter, Stella Morelli?' Her voice had turned into a rasp.

'Unfortunately for Stella, it's not legal as it is not signed or witnessed,' Perillo said, 'but he did want to make this his last will and testament. He had an appointment with his lawyer for the day after his death.'

'The man was delusional!' Tilde slammed the draft of the will on the desk. 'Even if he had signed it' – her face was white with anger – 'Stella would never have taken that money.'

'It would have changed her life. Yours and Enzo's.'

'My Stella is not his daughter.'

'She was born nine months after the rape, give or take a few days.'

'She was born premature.'

'Her eyes are the same colour as Robi's.' Thanks to Daniele's research he could add, 'Only two percent of the world's population has green eyes.'

'Stella's eyes are the same colour as Enzo's grandmother's.' Tilde filled the empty cup with water again and drank all of it down. Some colour returned to her face. 'Stop being the maresciallo for a moment. What are you getting at, Salvatore? Do you really think I could shoot a man's face off?'

'I'm getting at something you don't want to say out loud.'

'What? I'll repeat it over and over until there's no breath left in me. I didn't kill the man who raped me. And I never told anyone I was raped. Not a single person.' It was a lie, but she wanted to keep Enzo out of this. She had told him only after he'd found the paper results from the lab. He had cried with happiness. She hadn't realised that he too had had doubts about being Stella's father. On January 1, 1997, they'd been engaged for five months but had not yet made love.

'How are you so sure Stella isn't Gerardi's daughter?'

Tilde crushed the plastic cup in her fist.

Perillo turned to Daniele, crouched behind his computer, inputting Tilde's words. 'Dani, please take the bar tray back. They're in short supply over there.'

Daniele shot up, grabbed the tray and happily rushed out of the office. Tilde's story had upset his stomach.

'Thank you,' Tilde said.

Perillo acknowledged her thanks with a nod.

'To answer your question, I had Stella's DNA tested. They confirmed she was Enzo's daughter, as I had hoped. If you want, I can show you the lab report.'

'I'll take your word for it. Why didn't you want to tell me?'

'You don't understand the shame I've experienced. Of being raped first of all. And again, for doubting she was Enzo's daughter. A mother should know.'

'You had every reason to doubt. Thank you for bringing in the hundred-dollar bill, and thank you for telling me the truth.'

'You believe me, then.'

'I do.'

'Will you question Gianni?'

He spread his hands in a gesture of regret. 'I'm afraid I can't discuss police matters with you.'

Tilde rose from her seat and took back her tweezers from the desk. 'Well, I'm glad to hear it's a police matter.'

Perillo stood up and took Tilde's hand. A good, solid woman who had gone through something no one deserved.

'Take care of yourself, Tilde.'

'I don't have to. I have a good husband and a wonderful daughter, and Zia Rita has left me the gift of Nico. Bring your wife to the restaurant every once in a while. She deserves a night off.'

'Yes, she does.'

Perillo walked Tilde to her car. As soon as she drove off, he smoked a quick cigarette. Daniele walked back from the lounge. 'Get into uniform,' Perillo ordered. 'We're paying an official call. Meet you at the car in ten minutes.'

Upstairs, Perillo hurriedly got into his own uniform and went to the kitchen, where Signora Perillo was sautéing onions. 'I'm not going to make it back for lunch.'

She kept stirring without even turning around.

On the counter next to the stove, Perillo noticed a box of Arborio rice. 'What am I missing?'

'Risotto with porcini mushrooms.'

'What bad luck! Can you make it for dinner instead?'

'You might not be here for dinner, either. I'll save you some.'

He kissed the back of her head. 'I'll miss you.'

'You'll miss my risotto.'

He gave her behind a loving pat. 'That too.'

CHAPTER EIGHTEEN

At the Ferriello Winery, Perillo found Aldo watching over the machine that placed perfectly positioned labels on his wine bottles. In the open adjoining room, Arben was stacking bottles in wooden crates with two Kosovian helpers. 'We've got a big shipment going off to China in two days,' Aldo said.

Daniele stood near the machine, transfixed by its seamless automation. His grandfather had labelled his wines with a brush and a bottle of glue, but then, he produced a maximum of thirty bottles in a good year.

'Why the uniforms? Are you here to arrest me?' Aldo had a grin on his face. The Chinese order they were fulfilling was a big one.

'No, we need to talk to Gianni.'

'He came in this morning in a coal-black mood. What's he done?'

'Nothing for you to worry about.'

'He works for me. Of course I worry about it. Anyway, you missed him. He ran off about ten minutes ago.' Aldo kept his eyes locked on the labeller. It was an old machine, and sometimes it hiccupped, mangling the labels. 'Bad timing on his part, but I remember what it's like to have troubles in love, so I let him go. I expect him back in half an hour. Cinzia's in the reception room. She'll give the two of you a glass of red while you wait.'

'Thanks, but we have to attend to something else. Call me when he gets back, but please don't mention to him that we've come by. That goes for Arben too.'

Aldo looked up with a frown. 'This sounds serious.'

'It isn't, but some people get nervous about a visit from the carabinieri.'

Back in the car, Perillo called Nico. 'Are you at the restaurant?'

'Outside.' He had gone there hoping to find out from Tilde how her conversation with Perillo had gone.

'You can't talk?'

'That's right.'

'Gianni's there.'

'Very much so.'

'Keep him there. We're coming.'

'Who was that?' Gianni asked Nico, his handsome face scrunched up with suspicion.

Nico slipped the mobile phone in his back pocket. 'Luciana, the florist.'

Tilde had arrived fifteen minutes earlier and told Nico, 'Keep him out of my restaurant.'

Gianni heard her and leant against the wall under the lamp outside the front door, resigned to waiting. 'It's the only exit,' he muttered to himself.

Nico grabbed Gianni's arm and led him to the church steps, always a good place to talk, maybe even to get him to come to his senses. Perillo could take his time. There was no danger of Gianni leaving, not until Stella was present to hear him out. 'Come on, let's sit.'

Gianni let himself be pushed down onto the steps.

'Stella is rightfully upset, you agree with that, don't you?'

'Yes, yes, yes! I was awful, but she has to understand that she's my woman. She's mine and I'm hers. I'm going to marry her. She can't just leave me. It's not fair.'

'Why were you so upset when you couldn't find the money?'

'It's what I was going to use to pay for the hotel. We were going to celebrate. She just didn't understand how important it was for me.'

'The celebration or the money?'

Gianni turned to stare at Nico like he was dumb. 'Both. I needed one for the other.'

'Your reaction was very strong.'

'And how would you have reacted? I put the money in the backpack, and when I went to get it, the money was gone. The only other person who had access to the backpack was Stella. What was I supposed to think, that it flew away?'

'Maybe that it dropped out the way it dropped out from somebody's wallet or pocket in the supermarket. That's how you found it, isn't it?'

Gianni looked at Nico with narrowed eyes. 'Stella talks too much. And so do you.' He leant back on the stairs, crossed his arms and didn't say another word.

Eight or ten minutes later, Perillo and Daniele appeared from the side street next to the church. 'Gianni Baldi.'

Gianni sat up and stared at the two carabinieri standing above him. 'That's me.'

Perillo introduced himself and Daniele. 'I have some questions I need to ask you.'

Gianni scrambled to his feet. 'God, don't tell me Stella filed a complaint against me. I only yelled at her. I didn't touch a hair on her head, I swear it.'

'Your treatment of Stella is not the reason we're here. Your home is just down the hill. Anyone home now?'

'No. My parents are at work.'

'Good.' Parents only got in the way. 'We found the hundred-dollar bill.'

Gianni's face did not light up. 'Where?'

'A woman brought it in.'

'Where was it?'

'That's not important. Let's talk at your home.'

'Like hell it isn't. Stella is going to chop my head off.'

'Hasn't she already?' An unnecessary comment, Perillo realised too late.

'You talked to her?'

'Let's just say I heard a rumour.'

Gianni started stomping his feet on the cobblestone. 'Shit, shit, shit!'

'Let's go to your place.'

'You want to know about that money? I found it. Right on the floor of the Greve Co-op, that's all there is to it.'

'I need a few more details.'

'Can't this wait? I need to talk to Stella.'

'Afterwards.'

'I need to go back to work. We're preparing a big shipment to China. Three thousand bottles.'

'Afterwards.'

Gianni glanced at the door of the restaurant, probably hoping Stella would appear. 'Can't we talk here? Nico's a friend.'

Perillo held out his arm to usher the way. 'Let's go.'

Gianni turned to Nico. 'You come too. I want you as a witness.'

Perillo snorted. 'We're not going to beat you up. Answer a few questions and it's all over.'

'I don't trust anyone in uniform. If it's only questions, you can ask them here.'

'Come on, Gianni. Love can wait.'

Gianni dug his heels into the cobblestones. 'Not without Nico.'

Perillo let out a long, noisy sigh for effect. He was happy to have Nico come along. The more eyes and ears, the better. 'All right. Nico, you come too.'

Gianni, sandwiched between the two carabinieri, walked halfway down the hill. Nico followed. Going along suited him fine, but he had to remember to keep his mouth shut and be the fly on the wall. In the meantime, two questions whirled in his head like lotto numbers waiting to be extracted from their cage. The hundred-dollar bill. Had Gianni really found it on the floor of the Co-op? Had he found more? Gianni claimed he was going to use the hundred dollars to pay for the hotel, but Stella had said they planned to celebrate somewhere fancy. A room in a fancy hotel in Florence cost a hell of a lot more than a hundred dollars a night.

Gianni lived above the only laundrette in town. As they walked up the narrow flight of stairs, they could feel the pulsing of the washing machines underneath their feet. Gianni unlocked the door, and they entered into a large square room filled with light from a large sparkling window. One half of the room was a well-furnished kitchen. The second half, divided by a long table, was used as a living room. Underneath the window was a sofa covered by a blue-patterned cloth Nico had seen at the Greve market. One armchair. On the wall hung a calendar featuring Our Lady of Sorrows.

'So, ask,' Gianni said, standing on the kitchen side of the table with his arms crossed.

Perillo took his time sitting down on the sofa. Daniele took out his notebook and pen and seemed not to know where to place himself. Nico sat on the armchair and leant over to feel the texture of a jade plant. 'Who's got the green thumb in the family?' Okay, so he wasn't keeping quiet, but he'd found that asking inane questions usually loosened up interviewees.

'Papà,' Gianni answered, his eyes still on Perillo. 'Go ahead, then. I'm not planning to offer you coffee.'

Perillo patted the seat next to him. Daniele sat.

'Tell me how you found the money.'

'I already told you.'

'Tell me again.'

'Are you hard of hearing?'

Nico intervened. 'There's no need for hostility, Gianni. Just answer as best you remember.'

As Gianni walked around the table and straddled a wooden chair, Perillo shot a glance of approval at Nico.

'Okay,' Gianni said with a put-upon tone. 'Let's get this over with. I found the bill on the floor at the Greve Co-op.'

'When did you find it?'

'I don't know. About ten days ago.'

'Give me all the details.'

'I was with Stella, who needed to do some shopping for her mother, and this guy kept staring at her, which freaked Stella out. I told him to get lost and he left. That's when I saw the money on the floor. I guess it belonged to him.'

'You didn't find any other money?'

'I wish I had.'

'Did you ever see this man again?'

'No.'

'Do you own a shotgun?'

'Sure I do. Doesn't everyone?' Gianni raised his voice. 'What the hell are you getting at? Do you think I killed

355

that man because he was staring at my girlfriend? You're out of your head!'

'So you know the man from the Co-op is the dead man. Why didn't you mention that before?'

'You didn't ask. What's it matter, anyway?'

Perillo fought hard to contain the urge to slap this young man. 'There was blood on the hundred-dollar bill you found.' He hadn't got confirmation it was Gerardi's yet, but he wanted to shake Gianni up a bit.

'So the guy cut himself. What's that got to do with me?'

'It depends on when the blood got there.'

Gianni lifted his palms in the air. 'I don't know what you're getting at. I told you how I got the money. I've got nothing else to say.' He stood up and pushed the chair back under the table. 'No, I do.' He turned around, a finger pointing at Perillo. 'You're fishing around because you've got nothing. And I bet Tilde has something to do with you being here. She can't stand me, and the feeling is mutual. Stella and I are going to get married whether she likes it or not.'

Given Gianni's arrogance, that 'she' could refer to Stella as well as Tilde, Nico thought. Stella had been wise to break up with him.

Nico stood. 'I'm sorry, I need to use the bathroom.' An old ploy. Whatever he found couldn't be used in court, at least not in the States, but it might give Perillo a leg up. He was also tired of just being a witness.

Gianni pointed a thumb to his left. 'Second door to the left. Pull hard on the chain. It gets stuck sometimes.'

'Thanks.' Nico made his way carefully past the plant-laden coffee table and turned the corner to face a narrow corridor. He waited for Perillo to start talking again before opening the first door.

Perillo was going to ask to see Gianni's shotgun, but right now, they all needed to stay right where they were until Nico came back. 'Where were you last Monday morning around six o'clock?'

'Here, asleep. Where else?'

Perillo smiled in answer to Gianni's sneering attitude. Was his antagonistic tone a cover-up for fear? 'Was anyone with you?'

'My parents. My mother woke me up at seven-thirty with my caffelatte. She does that every workday. I've got to be at the winery at eight-thirty.'

A mamma's boy then, Perillo thought. That explained some of his attitude.

Daniele, who had been quietly and quickly taking notes, felt a pang of envy. His mother had stopped offering him caffelatte in bed on his tenth birthday.

'Can anyone else corroborate that you were here at that time?' Mothers never told the truth about their children to the authorities. 'Your father?' Not that fathers were much better.

'Papà leaves at five, except on Sundays. He's a mason working on that five-star hotel Vigna Maggio is building in Vitigliano. It was just me and Mamma.' He leant back against the table with a satisfied smirk on his handsome face. 'Now, I've really got to get back to work.'

Perillo stood up slowly and adjusted his uniform, taking up time and waiting for Nico. Daniele followed his lead. It wasn't like the maresciallo to waste time, but Nico hadn't come back yet.

'I'll need to speak to your mother,' Perillo said. He would also have to speak to Stella, who had been with Gianni when he'd supposedly found the money.

'Sure. Mamma'll vouch for me.' They all heard the toilet flush. Gianni walked to the front door, twirling the key chain. 'You'll find her at the post office in Panzano.'

'I'm not finished yet,' Perillo warned, not moving.

Gianni spun around. 'God Almighty, now what?'

'You need to come to the station and sign a statement.'

Gianni pointed at Daniele. 'He's been taking notes all this time. I'll sign them here.'

'Notes won't do. We need a formal statement. You can come with us now.'

Nico walked in from the corridor, pushing his shirt into his cargo pants. 'Everything okay, Gianni?'

'Well, you weren't much of a witness, and now they want me to go to Greve and sign a statement.'

'It's just procedure,' Nico said. 'Don't worry about it.' He turned to Perillo. 'Gianni's quite late for work. Can't he come this evening?'

Gianni looked relieved, and Perillo understood. Nico had something to tell him first. 'No later than seven. Now, we need to take your shotgun.'

'What for?'

'To eliminate it as the weapon that killed Gerardi.'

'I didn't kill him! How many times do I have to say it? No wonder you guys are known for being slow. How many carabinieri does it take to sink a submarine?'

'That one's old,' Perillo answered. 'Fetch your shotgun now. When you come to the station later, I'll tell you some better jokes.'

'Do I have a choice?'

'For the jokes, yes. The shotgun, no.'

'I'll get it for you, but I want it back by next Sunday. I'm going hunting with my buddies.'

'We'll try our best.'

Back on the street, Daniele asked Nico in a whisper, 'You didn't really have to go to the bathroom, did you?'

'No, but once you get there, why not?'

Daniele hugged Gianni's shotgun to his chest and smiled. He was catching on.

Nico was staring at the laundromat. 'Did forensics look at those machines for blood?'

'Then you think—'

Perillo cut Daniele off. 'They did. Plus the Caritas dumpsters where people leave clothes. Nothing. Now, let's get this shotgun back to the station. Vince will have to make another trip to Florence.'

'I can do it,' Daniele offered. He'd never been to the renovated Cathedral Museum. He'd finally see the real Baptistery doors.

'No, Dani. I need you with me.'

Daniele knew the real reason the maresciallo didn't

want him to go. He would take twice as long. Vince was a speed demon.

As the three of them walked down to the main piazza, Daniele asked, 'How many carabinieri does it take to sink a submarine, though?'

'I'll tell you a better one,' Perillo said. 'A carabiniere runs to his maresciallo. "Our squad car got stolen." "Did you see who it was?" "No, but I got the number plate."'

'That's not funny.'

'The police think it is. Don't get discouraged, Dani. Being the butt of jokes gives us a perverse pride.'

In the piazza, the benches were deserted. The old men were home eating a hearty three-course lunch, pasta and some meat with cooked vegetables. For dessert, whatever fruit was in season. For dinner later, it might be a light soup and cold cuts. A full stomach at night brought nightmares. In between, around five o'clock, they would come out again to chat, complain, maybe start up a game of cards. Luciana's flower shop was shuttered. The cafe had only a few clients. It wasn't coffee time yet. The outside tables at Da Gino were almost full. The best place to talk was in the squad car. As Perillo and Daniele were getting in, the lilac-haired waitress, Gino's daughter, Carletta, waved at the group.

'Why is her hair that colour?' Daniele asked.

'She's young. You've made another conquest,' Perillo said.

'No, she's waving at you.'

'Well, maybe. I got her out of trouble once.' He turned to Nico, who was sitting in the back seat. 'I'm listening.'

'I think you have your man. Unless Gianni can explain why he has a thick stash of euros in his house.'

'Where was it?'

'I got lucky, because his room was a holy mess. It looked like it hadn't been cleaned in a lifetime, which works in our favour. I took out a clean handkerchief' – a Rita must-have – 'and started poking around. I noticed the guitar was full of dust, except around the rosette and the strings over the sound hole. I took it down and shook it a few times. Some bills fell out. I pressed my eye against the hole and saw more. Lots and lots of hundred-euro bills, bills I suspect were originally dollars. I put back the bills that fell out, re-hooked the guitar and went to the bathroom.'

'You think Gianni killed Gerardi for his money?'

'The watch Gerardi wore did announce he was rich, but Gianni would have had to know the man was carrying that much cash.'

'But how would he get Gerardi to walk into the woods at that time of the morning?'

'Exactly. I think that cash was an extra bonus.'

Daniele snapped his fingers. 'Gerardi kept writing to his sister asking about Tilde, so much so that she thought Tilde was the mystery woman. When she told him Tilde had a daughter and the dates matched up, he assumed Stella was his. That's why he came back.'

Nico felt the blood drain from his face. 'She told you.'

'Yes,' Perillo said. 'Tilde also told me she has proof that Stella is Enzo's biological daughter. She's no longer a suspect.'

Nico's heart pumped fast with joy. 'Thank God.'

'The date on the bracelet charm, January first, 1997, is the date of the rape.' Daniele was on a roll. 'What Gerardi thought was the date of Stella's conception. He saw it as her real birthday.'

'Sick, but the only date he knew himself,' Perillo said. 'I wonder if he saw giving that bracelet to Stella as a form of apology.'

'If Gianni didn't kill for money, then why?' Daniele asked.

'That might not necessarily be the case. We'll ponder it later,' Perillo said. 'We've got to get this shotgun to Florence. If our luck holds out, it will have traces of Gerardi's blood. Gianni is obviously not good at thorough cleaning. Let's meet up at the station after lunch. Three o'clock okay with you, Nico?'

'Fine.'

'Thanks for thinking so fast.'

'The bathroom trick is very old. I'm surprised Gianni didn't catch on. By the way, his parents' bedroom is the last room in the hallway. Gianni could have easily slipped out without them knowing and been back in time for his caffelatte. Ciao for now, and buon appetito.'

'Buon appetito to you too.'

Nico wanted to walk up the steep road back to Sotto Il Fico and give Tilde, Stella, Enzo and Elvira a big hug, but it was the height of the lunch hour. The hugs would have to wait. Right now he was hungry. A mortadella and caciotta sandwich was waiting for him at home, plus OneWag. He missed the little guy.

* * *

'What the hell have you done?'

OneWag hid his face between his dirt-caked paws. In front of him, the rosebush was lying on its side, roots exposed. Next to it, a deep hole.

Nico didn't move from the open garden gate. He wanted to be furious, but his good mood prevented it. 'Get out of there!'

OneWag stuck his face in lower. The little mongrel had been clever enough to figure out how to slip out the long wooden stick Nico used to close the gate. At least he'd ruined the one rosebush that wasn't doing well. But while digging for what?

'Out, I said.'

The dog turned on his back, legs in the air.

Nico stepped into the vegetable garden. 'That's not going to work.' He noticed OneWag had something in his mouth. He walked in closer. 'That better not be one of my vegetables.'

No, it was something plastic. He tugged at it. OneWag let go. A sheet of thin plastic. Nico took another step and looked into the hole OneWag had dug. It was full of small pieces of soft, clear plastic. He reached into his pocket and took out his phone.

'Has Vince left for Florence yet?'

'He's leaving now,' Perillo said. 'Why?'

'Tell him to stop by my place first. My dog dug up something forensics needs to look at.'

Taking advantage of the moment, OneWag snaked his way behind Nico, his long ears dragging dirt. It was back to the streets for him.

'What is it?' Perillo asked.

'I think it's the plastic poncho our murderer used to keep the clothes clean. It's been cut up into slivers.'

'Bravo, Rocco. I'll send Vince over right away.'

'His name is—' Nico started to say, but Perillo had already hung up. By now, OneWag was past the gate, ready to start running.

'Where do you think you're going?' Nico asked. 'Come here.'

OneWag started to snake his way back, his small body tensed for a kick or a whack with a stick.

'Walk on your paws. You're dirty enough as it is.'

OneWag stopped. Nico saw he was trembling and picked him up. He brushed the dirt off his face, his ears, his silky fur. He held the dog tight against his chest to soothe the tremors. He remembered the poor dog had likely experienced some terrible things. 'It's okay. You did a good thing this time.' He turned OneWag's snout so they were eye to eye. 'No more digging in our vegetable garden, okay? You got that?'

OneWag blinked. Nico let go of his snout and got a lick in return. Nico put him down. 'Off you go.' OneWag trotted out, tail held high, and dropped down on the grass outside the gate.

Vince showed up five minutes later, and he and Nico gathered all the plastic pieces and carefully dropped them in the evidence bag. On the way back to his car, he dropped a cowhide bone for OneWag. 'Rocco should join the carabinieri,' he called out as he gunned the motor and raced out of the driveway, spitting gravel in every direction.

* * *

The three of them sat on a shaded bench in the park facing the carabinieri station. Perillo was in his usual jeans and crisply ironed shirt. Daniele had kept his uniform on. OneWag sat at Nico's feet, chewing on Vince's gift. At three in the afternoon, no one was around. They could speak freely, and Perillo could smoke.

'All right, we think Gianni is the killer,' Perillo said. 'Now, let's go over the possible scenario. He sees Gerardi staring at Stella at the Co-op and confronts him.'

'What's more important is that Gerardi sees him with Stella,' Daniele adds. 'Am I right?'

'Yes. Gianni is a possible conduit to Stella. After Gianni confronts him, Gerardi asks him to meet somewhere else so he can explain his interest in Stella. I don't think he makes his plea outside the Co-op with Stella nearby. They meet that day or the next, and Gerardi explains Stella's his daughter, and that she's going to inherit a lot of his money. He begs Gianni to convince Stella to see him. From how she reacted in the Co-op, he knows she's scared of him. Maybe he offers Gianni some money. Gianni sets up a fake meeting early in the woods behind Nico's house. Unaware that Gerardi is a dying man, he kills him.'

'The woods behind Nico's house,' Daniele repeated. 'I forgot to tell you, I got the report from the other land experts. No vines are going to grow on the land Gerardi bought.'

'Good,' Perillo said. 'Aldo will be happy to hear he wasn't cheated.'

'So Gianni kills Gerardi,' Nico said, 'and in his mind, Stella inherits, which to Gianni means he won't lose her

365

to some Florentine. She stays in Gravigna, and they get married and live happily ever after on her money. I do think Gianni is arrogant and stupid enough to think that's how it would have worked out.'

Perillo stubbed his cigarette out on the sole of his shoe. He was about to toss the butt when he caught Daniele looking at him. 'We'll have to wait for forensics to nail him.' He pushed the butt into his pocket. Daniele turned away to hide his smile.

'I have a hunch,' Nico said. 'If it's right, maybe we won't have to wait for forensics. May I make a suggestion?'

'Why do you think I asked you to get involved?' Perillo asked. 'Make all the suggestions you want.'

'I only have one.'

CHAPTER NINETEEN

Gianni showed up at the carabinieri station at seven o'clock sharp, still in jeans and his Ferriello T-shirt. He ignored Perillo behind his desk and walked over to Nico sitting in a chair a few feet away. 'Did you talk to Stella?'

Before Nico could answer, Perillo said, 'You'll talk to Nico about your love problems later. Normally, I don't allow people not officially involved in an investigation to sit in, but at your request, I made a concession this morning, and I'm making it again tonight. You consider Nico a friend, and I want you to feel comfortable. Now please sit.'

Gianni sat in the chair placed in front of Perillo's desk. He was still looking at Nico. 'She isn't picking up or answering any of my texts.'

'Let us proceed with the matter at hand, please,' Perillo said in a cutting voice.

Gianni reluctantly turned to face him.

'Brigadiere Donato has typed out what you stated this morning in your home.' On cue, Daniele got up from his post in front of the computer and brought the two typed pages. Perillo read quickly, then summed up the contents. 'You stated that you found the hundred-dollar bill at the Co-op here in Greve after a man, who turned out to be Roberto Gerardi, stared aggressively at Stella and you confronted him. You did not find any other money. You never saw Gerardi again. At the time of the murder, you were home asleep. Your mother brought you a caffelatte at seven-thirty, as she does every workday morning. You did not kill Roberto Gerardi.'

'Yeah, that's what I said.'

Perillo held out the pages for Gianni. 'Please read it carefully before you sign it. Making a false statement is a serious offence.'

Nico noticed the slight tremor of Gianni's hand as he turned the page.

Gianni looked up. 'Can I have a pen?'

Nico leant forward in his chair. 'Gianni, before you sign, I think there are some things you need to know.'

'Like what?'

'When you confronted Gerardi outside the Co-op, did he tell you why he was staring at Stella?'

'He didn't have to. She's beautiful.'

'She is, but that's not the reason.'

'Who cares what the reason was? I didn't like him looking at her like he was going to swallow her whole.'

'He stared because he thought he was looking at his daughter.'

'What the fuck are you talking about? No way is Stella his daughter.'

'You're right. She isn't, but he thought she was.'

Gianni shook his head, laughing. 'No, he didn't.'

'Why don't you think so?'

Nico's question silenced his laugh. Gianni stared at Nico for a few beats before answering. 'Because, well, it makes no sense.' His voice was loud. 'She's Tilde and Enzo's daughter. She'll inherit the restaurant one day, and I'll help her run it.'

Perillo intervened. 'Do you know Maria Dorsetti?'

Gianni shot a surprised look at Perillo, as if he'd forgotten he was there. 'No.' The word came out as a spit.

'She's one of your mother's Friday-night canasta friends.' Gianni's mother had told Perillo when he'd gone to the post office to check on Gianni's alibi.

Gianni ran his hands through his hair, his face flushed. 'I don't know their names.'

'Stella is Tilde and Enzo's daughter,' Nico said in the soft, calm voice he'd always found useful. 'What's important for you is that Gerardi, who was a millionaire, thought differently. He was dying, and he wanted Stella to inherit most of his wealth, but he needed to talk to her first. He had important things to get off his chest. Unfortunately, he never got to meet her or make official the will that would've given Stella more money than she could ever dream of. He was murdered, so the money goes to his sister, Maria Dorsetti.'

Gianni leapt to his feet, knocking down his chair. 'No!' he yelled. 'You're lying. You're all lying! Stella had nothing to do with that man.'

Nico picked up the chair from the floor and set it back in front of Perillo's desk. 'Sit down, Gianni. Yelling is what got you in trouble with Stella. It will get you into even more trouble here. If you sit down, Maresciallo Perillo will show you we're telling the truth.'

Perillo pushed the copy of the handwritten will Gerardi had kept in his safe-deposit box across his desk.

'Read it,' Nico ordered.

Gianni continued to stand and read, his lips quietly forming the words, eyes darting over each sentence twice. He turned to Nico when he was finished. 'I've lost her for good now.'

'Stella will want the truth.'

'It won't win her back.' Gianni slumped down in the chair and, with a grim expression, faced Perillo. 'Well, here it is, then.'

By the time Nico got back to Sotto Il Fico, the restaurant was empty of patrons. He walked in with Enzo, who'd just driven his mother home. He called Stella and Tilde in from the kitchen. Alba, their helper, had already left.

'Please, sit down,' he said. 'I have some sad news.'

'Someone died,' Tilde said.

'No.'

'Thank God.' Tilde sat at the corner table and raised her arm to invite Stella to sit next to her. Parental instinct taking over, Enzo sat on Stella's other side. The yellow light from the lamp above them cast a shadow under their eyes.

Nico sat down and faced them with the painful knowledge that he was about to wound his goddaughter's heart.

'Well, what is it?' Stella asked.

'This evening, in Maresciallo Perillo's office, Gianni confessed to Roberto Gerardi's murder.'

Tilde gasped. Enzo wound his arm around Stella's shoulders. Stella stared, wide-eyed.

'Why?' she finally asked.

'He says Gerardi's sister offered him a thousand euros, to start with. After she inherited, she was to give him an additional hundred thousand euros.'

'He said so?' Enzo asked.

'Yes. And Maria Dorsetti is being questioned right now, I believe.'

'She'll deny it, of course. Does Gianni have proof?'

Gianni had kept proof, which he'd played for Perillo – two conversations with Maria recorded on his iPhone.

'I'm sorry, I can't say. I shouldn't even be telling you this much, but Salvatore Perillo is a friend.' So much a friend he was going to ask Della Langhe not to mention Stella's name when he talked to the press. Her name would have to come out at the trial, but the wheels of Italian justice turned very slowly, a blessing in this case. It would give Stella time to brace herself, develop some armour against long-kept secrets that weren't hers.

'I understand,' Enzo said. 'It's hard to believe Gianni's the killer.'

Stella shook her head in disbelief. 'He killed a man for money?'

'He said he was tired of living with his parents,' Nico said. 'He wanted to get his own flat. He needed a new motorcycle.' These weren't Gianni's main reasons, but he didn't want Stella to blame herself.

'It's not my fault, is it?' Stella asked as the lamplight illuminated the tears on her cheeks.

Tilde stroked Stella's hair. 'Of course it's not.'

'He thinks he did it for me, doesn't he?' Stella said. 'That if he had lots of money, I wouldn't go to work in Florence. That I'd stay right here and marry him.' Stella wiped her cheeks with the back of her hand. 'Poor Gianni. He's so self-involved he can't see reality. I fell in love with him at first because I confused that with strength. Shit! I can't believe this.' She slumped forward on the table and buried her head between her arms. No one said anything while she sobbed, then slowly regained her breath. After two or three minutes, she looked up and asked Nico, 'What's going to happen to him?'

'He's being driven to a jail in Florence, if he's not already there. Eventually he'll be put on trial.'

She sat up. 'I'm going to see him.'

'Stella!' Tilde cried out. 'He's a cold-blooded murderer.'

'I'm sorry, Mamma, but I'm going to see Gianni tomorrow.'

Enzo squeezed Stella's hand. 'You'll need permission. Let me talk to Salvatore, and then I'll drive you.'

'I want to go alone.'

Tilde covered her mouth to keep from intervening again.

'Please, let me drive you. You'll be upset.' Enzo knew that on the way back, Stella's eyes would be too full of tears to see the road. 'Thank you, Nico, for telling us about Gianni. I'm sure it wasn't easy, but I'm glad we found out from you and not the carabinieri.'

'I've always thought bad news is best delivered by someone in the family,' Nico said. As a homicide detective, one of his roles had been the total stranger announcing the death of a family member. He'd hated every second of it.

Tilde stood up. 'Thank you,' she said, and gave him a quick hug. Stella and Enzo followed suit.

'Goodnight,' Tilde said as she was leaving. 'If you're up to it, I could use you for lunch and dinner tomorrow.'

'I'll get here early.'

'We'll cook together. Food is a great medicine.' Tilde linked her arm through Stella's. 'Come on, darling. Let's go home.'

Nico followed the three of them out of the restaurant with a heavy heart. It would take some time before their family would find peace again, but he would do everything he could to help.

CHAPTER TWENTY

Nico picked the last Sunday in October to celebrate Aldo's grape harvest with a cookout in his garden. Everyone needed a pick-me-up after the shock of Gianni's arrest. Nico had helped Tilde cook countless Tuscan meals in the past month. Now it was time for his Italian family and friends to be introduced to some old-fashioned American food. Not hamburgers and hot dogs, which they could find anywhere. Spare ribs lathered in barbecue sauce, accompanied by coleslaw and potato salad. If nothing else, the food would be a distraction, a conversation piece.

Tilde had resisted closing Sotto Il Fico for one day, even though the tourist season was almost over and fewer diners were coming to eat. To Nico's surprise, Elvira sided with him. 'It will be good for Stella,' she declared. It was what Nico hoped. Stella had become so withdrawn after her visit to Gianni. Nico suspected she still thought she

374

was somehow to blame for what he'd done. Nico tried to talk to her, but she kept repeating, 'I'll be fine, Zio Nico. Don't worry about me, I just need time.'

Just days before, Nico had bought a grill, two bags of charcoal and some wooden chips. That morning, Aldo and Arben had driven over two long tables and helped Nico set them up. Tilde and her family arrived early. She brought the restaurant's cutlery, plates and napkins, insisting that plastic and paper had no place in a celebration. Luckily, Nico had already brought down his armchair for Elvira. She let him peck her cheeks, sat down, spread her green flowered housedress over her lap and went to work on the *Settimana Enigmistica* crossword puzzle. Stella, looking too thin but still beautiful, hugged him. He hugged her back tightly. He noticed she'd attached the rabbit's foot he'd given her to her belt. The results of the museum exam hadn't been announced yet. While Tilde and Stella set the tables, Enzo watched Nico light the charcoal and asked what ingredients were in the sauce.

Fourteen people were coming. Only Jimmy and Sandro had declined, as there was no one to staff the cafe for them, but they'd provided two large thermoses of coffee and refused payment. As more guests arrived, their generosity overwhelmed him. Nico had specifically told everyone to come empty-handed. Not a single person had listened. Luciana brought two aster plants that she put at the centre of the tables. Enrico, a basket filled with his olive loaves. Signora Perillo offered a raspberry jam crostata and a smile, as Perillo stood beside her, happy his shy, pretty wife was willing to expose herself to what she would consider a crowd of strangers.

Daniele introduced Rosalba to Nico with blushing cheeks. He had never expected Rosalba to accept his invitation. He was sure her mother would prevent her from going; she had good reason.

'I hope there's enough for everyone,' Daniele said as he handed Nico a wide dish filled with tiramisu, made by him in Signora Perillo's kitchen.

Nico thanked him. 'A taste is all we need.'

Aldo had insisted on supplying the wine. Cinzia brought what she insisted was just an appetiser, 'in no way competing with the bones Nico is going to serve us'. Her 'appetiser' turned out to be a huge bowl of cacio e pepe spaghetti, which was devoured before it had a chance to cool. Nico understood it was Cinzia's payback for declining to celebrate the solution to Gerardi's murder with her and Aldo back when the news had first come out.

Perillo thanked Cinzia repeatedly, overjoyed to coat his stomach with cheese, pepper and spaghetti to protect him from whatever concoction his American friend was going to serve. Signora Perillo, on the other hand, stayed away from Cinzia's Roman dish. To be on the safe side, she had eaten at home.

Nico was tending the grill when Luciana cried out with her usual oversized enthusiasm, 'That one's one of your best, Nelli! The very best.'

'Thank you,' Nelli said, and kept on walking.

Nico turned around. She was coming towards him, dressed in a yellow skirt and a light blue blouse. It was the first time he had seen her without paint-splattered jeans. She looked lovely. 'I'm glad you could come,' he said.

'You sound surprised. I told you I'd be here.'

'You did.' Now he felt stupid.

'You don't take things for granted, then?'

'I don't know if that's true.' Stupid, and now embarrassed.

'I brought you this.' She handed over a small framed painting of Gravigna as seen from a few miles away. It was the same view he saw each morning on his run. He always stopped to stare at the town while catching his breath before turning back home. He had bought her painting of OneWag at her show two weeks earlier and asked to buy the landscape.

Nelli kissed his cheeks. He brushed his lips quickly against her cheeks. 'You said it wasn't for sale.'

'I wanted to give it to you.'

'Thank you. I don't know what to say.'

'There's no need for anything more than a thank you. Who's the beauty with Daniele?'

'Rosalba Crisani. She sold the charm bracelet to Gerardi.'

'Robi got it all wrong, didn't he?'

'What do you mean?'

'She's got his nose and his smile.'

'Oh,' was all Nico could say.

'I'll leave the painting inside the house, okay?'

'No, prop it up on that olive branch so we can all enjoy it.' His yard had one runaway olive tree from Aldo's grove. He was moved by the gift and wanted to keep looking at it.

Nelli did as he asked and walked away with a wave of her hand. 'Ciao, Nico. I'm going for a glass of wine. Want one?'

Nico lifted his untouched glass. 'Got it, thanks.' He looked over at Rosalba, laughing with Daniele. He couldn't see any resemblance, but then, Nelli had known Gerardi when he'd been Rosalba's age. 'Send Perillo over, will you, please?'

She smiled. 'Got it.'

Perillo made his way over quickly. 'I don't know anything about grilling, so I can't help.'

'Nelli just told me something.'

'Rosalba?'

'You knew?'

'Thanks to Daniele. Last night I walked into my office to get my cigarettes and found Daniele at his computer. The minute I walked in, he shut the screen off. It's not the first time he's done it – I thought he was looking at pornography. He can do that all he wants, but not on the station's computer. This morning I asked him, "What were you looking at last night?"

'He said, "Nothing."

'I told him to show me, and he did, albeit reluctantly. What he was looking at was Rosalba's birth date. She was born six months after Gerardi left. I suspect her mother didn't know she was carrying Gerardi's child when she broke up with him. She would've been only two months pregnant.'

'Gerardi should've at least entertained the idea when he found out Irene had a daughter.'

'Maybe he had too much anger towards her for rejecting him. Or too much guilt about the rape. A daughter from the terrible thing he did, someone he could compensate, would have made his guilt easier to bear.'

'Was Daniele upset you found out?'

'He pretended not to be, but I'm sure he wanted it to be his secret. There's nothing like knowing someone's else's secret to make you feel close to them.'

'Ehi, Nico,' Nelli called out by one of the tables. 'Gogol's here.'

A welcome interruption, Nico thought as he walked over. Enough with anything that had to do with Gerardi. As the Italians said, 'Basta!'

Gogol had brought himself and his overcoat, but he'd left behind the powerful cologne. The left-behind cologne was his gift, Nico thought as he welcomed him. Nelli hugged him. OneWag sniffed the hem of his coat and his shoes and waited for the old man to acknowledge him. Perillo introduced Signora Perillo, who smiled with a slight bow of her head.

Gogol grinned at her. 'You should be proud of your hero Ulysses, Signora. He took a mad leap and flew with swift wings and the plumes of great desire.'

'Is that Dante?' Perillo asked.

'*Purgatorio* Four. My adaptation to fit the circumstances. A good man, Perillo. He brought justice.' Gogol turned to Cinzia, who offered him a plate of cooled-down cacio e pepe. He dug into his pockets and showed her he'd brought his own lunch: yesterday's crostini from Sergio's shop. Then he took the plate anyway and dropped it to the ground.

OneWag didn't wait a second to bury his face in the pasta. Cinzia laughed, which brought Stella over. When OneWag looked up at her with bits of melted cheese on his whiskers, Stella laughed too. Then Tilde laughed, Enzo, Nico. Laughter spread down both tables. Daniele, Rosalba, Luciana, Enrico. Only Elvira paid no attention. Five Down was giving her trouble.

Once OneWag was through eating, the plate looked like it had just come out from the dishwasher. Nico hoped his guests would go home this evening with minds clean of the ugliness of murder and stomachs filled to satisfaction. He went back to the grill to work on the spare ribs. As he basted them with the sauce, he listened to the lively chatter amongst friends and family. He felt his body relax. The tension and sadness of the recent years seemed to melt away. He looked up at Nelli's painting of Gravigna, perched on a tree branch, and knew he was home.

ACKNOWLEDGEMENTS

Writing this story has been a joy, thanks to the many friends I made while researching in Tuscany. They welcomed me and answered a flood of questions with smiles on their faces. A huge grazie to Lara Beccatini, who first introduced me to the ways of a small Tuscan town and stayed close throughout. Grazie to the team at Il Vinaio in Panzano: Paolo Gaeta, Teresa Barba, Brian Garcilazo, Carolina Gemini and Manjola Kurti. They fed me their wonderful food and filled my glass with excellent wine while I took notes. I am grateful to Ioletta Como and Andrea Sommaruga for trying to teach me the complicated wine business, Lorenzo Guarducci for answering my questions about guns, Bibil Vangjeli and Gianluca De Santi for feeding me breakfast every morning and introducing me to the local Maresciallo dei Carabinieri. Maresciallo Giovanni Serra's help is a priceless gift, and I send him a thousand grazie.

I am lucky to have a wonderful New York team of readers who give me advice and spot my countless typing mistakes. A heartfelt thank you to Barry Greenspon, Barbara Lane, Rose Scotch, Elaine Gilbert and Willa Morris.

I am grateful to Kelly Smith for choosing my story, and I am proud to have become an Allison & Busby author.

To my patient husband Stuart, my love and trust.

CAMILLA TRINCHIERI worked for many years on films in Rome with directors including Federico Fellini and Luchino Visconti. She emigrated to the US in 1980 and received her MFA in Creative Writing from Columbia University. Under the pseudonym Camilla Crespi, she has published seven crime novels.

camillatrinchieri.com   *@camillatrinchie*